Also by K. Aten:

THE ARROW OF ARTEMIS SERIES
The Fletcher
The Archer
The Sagittarius

THE BLOOD RESONANCE SERIES
Running From Forever
Embracing Forever

MYSTERY OF THE MAKERS SERIES
The Sovereign of Psiere

OTHER TITLES
Rules of the Road
Waking the Dreamer
Burn It Down
Children of the Stars

Remember Me, Synthetica

K. Aten

Silver Dragon Books
by Regal Crest

ISBN 978-1-61929-442-4

First Edition 2020

9 8 7 6 5 4 3 2 1

Cover design by AcornGraphics

Published by:

Regal Crest Enterprises

Find us on the World Wide Web at
http://www.regalcrest.biz

Published in the United States of America

Acknowledgments

Let's start from the beginning. I want to thank Ted for his help in the chapter by chapter beta reading, as well as the full pass. My new helper this time around was Lex, who also gave it a read through in beta and provided valuable feedback.

I'd also like to thank my wife, Kari, who actually read this one. She said it may be her favorite, minus one particular part. (That I can't explain because... spoilers)

My main editor, Micheala, is detail-oriented and supportive and isn't afraid to keep it real concerning my biggest issues in any particular book. I've also got Mary at my back, cleaning up the last few bits that Micheala and I miss. Both are great at what they do!

Next is Ann McMan, who gave me such a gorgeous cover. The imagery was perfect for instilling the Asimov feel I was looking for, and the colors conveyed undertones (That I can't explain because... spoilers) that fit well with the story and underlying theme. I also want to thank Patty, who is efficient as always in keeping my eBooks tight. And last is Cathy. She is the rock who hasn't lost faith in me yet. Let's hope she never does.

Dedication

"One of the great things about science fiction is that it introduces you to notions and technology that don't currently exist yet have the potential to exist. Thousands of modern scientific inventions and concepts were first introduced and birthed through the medium of fiction." Dr. Falguni Nanjiani - *Remember Me, Synthetica*

This novel is a nod to all those masterpieces I grew up reading, the books that inspired me, and the authors that made me believe anything was possible.

Part One

Alex in Wonderland

Chapter One

Activation

AWARENESS CAME GRADUALLY with the sensation of muted darkness and steady *beeping* in my ears. A slow rhythm of breaths moved in and out of my chest as I tried to make sense of my surroundings. I opened my eyes, blinking four times in the light of the room. It wasn't bright, rather my eyes felt unused. Faces I didn't know stared back at me.

"Alexandra, can you hear and understand me?"

His question only left me with questions of my own. I contemplated the best response. "Who are you?" Another person I didn't recognize sat farther away at a portable desk, steadily typing on a laptop. I tried again. "What are your names?"

The man nearest to me responded. "I am Doctor Ryan Jones. I've been overseeing your care here in the bio-medical division of OAS. The gentleman at the computer is Doctor Baumgartner. He will be assisting with your cognitive and sensory tests later. Today he is recording initial observations."

OAS, or Organic Advancement Solutions, is my father's company and also my place of employment. I was still missing a lot of information. "Why am I here, Doctor Jones?"

"Alexandra..."

Another voice with a British accent pulled my attention so I twisted my head to look at the back right corner of the room. "Doctor Nanjiani?" Wait, that wasn't right. Memories flooded through my brain and I felt relief as I recognized my best friend and coworker. "Falguni. Your name is Falguni. Why am I here?"

I watched her glance toward Doctor Jones. His deep voice felt good in my ears. It was soothing when he answered her unspoken question. "Go ahead."

Falguni came closer and took my hand. The sensation was strange. All sensations were strange, like the feel of the sheets against my body or the way her skin slid against my own. "Alexandra, you were in an accident six months ago—"

"Alex."

"Excuse me?"

"I don't like Alexandra."

She glanced back at Doctor Jones again, even as Doctor Baumgartner began typing furiously on his laptop. I explained. "It sounds too...long. It's very formal, don't you think? I like Alex better." Everyone froze and I questioned my assertion. "Is that not what you call me?" I couldn't remember. Falguni smiled but it did not match the visual my mind remembered. This smile in comparison seemed forced. Her lips were pursed tightly, and her eyes weren't crinkled up at the corner. She looked...sad. Distraught.

"It's not what you preferred before the accident but I can call you Alex now if you'd like."

I nodded. "And please continue with the reason I'm here."

"As I was saying, you were in an accident six months ago. You were struck by a car and suffered a traumatic head injury. Mr. Turing, your father, had you transferred to the bio-med facility here at OAS after the hospital doctors determined the best course of action was to put you in a medically induced coma."

My mind raced and I recalled the textbook definition of the affliction. "Medically induced coma: a deep state of unconsciousness to ensure protection and control of the pressure dynamics of the brain, thus allowing the brain to rest and decrease swelling."

"That is correct, Doctor Turing. After running the most recent set of brain scans yesterday we determined that you were ready to be awakened."

I looked from Doctor Jones back to Falguni. "Six months?" She nodded. I thought back to the last thing I could remember. I was walking with Falguni and we were talking about a breakthrough in the— "Synthetica! We had a breakthrough and..." The next image that flickered through my mind was of the two of us at a crosswalk by our favorite coffee shop. I turned to look at her right before screeching car tires pulled my gaze the other way, then nothing. "I was hit by a car."

Her eyebrows went up. "You remember that?"

"Yes. I can see it clearly right until the moment everything went dark."

Doctor Jones spoke up. "Is that the last thing you remember?"

"Yes."

"What's your earliest memory?"

It seemed like a strange question but I tried to think back. Scenes played through my head like disjointed motion pictures:

the limited time I spent with my father, working with Falguni in the lab, and seeing a film at the cinema. But other memories like things from my childhood were mere images without motion or sound: an old picture of my mother who died when I was young, my father cutting a giant ribbon in front of OAS, and myself as a toddler in a blue dress. "I remember seeing *Castigation* with Falguni in the theater." I tried to place the movie with a time but was unable. "I don't remember the date."

Falguni gave my hand a squeeze. "That was two years ago."

The news was disconcerting. "Based on what is in my head and what you've just told me, it appears as though I've suffered some memory loss. Is this the case?" I looked around as a thought came to me. "Where is my father?"

Doctor Jones again had my answer, he seemed to have most of them. "I'm afraid he is on a trip overseas, tending to business and looking into a possible expansion of OAS. He recorded a video for you to watch when you're ready."

They weren't telling me what I wanted to know. "Do I have memory loss? Is there permanent damage from the injury?"

"We won't know for sure until—"

"Yes." Falguni gave me the straight answer. "The swelling on your brain affected different areas, including parts of the frontal lobe, parietal lobe, and the temporal lobe. What Doctor Jones meant was that you *do* have damage that can affect memory, sensory perception, and emotions but we don't yet know the full extent."

I listened to the diagnosis and felt empty. Or at least something that seemed like it could be emptiness. It wasn't really an absence of feeling, just that something was lacking. It's the difference between having a full data drive that was deleted versus having a drive that was never utilized, but yet you know something is supposed to be there. I didn't want to be in the bio-med facility. I sifted through my memories again and knew where I should be. "I want to go home."

"I'm afraid that's not possible." Doctor Jones's tone was firm and Doctor Baumgartner continued typing behind him.

It was Falguni, my friend, who came across as more reasonable. "Alexandra...Alex, what Doctor Jones means is that you need to stay for a few days under observation. It's simply to make sure there will be no detrimental lingering effects from your coma and injury."

"Yes and concerning your injury, OAS has an experimental

drug that we've developed that may help with your memory loss, though there is no timetable for how long it will take. Would you be interested in trialing the drug?"

I wanted my memories back but the scientist in me was curious. "What's it called?"

"Mendaxecall. It is ready for human trials but only just. If you want to be in the trial we'll need your signature on the release form."

I couldn't remember Mendaxecall being mentioned before my accident but then I had nothing to do with the bio-medical division of the company. My research was in robotics and artificial intelligence. But if there was one thing I was certain of, it was the quality of OAS products. I trusted my family's company since we were years ahead of the nearest competitors in all four divisions: bio-medical, prosthetic, nanotechnology, and robotics/AI. "I can do that." I rubbed the palm of my hand across the course white sheet of the bed, then moved it up to the thin light blue blanket. It was...soft. When I turned my hand over, the lines and whorls held my attention for a few seconds before I moved my free hand up to touch my own face and hair. They were soft too, in a different way. My finger ran across a ridge beneath my short hair toward the back of my head. I traced one vertical side down, followed the horizontal line across, and then ran my finger back up the other side. It was two inches square, with no ridge at the top. "What happened to my scalp?"

"That's scarring from the injury. I'm afraid the doctors were forced to clip your hair short after the accident."

Falguni reached into her back pocket and pulled out a cell phone, opening the camera app and turning it to self-photo mode. She held it in front of my face so I could see. "Don't worry though, we had a stylist come in and fix your hair before waking you. It's a lot shorter now than what you'll remember, but it's still cute."

There were no blemishes or marks left over from the accident and I wondered about the extent of my injuries. I tilted my head to the right, then to the left, and either way something was missing from my memory of *self*. "Where are my glasses?"

Her hand shook slightly before she pulled the phone back again. "Oh, well they were broken when you were hit by the car but they weren't for enhancing your sight so the doctors felt no need in replacing them."

That seemed odd to me. "Why would I wear something that had no use?"

"You were, um, documenting the world around you. It was a pet project of yours. The glasses were actually the only reason the police caught the driver. It happened so fast that I didn't see the license plate and all I could focus on was the blood..." Falguni's voice broke and something deep inside me, some emotion, twisted at her display of pain.

"It's all right, you don't need to tell me the details." When Falguni's expression didn't lighten I tried to be empathetic, something I remember not being good at. "I'm sorry you had to see that." She smiled sadly at my words and the room grew quiet. Even Doctor Baumgartner's typing had ceased. When I considered all the social cues I'd missed over the years I was able to describe the silence. It was awkward. Instead of speaking more I lifted my hand and ran my fingers across the nearly buzzed hair at the side of my head. I was thrown by the various sensations against my skin. "This is strange. It's like I'm feeling things for the first time but I can see myself and clearly remember touching other things. It's odd that I don't remember what they feel like. Is this a side effect?"

Doctor Jones nodded. "I'm afraid so, though it's one we've never seen before. You are truly a medical marvel."

"When can I go home?"

"Why don't you relax for today and Doctor Jones can start your tests tomorrow. Give yourself time to acclimate to being awake and aware."

I didn't like her suggestion at all. "But—"

"Alex, you're going to feel weak after six months on a liquid diet with minimal physical therapy, and you may need to practice basic things like walking and feeding yourself before you can go home, okay?"

Falguni's reasoning seemed logical. "Okay. If I can't go home and there are no tests today, I need to do something."

She tilted her head at me and I knew she was curious. I'd seen the look many times while working in the lab. The image was embedded into my brain. "Are you bored?"

"I don't know. But I require activity of some sort." Another bit of data came to me. "I don't like to be idle."

"You never have. I'm sure they can bring a TV into your room, or something. And if you'd like, I can stop by your condo and pick up your Kindle for you."

I was missing information again. "You have access to my condo?"

She smiled and appeared sad. "Yes, you gave me the code a long time ago. You're my best friend, you have a key to my place too."

Falguni was distressed. Her eyes didn't show happiness and the tone of her voice was more brittle than the one from my memories. "I don't remember that." Based on her expression, I presumed she was saddened by my lost memories, perhaps more so than even me. "I'm sorry that I no longer seem to be the Alexandra you remember."

Falguni's gaze grew glassy before she cleared her throat to respond. "Its fine...Alex. What was forgotten can either be remembered or relearned. And a strong friendship can easily be rebuilt."

Falguni still seemed unlike herself and I added more data to my hypothesis that perhaps a portion of her sadness was due to the fact that her best friend, me, had been in a coma for six months. Not only did I wake up with missing memories, I felt different. I directed my attention back to the doctor in charge of my care. "Is there anything else I should know?"

"I highly recommend you stay with someone for the first week after your release from the medical facility. Or someone can stay with you, it's your preference."

"I'm going to stay with her. I figured she'd acclimate faster if she were in her own space."

Doctor Jones smiled at Falguni. "That's very smart. Before I leave for the day, I have a few more questions for you. Are you hungry?"

"I don't know if I'm hungry."

Falguni saved me from confusion. "Do you feel empty?"

I did feel empty in a way that I knew meant I needed sustenance. "Yes."

Doctor Jones pointed and winked at me. "I think we should start you on some broth and Jell-O today and see how your digestive tract responds. If all goes well you can be back on solid food as early as tomorrow. How does that sound?"

"That is satisfactory. Thank you, Doctor Jones."

"Do you have any other questions for me?"

I shook my head, still feeling detached from the events I woke to.

"Wonderful. Now for my last question. How do you *feel*, Doctor Turing? As your friend pointed out, the frontal lobe was one of the regions of the brain that received trauma. You may be aware that region of the brain is responsible for a variety of things including thinking, planning, executive functions, organizing, and problem solving. However, it is also the part of the brain responsible for emotions, personality, and behavioral control."

"I am fully aware of what *every* part of the brain controls, Doctor, since I have to be able to program those very things as part of my work project here at OAS. As for my own emotions and how I feel, I—" Once again, I lacked proper information. I tried to analyze his question and searched my thoughts. "Feel? I, I, feel, feel—" I stopped speaking immediately at the wrongness of my speech. "That was a strange glitch, I apologize. I don't know how I feel, Doctor."

Doctor Jones frowned. "Glitch? That seems very—" He paused, looking as though he were searching for the right word.

It was in that silence that Doctor Baumgartner finally spoke from his position at the laptop. "Robotic. Cold."

"Doctor Baumgartner! That is highly inappropriate, not to mention insensitive."

Falguni didn't yell, but her tone made no secret of her displeasure. I smiled because the tone was familiar if not the exact words. I had vivid memories of Falguni as my savior before.

"Alexandra has a genius level intellect and has always...suffered a bit with emotional cues and responses. She lives, breathes, and sleeps robotics and using the terminology to relate to the world around her has always been what's most comfortable for her. But Alexandra *does* feel and there is nothing wrong with her. She's *not* cold."

"Genius?" He raised a sandy eyebrow and I understood his disbelief in that motion alone.

Facts assailed me as I thought more about who I was. My education unfolded in my mind like a file, a list of accomplishments and grades. Hyperthymesia had its advantages, but also made my lack of memories all the more disturbing. "I know I was tested at the age of five but seem to have lost my memory of it. Father had me tutored outside public education and I completed my seventh degree when I turned thirty-four, four years ago. I struggled to express myself emotionally, which manifested in social and cultural difficulty and father had me tested again when I was in my teens. Doctors found that the common alleles that contributes slightly to autism risk overlapped substantially and significantly with alleles designated for high intelligence. It wasn't conclusive proof of a disability but they recommended therapy and exercises to help me cope that were similar to those for people on the autistic spectrum."

Falguni nodded and smiled at me. "Yes, all those things are true. Your work takes up the majority of that big brain of yours and doesn't leave a lot of time for social niceties. You've always been extremely driven and socially awkward. I think it's just part of your personality."

"Seven?" Doctor Baumgartner appeared to be stuck on my degrees and I had no idea why he would disbelieve my declaration.

I listed the seven for him. "Bayesian networking including neural nets, computer science, cognitive science theory, engineering, physics, robotics, and mathematics. My great uncle, Alan Turing, also had seven degrees, though they weren't quite the same as mine."

"Alan Turing, creator of the Turing Test?"

I nodded.

"Jesus!"

"Doug, that's enough." Doctor Jones turned back to me with what I recognized as a kind smile. "Let's try again, Alexandr—Alex. How do you feel? Sometimes it's a hard question to answer so take as long as you need."

I thought about my predicament and the fact that I had lost memories of more than just my past but also of some of the simple things in life. Falguni was wearing a fuzzy sweater and I reached out to touch the sleeve. I didn't know the current status of my project or my career and I had no idea if I'd ever regain what I had lost with the injury and missing time. "I feel disoriented and empty. I...worry about my career and lost memories." I looked first at Falguni, then Doctor Jones. "I think that I'm...afraid."

"Fear?"

The word sounded fitting. "Yes. I fear what is to come for me." Doctor Baumgartner smiled where he sat at the rolling desk. It seemed like a poor response to my statement until Doctor Jones spoke again.

"Emotional response is a good thing and we'll do what we can going forward to allay some of those fears. For now, I'll schedule a liquid meal and have someone bring the trial paperwork to your room. We'll also have a media cart sent up for entertainment. I believe Doctor Nanjiani has a copy of the video your father made for you, whenever you're ready. We'll be back tomorrow morning to begin your cognitive and sensory testing."

He waited and I realized that he required a response from me. "Thank you, Doctor."

"Perfect. With that, Doctor Baumgartner and I will take our leave but we'll be back first thing tomorrow morning." Doctor Jones spun on his heel and walked to the door of my room, then held it open while Doctor Baumgartner pushed the cart through and they both left.

I watched the heavy door swing shut. The only sound in the room was the quiet *beeping* from the machine next to my bed. I glanced at it and followed the wire to the electrode on my chest. I didn't like the noise. "Can we turn that off now? It's clear that I'm awake and no longer in need of such monitoring." When I spoke, I felt disconnected with who I knew myself to be from the memories in my head, and the person that I felt like since opening my eyes. I didn't want to be robotic and cold as Doctor Baumgartner had observed.

Falguni came around the bed and shut off the machine before reaching over and carefully removing the electrode pad from my chest under the edge of my gown. I found it curious that she rubbed her index finger briefly over the spot where the electrode was located before moving the entire thing away from me. "There, is that better?"

"Yes. Thank you."

Silence reigned again while she watched me carefully. I wasn't sure what to say to her so I spoke aloud those feelings of distance I had only just discovered. "Falguni,"

"Yes?"

"I feel a strange sort of disconnect between who I am and my memories. It concerns me." I watched her closely and the minute my words registered, her eyes widened and mouth dropped open slightly. A second later her face returned to a neutral expression. Falguni's shock wasn't there long, but I didn't need long to see it.

"Oh? What do you mean when you say disconnect?"

Putting into words something as intangible as feelings and thoughts was difficult. "What I mean to say is that the person that I am now and the way I feel, doesn't match with who I remember myself to be. I can clearly remember saying and doing things that I don't think I would ever do. Does that make sense?"

"What makes you think that you wouldn't do or say the things you remember?"

My forehead tightened as my eyebrows drew down and I

frowned at her question. "The things I see in my memories don't make me feel good inside. I remember being career driven, impatient, and short with people. Rude or inappropriate responses don't come from someone who is a good person, do they? Doctor Baumgartner said I was cold and I don't want to be. Was I a good person, Falguni?"

Falguni sighed and pulled up a nearby chair to sit close to my bed. She took my hand again and I reveled in the human contact. "Good can have different meanings and your question is difficult to answer. You were, *are*, a complicated individual but you were also good. I think my friend Alexandra was kind in her own way too, but I'll admit that there were times when she…you, could be abrupt and sometimes emotionally distant to the people around you. It wasn't your fault, it was simply your unique way of processing people and events. You were wholly devoted to your life's work. The Alexandra I knew always valued logic over emotion and you've always had trouble expressing yourself. Sometimes that comes across as cold to other people that don't know you. I definitely wouldn't classify you as *bad*. You were my best friend and I loved you."

I ran my tongue across my teeth as I took in her words and sucked in a breath when the new sensation hit my brain. My tongue was moist and the teeth felt smooth against it. I reached up with my left hand and felt the strange pebbled surface of my tongue. "Sthpongy." Falguni watched patiently as I moved my first and second finger to feel the surface of my top teeth. "Hard and smooth." I looked at her feeling a curious mix of worry and excitement. "I don't remember sensations and I want to feel more."

She smiled. "This new facet of your affliction comes across as nearly childlike wonder for the world around you. And I think you'll feel a lot more when you begin testing tomorrow."

I thought of the testing to come and of my life after, when I was allowed to go home again. I had more recent memories from when my friend wasn't with me and they caused me concern. "Falguni?"

"Yes, Alex."

"Sometimes I was mean to people and it had nothing to do with my social awkwardness. I…didn't have time to be nice." She made to say something, perhaps to contradict my words but I cut her off. "It's true, I remember being very driven toward my career goals, sometimes to the detriment of my relationships with the people around me. I can clearly see various memories where I treated you and my father poorly. I don't just want to be *good*. I want to be better. Life is about more than my science and my career. The accident has opened my eyes in a lot of ways and I can clearly see changes that need to be made." I looked into her brown eyes and tried to convey the depth of my conviction by sight alone. "I want to be good to others, both kind and patient." The look on her face should have been my first clue as to how much my personality had been changed by the injury.

Falguni looked shocked at first then smiled sadly, another look that didn't reach her eyes. "You will."

Chapter Two

Setting Data Parameters

IN TOTAL, THEY kept me in the bio-med wing for five days before releasing me into Falguni's care. I watched the video from my father on the second day and he seemed different than I remembered. His features were haggard and the tone of his voice lacked the warmth I could hear in my memories of our time together. Perhaps he was as negatively affected by my time in a coma as Falguni. I was told that there was a point when the doctors were certain I'd never wake, and I surmised that those closest to me would have suffered with the news. The fact that not only did I wake, but came through the trauma with all my intellect intact was surprising. Strangely enough, while I lost a great deal of personal memory, all the knowledge I'd accumulated in my years of education and across all my degrees was still inside my head. A medical marvel, indeed.

Chicago traffic was surprisingly light for a Friday afternoon and we arrived at my building a little after one. Falguni led the way past the security desk, waving at the guard as we walked by. "Afternoon, Pete."

"Good afternoon to you too, Doctor Nanjiani! And it's good to have you back, Doctor Turing."

I nodded and forced a smile for the guard I vaguely remembered. Despite not being familiar with the desk staff I recalled his name in an instant. "Thank you, Pete." I observed the surprised look on his face with my greeting and made a mental note to speak with him more often.

We took the elevator up to the top level, which was converted into four multi-story luxury condos, rather than the standard floor that featured six single-story condos. The building was high-tech, right down to the fingerprint scanner to work the elevator. Of course Falguni had that security access, but something made me want to scan into the door of my condo myself. Perhaps it was the need to feel the cool dark sensor beneath the pad of my index finger. Inside was exactly how I remembered except for the smell. I couldn't seem to remember any smells. The doctors called

it sensation amnesia. When they finished the testing it was determined that the only senses that suffered were olfactory, tactile,
and taste. Relearning everything was irritating but it came back
fairly fast. I discovered during my week of recovery and testing
at OAS that once I smelled something I had no problems assigning a source. I breathed deeply and identified four distinct scents.
"Lemon, cedar, coconut, and...pineapple?"

Falguni smiled stiffly. "Your cleaning service comes every
Thursday so that would be the lemon, which is your preferred
cleaner." She pointed to one side of the living space in my open
concept first floor. "The smell of cedar is from the chest that
belonged to your mother. You keep a soft blanket in there for
when you nap on the couch. And tropical fruit is the air freshener
plugged into your wall outlet."

As soon as she mentioned the cedar chest I dropped the backpack I'd been carrying onto the floor at my feet and made my way
across the room to open the lid. Inside was a large faux fur blanket and I pulled it out to rub against my face. It was glorious and
smelled like the cedar chest. The scent prompted images of my
mother but no true memory, which saddened me. I was told that
memories of my mother were some of the many I'd lost with the
accident. She died when I was four but I retained images in my
head of the way she used to smile at me. I never wanted to pull
the blanket away from my face and my thoughts prompted me to
mumble into the blanket. "It's the Proust Phenomenon."

"What's that?"

I turned my head to Falguni as she remained by the door, but
didn't pull the blanket away. "Odor-evoked autobiographical
memory."

She nodded. "I see. Your mother?"

"Yes, the one where she's posed with me in her lap. I think it
was taken shortly before her cancer diagnosis. I can see the date
written on the back of the photo in my head." I buried my face
into the soft blanket again and let the image wash over me as I
breathed the smell of cedar and fabric softener into my nose.

Falguni's voice was a little lighter when she spoke, and if I
had to guess I'd say she was smiling. "You remind me of a cat the
way you're rubbing against that."

I looked at her while still holding the extraordinarily soft
material against my skin. "Cat?"

"Yes, domesticated feline. They tend to rub against everything as a way of scent marking. Though truthfully there is no

scent for us to smell, instead it leaves an inordinate amount of fur behind."

I perked up at her words. "I *know* what a cat is. Do you think their fur is as soft as this blanket?"

Falguni shrugged. "I suppose. What would you like to do now? Are you tired or hungry?"

"I want coffee."

Her eyebrows shot up in surprise. "Coffee?"

"Yes, from our favorite place. The Bean Bag. Can we go now? Will you go with me?"

"Sure, we can do that. It's probably best if we walk though so I don't have to find parking." Falguni looked at my backpack. "Do you want to put that away?"

"No." I paused to rethink my answer. "Yes. Sorry, that was a strange response. Of course I'd like to put my belongings away." Then I remembered she was staying with me for a week. "Do you have clothing as well?"

"I dropped a suitcase off yesterday when I picked up your backpack. It's upstairs in the spare room."

I smiled and for the first time since waking at OAS it felt easy. "I'll be right back." I folded the blanket and returned it to the cedar chest. While upstairs I took the opportunity to use the restroom and marveled at the differences between my home and OAS. When I arrived back at the front door I remarked on one of the differences. "I like my toilet tissue much better here than in the bio-med building. My lady bits are a little sensitive."

Falguni snorted with the first laugh I'd heard since waking. I missed that laugh. "Lady bits...I can see some things haven't changed. You've been using that term for all ten years I've known you. And concerning the bog roll, your father might be practically a saint but the director is a penny-pinching asshole. Are you ready?"

My building was Fifteen Fifty on the Park, at the intersection of Lincoln Park, Old Town, and Gold Coast. Because of the prime location we didn't lack for any number of coffee shops and restaurants in the area. But there was one place I remembered visiting many times with Falguni. I stumbled over my best friend's name in my mind. "Do you like being called Falguni, or do you go by Fal as well?" The question rolled off my tongue before I could sensor it but rather than apologize, I reached out to tear off a leaf from a tree as we passed.

"To be honest, it doesn't actually matter to me. You've

always called me Falguni and I never requested otherwise."

"Do people ever call you Fal?"

Falguni looked at me curiously. "Some do."

I thought for nearly half a block as I rubbed the leaf between my thumb and index finger. The surface was waxy and the veins of the leaf were pleasing to touch. Finally I glanced to my left where she paced beside me with her purse strap slung across her chest. "Can I call you Fal?" I tried to explain my reasoning. "Falguni is a lot like Alexandra. It seems long and...overly formal. Best friends shouldn't be formal, right?"

She took the rest of the block to answer and I regretted asking the question. Before I could cancel my request she spoke up. "There are no rules dictating how best friends should be. I suppose this is part of learning this new you and re-establishing our friendship. I think it would be fine for you to call me Fal. I suppose anything is better than Falie, which is what my dad uses."

Her concession made me happy and my smile pulled the sides of my face. I touched my right cheek where the dimple was located then grew distracted by the scent wafting out the door we were approaching. "I think I smell coffee. It smells rich, and warm and...it's wonderful!"

Fal smiled and waved toward the store and I realized we'd arrived at The Bean Bag. "Coffee is all of those adjectives and more."

"It seems strange that I'd forget something so glorious, even temporarily." We entered and the smell of coffee increased tenfold. I recognized the layout and glanced toward the street side windows where Fal and I usually sat. I followed her to the counter by rote even as I took in the nook near the fireplace that featured a handful of comfortable looking beanbag chairs.

"I'd like two soy espressos please —"

"Wait!" Fal gave me a strange look. "I know that's what I've always ordered before, I can clearly see it in my memories. But I don't want that today. I want something new."

"Okay."

The barista waited patiently, having no idea why it was significant that I wanted a different drink. But with one look at Fal's facial expression, I knew it was important. It was another way that I differed from who I used to be. I glanced up at the menu. "I would like a caramel frappalatte, please. Size large to be consumed here." The barista gave me a strange look and I ignored it because memory told me I'd received a lot of those looks. I reached for my wallet and suddenly realized I had nothing in my pockets. "I, uh..."

Fal had already pulled her own wallet from her purse. "I've got it. Your wallet is in the top drawer of your desk at home. They gave me all your personal items after the accident and I left them there while you were in...while you were at OAS. You can catch me next time."

"Thank you." When they called our names a few minutes later we grabbed the large white cups and I guided Fal over to the beanbag chairs. There were little tables near each one to set our drinks and I awkwardly settled into the cotton-covered seat. "This is surprisingly comfortable but the fabric is as scratchy as the sheets at OAS."

Fal's frown reversed as she laughed at my observation. "I'll admit, this wouldn't be my first chair of choice but they're not bad. What made you choose to sit here when we've always sat near the windows?"

She sipped her drink and I suddenly remembered my own. I held the heavy cup close to my face and sniffed. It smelled better than what drew me into the shop. I tentatively took a taste and jerked back as the pain receptors in my tongue fired all at once. "Oh!"

Fal sat forward. "Did you burn yourself?"

"I think so? It doesn't feel pleasant at all. Is this normal?"

"No, the coffee is a bit hot. Blow on the top of the cup and take smaller sips, like this." She demonstrated the technique and I copied her.

The next sip caused an explosion of sweet and bitter flavors on my tongue. It was everything the smell promised and more. I could pick out the detailed notes in the coffee as well as the cream and the sweetness of the caramel syrup. I stored it all away in my memory and took another larger sip, careful of the steaming liquid. I moaned. "The smell was not disappointing. This is the best thing I've ever tasted!" I opened my eyes to see Fal watching me with her head tilted, curious. "What is it?" I thought about the movies I'd seen and books I'd read and held the cup out to her with a steady hand. "Would you like to try some?"

The frown was immediate. "No thank you, I'm lactose intolerant."

"Oh. I don't remember that."

"Its fine, Alex. It was something you learned a long time ago, when we first met and I suppose it hasn't come up again in the last few years."

The somber look on her face told me it wasn't fine but I didn't press her for more information. Instead I withdrew my cup and continued sipping, listening to the low chatter of the coffee shop. I searched through my scattered and disjointed memories for something to talk about. The need to connect with Fal was almost physical. When I looked up from my cup I found her watching me again. "You mentioned that we've been friends for ten years, but I only remember the past two. What is your favorite memory of us?"

Her face twisted as her eyes filled with tears and I recognized the expression as anguish. Fal abruptly set her cup down and stood from the chair. "I can't do this." Then she walked out at a fast pace, weaving between other customers until she pushed through the door. I was left with a coffee shop suddenly full of curious people. The cup in my hands lost significance with Fal's departure and I placed it on the table next to hers.

"You better go after her."

I turned to see a beautiful woman with golden eyes sitting at a table nearby. She had light brown skin with curly shoulder-length hair and held her own clear coffee mug cupped between her hands. "What?"

"Is that your girlfriend? She seemed pretty upset and every-one knows you don't let them walk away crying."

The woman's observation was unsettling. "She is my best friend, not girlfriend. I was in an accident and lost my memories. We aren't lovers."

"She was still crying."

I felt my eyes widen as my thoughts returned to the look on Fal's face as she rose from the chair. "Oh! She *was* crying." I quickly stood and called back to the woman on my way toward the door. "I have to go, thank you!" Fal wasn't in sight when I stepped through the door, which she would have been if she went back to my condo. I thought about where she could have gone nearby and the solution quickly came to me.

Around the corner and down another block was a small park with a fountain. I found her there on a bench near the fountain and sat down on the opposite end. "I'm sorry that I keep making this hard for you."

Fal wiped the tears from her cheeks but didn't look at me. "I'm sorry too. It's just...I lost my best friend six months ago and I grieved at the time. Then I have to—then they wake you up and you're just so *different*. You're clearly not her and I miss her so much — you, I miss you."

Her sadness was uncomfortable and I didn't know what to say to make it better. There wasn't anything I could say, events unfolded that led us to this place and there was no going back to the way things were. We all had to learn who I was, even me. I looked around the park, listening to the wind blowing through the leaves in the trees, the birds singing, and the gurgling splashes of the fountain. "I like this place. It's soothing."

Fal took a deep breath before lifting her head to meet my gaze. "How did you know I'd be here?"

"I remembered coming here with you. You tried convincing me to throw change in the fountain and make wishes, even though we both know that any wish coming true would be a simple mathematical configuration of probability odds combined with the inclination of nature to repeat itself."

She barked out a laugh that abruptly turned into a sob. When Fal covered her face with her hands I moved over on the bench and lifted my right arm to pull her close. I'd seen others do it and it seemed like a response that would bring the most comfort. When she leaned into me I admitted my failing. "I don't like that you're sad and I wish I could fix it. I excel at science, not emotions. If only this were something I could program away." My words only made her cry harder so I remained silent after that and just let her cry.

We stayed in the park until afternoon traffic increased and more people began passing by on the sidewalk. It was a fairly quiet walk back to my condo and while I remember that the old me was comforted by the silence, the new me remained unsettled. Two blocks from my building a tiny cat sauntered out of the alley and made Fal stumble forward as it weaved through her legs. I caught her but as soon as she had her feet again I approached the cat. It looked skittish so I slowed my movements as I leaned down and held out my hand.

"Don't touch that!"

I pulled my hand back at the tone in her voice. "Why? It's only a cat."

She grabbed my wrist. "Because it's a dirty stray, Alex. You don't know if it's carrying a disease or infested with fleas."

The cat was smallish, or I assumed it to be, not remembering seeing one in person. It looked like a tawny tiger and had bright green eyes. "But look at it, we have the same colors!" I wanted nothing more than to run my fingers through the cat's fur and wondered if it would be as soft as my cedar chest blanket. I pleaded with Fal. "Surely petting it can't hurt." When I saw the skin around her mouth soften and relax I knew Fal would give in. She released my wrist and I immediately squatted down. The cat came right up to me.

I saw Fal smile in my peripheral vision. "It's certainly friendly, I'll give it that."

Touching the fur for the first time was as much like touching my blanket at home as drinking coffee was like smelling it outside the shop. It was so soft and amazing. A rumble started below my fingertips as I moved down to scratch at the cat's chest. "I think it's purring." I smiled up at Fal. "This is the softest thing I've ever felt, why doesn't everyone have a cat? How could I forget the sense of touch when there are things like cats to pet?"

She shrugged and shifted her weight from foot to foot. "Some people are allergic, some can't have pets where they live, and others are simply unable to care for them properly."

I glanced at a post nearby with signs hanging from it. The decision was easy to make. "We need to find out who owns this cat. I can take it home and hang flyers, then—"

"Alex, stop. You can't take that cat home."

She was exhibiting anger that didn't make any sense. The emotion lacked logic. "Why ever not? I'm not allergic, I can have pets in my condo, and I'm fully capable of caring for another living creature." I smiled and attempted to make a joke. "Those seven degrees have to be good for something."

Fal crossed her arms. "Hello? You just came out of a six-month coma and no matter what the tests showed, the doctors still don't know if there will be any other issues from the injury. Not to mention, you hate cats!"

I tried to remember if that was true but nothing came to me. It was a blank when I searched for the information. "But...I don't hate cats."

She was adamant. "You do."

I waited for a few seconds but she remained unmoving. Finally I sighed and scooped the little cat into my arms. "Maybe I did hate cats, but I don't anymore. And no matter what I've gone through, this is still *my* life."

Her mouth dropped open in shock. "You're actually going to do this? Against better judgement and my advice?"

I pressed my lips together and nodded while an image

popped into my head of a scene from a comedic western Fal and I had watched last year. The protagonist and antagonist faced off across a dusty street, neither moving nor backing down. It was strangely humorous and my lips lifted in a secret little smile.

"Fine, but if you're going to do this you need to do it properly. Let's at least see if we can get it checked out today. It's still early afternoon, someplace should be open. Maybe we'll be lucky and get an appointment."

"There is a veterinary clinic four blocks back. We passed it on the way here. The sign said Old Town Veterinary."

Fal pulled out her phone and searched for the number, then waited for it to connect. "Hi, my friend found a stray cat and we're wondering if we can bring it in for an exam and see if it has a chip of ownership." She paused. "Yes, we're actually about four blocks away, we can bring it right in. Thank you." She hung up and leveled a hard gaze at me. "You're lucky, they've got a walk-in opening at three-fifteen. But let me reiterate that I'm highly against bringing that cat home with you."

I tilted my head. "Are you allergic?"

"No, but—"

"Then I'll decide what I'm going to do with the cat after we speak with the veterinarian. And it is my decision to make, Fal." I softened my tone. "Please...I've lost so much to the accident and I'm only just relearning who I was and who I'm becoming. Can't you understand that? And—" I glanced down at the cat in my arms and it purred louder as it head-butted my chest. "I have this need to help. I can't leave it here now."

She ran a hand through her hair before turning and retracing our steps toward the coffee shop. "Fine, you've made your point. Let's go, Doctor Dolittle."

I quickly caught up before asking the obvious. "Who is Doctor Dolittle, is it someone we work with?"

"Doctor Dolittle was a—you know what, never mind. You can look it up when we get back to your condo. For now let me fume at you a bit."

I smiled at her tone, I'd heard it before. She was definitely warming to the new me. "Okay."

The clinic was modern and well cared for, which made sense given the location. A lot of luxury condos had popped up over the past few years where the three neighborhoods converged. I remember Fal talking about it, remarking that the neighborhood had too much money and not enough entertainment. I pointed out that I liked it quiet and if I wished for entertainment I'd go to another neighborhood. That was the previous year and I marveled at how clear that inconsequential memory was when so many other more important ones were apparently lost. There was a man with a cat carrier to the right and an androgynous looking woman with a floppy-eared dog on a leash in a chair on the opposite side of the waiting room. The receptionist looked up as we approached and Fal spoke for us. "Hi, we called about a stray cat a little bit ago."

The woman smiled and gave us a form to fill out. I looked pointedly at Fal and she gave me the same look in return. "No way, this is all on you."

I looked down at the cat who had fallen asleep. "But my hands are full. Unless you want to hold it...?"

She didn't answer aloud but grabbing the clipboard was answer enough. I watched as she filled in all my information then handed it back. "You owe me for this."

"Do we usually owe each other for services?" The receptionist snickered at my words but I wasn't sure what she found humorous.

Fal's mouth dropped open for a second, then she groaned. "Cor blimey, Alex. It's a figure of speech. It just means you'll have to do me a favor sometime because I'm doing something for you that I really don't find pleasant."

"Oh." This notion of barter was not something I remembered between us. "Will I find the favor unpleasant as well?"

She sighed. "If you keep talking you will." The receptionist full-on laughed and I began to see the humor.

"Oh, okay."

The wall next to the entrance featured a large supply of pet products, from dishes and food to carriers for a variety of small animals. I spent time looking over the selection while Fal read a magazine. The little cat slept on in my arms. Both the other two people with animals were taken back before a younger woman in scrubs opened the door to call for me. "Alexandra Turing?"

"It's just Alex, please." I glared at Fal while she pointedly ignored me.

"If you'll come this way we can get you set up in an exam room."

I started to follow the assistant but paused to look back at Fal. "Are you coming with me?"

She sighed again and put the magazine back on the table. "I

suppose someone has to explain your *peculiarities* to the doctor."

I could see by the lift of one corner of her mouth that she was teasing me so I responded in kind. "You're very humorous but perhaps you should stick with robotics. You're much more adept with positronic brains than your own."

Fal and the veterinary assistant laughed. "Zing! Nice come back." She paused for a second. "I suppose that is another thing I'll have to get used to. Alexandra, the old you, didn't exercise her wit in the humorous way I've seen from the new you over the past week. And she typically preferred dry humor over sarcasm."

I smiled innocently. "I bet that worked out *very* well for me." She laughed again but quieted when the doctor entered the room.

My eyes widened with surprise when I recognized the same beautiful woman with golden eyes from the coffee shop, the one who told me to go after Fal. "It's you!"

The doctor smiled and I was drawn to the symmetry of her face and the contrast between her white teeth and darker skin. There was something about the woman that I found highly appealing. She had been wearing a blue shirt and khaki pants in the coffee shop, but both were now covered by a long white lab coat. "And it's you..." She glanced down at the chart. "Doctor Alexandra Turing. My name is Doctor Emily St. John and my assistant is Katelyn. I see you've found yourself a little friend." She gestured toward the cat. "You indicated on the form that you wanted a full exam as well as a chip scan. Please place the cat on the table so my assistant can hold it steady."

I followed her direction before stepping back to stand near Fal. I couldn't stop staring at the doctor. If Fal noticed she didn't say anything. "Yes, it came out of an alley near my condo. I was concerned that the cat was lost but Fal seems to think it's a stray." Remembering another expected social cue, I waved toward Fal. "This is my best friend, Fal. She was the one who tripped on the cat."

Doctor St. John smiled as she ran a hand down the cat's back. The feline raised its tail higher with the stroke. "Well, the kitten is a bit underfed but initially appears in good condition. This girl *is* most likely a stray, we see it occasionally around here. My guess is around four months old."

Katelyn took the cat's temperature, and the tiny kitten looked most aggrieved at the anal intrusion. Then Doctor St. John listened to its lungs and palpated the cat's abdomen. Her words suddenly registered with me. "Wait, the kitten is a female?"

"As she's lacking the proper bits to be a male, I'm fairly sure that she's a girl." The doctor paused to stroke the sides of the cat's neck and down her chest. "She's certainly pretty, isn't she?"

Strangely enough, I didn't think at all before I answered. "Not as pretty as you."

Fal coughed next to me and judging by the look of barely restrained humor on the assistant's face as well as the embarrassed countenance of the doctor, I'd erred with my admission. "My apologies, Doctor St. John, I don't think I was supposed to say that aloud."

"Alex!"

I turned to look at Fal who appeared as if she were trying not to laugh. "What?"

"You should quit while you're behind."

"I don't understand, I was just—" I stopped speaking as Fal held up her index finger. I remember that motion from before. It meant I'd missed some social expectation or had remarked inappropriately. My voice was quiet when I spoke again and the feeling inside me was different than any I remember since waking from the coma. "I didn't mean to embarrass or make you feel uncomfortable."

The veterinarian laughed gently and gave me a wide smile. "Its fine, Doctor Turing. I'm actually quite flattered."

"You can just call me Alex if you'd like. I don't go by Alexandra anymore and I'm not here in a professional capacity so Doctor Turing seems too formal. Fal filled out the form and is upset that I want to keep the cat so she wrote down Alexandra."

I heard Fal whisper "word vomit" quietly behind me.

Doctor Emily St. John leaned a little closer. "Perhaps I'll call you Alex the next time I see you at the coffee shop. I discovered it a few months ago and usually go there on my lunch break." She winked and I grew inexplicably lighter at her announcement. I knew with certainty I'd be having lunch at The Bean Bag again sometime soon.

Chapter Three

Establishing Network Connections

"I'M GOING TO call her Anna." I leaned the bag of cat food against the kitchen island and gently placed the new cat carrier on the floor next to it before opening the door. I watched attentively as the freshly washed and medically healthy kitten crept out to explore. I removed the cell phone from my pocket and took a picture of her.

"Why Anna?"

"Because at work we have ANN, which stands for artificial neural network. I added an 'a' to the end because the cat is very cute and sometimes the letter 'a' is added to cute things. At least it made logical sense to me. Artificial neural network animal."

"I'll admit that I'm still trying to follow your logic on this decision, Alex. I'm not even going to attempt to understand your reasoning behind the name. Where do you want this stuff?"

I turned to see Fal holding the rest of my purchases from the veterinary clinic. She had a bag of litter and covered litter pan, as well as another canvas sack of cat dishes and toys. I thought about the layout of my condo. "How about the utility room?" Fal huffed and strode across the kitchen and through the open door to the room that housed my laundry and pantry overflow.

Fal's voice called out from the room a little over a minute later. "Bring her this way so she can see where the food and litter is."

I quickly grabbed the little cat and the bag of cat food and made my way to the utility room, then placed Anna in the freshly filled litter pan. She scratched around for a few seconds but didn't use it. Instead she ran over to where Fal had filled her dishes with food that I bought at the clinic and water from the laundry sink. There were small crinkly balls among the cat toys so I grabbed one from the bag and threw it into the living room. Anna immediately sprinted after it and I followed the kitten so I wouldn't miss any of her antics. I sat on the couch and Fal took a seat in the nearby chair, watching me as much as I watched Anna. Fal's gaze felt heavy even though I knew it was merely my reaction to seeing her watch so intently in my peripheral vision.

I didn't question her curiosity, instead I spoke about how I was feeling, which was one of the recovery exercises that were recommended by Doctor Jones. "I'm really glad I brought her home. Watching Anna play makes me feel strangely happy."

"How does it make you happy?"

Her question was difficult to answer and it took me a minute and fifteen seconds to find a starting point. "Happy is hard to explain. I feel lighter, though I know that neither my mass nor Earth's gravitational pull have changed. It's like I have multiple emotions running through me at once whenever I look at her. Tenderness, protectiveness, joy, and worry. I've felt some of them for my work before, haven't I? I remember saying things that would indicate such."

"You have."

"I'd like to get back to work as soon as possible." Fal started to speak and I cut her off. "I know that you'll be staying with me this coming week and that you took it off to help me acclimate to life here at home. However, I think the Synthetica project would be best served if you used the time to update me on all that I'd missed during my absence. Work is the majority of my life and the thing I most need to feel whole. I want to feel vital...normal again."

Fal frowned. "I suppose we could do that. I have my laptop upstairs and yours is locked in the safe in your office. Your father put it there himself after the accident."

I touched the skin between my brows where I could feel a crinkle form with my thoughts. Memory was a complicated thing and I did my best to recall my final actions in the project before everything went dark in front of the coffee shop. "I remember that we'd just made a breakthrough on neural mapping for the positronic brain on the day of the accident."

"That's correct. Reconfiguring the various lobe networks allowed for a seamless simulation of human thought and even increased the learning instinct that was programmed in by Doctor Venga. That allowed the android to take whatever base program it was given and evolve it exponentially, from intellect to emotion. However, despite those advancements, the chemical synaptic gel that encases the primary CPU lobe requires a regular influx of Trichlorosilane. Without it the positronic brain suffers rapid memory degradation and eventual system collapse. The more the brain is taxed, the faster the decay.

The additive was unfamiliar. "What is Trichlorosilane?"

"It's a colorless and volatile inorganic compound. It rapidly decomposes in water to produce silicone polymer while giving off hydrochloric acid. The small amount of acid clears the circuitry and neural pathways and the silicone adds a protective layer after to help prolong the life of the system."

"Fascinating." Motion near the bookshelf caught my eye. Anna had jumped up to the third shelf and readied herself for the big leap to the mantle above the gas fireplace. My gaze moved with concern to the glass candleholders interspersed evenly along the dark stained length. "No, Anna!"

Fal began laughing. "She's not going to listen to you."

I looked at her, curious how she could know such a thing. "Why not?"

Her expression indicated that I was being particularly dense. "Alex, she's a cat. They do what they want." Both our gazes were drawn back to the fireplace when the little tawny tiger leaped from the bookshelf to the mantle. "You better stop her before she breaks your candles."

"I'm certain she won't damage any —" I stopped speaking as a little paw hooked around the candleholder and pulled it toward the edge of the wood. "Perhaps I should —"

My words proved too late as the glass holder dropped to the stone tiles in front of the fireplace with a *crash*.

"Oh, format me!" The remembered favorite exclamation slipped out before I could think about my reaction, and I jumped from the couch to retrieve the cat before she caused more trouble. Fal laughed but made no move to leave the chair to help me.

"You were saying?"

I scolded the kitten. "Anna, you're a very bad cat!" She rubbed her head against the index finger I'd been shaking at her and I smiled. Then, realizing the effect she was having on me, I walked over and deposited her in Fal's lap. "She is entirely too cute for me to function properly. Please hold her until I can clear the broken pieces."

As I used a vacuum to remove the glass pieces from the floor, my attention was drawn back to the chair. The smile returned when I witnessed my cat-opposed best friend stroking Anna's soft fur.

I LEARNED FAIRLY quickly that Anna was not calm, controlled, and easily maintained. She was wild and untamed and so very unlike everything else in my life. Science, computers, and programming were easy. Data in, data out, and functions were planned and thought out well in advance. But little Anna was spontaneous, destructive, and insanely curious. Rather than have Fal update me on their progress in the Synthetica project over the past six months, I spent Saturday morning until noon altering my condo to make it safe for cats and humans. Fal called it "cat-proofing" and again refused to help. When I finished securing the last cabinet I washed my hands in the sink and thought of what I wanted to do next.

"Fal?"

She looked up from a six month old issue of *Servo* she found on my end table. "Yes?"

"Do you want to go for coffee?"

The look on her face, with one side of her mouth turned up and a single raised eyebrow, appeared as if she knew a humorous secret. I searched through my memories for the word and it came within a blink of time. "Why are you smirking at me?"

Fal picked up her phone from the coffee table and turned it over to check the time before meeting my eyes again. "You know she won't be there, right?"

It was unfair that she could understand me so easily while I struggled to fully understand all her emotions and phrases. I didn't pretend to misread her comment, or pretend ignorance like I'd seen others do in movies and at work. "Why not?"

"It's Saturday. Even if she's working today, the hours on the door said they were only open until one so the staff probably won't take a lunch."

Her explanation made sense. "What if I just wanted coffee?"

She raised that bothersome eyebrow. "Do you *just* want coffee?"

I had to be truthful. "No."

"How does that make you feel?"

Fal probed my emotions, exactly as Doctor Jones had directed and I searched for the best way to describe how I was feeling. I watched Anna toss a toy mouse into the air and chase after it. "I feel...disappointment, irritation, and fear."

She stood and left the magazine on my chair, then joined me in the kitchen. "Start with the first, why do you feel disappointment?"

"I think the reason would be obvious. I wanted to see Doctor

St. John today."

Fal smiled. "And why is that? Why are you overly interested in seeing a complete stranger?"

My mind raced because her questions were difficult and provoking. I knew from a few haphazard memories and from Fal's descriptions of my personality that I never before went out of my way to socialize with people. So why did Doctor St. John spur such a reaction from me? "I...she...she pleases me."

"How?"

"She..." I grew frustrated with my own lack of explanation.

Fal came closer and placed a hand on my forearm. "Are you physically attracted to her?"

The image of Emily's face appeared in my thoughts and I spoke of what came to mind. "When I initially saw her in the coffee shop, I noticed her eyes first. They are the only golden brown ones I've ever seen. Then she smiled at me and her eyes crinkled at the corners. She had smiling eyes."

"Smiling eyes, hmm? And yes, her eyes were gorgeous and unique."

"Please refrain from interrupting if you want a full list of my reasons." She waved for me to continue. "Her mouth was full but not overly wide, her face showed remarkable symmetry, which is a proven indicator of general attractiveness. Her skin is a pleasing RBG one ninety-five, one twenty-eight, eighty-three tone, or hex C-three-eight-zero-five-three if you prefer that format. Though," I paused at the notion of skin tone then quickly continued. "I find all shades of skin pleasing so it can't be that."

Fal's mouth gaped open before she interrupted me again. "Wait, do you have all the color codes memorized?"

Her reaction seemed extreme. "Of course. I have a book on colors and computer programming on my shelf. Now please let me finish."

"Of course you do." My friend rolled her eyes like an adolescent.

"Did you see the way she held Anna during the exam? She was very gentle. She also told jokes and smiled easily—and the bones in her wrists! Her wrists were fine and delicate looking but her hands eminently capable as they performed their task."

Laughter met my drawn-out explanation. "Is that all?"

I pondered for a moment then nodded. Her laughter made me wonder if my reasons were flawed. "Are those not valid reasons for attraction?"

"Alex, attraction can't be quantified or plotted out. It's subjective, amorphous, and different for everyone. You may like the shape of a person's lips, and maybe my favorite feature is small ears with attached ear lobes.

I surprised myself by laughing at her strange remark. "Is it really?"

Fal smiled and shook her head. "No, I was merely making a point. I'm simply saying that it's not for me or anyone else to determine why you should or would be attracted to someone. And attraction doesn't end at the physical characteristics. You mentioned Doctor St. John's sense of humor and her gentleness during Anna's exam. Those are social and behavioral characteristics. As you get to know someone you'll find things that attract you, and other things that irritate. It's all part of the courtship process if the two people are romantically inclined."

"I like her laugh too."

"You liked a lot about Doctor Emily St. John."

I exhaled forcefully, still disappointed that I wouldn't get to see her. "I did."

"Cheer up, Turing. You can always see her on Monday."

My mouth dropped open at her suggestion, and I filed away what sounded like a familiarly used nickname to bring up at a later date. "But, we have to work on Monday."

Fal grabbed a glass from the cupboard and filled it with water from the door of the refrigerator. "We aren't going to the lab on Monday, I was planning on getting you up to speed on the project here at your condo. I have most of the newest data on my laptop and what isn't there can easily be accessed on our network with the VPN. I think The Bean Bag would be a perfect place to break for lunch."

"You've made a valid argument and I concede to wait until Monday to see Emily."

"Oh ho, so it's *Emily* now and you haven't even met her at the coffee shop yet!"

I grew alarmed at her comment. Was I allowed to call her Emily when we hadn't yet met as the doctor suggested? "Is that incorrect? Am I supposed to wait to use her first name?"

"Alex, relax! I'm only teasing you. You don't have to be so formal in the privacy of your own home unless the person is here with you and they specifically request it."

"Oh, okay." I looked around at my condo and spotted Anna running into the utility room. "I didn't plan beyond going to the coffee shop again and now I don't know what to do. Can we start updating my Synthetica knowledge now?"

Fal curled her lip up at my suggestion. "Absolutely not! You may be like a machine with your highly driven work ethic but I actually enjoy weekend downtime." She glanced toward my bookshelf. "Maybe you should read a book."

I followed her line of sight. "I've already read them all."

Fal shot me a look of disbelief. Perhaps she was surprised that I had memory of reading the books. "All of them?"

"Yes. You know that along with my hyperthymesia I also have an eidetic memory. I need only look at the title to clearly recall every last page of text. I have page upon page in my memory right now and can recall each in an instant."

She frowned and walked over to the tall shelf. "But...these are all text books!"

"I have seven educational degrees, what else would I read?"

She was silent for a few moments before pacing over to the front door. She grabbed her purse from where it hung on the coat rack. "Grab your wallet and let's go."

Her abrupt attitude shift had me concerned. "Where are we going?"

"It occurred to me that in all the years I've known you, I've never seen you read a single fiction book. I think it's time I introduced you to the grand master of science fiction."

I blinked in surprise, unsure who she was talking about. "Stephen Hawking?"

She actually growled at me, like an animal. "Wallet, now." She tapped her smart watch. We're leaving in sixty seconds!"

I retrieved my cell phone from the end table in the living room and grabbed my wallet from the bag hanging by the door where I had relocated it the previous evening. I slid each into the front pockets of my khakis. "I'm ready."

"Good. Prepare to be inspired."

"Inspired?"

"Absolutely. One of the great things about science fiction is that it introduces you to notions and technology that don't currently exist yet have the *potential* to exist. Thousands of modern scientific inventions and concepts were first introduced and birthed through the medium of fiction."

I considered her assertion. "I thought that necessity was the mother of invention, not fiction."

Fal laughed. "Well if necessity was the mother of invention, then imagination is surely the father. Come on." I wasn't about to decline her offer.

Two hours later I sat ensconced on my couch with a pile of books next to me. Anna was settled into my lap as I picked up the first book. The cover featured a bulky mechanical robot that looked like it came straight out of a post-modern design magazine. "I, Robot."

Fal looked up from a thick fantasy book and smiled. "He's the grand master, you'll love it."

I considered her excitement at the thought of me reading a stack of fiction novels and compared it to my memories of her and our interactions together. "Fal?"

"Yes, Alex?"

"I didn't do things that could be considered *fun* before, did I?"

She closed her finger in the book she was reading and met my gaze. "Not really. You were pretty focused on work and not much else, especially in the last few years. Occasionally we'd have dinner or I'd convince you to go to a park, but most of our socializing took place in the coffee shop."

"Will reading these books make me better?"

Fal shook her head. "I told you before that there is nothing wrong with you. And fiction books aren't meant to do anything but entertain and, if you're lucky, prompt thought."

"Prompt thought?"

She tilted her head and stared toward the far wall. I recognized the pose as one of analysis. I'd seen her adopt it many times in the lab. "Consider this, a book is a form of recreation, and recreation can happen in many ways. It can be mindless, it can require structured feedback, or no feedback at all. When I choose a book to read I'm looking for pure entertainment. However, all my favorite novels will do one or more of the following. They'll make me think deeply about the concepts or story line involved in the tale, they'll make me feel emotions so strong that I have a hard time stepping back from the novel when it's finished, or they will make me want to discuss the book with others. The last reaction is to compare experiences and takeaways from the story."

"I see. And you are hoping for a positive reflection on these novels because they are your favorites and you wish to talk to me about them?"

"Sure. But more than anything I hope they bring you as much

enjoyment as they brought me."

I opened the cover to look inside and was surprised to discover that it wasn't a single novel, rather a collection of short stories. "Are you sure about this?"

Fal opened her own book and lifted her feet to rest on my coffee table. "Trust me."

I copied her movements, nearly unseating Anna who mewled in a disgruntled fashion. "I trust you, Fal."

Her eyes moved up to meet mine after I spoke, then she quickly glanced down again without saying another word. She wore a strange expression upon her face but I didn't question her about it.

Two and a half hours and two hundred and fifty-three pages later I closed the book and placed it on the couch next to me. Fal noticed my movement and looked up with a smile.

"What did you think?"

I pondered. "I think the author is either brilliant or a complete fool."

She laughed at my description but didn't contradict my observation. "Do you want to talk about what you read?"

Too many thoughts were running through my mind and I needed a few minutes to process what I'd read. I stroked Anna's soft fur. "Not yet."

"Are you hungry?"

I felt my stomach but the motion didn't impart any information. However there was a feeling of emptiness and a desire to experience more of the flavors I couldn't remember. "I would like to eat, yes." I looked at the time on my cell phone. "Is it too late for eating? Or too early?"

Fal smiled. "We're adults, Alex. We can eat whenever we like if we're hungry, which I definitely am since we skipped lunch. How about Thai Guys today?"

I searched through my memories and could find none of that particular restaurant. "Have I had Tie Guys before? What kind of food is it?"

"It's Asian-fusion, Thai food."

Clearly I had misunderstood the name. "Oh, I thought you said — never mind."

She unlocked her phone and typed in a quick search, then held it out to me. "Here, I've brought up the menu. Look it over and when you decide I'll call in the order for delivery."

I grabbed the phone and quickly scrolled through the list.

"There are so many choices! Do I have to decide for myself or can you pick something for me?"

"Try to choose for yourself. Think of it as part of the acclimation process. If there is something that you don't care for I'll probably eat it as long as it's dairy free. I haven't met a dish from Thai Guys that I didn't like."

THE REST OF our weekend continued in much the same way. I read the books that I brought home from the library and we discussed each after I'd had time to process the thoughts they provoked. Fal introduced me to a variety of different restaurants in the area. Sunday she drove me to the grocery store to stock my refrigerator with fresh supplies for the coming week. Some items I remembered buying before my accident, others I'd discovered a fondness for only since waking at OAS the previous week. We made dinner together that evening using a recipe I found on the Internet. The combination of flavors was so delicious that I decided to make it again soon. Fal seemed pleased with it as well. After dinner and cleanup, I finished reading yet another book and felt unsettled. Fal looked up as I placed the book on top of the pile of completed novels.

"Well?"

I considered the story and its main character. "Friday Jones is an intriguing woman."

Fal tilted her head. "Do you consider her a woman?"

Her question was curious and confusing. "Of course I do."

"Why?"

"She's human."

Fal countered. "She's an engineered construct. You could argue that she was only ever a lab experiment."

I found her observation...distasteful. "Creation or no, experimental or not, she's self-aware and has feelings and emotions as any other person. She has love and passion in her life like anyone else. To me those facts indicate that Friday is a person and deserves protection, rights, and privileges as such."

"Interesting."

"Do you disagree?"

Her brow furrowed as her phone lit up with a text message. Fal met my eyes as she picked up the device and her voice turned suddenly serious. "In theory I agree with you."

"I sense you have a modifier to add."

Fal sighed and brought up her message app. "Ask me again at a later date."

"When—"

"At a later date, Alex. I don't have an answer for you right now."

Her voice carried the slight heat of anger and I regretted pushing for a more detailed response. "Okay."

After she elicited my agreement, I watched Fal respond to her text message and wondered if my accident and sudden recovery had pulled her away from her regular life. There were too many things I couldn't remember and I had no idea if my best friend was even romantically involved with anyone. I made a mental note to ask later when she didn't seem so angry and stood from the couch. I needed a break from reading and opted to find one of the sticks with feathers to taunt Anna. I grabbed my phone from where it rested next to my stack of read books in case I needed to take more pictures of my little kitten. Perhaps a scientific study could be conducted to find out how a small mammal could cause me to feel so much in forty-eight hours. It seemed too short a time to develop such strong feelings of affection on my part, but nonetheless, the emotions existed.

I found her upstairs in my bedroom, lounging on my bed. She'd clearly demonstrated zero understanding of English so I tried to simplify my speech in the hopes that she would learn basic commands and responses. "Who is my little baby cat? Who is my pretty girl?" I waved the feathered end of the toy through the air and was pleased to see her give chase. Despite the expense and chaos Anna brought into my life, I regretted nothing about my decision to bring her home with me. I continued speaking to her in a limited child-like vocabulary as she played. I'm sure I sounded foolish but I didn't care about that either. Anna brought me joy.

Chapter Four

Error Check

MONDAY MORNING I awoke without the aid of an alarm, though truthfully I couldn't remember if I ever used one before. I'd been waking each morning abruptly, fully aware and ready to start my day since I was brought out of my coma. My previous method of waking was one of the memories I'd lost with the accident. I couldn't remember a single time from before the coma. By seven a.m. I had taken my Mendaxecall pill, dressed, cleaned my teeth, and styled my hair as well as I was able. Fal had shown me the picture that the stylist used to match my hair and it wasn't too difficult to replicate each day. The sides and back were shaved short and the top had grown out into a layered pixie cut. At least that's what the description said in the magazine. I contemplated letting it grow out even more because I was used to seeing slightly longer hair in the mirror.

Fal came downstairs while I was cooking eggs and making toast. She seemed surprised to see me at the stove. "Breakfast will be ready in a few minutes. Would you be willing to watch the toast and spread the butter substitute when it pops up?" She was dressed casually in yoga pants and a hoodie with the Union Jack flag on the front, not at all like the professional I knew her to be.

"Sure." Her timing was ideal and she finished the toast as I slid her eggs onto a plate. I cracked two more for myself and passed her plate down the counter so she could lay her buttered toast on it. I applied seasonings as she lay a piece of toast onto my plate. "Would you like some sliced avocado?"

The mere mention of the strange green fruit had my mind contemplating the flavor. I had read about it and seen plenty of pictures. It was one of the things I purchased from the grocery store because I wanted to see what it tasted like. Fal cut one up for us the previous evening to have with our nachos and I loved the taste and texture. "Yes, please."

I watched Fal out of the corner of my eye while I waited for the eggs to be ready for flipping. She deftly cut the avocado all the way around the skin, then twisted the halves apart before using the knife to hack into the pit and remove it with yet another twist. After that it was a matter of scooping the flesh out with a spoon and cutting it in to slices. I made a mental note to remember the way she did it so I could replicate it later. I slid the seasoning down the counter to her and she caught it before sprinkling a little over the avocado. It was strange how easily we fell into a routine around each other after only a few days.

Once my eggs were cooked sufficiently we took our plates to the far side of the island to eat. I brought up my strange sleep patterns from the night before. "I think all the books I've read this weekend have my brain processing things in my sleep. My dreams have been strange." Her fork clattered to the stoneware plate and I looked up to catch her staring at me. "Did I say something wrong?"

She quickly looked down and picked up her fork then cleared her throat. "No, not at all. What did you, um, dream about?"

"I don't remember everything from my dream but based on scientific journals I've read, I know that is a common occurrence. There was no real story or plot to my dream, mostly disjointed images and bits of action. Last night was quite strange with four of the books I read morphing into an odd and fantastical tale in my head. I can still recall the vivid images of that dream sequence but can't make any sense of them." I ate a few more bites of my eggs before meeting Fal's intense gaze again. "Do you think I should keep a dream journal? I don't recall if I ever did that before but logic says I would have found evidence of such by now."

Fal swallowed her own bite and wiped her mouth. "You've never mentioned keeping a dream journal but I don't see why you couldn't start something like that now if it interests you."

"Is there a store where I can buy such things? I'd like to write out my dreams manually, rather than store them on my computer. That way I can leave the notebook in my nightstand for easy access."

She nodded. "I think we can find something after lunch today. We'll already be near the small shopping plaza when we go to the coffee shop."

I smiled. "Yes, the coffee shop! I'm very excited to see Emily again. She didn't give me a definitive schedule, but it is a standard work day so the odds are in my favor that I will encounter her."

"I would have to agree with you there."

After eating my last bite of toast I gathered my empty plate and utensil to put into the dishwasher. "Speaking of Doctor Emily St. John, I dreamed of her last night as well. It was quite...strange."

Fal gathered her own plate and loaded it while I hand cleaned the pan. "Strange how?"

"It was...titillating. I—" My interest in Doctor St. John defied explanation and I suspected that was the reason why her face would show up in my dreams. What was odd was how she talked to me and spoke of things that she never actually mentioned in our limited interactions with each other. I'd seen movies with romance between two characters. Recently I'd read books with explicit sexual intercourse mentioned and neither had made me feel quite like my dream of the doctor. "I dreamed of her last, near the end of my night. She did things and said things that never happened in real life. I don't remember my dreams from before the accident, is it normal for your brain to create fictional stories and images from real people and events?"

"Oh! Fascinating—um, I mean yeah. My brain does it all the time. Some people don't remember their dreams at all and some people have completely fantastical dreams that are almost like movies in their head every night. Both are normal."

She appeared distraught. "Is something wrong, Fal? Is it...improper for me to have such dreams about Doctor St. John?"

Fal stopped wiping the counter at my words and turned to meet my eyes. "What do you mean when you say *such dreams*?"

I glanced at the clock on my microwave. "It's nearly eight a.m., should we begin working on the project now?"

Fal quickly hung the rag on my faucet and gently guided me by the elbow into the living room. "Nope. I want to start the recorder on my phone and have you sit down and tell me about your dream."

I tilted my head to the side, confused as to why she was interested in my dreams. "Does this have any bearing on my recovery?"

She shrugged. "I'm not certain, but it seems like it would fall under the parameters of data that Doctor Jones is looking for. He left us explicit instructions as to what you should eat for the first few weeks after waking to prevent intestinal upsets."

"Yes, I've been keeping a log of my urination and bowel movements, as directed."

"Good. He also suggested we establish a daily routine as

soon as possible and discuss any strong emotions you feel each day, as well as their source. His last item on the list, as you know, is to record anything significant. I would hazard a guess that you dreaming about a woman you just met and admitted a strong attraction to her could be considered significant. Do you concur?"

I conceded her points. "You're right, my apologies."

It took four seconds for Fal to bring up the recorder app on her phone and set it on the arm of the couch near where I was seated. She tapped the record button on the screen. "Okay, tell me about this dream."

"In the beginning we, that is to say Doctor St. John and myself, were both sitting in chairs in the coffee shop, talking about the difference between animal brains, human brains, and positronic brains. The next instant we are in a beautifully appointed bedroom with a large bed, the very same one that Friday Jones finds herself in with Janet Tormey in the book *Friday*. Only in my dream, I was Friday and Emily was Janet and I—" I wasn't embarrassed to admit what I had dreamed about, but I was concerned about my reaction to it.

"You what?"

I met her eyes. "The sexual encounter played out between myself and Emily exactly how I imagined it did between Friday and Janet. It was very...stimulating. I woke in the exact moment of sexual culmination to find that my body had reacted to the dream. I was extremely sexually aroused and I had leaked a significant amount of moisture onto the sheet. Is that a normal reaction to a dream as well? It was an uncomfortable way to wake so I researched it this morning while I lay in bed. The sexual health website says that unlike men, a woman's experience with sexual dreams is less wet but still quite intense. It mentions physical reaction to sexual dreams, which can include vaginal lubrication and orgasm. While I don't remember orgasming last night, or any night really, the wetness I discovered this morning indicated that vaginal lubrication did occur. Did you know that women's orgasms during sleep have not been studied extensively?"

Leaning forward through the explanation of my dream, Fal suddenly sat back against the chair she favored. "Fuck."

I grew alarmed at her expletive. "What's wrong? Is there something wrong with me that I'd have such a reaction without another present? I didn't think there was based on what I read but I also don't recall ever waking so aroused in the past. I don't recall being aroused at all."

Fal rubbed her left earlobe in what I recognized as a familiar nervous tic. "No, there is nothing wrong. It's uh—"

"Are you sure? Because you seem quite upset."

"No, well...I'm not upset, it's just awkward. I feel like I'm giving the birds and the bees talk to you when I know for a fact that you're quite capable in—shit." She stopped speaking abruptly and rubbed her temples with the first two fingers on each hand. "Can you forget I said that?"

Her words indicated knowledge of my sexual past that I didn't possess. "I can't forget anything." My own declaration gave me pause. "With the exception of everything I lost to brain injury."

"Don't remind me."

"Fal?"

She didn't open her eyes. Her response sounded tired despite the early hour. She sighed. "Yes, Alex."

"I don't remember any of my sexual experience. Did I have a lot? I don't even recall kissing anyone. If I had relationships prior to my accident, then I have no knowledge of them." I watched as Fal opened her eyes and sat back on the chair but still refused to meet my gaze. Instead, she watched Anna where the little cat sat atop the mantle. I gave up trying to keep her off the wood shelf and opted instead to remove the candles that had been placed there.

"You were always a very private person. It's true that most of your life was devoted to science, OAS, and the AI project specifically. You didn't typically bring your private life to work with you and didn't really encourage the rest of us in the lab to do it either. You preferred to keep everything as professional as possible."

I didn't like how she was describing me. "When you tell me details like that it makes me sound like a..." I contemplated the best term. "An arsehole." The word was Fal's. It was crude but fit the meaning I was looking to impart.

Fal snorted a quick laugh. "No, as I said before, you were very driven and brilliant in our field. But you have to understand who Alexandra Turing was before the accident. Some people dream of getting married and having children but she...you...to you, marriage was a social construct. And while you did speak of previous lovers fondly if sparingly, relationships weren't your focus in life. What the old Alexandra wanted more than anything was to create life, but not through something as simple as biological means. She dreamed of creating the first AI that could pass the Turing Test." Fal paused. "There wasn't a single one of us in the lab who didn't look up to you or idolize you in some way. It was in your very nature to inspire."

Her words held more meaning than I was able to discern. "Even you?"

She laughed but it didn't reach her eyes. "Oh yes. The truth is, Alex, I only know of one *serious* relationship that you've been in and it occurred about eight years ago. You dated someone for about a year and a half before you both called it off."

This new bit of information was fascinating and worrisome given that I didn't remember it at all. "Who was I in a relationship with?"

Fal sighed again and when she turned her head to meet my gaze she looked sad. "It was me."

Shock froze me completely for a number of seconds and I grew aware of the way Fal's gaze sharpened and moved down to my lap. When I followed the motion I noticed that both my fists were clenched, a motion I didn't remember performing. I said the only thing that seemed appropriate under the circumstances. "I'm sorry. I don't—"

"Don't remember. Yes, I'm very aware of what you do and don't remember."

"Fal?"

It took forty-seven seconds for her to answer me. "Yes, Alex?"

"You're a pretty amazing and kind person. Not to mention very beautiful. I bet the memories I lost of us together were really good."

Suddenly she smiled. "They were the best, *Pyaar*, but the friendship we got out of the experience was even better. The way you are now reminds me a lot of the Alexandra I first met all those years ago. Maybe..." She trailed off then reached over and stopped the recorder. "Maybe I'll show you pictures sometime."

The word "pyaar" was unfamiliar but I sensed that it was positive so I smiled back at her. "I would appreciate that."

Fal stood abruptly from the chair and grabbed her phone. "We should get to work. If we start now we can cover a lot of data before we head to the coffee shop later. Are you ready?"

"Sure. I only need to retrieve my laptop from the safe in my office. Do you want to work at my dining table or the table in my office?"

"Your office. You have the large monitor mounted to the wall there and I can display some of the schematics and network scans to that instead of your laptop."

"Okay." I stood and we both walked toward the stairs. "Hey, Fal?"

She was two steps ahead as we walked up. "Yes, Alex."

"Should I touch myself next time I wake up sexually aroused and uncomfortable?"

Fal stumbled and I caught her easily. She whipped her head around to stare at me. "Jesus, Alex!" She laughed and I could tell the question made her uneasy again. "Do whatever feels right at the time, just don't let me hear you, okay? While some people are voyeuristic with their sexual interests and *like* hearing others get off, I'm not one of them."

Get off. I thought about the term and nodded. I made another mental note to find books about sexuality and sexual response the next time I went to the library. I had lost so much but I was going to do my best to get it back. I hoped more than anything that the Mendaxecall would work for me. "Do you think it's possible to program sexual pleasure into our positronic brain, or is that too human a concept?"

Fal glanced back as she neared the top of the stairs. "I think that if anyone could perform such a feat, it would surely be Alexandra Turing. You're the best in the field, Alex. And on that note, let's get to work."

Her words triggered something and disjointed pieces of memory came to the forefront of my mind. "I think I did write code for that...and many more things relating to human function and psychology. I clearly remember seeing myself typing it out. But...the thought is vague." I grew frustrated. "I hate that I can't remember!"

Fal sighed where she stood in the doorway to my office. "Perhaps you'll remember more once you've had a look at your files."

I had no choice but to let her unrealistic hope placate me. "Okay."

WE WALKED INTO The Bean Bag at twelve-eleven p.m. I immediately scanned the crowd for Doctor St. John and felt disappointment when I didn't see her. I tried to distract myself with the thought of food. Every day since I had woken had become a culinary adventure as I discovered new tastes and flavor combinations. I smiled at the person taking orders at the counter. "I'll have a McMorris and a cup of the homemade vegetable soup." I was excited to try the new sandwich because when I looked up the coffee shop menu on the Internet Saturday, I saw that the corned beef and coleslaw sandwich was highly recommended.

"Alex, you're a vegetarian."

I looked at her in shock, doing my best to pull up memories of such a thing. "I am?"

She held up a hand to stay the woman behind the counter. "Yes, you are. That's why I ordered the vegetable stir fry from Thai Guys the other night when you couldn't decide."

"Oh. I suppose that explains why I have no memory of ordering meat products. Was it for health or ethical reasons?"

Fal frowned. "Neither. You told me that you simply didn't like the taste of meat."

"That's the problem isn't it? I don't know *what* I like any more so," I smiled at the woman behind the counter. "I'll take the soup and sandwich as previously ordered. Thank you." Fal frowned and spent the entire time texting on her phone while we waited.

When we received our food, I followed Fal to a table near the windows and recognized it as the one from my memory. I grew melancholy between the fact that Emily wasn't there for lunch and the thought that I'd disappointed Fal with my curious need to explore what felt like a new world around me. I kept glancing at the door as I pushed the soup around the bowl with my spoon. Fal must have sensed that my mood was low because she reached across the table and squeezed my hand. "She may not have been scheduled to work today but we can always come back for lunch tomorrow too."

"I know, but—"

"Good afternoon, Doctor Turing, it's nice to see you again."

I twisted my head to the right when I heard that longed-for voice and saw her standing slightly behind me holding a tray with a salad and drink. "*Emily.*" Fal snorted and I corrected my social blunder even as I quickly stood to greet her properly. "I meant to say hello, Doctor St. John." She laughed and I felt a pleasant twist inside. It was warm.

"I believe I already said you could call me Emily."

"Thank you, Emily. And of course you can call me Alex." I glanced around, taking note of the full tables. "I see there aren't any other available seats, would you like to join us?"

She frowned. "I wouldn't want to interrupt..."

"Actually, the only reason we are here for lunch today is because Alex was set on seeing you again."

My mouth dropped open. I was fairly certain that best friends weren't supposed to expose a person's feelings and emotions to the one they were attracted to. We watched two romantic comedies over the weekend where such things were met with irritation and embarrassment. I called out a warning. "Fal!"

"Alex, it's okay. I'd be delighted to join you."

Once the food was unloaded I grabbed both empty trays and took them over to the table near the trash bin, then quickly returned to our table to begin my own lunch. Even though I enjoyed speaking with Fal, I could not wait to learn more about Emily. I swallowed two spoonsful of my soup before my curiosity got the better of me. "How long have you worked as a veterinarian? Do you have any pets of your own? Are you from Chicago?" I felt something strike my leg under the table and looked up to see Fal holding up a single finger. I took a deep breath and fell silent. When I met Emily's gaze I warmed to see her smiling eyes.

She lowered her fork and wiped her mouth. "In order? I've been practicing for fifteen years but I've only owned my own practice since I bought out my dad four years ago. I used to have a dog named Joe but he died last year. And I grew up in Lincoln Park, as did my dad, but my mom is from Diego Martin, in Trinidad." She took a sip of her coffee. "What about you? I only know that you're both doctors but not what kind."

"I..." I looked at Fal, unsure how I should answer given the unique circumstances I'd recently found myself in. Lucky for me, Fal rescued me with an explanation. I preferred verbal rescues over kicks under the table.

"We're both roboticists working at OAS."

Emily's eyebrows lifted with the information and she turned to me. "What's your degree in? Your doctorate."

Fal smiled and stifled a laugh with her hand but I couldn't understand the reason behind her sudden humor. "I actually have multiple degrees. I have PHD's in cognitive science theory and mathematics, and bachelor's degrees in Bayesian networking, computer science, engineering, physics, and robotics."

Emily's mouth dropped open and she moved her gaze from me to Fal. "She's kidding, right?"

"I'm afraid not. Don't worry though, I've only got a bachelor's degree in computer programming and a doctorate in experimental psychology. While OAS is known to hire the best in our field, not all of us are prodigies like Alex here."

I looked down at my soup at Fal's words, suddenly feeling uncomfortable with how different I was compared to most other people. In an instant of cognitive self-awareness I realized that without the intense focus on my career goals that I apparently used to have, my only other option was to turn my gaze inward. The difference between me and the world around me seemed like a chasm. It felt socially insurmountable. How could I ever connect with someone like Emily?

"I can honestly say I've never met a prodigy before, but..." I looked up when she didn't finish the sentence and Emily smiled at me, the little wrinkles visible at the corners of those golden brown eyes. "I find it incredibly intriguing." She picked up her fork again and winked at me. "Oh...and attractive."

Initially I was elated by Emily's words, that despite being so incredibly different from the people around me, she didn't care. But she didn't know how different I really was. The problem wasn't that Emily didn't know all of me, the potential issue in that ignorance would be found in the fact that *I* didn't know all of me. I was morally obligated to tell her the truth about how damaged I was. "Emily, I think in the spirit of full disclosure, I need to tell you that I was in an accident six months ago and only just woke from a coma last week."

Emily gasped. "Oh my God, are you okay? Wait, you briefly mentioned something about that the day we first saw each other in the coffee shop."

Fal jumped in. "She's physically healthy, but she suffered a traumatic brain injury and has lost a lot of memories of her past. Alex also experienced something never seen before in that she can't remember the way things touch, taste, and smell. So, she's relearning a lot."

"Wow, that's...I don't even think I have words for what it is." Emily's gaze moved from where Fal sat on the right, to where I sat on her left. "That must be so frightening for you. How do you feel?"

I looked back at her, sparing a quick glance for Fal. "Honestly?" Emily nodded and Fal's eyes narrowed as she focused on me. "It's disheartening to discover that I'm missing so much of my life, my memories of childhood and normal human experiences. I want to learn as much as possible so I can resume life where I left off at the time of the accident. But..."

Fal prompted me. "But?"

"But at the same time, everything feels brand new. I'm having all these new experiences, meeting new people, and enjoying being alive. I feel...reborn. Is that strange?"

Emily reached over and gently patted my hand. "If anything, I'd say that's a normal reaction to a traumatic or near-death experience. You've been given a new lease on life, its best if you don't waste it."

We were interrupted by vibrations from Fal's cell phone and she frowned when she saw the display. "Hey, sorry to interrupt but I have to return a call. I'll be back in a few minutes, okay?"

I shrugged. "It's fine, take your time. You've already given up a week to help me acclimate and that's more than enough."

She smiled back at me but it was another one that didn't reach her eyes. Her lips were tight and there were small vertical wrinkles between her brows. I wondered who was calling. "Thanks." Fal turned to Emily. "It was a pleasure meeting you again. No offense but I hope I never have cause to return to your clinic because this one," she pointed at me, "decides to pick up another stray animal."

Emily laughed. "Yes, well, that just means that Alex has a big heart and an abundance of love to give."

Emily's defense embarrassed me but I didn't want to show it. I chose to answer Fal instead. "Go on, we'll be fine." She acknowledged my assertion with a nod but was already heading for the door.

Emily watched Fal walk away then turned her full gaze on me. It made me nervous. "So—" I was horrified to realize that I had absolutely nothing to say. Decades of education and research and I may as well have been a formatted disk when it came to asking the things I really wanted to know.

She prompted. "So?"

I flipped through what memories I could access, like images in a catalog. But trying to come up with something unique and interesting to speak with Emily about was like calculating pi to the one hundredth digit in my head. No, calculating pi was easier. Wait...pi was the answer! I met Emily's gaze. "Do you eat?" She pointedly looked down at her nearly empty dish and I felt like a complete idiot. "I mean, would you like to eat with me?"

"I have enjoyed it so far." I sighed. It was such a weak and human sound but it truly conveyed how I felt. Emily's smile let me know that she enjoyed making things difficult for me.

"I'm sorry. I'm not good at this."

Dark curly hair bounced as Emily tilted her head to the side. "Is your social difficulty something you've developed as a result of your memory loss?"

I rubbed my finger over a gouge in the wood table as I gave her the honest answer. "I don't think that social norms were ever something I excelled at. From what memories I can recall, I've always struggled with social interaction. People are hard to connect with. They aren't like machines at all."

Emily nodded sagely. "That's certainly true. Social interaction takes a lot of work from both sides and nobody is perfect, so don't feel like you have to be. Just say what's on your mind, Alex."

I inhaled and exhaled slowly. "Emily St. John, I like you."

"I gathered that."

Courage is a thing that is spoken about once and felt twice. I dug for mine within the depths of my scattered and torn psyche. "Would you like to eat dinner with me sometime soon?"

Her smile was blinding and the warmth returned to my chest with her response. "I would love to have dinner with you." The smile didn't stay because the minute she looked at the time on her phone was the very same instant her expression turned to one of sorrow. "Damn. Unfortunately for this meal, I have to get back to the clinic. But," She reached into her purse and withdrew a business card. "I'll give you my card so you can program my phone number into your cell. Text me when you have time to talk about dinner." She stood and I stood as well.

I felt extremely lucky with how things had gone. "Thank you for saying yes. I've really enjoyed seeing you today and I can't wait to learn more about you over our dinner date."

Emily St. John opened her arms for a hug. "I feel the same way." I met her embrace and reveled in the new feeling of touch, the warmth of her skin, and pressure as she pulled me against her. She pulled away and smiled back at me. "Until next time, take care, Alex."

She was out the door before I could fully process what had just happened. I sat down at our table and sixty-four seconds later I was studiously avoiding thinking about the ramifications of what I'd done. The metaphorical bubble burst when Fal came back. "Hey, where did Emily go?" She sat down at the table.

"She had to get back to work."

"And?"

"I need another minute to process."

"All right, go ahead." Fal balled up her paper trash while she waited.

It took another two minutes and fifteen seconds before I was ready to speak again. "Hey, Fal?"

"Yes, Alex?" She looked at me curiously.

"Do I have anything I can wear on a date this weekend?"

Her mouth dropped open in shock. "Shit."

I frowned. "That wasn't the response I expected."

Fal's frown deepened. "Yeah, well that wasn't the question I expected."

"So do I?"

Fal sighed and rubbed her ear. "I think we can find you something."

Joy was a freeing thing that washed away some of the lingering sorrow that ebbed with my awareness of the missing memories. "That's wonderful." Then I thought of Emily again, and the beauty of her smile. "*She's* wonderful."

Fal stood and picked up her trash. "Come on, Romeo. We still have work to do today."

I followed her as she went by the trash bin and walked out the door. "Isn't the story of Romeo and Juliet a tragedy?"

"Yup." She didn't speak the rest of the way back to my condo.

Chapter Five

Installing New Hardware

"AS YOU CAN see, by altering the blocks of code here and here, we were able to insert the algorithms developed to facilitate Doctor Venga's 'learning instinct' sub-routine. N-T had a break-through in the filament lab, which made for a more abundant and cheaper supply of nanowires. Shortly after increased production, Purchasing approved our request for more sample strands for the Synthetica project. We switched to nanowires throughout the brain and peripherals, instead of using them sparingly to only connect the four positronic lobes."

I studied the schematics for the new hardware and software that had been inserted after my accident. I remember speaking with my father about the nanotech division of OAS. It was in one of my last conversations that he mentioned they were on the cusp of a major change in nanobot production. "Did they figure out how to create the assemblers and cascade the production pro-cess?"

"Yes. The nanoscopic machines were programmed to repli-cate themselves, with each generation building the next in pre-dicted exponential growth until they could create actual life-sized objects. Their end intention is for the assemblers to keep building themselves until we can successfully achieve molecular manufac-turing on a larger scale."

Her words triggered another article I'd read the previous year. "Molecular manufacturing is the key to changing the world. Assemblers and replicators together could replace traditional manufacturing methods." I grew excited as I considered the rami-fications of the nano project. "Eventually we could replicate any-thing, including food, metal, and diamonds. We could end world hunger, Fal!"

She laughed and I had memories of her teasing me about my boundless energy when it came to all things tech. "Eventually perhaps. However the project definitely isn't there yet. For now I'm happy they were able to significantly increase our nanowire supply. And lucky for us, Director Devos wants us to collaborate on this project as much as possible so we've been borrowing tech and ideas from all four divisions."

I brought up one particular block of code that was tasked with moving an attached prosthesis. "This is my code, isn't it?"

Fal nodded. "How did you know?"

"I recognized it and remember spending hours working on this exact program. It also bears my distinct logarithmic signature, a signature found within each block of code I write."

"What? You have memory of this signature?" Her voice was sharp and I looked away from the large screen on the wall of my office to meet her wide eyes.

I tried to explain. "Yes, visual memory of typing the code. I have a...pattern to my programming. I clearly see it in my head and remember putting it into this one and many others. There is a cadence to the various sequences and notes I create. I can always tell what's mine and what's not, even without my code signature. I honestly doubt anyone would notice it but me. I seem to be drawn to patterns no matter how subtle or spread out they are."

She pursed her lips and muttered. "Program within a program...Jesus Christ."

I heard her clearly but was aware enough to know that muttered comments, especially from Fal, weren't always meant to be heard or reacted on. "What was that?"

Fal shook her head, confirming my thoughts. "Nothing. And your explanation makes sense." Fal looked away as if she were disinterested in my answer but her body remained tense as she typed something on her laptop.

I scrolled through a few more blocks. "What about API? One of our goals was for the brain to be self-contained. We were trying to get the reconfigured data function to work seamlessly with the peripheral inputs. If I recall, the application programming interface was going to be one of the last things we focused on."

Fal stopped typing. "Yes, well in the end we decided to go with standard wireless transmission for programming updates. An external access port to the brain pod would still be in place but used only in the event that the wireless receiver was offline. There is one standard output jack to connect an expandable wiring harness to power and control all attached peripherals."

I smiled, recognizing one of Fal's pet projects based on conversations we had in the past, before I forgot so much of my life. "The wireless updates were your idea, weren't they? Did you decide on a single controller interface, or can the positronic brain be updated from any properly formatted wireless capable machine?"

"Any machine, with the right software of course. Though there is a safeguard in place that prevents the wireless update function from being altered via wireless update. That was Devos's requirement." She looked proud of her part, which was justified given the undertaking of such a task.

"Speaking of safeguards, what about security?"

Fal typed a few lines on her laptop then projected her screen up to the TV on the wall. "Biometric authentication. We've programmed Synthetica to control any and all android peripherals that are permanently synched to it, using both hardwire and encryption secured software. So if any peripheral needs updating, or changes made to the wireless update program, it can only happen through the positronic brain and the harness. While the updating can technically happen on any computer with boost capability, it would require intimate knowledge of the encryption algorithms we have on our OAS machines to replicate proper security protocol, which is where the software comes in. On top of that, the wireless update and control program requires a multi-level biometric key match."

I thought about what OAS had been working on before my accident. "Fingerprint and retinal?"

She shook her head. "Four biometric keys. Fingerprint, retinal, voice, and blood."

Her list of keys baffled me for a nanosecond until I remembered the cross-collaboration between all OAS divisions. "Were you able to develop a security peripheral from bio-med's flash glucometer?"

Fal smiled and pointed at me. "That's exactly what we did, only we had all biometric security read features built into a single plug and play device."

"What about spoofing?"

"Not with a four key biometric test."

The network seemed pretty secure, which was one of my fears once we got the Synthetica project functional. I didn't want someone hacking into our positronic brain with less than honorable intentions. Without limiters set, the brain would have immense computing potential coupled with human-like intelligence and reactions. In order to prove we had created something worthy of passing my great uncle's Turing Test, it had to be above reproach. "So, not only do you need the correct program with security protocols in place, but you can't access the update function unless you do it wirelessly via a four point biometric scan, or through a proprietary OAS program and the harness plugged directly into the shell."

"That's correct." Fal grinned. She, more than anyone else, knew how important the security of Synthetica was. I had quite a few memories of me telling her my fears over and over again in the lab.

But there was one other concern. "Who has access? You mentioned the four-point scan, and I'm assuming you have to *have* access to *give* access. But who is on that list?"

"As of right now, only three people. Myself, Director Devos, and your father."

All three people made sense, given the sensitive nature of the project. "When can I be added to the list?"

Fal frowned. "Alex, we're still in the testing phase. It's not really necessary to go through the scans to give you access just yet. Not to mention, we only have the one prototype scanner and it's at the lab."

"Soon?"

That unreadable look came over Fal's face again, one that I could never decipher. "When you're up to speed on everything, sure."

I let it go and took her word as truth. "So, moving on, what is the biggest obstacle the project is currently facing?"

"Well, until you woke last week, we've been working on solving the portability issue. If you remember we wanted this positronic brain to have a variety of potential real-world applications?" I nodded. "In order to do that the brain pod had to be reasonably self-sustaining and portable with the aid of peripheral attachments, such as a power supply and mobility apparatus. While we've been able to solve a lot of issues over the past year, we're still struggling with how to get the Trichlorosilane into the system. To be truly self-sustaining, Synthetica will have an organically-fueled power generator versus a chargeable battery. The generator can convert organic base matter to energy and use the waste for raw material before expulsion from the system. The problem is that Trichlorosilane is an *inorganic* compound so we have no way of replicating it within the peripheral unit. Without Trichlorosilane to temper the effects of the high heat and the moisture content in the suspension gel, the system degrades and neural pathways corrode."

"What are the measurable effects of the degradation?"

Fal opened two documents on her laptop. One was an imaging scan and the other a spec sheet with measurements. "These are scans from the first positronic brain we built shortly after your accident, AL-1, for Artificial Life, Mark 1. It was the prototype you'd been working on before...the one we were trialing the rudimentary programs on, eight months ago."

"What number are you on now?"

She flitted her gaze toward me then back at the large screen and frowned. "We are currently on AL-10."

I remembered hours spent programming in the lab and watching and murmuring with delight as the small circuits came to life with each new connection to the power supply. Strangely enough, I couldn't pinpoint a date for those memories or remember an actual trial. It must have happened right after I was put into a coma. I shook my head in frustration at the lack of memory and waved for her to continue.

"In the first few versions we ran multiple simulations by throwing programs requiring heavy processor function and setting up monitoring instruments around the positronic brain shell. We tried running the simulations with a variety of cooling mechanisms."

"What did you use?"

Fal ticked the items off on her fingers. "I'll list them in order from shortest time-to-failure to longest. The first system we tried was a small CPU fan, which did nothing for the internal temperature of the positronic brain. Next we attached ten cooling probes, evenly spaced around the shell. While we saw obvious improvement in the immediate area of the probes, it didn't cool the rest because most of the heat was generated from within the positronic core, where the four lobes connect to one another. For the third test we wrapped the entire thing with a gel cap, which worked well for short bursts of heavy processor function. Unfortunately if the processor load continued longer than twenty minutes the gel cap reached heat absorption capacity and failure still occurred."

I watched as Fal switched between various thermal scans and scrolled down through the performance readings for each test. "I'm assuming you solved this particular problem since it wasn't on the list of current issues you emailed to me."

She pulled up the schematics for a small pump. "Of course. We were able to siphon the heat energy but were unable to solve the long-term degradation problem. For cooling, we altered the gel cap and changed the cooling formula so that it was more viscous."

"What did you use?"

Fal smiled. "Believe it or not, ethylene glycol."

Her answer shocked me, though it probably shouldn't have. In truth it made complete sense. "Antifreeze? That is fairly brilliant."

"Thank you." She blushed lightly. "Anyway, antifreeze has the same viscosity as human blood and was the perfect thickness for coating the inside of the cap without being too difficult to circulate. The gel cap has four lines that provide inflow and outflow to a circulatory system. The prosthetic division had a prototype micro pump that we altered to both cool and facilitate circulation of the fluid."

Fal switched images to another diagram of the brain shell, with the added gel cap and circulatory lines. "The pump has three chambers: staging-entry, hyper-cool, and staging-exit. The two cooling lines run down the back and bottom of the positronic shell before merging together and connecting to the exit valve. The hot lines run down the sides before merging and connecting to the entry valve."

I traced the system with my finger. "So the heated ethylene glycol exits the gel cap, flows down into the pump through the entry chamber into the second chamber, where it's cooled, then flows into chamber three where it's pumped back up to the gel cap. Is the flow mechanism at the exit or entrance of the device?"

"There are actually two pumps working in tandem, with the valves opening and closing right after one another. You can see it operate here," Fal opened another file and pulled up a short video clip of a small prosthetic pump. "This is the next-gen version of the artificial heart that OAS marketed two years ago, which we've tailored to suit our needs."

She increased the audio and the familiar *lub-dub* of a heartbeat filled the room. "If I recall, the original artificial heart had a faint whooshing sound, which received minor complaints from the recipients because it didn't seem natural. But this solves the problem perfectly, it's brilliant!"

Fal shrugged. "Yes, well OAS phased the old pumps out of production so the second generation pump is what we got for the Synthetica project."

I couldn't stop smiling at the level of innovation that my

family's company had brought forth into the world. I was very proud of OAS's dedication to advancing society and making a positive impact on the world. "So you solved that portion but you're saying the very nature of the suspension fluid inside the positronic brain shell causes the heat-exacerbated circuit degradation?"

"Yes. We bought processing time with the cooling system but couldn't prevent eventual failure without the addition of the Trichlorosilane."

I considered the problem. "What about switching to an organic compound or using the nanotechnology to perform the same task?"

Fal sighed. "We've considered both options but to be honest, without you here we haven't really had the brainpower to solve this one. We've been primarily focused on all the other issues."

I typed out a few quick notes on my computer before looking up at her again. "I'll ponder the problem at a later date. I would definitely like a solution, if only to make it more convenient and practical."

"Precisely! Some of the applications for this tech, for Synthetica, are incredible. We could create medics with computer knowledge, memory, and speed, with the added benefit of human ethics, morality, and reasoning. The benefits in the emergency and disaster relief fields alone would be tremendous. Then if we look at government and military projects, the potential uses for Synthetica increase exponentially!"

I followed her list of suggested applications for the positronic brain technology to a point, then grew alarmed. "Fal, no one said anything about military contracts. The purpose here isn't to build some super-soldier. It's to save lives, to do something that no one else has done before."

Fal rubbed her left earlobe. "Alex...I don't think you're aware of exactly how much money has been funneled into Synthetica. Or how many resources OAS has allocated to make your AI project a reality. I sat through the meeting with Mr. Turing, Director Devos, and the vice president of finance, George Valparaiso. Devos made me the project lead in your absence, which was why I had to listen to the concerns given by Valparaiso. He stated definitively that OAS can float this project through the end of next year, but after that we need to start seeing a significant return of investment. He even suggested that your father go public with Organic Advancement Solutions to raise a major amount of money while spreading the risk of ownership to a large group of shareholders."

I searched my memories for all the discussions I'd had with my father. I was certain of my response. "He would never do that."

"Synthetica is millions of dollars and rising, Alex, and we've already had some of our team members reassigned since your accident. Your dad...he's considering the public option. The reason Synthetica hasn't cost more is because, for the most part, nearly all the material and tech is produced in-house. They've also been shuffling the budget to spread some of fiscal responsibility to the other divisions, making Synthetica an R-and-D project for OAS as a whole and not just the robotics division. The only way to avoid going public would be to secure a high dollar contract and everyone knows that the government has all the money."

I felt a new emotion with her words, one that I hadn't yet experienced since waking a little over a week ago. Anger. "No! I won't let that happen. I'll find a way to make parts of our research profitable without compromising our moral and ethical standards."

Fal gave me a strange look, another that I had a hard time interpreting. "Alex, the original designs had combat applications, created by one Alexandra Turing more than three years ago, very specifically listing the military as the prime target for Synthetica marketing."

Her words couldn't be true. I was certain that I would never do something like that, that I wouldn't promote such a twisted vision of my creation. "I don't believe you."

She didn't answer. Instead with a few keystrokes and the click of her mouse, Fal brought up a file located on the OAS network. A few more clicks and the contents of the file were displayed on the wall of my office. Each document located within had a different title, covering the range of potential applications for Synthetica that we'd been speaking about. Fal opened the one titled M.A.C. and brought up the summary. "This is the detailed write-up on the limitations, as well as the practical and ethical ramifications for the Military Android Conscript, or Mac."

I narrowed my eyes and gave her a sharp look. "Did you write that?"

Rather than answer, Fal closed the document then selected the file it was in and brought up the details for the doc. Both last created by and last edited by names were mine. My anger was interrupted by a cracking sound beneath my palm. I quickly moved my hand to see that my emotional grip had broken my mouse. "Data wipes and file dump!"

Fal glanced at the broken peripheral and pursed her lips. Then she closed the projection to the large wall screen and began rapidly typing. I didn't interrupt her since it appeared as though she had something important to get down. Instead I made a vow, more to myself that to her. "I will find a way around our financial issues without selling out to the military. No matter what the old Alexandra Turing was willing to do, I'm clearly no longer her. And right now the thought of military androids doesn't sit well with me." To lock in my statement, I quickly navigated to the network file she found the Mac project inside and deleted it and the two others with obvious military connotations. "I want all copies of those files scrubbed from the system or I pledge to create a bot that will scour our network and delete similar until they're gone."

Fal abruptly stopped typing and looked at me in shock. "You can't do that! Devos has already —"

"I can and will. I highly suggest you get rid of them before I program the bot. Opening this project to the military will cause nothing but harm and I won't have it! I don't care what kind of pressure we get from Devos or Valparaiso."

She tilted her head. "And if the order comes from your father?"

"I'll talk to him. I'm certain he'll see reason as long as I come up with a profitable alternative."

"And you think you can do that?" She snapped her fingers. "Just like that?"

I smiled at her and tried to lighten the mood. "Those seven degrees have to be good for something, don't they?"

My words elicited the smile I was looking for and she even seemed to concede a bit. "Perhaps we can entice a government contract with Bio-med's H-E-S project instead. I've heard they've shown promising results in lab rat tests."

Curiosity prompted my question. "What is H-E-S?"

"Human enhancement serum. We've been conducting human population studies for years. What OAS discovered was that the single-nucleotide polymorphisms in the serum's DNA repairs genes and cause up-regulation of their expression. It was a breakthrough discovery that found a correlation to increased longevity.

The paper also mentioned being able to turn on and off genetic limiters. I don't know much more than that because I only read the cursory article that was sent out in an internal memo." She waved a hand through the air. "It was interesting but ultimately not my field of study."

"Not mine either but I'd love to read about it some day when I'm fully caught up on the Synthetica project." I paused because Fal's friendship was important to me and I knew that our previous conversation before getting off track didn't end on a happy note. I watched as Fal fidgeted with her hoodie string. "Are we in agreement about the military applications? Can you understand why I don't want my creation to be used for something like that?"

Fal sighed. "Yes, Alex. I understand why you feel the way you do and I'll accept your direction on the matter."

While she still didn't seem happy, I think she accepted that there was a new line that I refused to cross. Perhaps I had been so overly focused on the successful completion of the Turing Test that I didn't truly grasp the ethical ramifications of creating such a thing. But the accident and losing my memories had allowed me to step back and look at Synthetica from a distance. Instead of the micro picture, I was now aware of the macro picture and knew deep within that we had a duty to the world around us. A few negative factors should not lead to the collapse of our principles and humanity. I wasn't going to give way on this topic and Fal knew it.

THE NEXT FEW days progressed much the same way, with the exception of our daily coffee shop visits. I got so engrossed in the project that I didn't want to take time away from working in my office, thus skipping lunches at The Bean Bag. Once I'd re-familiarized myself with the current status of Synthetica, I began scouring the OAS network for articles and journals relating to the technology that had crossed the barrier between divisions, like the artificial heart-turned-circulatory pump for positronic brain cooling.

I knew from earlier memories that we had opted for a vanadium positronic shell when initially putting the project together. The material impressed me with its strength and energy storage capability. However, I was even more fascinated by the other prototype OAS products that we hadn't yet put into production. In the course of my research I read about the newest advancements in artificial skin. OAS had developed a prototype that was indistinguishable from real skin in group blind trials. It had the bonus of being self-healing as well as capable of touch sensitivity. Items as small as needles easily registered on the subdermal sensors. The nano-aided skin also registered temperature, pressure, and texture. They could even make it porous to secrete in a way similar to sweat glands. Simply amazing!

In a matter of days I scoured the OAS network, reading files that were flagged by Fal for their Synthetica potential. Research reports about the newest prototype prosthetic limbs may have been dull to others but I found them utterly intriguing. She sent an email remarking that Synthetica would be best served using the new graphene skeletal system. The prosthetic limbs featured sponge-like 3D geometry that made them lightweight and strong. I agreed.

And though the papers and research made for fascinating reading, I still devoted time each evening to speak with Fal about my thoughts and feelings. We also read library books and watched TV shows she thought could help me remember, or at the very least, function a little more normally while in public.

It wasn't until Thursday morning that I caught up with myself again, and only with Fal's help. I was sitting on my couch with feet propped up on my coffee table when she spoke. "Do you want to go to the coffee shop for lunch today?"

I looked up from my laptop in surprise. "The coffee shop! Yes, I miss trying all their sandwiches and soups. And coffee."

Fal tilted her head and frowned. "You texted Emily to let her know you wouldn't be there for a few days, right?"

I rubbed the arm of the couch with the first two fingers of my right hand. I liked the way the soft microfiber felt against my bare skin. Her question baffled me. "No, was I supposed to inform her of my absence?"

"Please tell me you at least texted to arrange a date for dinner."

"I haven't done that yet. When we spoke Monday and I told you of my plans to find profitability within the Synthetica project, my focus narrowed significantly and the notion of dinner with Emily must have been shunted to the periphery."

She made a face. "You mean you forgot."

"I don't forget anything. I merely prioritized other things above the dinner and have not made time to arrange a date."

Fal rubbed her forehead. "Alex..." She trailed off and I grew concerned with her sudden sadness.

I didn't want her to be sad but I also didn't know how to help. "What is it? Did I do something wrong?"

Fal met my gaze. "No, you actually did something very *Alexandra* for a change. Your focus, while it has always made you a brilliant and unstoppable scientist, is a terrible trait when it comes to establishing and maintaining interpersonal relationships."

Her words concerned me and I worried that I'd perhaps jeopardized my chance at connecting with Emily before we'd even had one evening together. How would I recognize my mistake going forward when all my decisions leading to this moment made logical and rational sense? "How can I fix this? I had no idea that prioritizing the project ahead of everything else would cause a rift between Emily and me. Nothing I've done was illogical, Fal."

It became obvious in the way Fal's body slumped in the chair and her huff of exasperation that she was frustrated with me. "Human emotions aren't logical, they're messy and require constant maintenance. You want some advice?" I nodded. "Unless it's a life or death emergency, always prioritize the people you care about over your work."

Sporadic memories of the past two years played through my head like disjointed movies and what I saw of myself upset me. Time and time again I had done exactly the opposite of Fal's advice. Dinners and visits with her, my father, and a few women I had only sparse visual memory of, none of it too personal. I'd put my work ahead of them all. Something in my expression must have shown the depth of my dismay because Fal quickly moved over to sit next to me. "I've disrespected Emily, haven't I? She'll have no interest in me after what I've done!" Regret was bitter, almost like a flavor, and I didn't like it.

"Hey, it's okay. Albert Einstein once said that anyone who has never made a mistake has never tried anything new."

Her words brought no solace. "What does that mean? If everything is new to me right now, am I predicted to do nothing but make mistakes until familiarity returns?"

Fal smiled and patted my hand. "How about this one, then? A life spent in making mistakes is not only more honorable but more useful than a life spent doing nothing."

My panicked mind gave pause. "I don't know that one, it's not something I've ever read before."

"George Bernard Shaw. And what I'm trying to tell you is that mistakes are human, they are a learning opportunity, Alex. Nobody expects you to be perfect. The only reasonable expectation someone should have for their fellow man is to learn from their mistakes and make amends if there is harm caused in the course of their education."

"You make me sound horrible, like everything I did in the past was an educational opportunity. Were we really friends?"

Fal laughed. "I think you can answer that one for yourself. Here's one last quote for you. Truth without friendship is a harsh reality, friendship without truth is no reality at all."

I thought for a second. The quote seemed familiar but wasn't one I could place with what was in my memory. The cadence sounded similar to another author I'd read so I made an educated guess. "Sophia Kent?"

She shook her head. "No, Leo Durand. But they do have a similar style. Listen, all I'm trying to say to you is that you can't change the past. If there is something you don't like about yourself, only *you* have the power to change it. The old Alexandra was a good person, brilliant, driven, and successful in her field. The world is a better place for having had her in it." Fal swallowed and appeared to be emotionally overwhelmed but after a deep breath she continued. "But you're at a crossroads right now with so many things and experiences coming at you at once. You have a choice here. You can continue down the path of Alexandra Turing and see how far your success takes you. Or, you can give up a little of that drive and single-minded purpose in order to better connect with the people around you."

Fear grew cold in my heart. "But what if the people around me think I'm too aloof, or too awkward?"

Fal suddenly put her arm around my shoulders and pulled me into a rare hug. "The people who are most important in life will see that you're trying, and will love you for you."

I sank into the embrace, reveling in the strange feeling of security and comfort, the rasp of her skin and clothing against my own skin. She pulled back after a few minutes and I used the opportunity to place my laptop onto the coffee table. When I stood she raised her eyebrow curiously.

"Where are you going?"

I smiled. "I'm going to text Emily and pick out clothes I want to wear to the coffee shop during lunch hour."

Fal's laughter followed me up the stairs.

Chapter Six

System Updated

I TEXTED EMILY first, then waited impatiently for the next half hour for her to respond. I was worried that she was angry with me until she said she was in an appointment, then asked if I'd be at the coffee shop later. I told her yes. Fal knocked on my doorjamb as Emily's response came back.

"What did she say?"

I looked down at my phone. "She asked if I was going to be at the coffee shop later and when I said yes, she texted me a thumbs up emoji."

"Oh."

Her lack of inflection left me feeling concern. "Oh? What does that mean? Is it a bad response?"

Fal walked all the way in. "No, not really. It's just a little...reserved. Impersonal."

My phone vibrated and I was glad for the opportunity to look away from Fal's pitying gaze. Emily had sent another message and it made me smile. "She just sent another that says 'good,' and that she 'can't wait to see me!' That's better, right?"

My friend laughed and walked toward my closet. "It's wonderful. Now text the pretty lady back and tell her you feel the same way. You can apologize for ghosting her when you get to the coffee shop."

The word was unfamiliar. "Ghosting? What's that?"

Fal sighed. "I'm not explaining every word you can't remember or didn't know the meaning of. You have a smart phone, use it."

I did as she asked and gasped at the meaning. "Oh, format me! I did that to her, didn't I?"

Fal walked over and took the phone from my clenched hand. "Easy there, Turing. We don't want you to break something else when we have yet to replace your mouse. Everything will be fine, what was done can be undone." She held out a hanger containing a crisp cream button down shirt. "Here, change your shirt and wear the tall brown boots and you'll knock her socks off."

Despite the fact that it was only ten in the morning, Fal's tone was familiar and I knew better than to argue with her when she used it. It wouldn't hurt anything to change into my lunch outfit a few hours early. "Okay."

EMILY WAS ALREADY at a table by the window when Fal and I arrived at The Bean Bag. She smiled and waved to us as soon as I walked through the door. Fal scowled when I chose to order the Juliet vegetarian sandwich along with a cup of beef and barley soup. I smiled at her as I pulled out my wallet to pay for both of us. "It's a culinary adventure, Fal. Let me *live* a little."

She stilled abruptly with my words, not meeting my eyes. Then after a deep breath she responded. "You're right and I'm sorry. Get whatever you want, Alex. New experiences are an important part of life and I'm sorry if I made you feel bad."

Fal seemed fine until we got to Emily's table with our food. "You know what, I think I'm going to sit over there and check my email." She pointed at the next table over that had opened up.

My mind immediately assumed she was still angry. "Are you sure? Did I do something wrong?"

I was reassured by the way the corners of her mouth rose with her eyebrows in a clear expression of mirth. "There's nothing wrong, Turing. I just don't feel like being a third wheel today." The confusion must have shown with the unfamiliar phrase and she held up a finger to keep me from speaking. "Look it up. But wait until after your lunch. Now go sit with the nice doctor."

I glanced toward Emily where she watched us with a curious head tilt. "Hey, Fal?"

"Yes, Alex?"

I felt very happy. "Thank you." Rather than answer me, Fal gave me a little shove toward Doctor Emily St. John's table.

Emily stood as I approached and I was unsure what her purpose was. I placed my tray on the table and held out my hand as Emily opened her arms for a hug. I awkwardly switched my motion and gave her what I thought was an appropriately casual embrace. I heard a laugh from Fal's table and pulled back, which prompted me to apologize as we both sat down. "I'm sorry, that was awkward."

"It's fine, Alex. How have you been?"

"Busy."

"I gathered that based on your radio silence." She winked to let me know she was kidding.

I ate a spoonful of my soup and let the hearty, rich flavor of the broth burst across my tongue. The little tiny white bits of barley delighted me with their texture. "This is amazing!" I looked up to see those smiling eyes and realized that I hadn't yet apologized or explained my absence. The spoon gave a *clink* when I released it to fall against the side of the cup. "I feel as if I owe you an explanation for my lack of contact the past few days. I...in the past I've gotten so caught up in my work that I often forget about the passing days, let alone the passing hours and any other personal things on my agenda."

Emily gently touched the back of my hand. "It's okay, really."

I sighed because it felt like the right thing to do. "No. Fal has made me realize that while my past behavior was beneficial to my professional life and career, it was to the detriment of my personal life. It is true that lack of skill cannot be improved if the person doesn't go out of their way to practice it. So my difficulty in connecting with the people around me has not been helped by the fact that I've always put my work first." I met her golden brown eyes and felt nothing but sincerity. "I don't want to be that person anymore. I need to create new pathways and habits so that I can learn to be better at social interactions and connections."

She looked curious, the head tilt returned with my explanation. "And how do I fit in with your new path? Am I a test subject, a practice partner in social interaction?"

Emily made it easy to smile. "No. I'd like to think of you as a friend, first and foremost. Beyond that," I shrugged, "I don't know. I've got a lot of learning to do still, and despite my newly-discovered wish for balance, I remain busy with OAS."

"I think that sounds like as good a plan as any. And I hear that you can learn a lot about connection and human nature from your friends." She smiled and went back to her salad.

We talked easily for the next twenty minutes while we ate. Emily told me some of the funnier stories from her practice, and I told her about some of our non-proprietary projects OAS was working on. She was especially interested in the prosthetics division. When I mentioned our rapid prototype lab she got really excited.

"Every so often we see patients that come in with paralysis, and others that require limb amputation. For the most part, dogs and cats adapt pretty well to the loss of a single limb. After all, they have four to start. However, that really only holds true for the smaller animals. Once you get into the bigger breeds of dog and other types of animals, and ones with more than one lost limb, a prosthesis is the only real hope they have for mobility."

I thought for a second then recalled something I'd seen nearly two years ago in a science journal. "I read a story a few years ago about how a dog received 3D printed, spring-based, front legs and was able to run again. Right now OAS is working on two things for that part of the medical industry, realistic looking prosthetics, and ones that can be connected to the human nervous system for full motion control. I believe they have the first part of that goal complete."

"Oh, I'm all about advancements in human medicine because sometimes they carry over into animal medicine. Once human prosthetics can be made more efficiently at significantly lower cost, it won't be long before they can do the same for pets."

There were plenty of times I'd been proud to be a part of the OAS team, to have it as my family's legacy, but none made me as happy as the simple look of admiration that Emily directed toward me. "Advancing humanity, one innovation at a time."

"Ah yes, Organic Advancement Solutions's timeless motto." I nodded. Emily paused to take a sip of her drink. "So...dinner."

The change in topic was abrupt and confusing. "Dinner?" Then I remembered how we left off the last time we spoke in person. "Dinner, yes! Full disclaimer, I don't really know a lot of restaurants and I'm still learning what I like to eat."

"Hmm," Her brows drew down in thought. "So no preference then?"

I shrugged. "I'll try anything at this point, since I haven't found anything that I dislike yet. Do you have a favorite food?"

Emily laughed. "I know you've pretty much only seen me eat salads in all our interactions but I really do like most things. Some of my favorites include sushi, Cajun food, Tex-Mex, and even a good beef pho."

I thought about her list. "Cajun is spicy, that sounds fascinating. Do you have a preferred restaurant for that?"

"My favorite? Fifolet. It's over near Wicker Park. It's a casual eatery and bar, and the food is to die for!"

I was glad she had a feasible suggestion, since I had an admitted lack in my restaurant knowledge in the Chicago area. Or any area really. We simply needed to work out the logistics of the rest of the date. "Do we need reservations? And how does Saturday sound?"

"No, and Saturday works for me. Do you want to meet there?"

I'd have to research the location and see what sort of public transportation was available, or use Uber. Fal had shown me the app on our last trip to the grocery store. "I'd offer to pick you up but I'm not cleared to drive yet."

Emily frowned at my words. "Oh, I'm sorry! I didn't even consider any issues you'd have with transportation. If you want I can pick something closer."

I rushed to reassure her. "No, what you suggested sounds really good and now I can't wait until Saturday."

"For Cajun food?"

I smiled, feeling strangely giddy. "No, to see you." Emily ducked her head shyly at my comment and I thought of things nearby. "I know you probably see your fair share of animals during the day and I don't know if you live nearby, but would you be interested in going to Lincoln Park Zoo before dinner? Then we could ride together to the restaurant." A sudden thought occurred to me and I amended my statement. "Or I can take an Uber to the restaurant so you're not obligated to take me home if the date goes poorly."

Emily winked. "I thought I only got to take you home if the date was going really well?"

Sexual innuendo. I'd read it, I'd seen it in movies, but I had no memory of having it directed toward me. The fact that it was coming from a woman with whom I greatly admired and thought was stunningly attractive made me squirm in my seat. "I, uh, I..." I could find no words nor phrases in my vocabulary to express how I felt right at that moment and was certain I'd heard a quiet laugh from Fal's table.

Perhaps it was the flummoxed look on my face but Emily spoke up to save me from another potentially awkward response. "I'm sorry, was that too forward?"

She looked a little distraught and I wanted to reassure her that it was fine. I loathed the thought of causing distress to someone else. "No, not at all. It actually made me feel...I'm afraid I don't have a word to describe the emotion but it wasn't negative."

Emily leaned closer and lowered her voice. "Alex, when you said that you lost a lot of your memories, does that include ones of dating or relationships?"

I froze, stopping all motion, including my breathing. I knew from reading and television that experience was a boon when entering into a relationship. Not only sexual experience but the action of exchanging conversation, emotions, and dealing with interpersonal conflicts along the way. I wondered if my lack of experience, or lack of memory of it, would cause Emily to take another path in our interactions. I attempted to analyze my reticence, my fear. I didn't want Emily to discount me for my lack of experience or knowledge of sexual history. But I owed it to her to be honest. My sandwich was momentarily forgotten as I met her eyes.

"I don't remember anything of that nature." I paused after the initial words, but went on quickly to prevent her from speaking. "I will understand if you find that off-putting. It would be a logical response. From what I've seen and read, it's a risk to someone's heart and emotions to invest in a relationship with someone who has no previous experience. And if that's the case I'd still like to go to dinner with you because even discounting the attraction or romantic potential, I find you utterly fascinating and would like to remain friends."

"You know, my ma has a saying that goes something like this. Ya doh be lucky an' coward."

The words made no sense, even after remembering that her mother was from Trinidad. "I don't understand. Do you have a translation?" She smiled at me, and the action made me feel both calm and nervous. It was an unexplainable reaction on my part. I figured I could ask Fal about it later.

"What it means is you can't expect to be lucky and afraid at the same time. Every achievement in life is made with a degree of risk. Perhaps you will recognize this quote better. Hellen Keller once said that optimism is the faith that leads to achievement. Nothing can be done without hope and confidence."

I nodded. "Yes, that computes much better. Thank you. As for hope and confidence, while I may be lacking in the second, I've got plenty of the first. All things considered, I have a new lease on life and if a person can't have hope after that then hope is truly lost."

The smile Emily gave me was the brightest I'd ever seen. "It's all settled then, proceed forward..."

"Slowly."

"Yes slowly." She paused for a second and a brief look of

concern flitted across her features. "You are attracted to women though, right? I mean, this isn't a sexual experiment for you?"

Emily's words shocked me for a moment. "Do people do that to each other?"

She frowned. "I'm afraid so. Though for many it's just part of learning who they are and no harm is intended."

"I'm definitely not experimenting. And from what I have observed since coming out of my coma, as well as what I've been told, I'm attracted to all types and genders. Though in an honest admission, I've been more drawn to you than anyone else I've met since waking, or even remember meeting. It's more than your aesthetic, it's your style, your voice, the way you smile with your eyes—" I was interrupted simultaneously by loud throat clearing from the next table and gentle laughter from Emily. I grew uncomfortable as I realized that I'd said too much too soon. "I think I was supposed to wait to admit all that."

Emily reached over and squeezed my upper arm. She was a very tactile person. "Well in the spirit of honest admission, I find your truthfulness and innocent curiosity a refreshing change of pace. Even though we've only just met in the relative scheme of things, I'm drawn to you as well. And so far," Emily paused and lowered her lashes slightly as she gave me a slow smile. "I find you very appealing."

"Oh." There was a strange rush through my body following her admission and I thought perhaps if I could program *that* bit of emotion into a positronic brain I'd pass my uncle's test for sure. Future goals were good, I told myself, but the present felt much better in that moment.

I was left in a bit of a daze from her words and much to my dismay lunch passed by too quickly. I felt as though I had merely blinked and found Emily frowning down at her cell phone. "I hate to say it..."

I sighed. "But you have to go back to work."

"Yes." She said, regretfully. Emily stood to gather her trash when her tray accidentally knocked a glass that was half full of ice water over the edge of the table. Without thinking about it and not quite aware of the motion, I moved to catch it. We both paused to see the glass held firmly in my hand with only a small amount of splash on the back of my fingers. Dark brows rose as Emily looked at me in surprise. "Wow. That was quite a catch."

I didn't know how to respond other than to carefully place the glass back on the table. The ensuing silence was broken by the scraping of a chair as Fal quickly made her way over to us. I stood when Fal held out her hand to Emily. "It was good to see you again, Doctor St. John."

"Please, just call me Emily. Unless I'm at work, Doctor St. John makes me sound like my dad."

Fal smiled. "Emily then. Well, unfortunately we have to get back to our project as well." She turned to me and I couldn't read the look on her face. "Are you ready, Alex?"

"Oh, yes. I need to take care of my tray." There was a slight bottleneck as the three of us took turns disposing of our lunch dishes then stepped outside the coffee shop. Fal distanced herself again and began texting on her phone as Emily and I walked a few feet from the door to say our goodbyes. I led with the first thing that popped into my head. "I'm sorry that I'm so awkward." I held out my hand.

Rather than shake it as I intended, Emily used my hand to pull me into another hug. Her whispered words into my ear caused a strange physical reaction, another which was new to me since waking. I shivered. "I find you very charming and can't wait to continue this conversation while on an actual date with you." Then as she pulled away she placed the lightest of kisses on my cheek near the corner of my mouth.

Emily left me there with the fingers of my left hand pressed to my cheek, watching her walk away. Her figure was very appealing from behind. Eventually Fal finished texting and came over to stand beside me. She glanced from Emily's departing figure to my gobsmacked face. "If you're finished ogling, we have to go."

As far as I was aware, we had no real schedule this week. I looked at her curiously. "Go where?"

"David Devos wants to meet with us. We're going to OAS."

Her words surprised me and I grew apprehensive. I hadn't been back to the facility since coming out of the coma and was unsure what this meeting could be about. "Did he say what he wanted? Do I need to bring my laptop?"

She waved off my concerns. "No. I suspect he only wants an update on your condition and feedback about what we've been going over this week."

"You haven't kept him updated?"

Fal stumbled over the uneven sidewalk but I quickly caught and righted her. "Oh, I've informed him of our progress but you know Devos. He likes to see things for himself."

I actually *didn't* know that and didn't remember such a thing. I could picture the man in my head and remember face-to-face conversations with him, but had no memory of his personality. Rather than say as much to Fal, I decided to keep the information to myself. It wasn't a long walk back to the parking garage at my condo where Fal had left her car. From there it was nearly a half hour to OAS in Chicago's early afternoon traffic. When we arrived, Fal made to get out of the car but I didn't move. She paused in opening the door, then turned back to me, her eyes narrowed with worry. "What's wrong?"

We were in the lower level of the parking garage and I stared at the employee entrance to the building, one that I remember using many times. I could see myself pressing my finger on the scanner and swiping my badge as the indicator light turned from red to green. I watched my hand pull open the door and knew the exact layout on the other side. But I couldn't remember the feel of the cold metal handle, or any emotions attached to the place. "I don't know."

"Alex." I turned to look at Fal. "You have nothing to be afraid of here. This is your company, these are your people. We're just stopping for a brief update and to pick up a few files."

My strange reticence was irrational. "I," I sighed and pushed through the feeling that prevented me from leaving the car. "Okay." Then without waiting for her response I opened the door and stepped out. I was the one to scan my way through the door first but had to wait for Fal to secure scan as well. We had software in place that prevented tailgating of employees. The camera on the other side of the door was capable of standard and thermal imaging. So if two people entered the vestibule without both scanning, the second door wouldn't unlock. Both had to exit and scan again to gain entry to the building.

The security door opened into sublevel one of the nanotech wing. From there we followed a series of hallways and doors with additional security scan locks to get to the elevators. Fal surprised me though when she scanned and selected sublevel three, rather than go up. Bio-medical, prosthetics, and corporate offices were located in the seven floors above ground. Nanotech had sublevels one and two, while robotics had three and four. The fifth and deepest sublevel was for storage and mechanical. "I thought you said we were going to see Director Devos?"

Fal didn't meet my eyes when she answered and I found it curious the way she stared at the elevator doors while she spoke.

"Devos has been in the robotics labs a lot more since the accident."

"Why? He never involved himself in our projects before. I have memory of him personally telling me that he was content on the corporate level and that he trusted us to get the project done in a timely manner."

She shook her head and stepped through the doors when they opened. "That was then, this is now." Fal paused and her abrupt stop in the middle of the hallway made me look around. Robotics and AI had never enjoyed the staff size that other divisions were allotted. But you could usually see one or two people heading somewhere in the halls.

"Where is everyone? For that matter, staff size should be even greater with interns this time of year."

Fal sighed. "Alex...when you di—" She stopped and sucked in a shaky breath. "When you didn't wake right away we had to restructure the project. We lost a major resource, you. The director shut down the entire department for two weeks to evaluate where we were and what resources we needed going forward."

To stop a project midway like that was unheard of without reason. "But we had just made a major breakthrough! He can't do that."

She held up a hand. "Wait. The breakthrough was driven by you and you were no longer available. At the end of the two weeks Director Devos, *and* your father, decided to reassign the majority of the scientists working on the project."

Her words shocked me. "Who is left?" At first Fal didn't say anything and I wasn't sure if she was more afraid of my reaction or something else. She, more than anyone else, knew what the Synthetica project meant to me.

"Myself, Sam Venga, and Li Min. And of course, Director Devos."

I froze. Previously we had twenty people working on the Synthetica project, including interns. There were a lot of coding programs that needed to be written, as well as an abundance of testing. To strip everyone from my project, my life's work was...devastating. I had so many memories of working in the lab, and each new breakthrough we made was like a gift. I felt a multitude of emotions when I met Fal's eyes. "Do you know how long I've wanted to make Synthetica a reality? My entire life! Everything I've done, all the hours of my career, the sacrifices I didn't even know I was *making*, only to see my creation come to life. And you all just...let it fade away." The more I spoke, the angrier I got and my volume increased with the level of emotion I felt. "You let it die!"

She looked shocked at my yelling but rather than back away from my shout, Fal stepped toward me. It was as if my outburst of emotion released the fetters on her own. "No, *you* died, Alexandra!" She abruptly paused and grew pale, then immediately clarified her statement. "You died on the table after you were hit by that car, and then we found out that you were put into a coma and might never wake. It was a lot to take and we were all in mourning, okay? I know this was your life's work but we didn't have *you* to make it real." She swallowed and grew quiet. "You were no longer available and we needed time to adjust. Without you the project wasn't going to advance as far and as fast and we had to offset cost by moving some of the scientists to more profitable projects."

The distinctive sound of an approaching Sentinel interrupted our conversation and I turned my head toward the end of the hallway, expecting to see my personal pet project, Artemis. I never cared for the appearance of OAS's security droids and worked in my spare time to give the one assigned to our department a little more personality. Perhaps it was a day for surprises, and maybe I should have expected yet another change, but it wasn't Artemis that walked around the corner. Nearly two years ago, shortly after the Sentinels went online, Fal joked that we should decorate Artemis somehow so the droid didn't look like the ones on all the other floors. I gave her permission and even worked on a program that would alter Artemis's voice and lexicon. The robotics division now had a Sentinel that wore a permanently affixed tin badge, told jokes, and had a pleasing British accent.

I wasn't sure which one approached us but I knew it wasn't Artemis. Sentinels were large at a little over six feet tall. The white powder coated metal gleamed in the LED lights of the corridor. While the android had arms, legs, and a big box-like torso, it didn't have a head. Instead there was a sensor dome in its place with an ominous looking LED light to indicate activity. OAS had a Sentinel assigned to all the divisions, walking the halls of each floor and demanding badge scans from everyone they encountered. If you didn't pass the security check the android was equipped with a cuff system. If the person encountered was violent or threatening, the Sentinel was also equipped with a Taser and would automatically contact the security desk and the police.

The Sentinel that approached us seemed loud and abrasive, not at all what I was familiar with on the AI floor. "This unit registers the physical and NFC idents of Doctor Alexandra Turing and Doctor Falguni Nanjiani. Please present badges for security scan."

My badge was clipped to my pants pocket and Fal's was on a lanyard around her neck. We held them out so the Sentinel could scan. I questioned its identity. "Which unit are you?"

The sentinel answered in its stilted robotic voice. "This unit is designated as Apollo."

I looked at Fal. "Wasn't Apollo assigned to sub-level five, the Maintenance level? Where is Artemis?"

Fal's hand trembled as she answered me. "Artemis is scheduled for a security upgrade so Apollo is temporarily reassigned to our floors."

"Are all the Sentinels getting upgrades?"

"Yes. Eventually."

The indicator light in Apollo's chest turned from red to green and the android stepped away from us. "Thank you for your cooperation." Then without any more input, Apollo continued down the hall in the direction we had come from, probably to take the elevator to the other robotics level. I grew tired of so much change and wanted to return to my condo where things were familiar. "Let's get our meeting with Director Devos over with so I can go home."

Fal gave me a curious look. "Why do you wish to go home? All week so far you'd done nothing but want to come back to OAS, yet now that you're here you want to go home?"

It was a strange conversation to have in the middle of the corridor but it wasn't as if there were others that could hear us. Only the ever-present cameras spread out to give full visual coverage of the facility to the security office. "I...I don't feel comfortable here. I assumed from the memories that remained that OAS would be familiar and make me happy. But there are too many things that are different from my memory, leaving me uncomfortable and sad."

We stood there in silence until finally Fal relented. "Okay. Let's get this meeting over with then we can go back to your place. We can even order Thai Guys for dinner if you like."

I smiled. "I would enjoy that." She led the way through the empty halls until we came to the wing with our private offices. I voiced my biggest fear as we approached our destination. "Fal?"

"Yes, Alex?"

"Am I ever going to feel normal again?"

She stopped in front of the director's door and met my eyes with sadness. "I don't know."

I sighed and reached out to knock on the door below the nameplate with the word Devos engraved in it. Before making contact I gave Fal one more look. "Perhaps I can find a new sort of normal."

Fal gave me a tight smile. "If anyone can, it's you."

Chapter Seven

Error Detected

I KNOCKED ON the door and the director's familiar voice called out from the other side. "Enter."

He stood from his chair and stilled as I crossed the threshold into his office. I smiled and Fal entered behind me. "You wanted to see us?"

Whatever had frozen him quickly thawed and he gave a physical shake. "Sorry, it's just that I haven't seen you since you were, uh, came out of the coma. I, um, my apologies, Alexandra. How are you doing?"

I automatically corrected him, figuring that it was best to get that part out of the way first. "It's Alex, please."

He glanced at Fal. "Oh yes, of course. Doctor Nanjiani mentioned something about you feeling more comfortable with the shortened version of your name. I simply forgot."

"It's completely understandable since it seems like every day I discover a new facet of myself, post-coma. I can't expect everyone else to keep up when I barely can."

The director looked in turns, nonplussed and giddy. He smiled. "Please be seated." He didn't give us time to wonder about the purpose of the meeting, instead launching right into the crux of it. "Falguni tells me that not only have you rejected all military applications of the Synthetica project, but you've recently begun researching the potential profitability of other OAS prototype ventures."

I looked at Fal, feeling the first stirrings of irritation and what I recognized as slight betrayal. "I wasn't aware that Fal was reporting on my actions so extensively."

For a moment, she looked apologetic but it quickly switched to a more neutral expression. "Alex, it's part of my job to report any out of the ordinary behaviors and actions. We're still not sure what effect—"

I stood from the chair in a fit of hot anger. It was another unfamiliar emotion and the lack of immediate motor control in the face of such anger shook me. I shunted the thought away to process later. "I think it's pretty obvious by now what the lasting effects are from the accident. While I have full memory of my project and the people around me, I've lost a lot of long-term memory and some of the more personal memories of my past. In the face of those things, the sensation amnesia seems miniscule. I think the real problem here isn't what I've lost to the coma, but rather what has changed since. Apparently you all enjoyed the fact that I was nothing more than an unfeeling cog in the OAS machine but that's *not* who I am now!"

"Alex, we have never thought that about you."

I looked straight into Fal's eyes. "Am I not performing to my expectation?"

"Of course you are, but—"

I waved a hand to cut her off. "And have I been acting improper or hurtful to the people around me?"

Fal frowned. "You know you haven't."

"Then let me live my life!" I turned my head to include Director Devos in my next statement. "Stop with the constant monitoring and worry. I'll get us back on track but you're going to have to accept that I'm not exactly the way I was before. However, I still have my intellect, my drive, and my passion to see this project through. If anything, what I've gone through has made me care *more* about the project and people around me."

The room was silent in the wake of my outburst until finally broken by Devos's long indrawn breath. He released it with equally as long a sigh. "Very well. If you are so invested in OAS and are determined to help Synthetica see early profitability, then by all means you are invited to return to work next Monday morning."

Fal spoke up. "And as long as Alex's doctor thinks it's okay, I plan to return to my own apartment this weekend as well. If you like, I can still swing by and pick you up each morning."

I didn't remember Fal ever doing that before so I asked. "Is that something you did for me often? I don't have memories of me driving but you mentioned that I have a car."

"You actually have a few cars at your father's estate. However the *old* Alexandra didn't like to drive, said it was too distracting and couldn't hold full focus enough to be safe."

"Then how..." I trailed off as I turned my thoughts inward, picking through the fragments of my bombed-out memory. A few images came through. The first was me holding a pair of cycling goggles. I could see myself shaking my head before putting them back in a case and stowing it away in a pouch strapped to my bike frame. The second was of me zipping along the streets of Chicago, maneuvering through traffic while avoiding car doors and illegally crossing pedestrians. "Where is my bicycle?"

Fal cleared her throat. "I wondered if you'd remember that particular detail. It's actually stored in the walk-in closet of the large guest room that I've been staying in. I was going to see if you wanted to take it for a spin this weekend. But my offer still stands for a ride."

I looked at her curiously. We'd discussed where Fal lived, and the fact that her neighbor was watering her plants while she stayed with me. "I'm a bit out of your way for you to stop on the way to OAS. You'd have to backtrack during rush hour traffic."

"It's not a big deal, Alex."

I shook my head because it *was* a big deal. I wanted to be independent because to me that was the biggest indicator that my life had returned to something resembling normal. "It is to me. I'll look at my bike tonight and if I'm not comfortable riding to work then I'll take public transportation or an Uber."

Director Devos cleared his throat. "I don't think that's a wise course of action given that you've only been out of your coma less than two weeks. It might be best to give yourself more time to physically acclimate before you take on something as strenuous as biking to work each morning. You need to be cautious, Doctor Tur—I mean, Alex."

I pondered his suggestion, and while his points made logical sense I couldn't discount my feeling of powerlessness when it came to others making life choices for me. "Let me counter propose this: I'll stop in today and see the physician that is in charge of my case and if he recommends that I wait, I'll allow Fal to transport me to and from work. Is that cautious enough?" Fal and Devos shared a long look. I knew it had meaning, as any long bit of eye contact does, but I had no way to decipher it.

I could see that Devos still wasn't convinced and his next words confirmed my assumption. "I'm not sure—"

"It's not for you to decide though, is it?" I cut him off, resolute in my decision. "The bottom line here is that neither of you are my doctor, and while you, Director Devos, are my manager when it comes to my job, I *am* part owner of this company, which in turn makes me *your* boss in a roundabout way. I'm not asking permission to make my way to work as I see fit. You already told me I could return on Monday morning, it's not for you to decide how I get here." I stood from my chair. "Now...if there are no other concerns or questions to address?" Devos remained stunned into silence. "Good." I turned to Fal. "I'm heading up to the bio-medical wing to find Doctor Jones. I'll let you know when I'm ready to leave."

Fal nodded. I left the room then but overheard Devos's quiet whispers to Fal before the door shut completely behind me. "You told me you had it under control. What the hell was *that*?"

Doctor Jones did a basic physical exam, listened to my heart and lungs, and then asked a series of questions. Afterward he pronounced me physically healthy and cleared me to resume work at OAS. I mentioned my dream journal and he thought it was a good idea. He also suggested that I continue to talk things out with Fal and make a log of anything I felt or thought that seemed out of the ordinary, or that wasn't well received by the people around me. He even recommended a psychotherapist on staff at OAS if I wanted to talk to a neutral party but I didn't feel comfortable with that. His lab had a long section of windows facing the hallway leading back toward the elevators. It was easy enough for me to watch him immediately walk over and pick up the phone as soon as I left. Logic dictated that he was probably contacting Director Devos and I wondered if I had any privacy left.

The ride home was quiet and as soon as I walked in the door of my condo I made my way upstairs to the guest room where Fal mentioned my bike was located. There were actually two bikes inside the large walk-in closet. The first was the one I was riding in my memory, a Specialized CrossTrail Hydraulic Disc upright bike. The other was a Giant SCR 1 Road Bike. Both had fenders and racks on the back, and water bottle holders, and there were numerous accessories on one shelf of the closet. A few helmets, gloves, goggles, and backpacks. There was also an electronic keyless shackle lock on the wheel of the CrossTrail. Sudden memory of the lock had me pulling the phone out of my front pocket as Fal stepped into the closet with me.

She saw me looking at the upright bike. "You liked that one more than the road bike. You said it was more stable and handled pot holes and wet pavement better."

I opened the app on my phone and with the press of a button the lock clicked open. "I want to go for a ride." Fal's mouth opened but nothing came out for a few seconds. I turned to look at her straight on.

"Right now?"

I nodded.

She pulled her own phone out to check the time then shrugged. "It's early still, plenty of sunlight to do a test run."

I waved toward the road bike. "Do you want to go with me?"

"Nope. Not even tempted in the slightest." Her British accent was strong in her response.

"Fine, I'll be back in about thirty minutes. Would you call in the promised Thai Guys order for us? You said we could get it earlier in the car."

"I remember." The look Fal gave me was a mixture of concern and curiosity. I grabbed what I needed from the shelf and rolled the bike out of the closet while she answered. "I can do that. Are you sure you remember how to ride that thing?"

I smiled back at her. "How hard can it be? Riding a bike is like..." I sorted through my thoughts to come up with an appropriate analogy. "Riding a bike is like riding a bike. If I fall off I'll get back on and keep going."

Fal rolled her eyes. "Now you're being a smart ass."

It was my turn to give her a curious look. "Am I?"

She shoved me lightly. "Get out of here, Turing. I'm famished and if you're not back in thirty I'm going to eat both our orders of spring rolls." She followed me as I carried the bike down the stairs. It was surprisingly light.

I turned to her, affronted at such a suggestion. "You wouldn't dare!"

She emphasized her condition. "*Famished!*"

"Fine, I'll be speedy." When I got to the front door of my condo I clipped my cell phone onto the specialized holder that synced with the small digital display. I took note of the fact that it was nearly seven p.m. No wonder Fal was so hungry. She interrupted my musing.

"I'm more concerned about staying safe than being speedy."

I put on the helmet and made my way down the hall toward the elevator. I turned back when I was nearly there and found her watching with that same unreadable look. "Well then, I shall endeavor to be both safe *and* speedy. If only for the sake of saving my favorite part of the meal."

It took me until halfway down to the ground floor before I realized that I too was abnormally hungry. Perhaps I'd cut my bike ride a little short. Surely twenty minutes would be sufficient to gauge how familiar I was with the act of city riding.

It wasn't as busy as mid-rush hour and the air had cooled significantly by the time I set off. I had it in my head to ride to the little park with the fountain that I'd visited so often with Fal. There was something exhilarating about the feel of the wind against my face. My speed wasn't fast because I was simply reacquainting myself with the bike. I wasn't even wearing proper riding clothes and based on the equipment I saw in the closet, it was logical to conclude that I had such things in a drawer at home. At one point during my trip I turned onto a long block and I increased my speed to see how it would feel. The bike was amazingly easy to handle and it felt as though I'd exerted no effort at all to keep it going.

A short time later I arrived at the park and dismounted the bike, pushing it along with me to go look at the fountain. I didn't have any change but took delight in watching the water fall down the bronze leaves of an intricately designed tree. A bronze cloud was sculpted above the tree and the water fell downward like rain, only to be caught in the basin below to begin its journey again. Tiny *pings* sounded as each of the little droplets hit the thin leaves of metal, and it made a calming music if a person didn't mind a lack of rhythm or harmony.

I had a feeling that time was nearly up and when I checked my phone my feeling was confirmed. I'd been gone nearly fifteen minutes so I quickly made my way back to the entrance of the park and remounted the bike. The return was equally as swift until a car door swung open into my path. I veered to the left around the door, then immediately veered to the right to avoid the car approaching from behind. My new trajectory took me toward a drive and the sidewalk, which was full of pedestrians. I braked hard but couldn't bring myself to a stop before my front tire hit a low brick wall surrounding some decorative landscaping. Thinking fast I twisted myself and rather than connect helmet first into the unyielding ground, I did a front flip and landed on top of the wall on the opposite side. Of the few people that had seen the incident only one came over to me.

"Oh my God! Are you okay?"

The woman was older with a liberal amount of gray sprinkled into her hair. She had a clipped Midwestern accent and I took a few seconds to hop down from the wall and straighten my clothes before answering. "I seem to be fine, no injuries or strains." I walked over to my bike and inspected the front tire. "The tire is also undamaged."

She nodded. "You weren't going terribly fast when you hit, but it was enough to pitch you from the seat." She paused and chuckled. "It's a good thing you've got fast reflexes or you'd have scrambled your brain on that wall! Probably broke your neck too."

I looked at the wall in question, the one I had inextricably landed atop. "Yes. I certainly can't afford to do any more scrambling."

The lady gave me a strange look and patted my arm before continuing her journey down the sidewalk. Lifting my bike upright, I glanced at my cellphone in its holder and cursed. "Holy Hadron, I'm going to be late!" Then carefully pushing the incident to the back of my mind, I steered out onto the road and pedaled quickly to make it back to my condo in the allotted time so Fal didn't eat any of my food.

When I entered my apartment less than ten minutes later, Fal called out from the laundry room. "How was your ride?"

"It went well." I pushed my bike across the living room and left it in the corner, where there was a large open area against the wall to the right of my bookshelf.

Fal came out of the laundry room carrying an empty can for recycling. "I fed the little beast but it's up to you to clean the litter. And you're in luck, dinner has only been here a few minutes so I haven't eaten any of yours yet."

I smiled. "Good thing!" Little Anna was in the laundry room going back and forth between her wet food and dry food, seeming as though she couldn't decide which she liked better. I took a short video in case I got a chance to show Emily later in the week, then returned my phone to my pocket and went about the chore of scooping her small poops from the box. It was the only thing I didn't like about my pet. That and her penchant for breaking things.

The incident with my bike moved back to the forefront of my mind as we sat down to eat. I continued to ponder it all through dinner and even after we settled in to read. Fal was in her normal spot on the chair and I sat with little Anna on my lap. While I was able to read the words of the new fantasy novel that Fal recommended, I couldn't properly process the tale while my mind was focused on what had happened earlier. Finally I gave up any pretense of reading and set the book aside. "Fal?"

She paused in her reading and closed the book on her finger to mark the page. "Yes, Alex?"

"What were my reflexes like before the accident? I assume that if I rode my bicycle to work every day that I was fairly well conditioned. But physically, what was I like?"

Fal opened the book again and wedged her bookmark inside, then closed it. She leaned forward and placed the book on the coffee table. My eyes were caught by the cover. It was colorful, with red, orange, yellow, and greens, and showed the profile of a woman's face superimposed over what looked to be a computer constructed city, or perhaps even a circuit board. The title, *Waking the Dreamer*, was written in simple white letters. Fal's voice pulled me away from my inspection. Her tone, neutral. "Why do you want to know?"

I attempted to put into words the small things I'd noticed since coming out of the coma. "I don't remember what I was like in that regard but I appear to be extremely agile and have displayed reflexes above what I'd consider normal. At least when I compare myself to others in similar situations."

Her tone was cautious. "Can you give me an example?"

"The incident in the coffee shop earlier today. Emily was very surprised to see me catch that glass and you acted strange after. Then tonight..." I wasn't sure how to tell her about the incident with the wall.

Fal abruptly leaned forward. "Tonight? Did something happen?" She stood and took a step toward me. "Were you injured?"

I held out a hand to stay her. "No. But I would have been seriously injured were I not saved by my own reflexes. A car door opened in front of me causing me to swerve into traffic, and back out again. In my efforts to gain control of the bicycle I went up onto the sidewalk. I'd nearly come to a stop when my front tire hit a low wall and my momentum pitched me over the handlebars. Instead of striking head first against the wall on the other side, I did a forward flip and landed on my feet on top of the wall. The older woman who saw me appeared quite shocked."

My friend and coworker sat down and pressed her face into her palms, rubbing at her eyes with the first two fingers of each hand. Her single word response was quiet, perhaps not even meant for me to hear. "Fuck."

"Fal?"

She didn't lift her head. "Yes, Alex?"

"Is this abnormal behavior? Should I inform my doctor or write it down?"

I grew worried as Fal physically gathered herself before she finally answered. She lifted her head and met my gaze with a tight smile. "No, it's not abnormal. You've been nothing less than exceptional from the moment I first met you. You're capable of more than I think even *you* realize. It doesn't surprise me that you reacted how you did, either time. I'd say that in the past you've always been reticent to display the full extent of your abilities."

I had no idea why I would do such a thing, why I would limit myself. "Why?"

Fal shrugged and leaned back in the chair, appearing exhausted after a few short sentences. "I don't know. But honestly, I wouldn't worry about it too much. Just be glad that your quick thinking and reflexes saved you. Are you sure you don't want me to pick you up Monday morning?"

Something seemed off about her tone and behavior but if my best friend wasn't worried then I refused to waste more thought resources on the subject. Instead I answered her question. "No, I still plan to ride my bike. I let my attention lapse for a moment and to be honest I was going a little too fast, in a hurry to come home for dinner."

Fal finally gave me a genuine smile and a small laugh. "Oh, so it was Thai Guys's fault that you crashed?"

"No, it was yours. If you hadn't threatened to eat my spring rolls I would have been going slower."

I got a glare for my words. "You wound me!"

Her tone sounded serious and for a nanosecond I was concerned. "I would never — "

Fal waved her hand through the air with another laugh. "It was a joke, Alex. Chill."

I was glad to see the smile reach her eyes again. "Okay."

That night I dreamt of golden brown eyes and a bright smile and when I woke in the early hours with Emily's name on my lips, I explored another part of myself that I had forgotten with the long sleep. The rush of orgasm was a mind-blowing experience and I wondered how I could ever have forgotten such a thing, brain damage or no.

FAL RETURNED TO her own apartment Saturday around noon, but not without helping me pick an outfit for my date that evening. Because Emily said yes to the Lincoln Park Zoo suggestion, we agreed to meet there at three-thirty p.m. since it was only open until five. After we planned to ride share to the restaurant for dinner. There was a sense of anticipation as well as a good bit of nervousness as I approached the park entrance. It was very similar to the way I felt when Fal and I ran a human sense program simulation the day before. Excited because I wanted to see if all the hours of programming we put into the routine would work, but nervous because we put so much work into it and I didn't want it to fail.

Emily and I agreed that casual dress was best for a walk in the park and dinner, so I had dark jeans and a collared button-up shirt with the sleeves rolled up. My loafers were comfortable, if not terribly stylish, at least according to Fal. But Emily was stunning in her summer dress and slip-on shoes. She was very attractive and I was unsure of how I should greet her for our date. I went with the standard meeting protocol and held out my hand for a shake. "Hello. I'm glad that the weather is nice enough to walk around today."

She snorted and ignored my hand. Instead Emily walked straight up to me and pulled me into an embrace. "Relax, Alex." When she stepped away again I got the smile I'd grown to treasure in such a short period of time. "I'm a hugger remember? And you have nothing to be nervous about, just be you."

"But, what if I don't know who *I* am?"

Emily looped her right arm through my left. "Then do whatever comes natural. Let's walk. We don't have a lot of time before they close and I want to at least see all the large cats. That's my favorite building."

I paused, dragging her to a stop as well. "I didn't think to consider whether or not you'd been here. I assumed that by agreeing to come you'd never before visited Lincoln Park Zoo. Would you like to leave and meet me at the restaurant later?" I rushed to come up with another option because my immediate suggestion seemed like a wasteful bit of traveling. "Or, we could go do something else until dinner?"

Emily pulled me along again, looking at me out of the corner of her eye while she steered us toward the seal pool. "Nope. I love the zoo so we're staying."

"Okay."

I could instantly recall pictures of any animal, every fact I'd ever read about in a book or seen in a television program, but none of it compared to watching the large majestic creatures in person. There was something awe inspiring about being up close and personal with an elephant, to see exactly how small you were in comparison. Even that didn't render me speechless quite like the large cat exhibit. A lioness lay sunning herself in the outdoor enclosure. The sense of peace that watching her brought was like nothing I'd felt before, or at least nothing I *remember* feeling. And inside the building I saw more lions, a pacing panther, and an ocelot that was playing with a tire. I gasped as one of the outside lions roared, sounding muffled while we were in the building.

I turned to Emily as we walked down the ramp outside. "I feel so small now. But at the same time, I feel very connected to the world and...gigantic. Is this normal?"

She laced our fingers together and I marveled at the feel of her smooth skin against my palm and between each finger. There was strength in her grip, but not an excessive amount and I tried to match it. "Anything you feel is normal and don't let anyone tell you different. I think one of the reasons I love the great cats so much is exactly how you put it. I feel connected with the world around me. They have a graceful beauty that exudes danger, yet they're still cats, which makes me want to cuddle. It's the sheer dichotomy of emotions they prompt that make me love them."

It was a few minutes before five when we walked through the gates away from the park. Emily was still holding my hand and she used it to pull me to a stop near one of the large statues. "Let's take a picture. You don't mind, do you?"

I looked at the one she had stopped near. "Siblings by Rosetta. I like this one because it has lions."

"Yes, it's my favorite." We sat down and Emily held the camera away from us and wrapped her free arm around me, pulling me close. The pressure of her embrace and smell of her perfume left me feeling a pleasurable kind of strange. Unfamiliar but nice. She carefully lined up the cell phone camera in selfie mode so we could see part of the lion statue in the background. "Say cheese."

I cut my glance to the left. "Why would I say—" The shutter sound of her phone went off while I was mid-word. I glanced at the phone then back to Emily. "I apologize, I seem to have ruined the photo."

"Nonsense." She took another picture while I wasn't looking, then quickly kissed me on the lips as I heard the digitalized shutter sound again. She pulled back with a smile. "Now, let's try it again. I'll count down, three, two, one, then I'll take the picture. Just smile, okay? Saying cheese is a dumb expression when people are taking pictures because it leaves your mouth in a funny shape."

"Do people like to say it because cheese tastes so good?"

"Alex?"

I turned my head to look at her. Our faces were so close I could see multi-colored flecks in Emily's golden brown eyes. "Yes?"

"Look at the camera." I turned to look at the camera. "Now smile." I also smiled, but I was watching Emily's eyes through the selfie screen. "Good." The last picture came out nearly perfect with both of us smiling. "Do you want to walk around a bit before heading to the restaurant, or get a cab now?"

I felt my stomach, somewhat confused still about the concept of hunger. Fal said my appetite might be off for a bit after waking but to follow my instincts and not forget to eat like I'd done many times in the past. I don't remember skipping meals but I trusted Fal and promised to do better. I thought about my food intake for the day and realized that I had already failed. "I haven't eaten anything but an apple since breakfast. My stomach feels fairly empty now, I could definitely eat."

Emily sighed. "Alex, why didn't you eat lunch?"

"I was busy picking out an outfit with Fal for my date tonight with you. Then I wanted to finish the book I checked out from the library this morning."

She looked at me strangely for a moment. "You read a whole book today?"

I nodded. "Yes, I usually read one or two a day."

"On your days off?"

I frowned. "No, every day. I also try to watch a movie or show to reacquaint myself with all the pop culture I've forgotten. Fal introduced me to fiction novels, specifically books of the science fiction and fantasy types. They're highly entertaining. I can read more books on my days off but today I had plans...so only one." I think I surprised her because Emily's mouth opened slightly but no words came out. The white of her two top teeth was bright against the darker full lips. I watched with interest as her tongue came out to caress the lower one.

"Jesus, Alex, how fast do you read?"

My gaze moved back up to meet hers after the exclamation and I noticed the crinkle between her eyes. "It depends whether I'm reading for pleasure or for deep comprehension. If it's for pleasure—"

Fingers against my lips cut off my answer and I delighted in the softness of her touch against my sensitive skin. "Never mind,

I really don't want to know. I'll just assume that your genius brain absorbs everything ridiculously fast. What I wouldn't have given to have *that* particular skill in vet school!"

I regretted the loss of her touch when she pulled her hand away. "It has certainly facilitated earning my seven degrees in fairly rapid succession while working at OAS."

Emily rolled her eyes and threaded her arm through mine again. "Come along, Einstein. Let's go flag down a taxi. I haven't eaten since breakfast either so I could definitely go for an early dinner. Besides, it will be a breeze getting a table this early."

"Einstein was a brilliant man, I'm flattered that you would compare me to him." I paused as my brain analyzed the rest of her statement. "Wait, you didn't eat either? Why not?"

She shrugged and gave a smile that was different from others I'd seen from her. "I was nervous."

"Oh." I gripped her hand a little tighter, but not hard enough to hurt. I liked holding Emily's hand.

I thoroughly loved my first Cajun meal. Mine made my tongue uncomfortable with the spice level, but it was nothing compared to the bite of Emily's jambalaya. That was one food adventure I didn't enjoy. While delicious, the jambalaya exceeded my pain tolerance by a large margin. Near the end of dinner she told me a story about a client that she took an x-ray of, a big lab with a full belly and no appetite. She had to do exploratory surgery and removed half a dozen sausages and fourteen small potatoes. And that one wasn't as funny as the dog that ate a Brillo Pad. I laughed so loud that people turned to stare in our direction. The meal ended when the server placed the bill on our table. Emily tried to reach for it but I was significantly faster, having seen the man approach from behind her.

"I'm afraid I can't let you pay for our dinner, Doctor St. John. I read two books on etiquette and watched three movies before this date. I know that the person who does the asking is usually the one to pay."

Emily raised an eyebrow at me. "Usually, but not always."

"Hmm, true. But I would genuinely like to treat you to dinner so I can feel like this is a real date."

She placed a hand over mine where it rested on the bill. "Alex, whether you pay or not, this is definitely a real date. One of the best I've had in years, actually."

I tilted my head at her strange words. "I know you wouldn't lie to me but it seems inconceivable that someone as beautiful, smart, and funny as yourself would lack proper dinner companionship."

Emily winked and raised the rest of her wine glass to finish the drink. "Flatterer."

I searched my thoughts for a compromise because I sensed that she wasn't completely comfortable with me paying. "Why don't you pay for our next dinner then?"

"Look at you! This one's not even done yet and here you are asking me on another."

I faltered at her teasing. "I...I guess I am. But you can pay next time if it makes you feel better, even if I am doing the asking now and etiquette dictates — ."

Quiet laughter and a soft voice cut me off. "Alex...the answer is yes."

The simple response to my question left me with immense pleasure and a buzzing feeling in my chest. "Stupendous!"

She shook her head and smiled. "How do you feel about a ride back to our coffee shop to finish out our first date?"

Her question had merit. "Perhaps we could take the drinks to go and walk down to my favorite park."

The server had taken my card away with the bill while we were discussing future dates and returned as I awaited Emily's answer to my suggestion. I quickly calculated the appropriate tip in my head and signed the slip. Emily stood and held out a hand to me. Of course I took it. She smirked as she pulled me toward the door. "A park, huh? It almost sounds like you're hoping for a kiss."

"Do parks prompt kissing?"

She smiled again and hailed an available taxi that was passing by the busy restaurant district. "I guess you'll have to wait and see." I felt...giddy at the thought of deliberately kissing Emily. Like many others, the emotion was unfamiliar but based on the textbook definition, it fit best.

It didn't take long to arrive at the coffee shop in my area of the city, nor did it take a significant amount of time to walk to the park after acquiring drinks. Emily was especially fascinated by the tree fountain. "This is gorgeous! How have I never been to this park before?"

"I'm not sure. Perhaps it's because it is not near any business, surrounded as it is by a mostly residential neighborhood." I gestured toward the water basin. "Fal usually makes a wish when we come here."

Emily gave me a serious look, one of the few for the night. "And do you?"

I shook my head. "No. Wishes are illogical."

"Well, illogical or not," Emily reached into her small purse and pulled out a quarter. "I'm not passing up an opportunity to make my own." She closed her eyes for three seconds, then tossed the coin into the basin. It made a dull *thunk* as it hit the bottom.

After that, we walked clockwise along the brick path toward the back of the little park. It was more like a small garden paradise with the way the path meandered between large and small groupings of flora. Our hands remained clasped for the entirety of the walk and in the darkened back corner where two ivy-covered walls met, she pulled me to a stop. We stood facing each other, closer than two friends would normally stand. I was drawn to the beauty of her face and expressive eyes. My own were in motion as I took in the delicate part of her ear, then those eyes I loved, before finally settling on her lips. The word that had been sitting on the tip of my thoughts was 'adoration.' It was illogical to feel such a thing for someone who was very near a stranger. Even so, I wanted to kiss Emily but I had no memory of the act and was afraid I'd do it incorrectly.

Maybe she sensed my dilemma but Emily smiled and moved a little closer. Then in a move that both surprised and entranced me, she lifted a hand to caress my cheek. "So soft. Every time I touch your skin I am surprised by how soft it feels." Much like the moment in the director's office, but in a nicer way, I lost control of certain functions and my eyes closed against my will. It felt like a natural response to her touch. My eyes fluttered open again in time to see Emily tilt her head and lean in. The first touch of her lips to mine was a mere caress, the slightest brush of skin against skin.

I opened eyes that I didn't realize I'd shut when Emily spoke in the silence of the moment after. "Was that okay?"

I breathed out an answer. "Yes." Then before Emily could back away I asked, "Can we do that again?"

She leaned toward me again and the kiss lasted longer the second time. I felt a strong urge to move my lips against hers in response and gave in to it. I'd seen the movies, I tried to replicate motions of actors as well as possible. I was taken off guard when her mouth opened slightly, and the wetness of her tongue caressing between my lips caused me to feel a tumultuous cacophony of different emotions.

A rush washed through me and I tentatively met her quest with my own tongue. There was a certain kind of excitement that came with the feeling of the two textured organs sliding together, or the way her exhaled breaths puffed into my mouth. The hand that had been touching my cheek moved up to gently grip the back of my head and we kissed for another sixty-seven seconds longer. At least I think it was sixty-seven. Her kisses made me forget to count. I sensed her slow withdrawal from the kiss and knew enough to pull back at the same time, though we were left standing quite close together still.

I would have been concerned about the tremulous feeling in my limbs if not for all the books I'd read about romance and sexual response. My words were as honest as I could make them. "I've never felt like that before."

"You don't remember?"

I sighed. "I don't know." Needing to be closer after the intimate moment I moved my hand to clasp hers again. Emily moved our hands up between us so she could thread our fingers together palm to palm. I looked at our point of contact then move my gaze up to meet her smiling eyes. "I'm really drawn to you, Emily St. John."

"That's probably a good thing because you've definitely made a mark on me, Alexandra Turing."

I took a breath and pulled back a little to make an attempt at focusing on something other than the way her throat moved when she swallowed, or the smoothness of each of her fingers where they lay between my own. "What do we do now?"

Emily gave me a smile that appeared more playful than her normal affable expression. "Now I walk you home like a gentlewoman."

Her words were curious and I tilted my head to see if I could puzzle out deeper meaning than the obvious. "Is that what you wished for at the fountain?"

Emily backed away slowly, stretching our arms out straight as they pulled taut, and I had no choice but to follow since she wasn't letting go. "You have to wait for our third date before I tell you that bit of information."

"Oh." After that I grinned happily and let her walk me home.

Chapter Eight

Open System

I DIDN'T HESITATE before scanning into the building on Monday morning. My odd reticence disappeared after my previous visit to OAS. The halls were still strangely empty from the images in my memory. The mundane walk from the elevator to my private office was broken when Apollo strode around the corner. The computerized voice was jarring and I mourned the remembered tones of Artemis. I made a mental note to check on my personal side project later in the week. It shouldn't take long to make a few upgrades so hopefully Artemis would be back in the robotics division soon. I held out my badge when he was within ten feet.

"This unit registers the physical and NFC ident of Doctor Alexandra Turing. Please present badge for security scan." I watched the Sentinel curiously as it checked my badge. Clean white lines of the torso, gleaming metallic limbs and various blinking sensors, the most important of which turned green after the android completed the scan. "Thank you for your cooperation."

"Don't you wish you had a personality?"

The droid wasn't allowed to continue its journey in the face of human interaction. It was programmed to answer basic questions, render limited aid, or call for medical or security backup. Clearly my question was too complex. "Question does not compute."

Even knowing the limits of their vocabulary and responses, I had to try. "If I could program you to think for yourself, would you like that?"

"Question does not compute."

"Apollo, where are you headed next?"

The Sentinel finally found something it could answer. "The next destination on my patrol is the secure elevator leading to sub-level four."

I sighed and *knew* I could do better than that. Perhaps I'd update all of the Sentinels' programming to give them some sort of character. Anything was better than the mindless automaton that lumbered down the hall in the opposite direction I was heading.

The next person I met was Doctor Li Min. She came out of her office as I turned down the corridor where our offices were located, heading away from me. She didn't see me and I quickly went through what memories I had of her to find what she preferred to be called. Again, the memory I had seemed too formal, definitely more so than I preferred.

"Doctor Min!" The woman spun around as soon as she heard my voice and even from where I stood it was obvious the way she paled.

She answered and remained where she was as I drew closer. "Doctor...Turing."

"Is something wrong?" I could see that along with the pale features, her eyes were widened as she scanned down the hall behind me, a sure indicator of nervousness.

Doctor Min cleared her throat and brought her eyes back to meet mine. "No, not at all. You startled me when you called out. I didn't see you come around the corner." She paused and tapped the file in her hand against her leg. "Have you officially returned to work then?"

I smiled. "I have! I'm very excited to get back into the swing of things. I've been gone too long."

"Will you be taking over the program again from Doctor Nanjiani?"

The laughter came unbidden when I found her question strangely humorous. "Oh no, I'm only now reacquainting myself with where we left off. I'm happy to let her stay in the lead. Like I said, I really only want to catch up with everyone and re-familiarize myself with Synthetica. Do you have time to eat lunch with me later? I thought perhaps you, Doctor Venga, Fal, and I could catch up since apparently we're all that's left of the team."

She looked at me curiously. "I think I could make sure my schedule stays free around noon. Perhaps we can order in and all eat in the small conference room in the north wing?"

"Great!" Her idea pleased me. I still had to see if Doctor Venga and Fal were on board with it. "Oh, and before I forget, I wanted to ask you if you prefer to be called by your professional name or if you wouldn't mind shortening it? I'm sure you've already been informed by Director Devos and Doctor Nanjiani that I've suffered some memory loss and...personal changes since the accident. Waking from my coma made me realize how short life is and I wish to better connect with the people around me. I would like everyone to simply refer to me as Alex. Doctor Turing is too formal for my preference when we're not in a meeting that dictates such titles."

Her face went through a range of emotions that weren't easy to read but I was pretty sure I puzzled them out. Surprise, shock, unease, and finally finishing on pleasure. "I think that is an easy enough request to comply with," She paused before finishing with a quiet, "Alex."

I smiled again, wishing to put her at ease. "Would you prefer your first name in day to day settings as well? Or do you like the formal address?"

"Well if I'm calling you Alex, it seems only fair for you to call me Li."

One down, and one to go. Now I needed to find Doctor Venga. "Wonderful! I'll send out an in-sys message around eleven to confirm lunch orders. I can't wait to work with you again."

She gave me a strange smile and tapped the file folder against her leg. "I feel the same way. See you in a few hours, Alex." With that she turned and continued down the hall, heading toward what I knew to be the level three testing labs.

Inside my office everything was clean and precisely organized. I sat in my cushioned desk chair and glanced around the room, taking note of the minimalist style from my memories. Every book was pulled to the front of the shelves, exactly like the public library near my condo. Each implement, paper, and personal item on my desk was in precise alignment with everything else. Nothing crooked, only parallels and right angles to each other. It didn't appear as though anything was missing but then I never left anything out so it wouldn't be obvious.

I unpacked my laptop from the messenger bag that had made the trip to work with me and docked it in the station then logged in. Out of curiosity, I accessed the security network and brought up the scan log for my office. It was a short list consisting of my father, Fal, and David Devos. All names that could be expected given the circumstances.

Checking my email took barely any time at all. I guessed they had all emails routed to other people after the accident to prevent a massive pileup. I minimized the email and went to the corporate information page that had all our recent developments and announcements. There was nothing of my waking from the coma, nor of my return to work. I did a search of news from six months prior and clicked on the first linked article that popped up. It was from a science digest, one that I myself used to collect. I read the article's title aloud, and the sound of my voice felt strange in the empty space. "Doctor Alexandra Turing, daughter of Organic Advancement Solutions founder, Matheson Turing, remains in a medically induced coma following a car accident last week."

I continued reading and the first few lines of the article made me feel things I didn't like, things I couldn't fully identify. "Sources report that she has been transferred to the bio-medical division of OAS after specialists at Northwestern Memorial Hospital declared it unlikely she would ever wake. Neither Matheson Turing, nor the company spokesperson, has commented on the situation." My voice didn't break on the last word, but my mouse did. I looked down in shock to find my hand tightly clenched around the small plastic peripheral.

"Oh, format me! Not another one." I was going to have to order a replacement from IT because I disliked using the small touch pad. Rather than put it off, I quickly closed the article and clicked on the IT report link. After filling out the online form, I contemplated the one email I had already read three times. I had some time available while I awaited the confirmation that would surely inquire why I needed four wireless peripherals. The email from my father was curious. He welcomed me back to OAS and inquired about how I was feeling. He mentioned that he was currently at one of our subsidiary locations in Germany.

When I spoke with Fal the previous week about the person I was before waking, one of the things that bothered me was my spotty memories of my relationship with my father. It didn't help that we had completely different personalities. We seemed at odds more often than not over the past few years that I could recall. Conversations between us played through my head like movies, where he wanted me to spend more time at his estate outside the city. I always turned him down, citing distance and wasted commute time as the reason. Even now, I couldn't escape the realization that I had put my obsession with AI and my great uncle's test well ahead of any and all personal relationships. While I had no memory of our time together, and despite Fal reassuring me that the breakup was mutual, I had no doubt that it was completely my fault in that instance as well.

Suddenly full of purpose, I looked at the smart watch on my

wrist and bent down to grab the cell phone from my messenger bag. I wasn't about to waste another second on that cold and driven roboticist. I'd been given a new lease on life and it was time to start living. I used video call because I had an intense desire to see my father's face, to watch his lips form words, to laugh, or even smile. I needed that from him to feel real. There was a seven hour time difference between here and Germany so it was about twenty minutes after three his time. I assumed he would still be in the office.

The digital *blurbling* sound of the video ringer was jarring in the silence. After four rings the weathered face of an older man came on the screen. There were so many similarities between us, despite the difference of age and gender. We shared the shape of our mouths, the arch of brows, though his were thicker and gone nearly white as had his hair. We also shared the same rare shade of dark green eyes. Our features were nearly opposite of my great uncle, Alan Turing. The infamous and long-maligned man had black hair and dark brown eyes. The clink of ice in a glass roused me from my frozen state. I watched as the father from my memories raised a glass of amber liquid to his lips while he observed me. He finished his sip, never taking his eyes off the camera. "Hello, Alexandra. To what do I owe the pleasure of your call?"

"Hello, Father. Did I catch you at a bad time?"

He placed the glass on his desk off screen with a *thunk*. "Not at all. Is there something you need?"

"I...I, there isn't anything I need. I guess I just wanted to hear your voice, to see your face and speak with you." I paused to think, then continued before he could answer. "I miss you. A lot of things are different for me, memories missing and parts of my personality that people have told me are completely different, but I remember you."

He looked at me curiously. "What do you remember?"

"While I do have memories, or rather, remembered images from my childhood, of us together, it's mostly something I feel inside. My more recent memories are not as good. I have recollection of us in disagreement much of the time, of me not making time to spend with you and that bothers me. If nearly dying has taught me anything, it's that I don't want us to be so distant. I...I want my dad."

I watched as my father's eyebrows lifted in surprise, and I took note of the glassy look indicating imminent tears or perhaps due to alcohol consumption. "I...I don't know what to say, Alexandra. You haven't called me that in a long, long time."

"It's Alex. I prefer to go by Alex now and would appreciate being addressed as such."

"I think I can manage that, though I may slip once in a while."

I smiled at him. "It's fine, completely understandable given the circumstances. Do you have time to talk for a bit?"

"I suppose I have time to talk to my own daughter." He looked around the office, and I watched the wrinkled skin at the front of his throat move as he swallowed. The camera jiggled and I could tell that he was placing the phone in a holder rather than keep it in his hand. I opened my drawer to pull out my own stand and did the same. Once the logistics of the video call were worked out he gave me a tentative smile. "So how are things going for you so far? Is Doctor Nanjiani helping you acclimate?"

"She stayed with me the first week home, though she's since returned to her own apartment. Today is actually my first day back to work at OAS."

My dad nodded. "Good, good..." The conversation trailed off, awkwardly. We clearly needed to find new common ground, to learn to share our lives with each other again.

I searched my memory and found the one thing that always made me smile. "I adopted a kitten!"

"Oh?"

"Her name is Anna and she's a small torbie, which is a tortie and tabby mix. Her tawny hair and green eyes perfectly match my coloring. My new kitten is an adorable little creature but extremely destructive. If you want I can send you a picture of her. I even have video."

He smiled and relaxed. "I think that would be wonderful."

We spoke for over an hour and at the end of the conversation agreed to a standing phone call every Monday, Wednesday, and Friday at the same time. He also said that he was thinking of coming back to the States soon and I cheered within my own mind. While talking to him made me happier than most things I'd experience since waking, it would be nothing compared to seeing him in person or receiving a hug. Many of my memories were spotty and broken, but one thing I knew for certain was that I loved my father.

BY THE TIME lunch arrived I had made a list of things I wanted to discuss with each division head, had confirmed and ordered lunch for the four of us remaining on the Synthetica project, and had a number of files marked for investigation. I was looking for current prototype items with potential for faster profit to help boost OAS in both profitability and brand recognition. Since lunch was the first I'd seen of Doctor Venga all day I immediately broached the subject of preferred names. He didn't act strange or reticent the way Li had. On the contrary he was jovial and curious about how I'd been since waking.

"I've been well actually. But on the topic of my condition, I've made a few personal and professional changes since coming out of the coma. Life is too short to hold people at arm's distance and with that thought in mind I'd like all my friends and coworkers to call me Alex. Unless of course we are in a professional meeting or other such venue that titles would be expected."

Doctor Venga was a tall, whip-thin man in his fifties with a very expressive face. His smile was broad as he grabbed my hand and pumped it into a vigorous handshake. "Well then, Alex, it's my pleasure to meet you. You can call me Sam, I prefer it actually. It's that Alexandra...er, you..." He glanced over at Fal and I assumed he was trying to approach the topic of my old personality delicately.

Like a professional, Fal picked up his explanation without pause. "It's just that the old Alexandra preferred formality at all times. She, you...sorry, it's so hard to reconcile the two very different personalities. Uh, you were a bit of a—"

I held up a hand and gave them all a chagrinned smile. "Say no more. I've recalled enough about who I used to be to know I wasn't the easiest person to work with. Bit of a stickler for the rules, and I was against fraternization." I looked intently at Fal. "Honestly, I'm surprised I maintained my friendship with you at all."

Fal made a face. "I'm not going to lie, Alexandra...*you* were a lot of work but certainly worth it." She looked around at the three of us. "Now instead of chatting and letting our food get cold, let's put away talk of the past and discuss the future now that we have Alex here."

We settled around the table and I watched the other three open their food, filing away each one's mannerisms and eating habits. Li used her chopsticks to eat every bite of the poke bowl, savoring the pieces of raw fish. Sam was a vegetarian and had no meat in his order but also used chopsticks. And Fal had opted for sushi instead of the bowl, using a fork. I too ordered the poke bowl and picked up the chopsticks curiously. Fal and I hadn't used them while she was staying with me. I had memory of holding the eating utensils on more than one occasion but couldn't remember how to use them. I turned my head to watch Li and mimicked the way she held them. Then as she picked up each bite of food I also copied the motion. The chopsticks snapped on my first attempt at grabbing a piece of shrimp.

I looked up to see Fal watching me intently. She smiled and shoved her set of chopsticks across the table. "It's okay, you can have mine. Try again with less pressure."

I opened the paper and carefully broke them apart, then tried again, reducing my pressure significantly. That time I was successful and quickly got the hang of the new way of eating. Once my attention wasn't focused on getting the food to my mouth I took notice of the taste. "This is amazing!" I looked up to see everyone had been watching me intently with varying looks of pleasure and satisfaction. I tilted my head curiously. "What is it?"

Sam gave a little laugh as he shook his head. "Nothing at all. It's just that you picked up the art of chopsticks incredibly fast."

"Didn't I use them before? I remember holding them once or twice."

Fal also laughed. "You definitely held them a few times but never tried to use them. You said it was a waste of time to learn when a fork was more efficient."

I rolled my eyes. "More efficient maybe, but this allows me time to savor each bite."

Li smiled and pointed her own chopsticks at me. "Thank you!" Then she turned and gave Fal a smug look. "See?"

"Yes, yes, I'm a filthy American who refuses to learn new cultures."

With Fal's dark looks, her Indian name, and faded British accent, no one would mistake her for a *filthy American*. We all laughed at her statement. All in all, it was a pretty good lunch.

Later that afternoon I set up meetings with the other three division heads, prosthetics, bio-medical, and nanotechnology, to take place over the course of the rest of the week. I requested in the meeting invite that they bring lists of their top ten projects and their top three issues preventing the completion of each. My first meeting was set for Thursday morning and I figured that would give them plenty of time to compile the information I asked for.

EVEN AFTER THE busy day I had, the conversation with my father, touring the labs, and having Fal show me the current status on a number of Synthetica related projects, I found myself curiously full of energy as I rode my bike home that evening. What made my day even more perfect was being greeted at the door by Anna. I carefully avoided her while pushing my bike inside, then walked over to set my messenger bag on the kitchen island. Once my arms were free I scooped up the soft little cat to give love and attention for as long as she would tolerate it. That tolerance lasted for sixty-six seconds before she tried to wiggle free of my arms. I had no choice but to set her down and follow Anna's mad dash into the laundry room to give her dinner, listening to her incessant meows the entire time. She was a demanding little thing.

After eating my own evening meal, I settled onto my couch with another science fiction novel set nearly five hundred years into the future. Fal recommended it to me and so far she had pretty good taste. I found it to be a highly engaging book involving submarine pirates, romance, intrigue, and action. The novel was my favorite to date and I was only halfway through. My entertainment was interrupted by the chime of an incoming text message. It was Emily. We had been communicating every day in one form or another since last Saturday's date. During the day it was frequently via text message but we'd spoken on the phone a few different evenings.

```
What do you think of dinner and a comedy show
for our next date?
```

I couldn't remember attending a comedy show before, or any show on a stage, only movies. I quickly texted back.

```
I like to laugh and eat.
```

My phone vibrated in my hand and I smiled as I read Emily's response.

```
LOL, you're a comedian. Maybe we don't have to
go anywhere.
```

After thinking about her text I typed the first thing that came to mind.

```
I like you, so going anywhere isn't a require-
ment for me to have a nice evening. You alone
make it nice.
```

She responded.

```
Now you're being charming.
```

Emily's words confused me because I was trying to be honest, not charming.

```
I'm being me, isn't that what you want?
```

Her response made me feel things that were new and exhilarating.

```
Well you are both charming and sweet so it's a
win-win for me. Now about dinner…have you been
to Second City Comedy Club?
```

I considered the mental map I had of Chicago but didn't
know the address for the club she suggested. I closed the text app
on my phone and opened Google to search for the name. The
result made me happy.

```
That is mere blocks from my condo!

Haha, I know. So, are you interested?

Yes. When?
```

I waited impatiently for her to text back.

```
Will this Saturday work for you? We can get din-
ner before the show at the 1959 Kitchen & Bar
that's onsite.
```

I was about to answer her when another text message came
in.

```
I'm on the website now so I can get the tix and
reservations for dinner all at once.
```

My fingers sped across the keys, anxious that she'd change

her mind.

```
Yes, I would enjoy all those things. Should I
contribute toward this date since we're doing
two things?
```

Twenty-three seconds later she responded.

```
You text hella fast and no. You paid for my zoo
souvenir and dinner last time. It's my turn.
Also, I assumed I could park at your place and
we'd walk since it's so close to where you live.
Is that okay?
```

I sighed as Anna jumped onto my lap. She curled into a ball and began purring so I took the opportunity to snap a picture and sent it to Emily.

```
Anna says it is a purrfect idea and we can't
wait to see you Saturday. What time?
```

Waiting for responses was the most annoying part about the text message system.

```
Aww, she's adorable! I can't wait to see you
both. I'll text you what time I'm coming over
after I finish making these reservations.
```

Another text came through a few seconds later.

```
There are a number of shows playing, do you want
to look and help choose?
```

I shook my head even though she couldn't see it and the motion was illogical.

```
I don't really know what I like when it comes to
comedy, but I trust your judgement because
you're intelligent and you've made good choices
so far.
```

```
See? There you go being sweet again. Fine, I'll
finalize the details here and send them to you
when I'm done. I should let you get back to your
book now.
```

She remembered.

```
Thank you! And today's novel is quite good, if
you like pirates, futuristic dystopian fiction,
and f/f romantic themes.
```

```
Sounds depressing and a little weird.
```

I sighed again. I suppose it was outside the bell curve to expect Emily and I to share all the same likes and dislikes. I typed back.

```
I'm going to consciously ignore what you just
said so that your perfection in my mind is left
intact.
```

My eyebrows went up in surprise and curiosity when I read Emily's next text.

```
Oh, I'm too weird to be perfect so don't build
me up like that. Maybe it's the profession
because I've never met a fellow veterinarian
that WASN'T as weird.
```

```
I had no idea. Truly.
```

```
You're safe, probably. Just let me know if you
ever want to take a walk on the wild side.
```

I grew confused again, certain that I'd missed some hidden meaning or social reference.

```
Does this involve another trip to the zoo?
```

```
OMG, Alex! No. No zoo or any other animals. Only
me and you and some groovy music.
```

Honesty seemed like the best policy.

```
That sounds like a dream I had the other night
about the two of us.
```

When Emily didn't text back right away I worried that I'd sent something inappropriate. I counted ninety-four seconds before the phone in my hand rang with an incoming call. Anna *mewed*, displeased at the noise so close to her sleeping form. The smile came unbidden as I answered, though the worry remained. "Hello, Emily."

"Alex—" She paused for two seconds before continuing. "You can't just tell me that you've had dreams about us and expect me to not be curious."

"I'm sorry, was I inappropriate?"

Her snorted laughter over the phone made me feel lighter inside. "Not at all. But you have to be aware that I'm *insanely* attracted to you."

I tilted my head, accessing new memories of our time together. "I wasn't aware, though I could tell you were interested in me. You said as much when I admitted my interest in you. But regardless, I'm happy that we feel the same way about each other. It certainly makes this courtship easier."

Emily's new spate of laughter was loud as it peeled through the speaker at my ear. "Courtship, huh? You're funny sometimes. But yes, our mutual attraction is certainly reassuring." I didn't answer what I assumed to be a simple statement and she prompted. "So, a dream about us...care to tell me about it?"

I thought of the many book and movie plots I'd memorized since waking, and the movies I remembered from before. I contemplated some of the things I'd learned from Fal about romance. "I'm not sure I'm supposed to give you the details of my dreams."

Her voice deepened a little over the phone and sounded more playful. "What's the matter, afraid that you'll get turned on if you talk about it?"

The dreams involving Emily had all been vividly intense and I remembered the hot rush I felt after waking from the last one. The indescribable need to touch and be touched. The answer I gave her was simple. "Yes."

That seemed to throw her off a bit. "Oh. Well damn, Alex. I know what I'm going to think about tonight when I'm drifting off to sleep."

It sounded as though she regretted that. "I'm sorry."

"Don't be. I've got some catching up to do, or so it would seem."

Catching up. My thoughts on her statement glitched, then raced as I contemplated her meaning. My curiosity wouldn't let me leave it at so vague a statement, I had to know. "Catching up?

Does that mean..." I trailed off, afraid to voice the potentially indecorous thought.

Emily made a low little noise, and I attempted to imagine her making it in person, bringing up our time together in my mind to use as a reference. My concentration was lost when she finally spoke. "Mm hmm, that's exactly what that means. You know, I didn't comment on it after our last date but you're an incredibly good kisser for someone who doesn't remember their past experience."

"I've learned since waking that I'm good at a lot of things."

I could hear stifled laughter coming from Emily and I wondered what part of my statement she found humorous. I was disappointed when she didn't explain. "And on that note, I think it's time for me to say good night. I've got an early morning combined with a long day tomorrow, and a number of surgeries lined up, so I need to shower and get some sleep."

I was sad and disappointed. "Oh, okay. Good night, Emily St. John. I look forward to our date on Saturday."

Her voice was something I'd consider as warm when she responded. "I have a feeling I'm going to look forward to *all* our dates."

"Is that a good thing?"

"The best. Good night, Alex." And with those five words, the line disconnected. I made a mental note to ask Fal how my comment about being good at things could be construed as funny.

Chapter Nine

Relational Structure

"WAIT, YOU SAID *what* to her?"

Fal's reaction to my conversation seemed overly dramatic. "I told her I was good at a lot of things. Why is that funny?"

Fal covered her eyes, shaking with silent laughter while I counted the seconds in my head. She finally looked up at me with tears in her eyes. "You were talking about sex dreams and kissing, then when she comments on how good a kisser you are you tell her you're good at a lot of things. Put the topics together and what does it sound like you're good at?"

My mind analyzed the conversation over and over, even backwards once. Suddenly the context of Emily's laughter made sense. "Oh. It sounded as though I could be referring to sex. As if I were saying I'd be good at sex...if a person were already thinking about such things."

"Which she clearly was."

"We both were." I looked away for a moment to collect my thoughts and when I turned back, Fal gazed at me with her head tilted. It was a look I remembered as her curious one. "But what if I'm *not* good at it?"

"Good at what, sex?"

"Yes, foreplay and intercourse. I can't remember doing such a thing and the many pieces of literature I've read mention that inexperienced lovers are not highly sought after."

Fal rubbed her forehead. "But you're not inexperienced. Alexandra Turing had enough lovers to have cleared that hurdle successfully."

"I may not be what people would refer to as a virgin, but I am definitely inexperienced. After all, the definition of experience is knowledge or practical wisdom gained from what one has observed, encountered, or undergone. All my knowledge of sexual relations has been lost, wiped clean. I may as well be a virgin. What if I'm awful?"

Fal laughed and logged into the laptop she had placed on the bench in our test lab when she came in. "You're not going to be awful."

I wondered if she was relying on some knowledge of our history together to make her statement. Rather than speculate I simply asked. "How do you know?"

My friend and colleague turned her head away from the screen and winked at me. "Because you're good at everything." In a fit of pique at her non-answer, I turned and stalked toward the lab exit, intending to head back to my office. Her laughter followed me out the door.

WEDNESDAY MORNING I sat at my desk with a smile on my face, telling my father about the joke I played on Fal to get even for her laughing at me the day before. "When she returned from the bathroom she hit the button on her laptop to bring up the PowerPoint presentation. Only when she attempted to use her mouse, nothing worked. She unplugged it, then plugged it back in. Then she tried the touch pad, and that worked fine. Finally after shaking it uselessly she turned the mouse over and saw the sticky note I placed over the sensor."

My father held his stomach because he laughed so hard. I was surprised no one knocked on his office door to inquire what was going on. Then again, he was the owner of the company. It had been a long time since I had heard my dad laugh in person. He finally calmed down enough to speak. "However did you come up with that idea?"

"Emily told me about it. She said that she played the prank on a classmate in vet school."

He froze for a second, then relaxed again. "And who is Emily?"

I forgot that in our first call on Monday we never got around to speaking about Emily. I told him a lot about little Anna, and the ideas I had for OAS, but I didn't mention Anna's attractive and intelligent doctor. "Emily St. John is Anna's veterinarian but she's also someone I'm interested in romantically."

The surprise on his face was easy enough to read, even from the small screen of my cell phone. "Romantically? Are you...dating?"

"We've had lunch together twice, and dinner once. We have our second date this coming Saturday."

"That seems kind of sudden with you only recently waking from your coma. What does Fal think?"

I tried to express what I'd been feeling since waking in that patient room. "I feel like nearly dying has given me a fresh start, another chance to do what I want with my life while reprioritizing certain things. I've realized over the past few weeks that I can be passionate about my career goals and still be able to make connections with the people around me. And I believe that Fal likes Doctor St. John just fine. She's never said anything negative about Emily and even helped me select clothes to wear when meeting her."

He sighed and propped his chin on his thumb before rubbing a forefinger back and forth across his upper lip. "That is a definite shift from your previous attitude, Alex. You're certain this is the right thing for you?"

"I have no definitive way of measuring what is right for me. I only know that since waking I've discovered many pleasures in life that I believe the old me would have let pass by."

My dad leaned back in his chair, resting his hands on the desk in front of him. "I admire your drive and dedication, always have. I tried to do my best by you when you were growing up, providing every opportunity and educational benefit within my power. But I've always been concerned about Alexandra's...about your personal life. I could see the way you struggled to interact with the people around you. And I grew dismayed as you gave up trying, writing off interpersonal relationships as a waste of time and effort. What I'm trying to say, is that while I'm sorry for the circumstances, I'm glad that you've got this chance to do things differently."

I smiled at him fondly. "I am too." I glanced at the desk calendar that sat in the corner, to the right of my laptop dock. I had to tear away more than half the days to update it since I began working in my office again. In a blink, I calculated the passage of time in my head. I'd been awake for only seventeen days but it felt like half a lifetime. I missed my father. I glanced back at the small screen in front of me and my mind veered off on a tangent. "Why are we doing this on our cell phones when we have a state of the art video conferencing system?"

He tilted his head and glanced slightly away, probably to look at his own laptop. "I have no earthly idea! You'd think a genius and her father would have suggested the vidcom right off the bat." He laughed again and the sound soothed me. I missed him.

"When are you coming home?" I clarified because I knew he

had multiple homes, one of which he had been living in while working in Germany. "Back to Chicago."

"I don't know. I suppose I could come back any time. I did all the footwork I wanted to do at the facility here. There was nothing keeping me away except—" His words cut off as his brows drew down with grief, and the lines on his weathered forehead looked deeper.

I didn't want him to feel pain. "I'm sorry. Chicago probably reminds you of my accident and the fact that you thought you were going to lose me for good. I won't push."

My father brought his hand up to rub both eyes with his thumb and forefinger, then slowly lifted his head and met my gaze. It was in that moment that I realized how heavy grief could be. He slumped in his chair like the world had forced him down, or maybe the near-loss of an only child. "But I have you now, don't I?"

The differences between the new me and old me never felt further apart than when I was looking at my dad. "Yes. I know that I'm not the same person you knew before. Even *I* can see the differences between some of my memories and the way I feel now. But I'd like to think that with time and patience from the people around me, I can be equally as good. Maybe even better."

He cleared his throat and the look in his eye indicated that he'd come to a decision. "If anyone can do what they set their mind to, it's you, my dear. And how about this? I'll work on my schedule this week and next to set things in order here in Germany, then I'll head home. You can tentatively expect me a week from this coming Saturday. Maybe we can have dinner." He paused as if considering something. "Though we may have to push dinner back to Sunday. I'll be fairly jet-lagged. I'm not as young as I used to be."

I laughed. "Perhaps we can discover the fountain of youth and make you young forever."

"Maybe we already have." His reply was cryptic, but then he'd always been that way in my memories.

We hung up shortly after that and I opened my meeting calendar and added the tentative date of my father's return. Once finished I brought up the prioritized list of open Synthetica action items and began cross-checking that against returned data that I gleaned from the OAS network using a bot I programmed. I wanted to see what we'd already borrowed from the other divisions and investigate if the same items could serve more than one purpose. I found one intriguing project buried in a sub-folder of the bio-medical division. It was the project Fal and I spoke of my first week home, the one she speculated could be sold to the military. The file, titled *Human Enhancement Serum*, had last been updated a week before I woke from my coma and I wondered if the project had stalled. Fal made it seem as though it were an important ongoing project. I was pretty sure something like HES wouldn't help our project but it was an interesting enough idea that I flagged it to watch for more additions to the folder.

There were a number of innovations Fal had shown me that were remarkable, but they could definitely be improved upon. One of those things was the circulatory coolant system. But shy of inserting cooling rods at even intervals into the positronic brain, which would take up valuable processing space, the gel cap was a good enough solution for the time being. The issue that was at the top of my list was to solve the degradation problem.

I grabbed a pen from the caddy on the left side of my desk and pulled a notepad from my drawer. The first step toward problem solving began with identifying the problem. Our problem was that the current components within the positronic brain contributed to heat related corrosion and degradation and eventual failure, thus requiring the addition of Trichlorosilane to the system.

Next I defined my goals, writing them out neatly across the top of the page. Eliminate the need for Trichlorosilane, prevent system degradation in relation to heat, and prevent system corrosion in relation to the moisture content of the synaptic suspension gel. I began brainstorming each in order of how they were written across the page.

The first possible solution for the Trichlorosilane issue was to find an organic compound that could perform the same duties with the convenience of initial absorption in the organic power generation phase. Another possibility would be to eliminate the need for Trichlorosilane or any other organic replacement by introducing nanotech surface scrubbers into the system. I'd been doing a lot of reading about nanotechnology. I had downloaded a multitude of papers written by OAS scientists and after analyzing the relevant data, I was convinced that our current tech could be reprogrammed to work in conjunction with our positronic brain prototype. That was one of the things I wanted to speak with Director Vogel about in our meeting on Thursday.

One of the reasons I created separate meetings for the division directors was so I would get to know each on a personal and intellectual level. It was easier to do that when only faced with one person at a time. I also wanted to discuss the hardest hitting problems for each of the four areas of OAS, without wasting the time of the other directors. Bio-medical didn't need to hear about nanotech, and prosthetics probably didn't care at all what we were doing in robotics. At least not yet.

I moved over to the next goal, which was to prevent system degradation in relation to heat. That one was a little trickier. I couldn't think of any solution other that the current gel cap already in effect, or cooling rods which I had already discounted as being too large for the given space. Computer processing, especially at high levels, created heat. There was no current technology in existence that would get around that basic fact. Perhaps future tech would develop something similar to cooling rods but in filament size to weave through and between each lobe, but we weren't there yet.

The last goal was to prevent system corrosion in relation to the moisture. There were two ways to accomplish this goal. One was to change the composition of the synaptic gel that connected the outer lobes of the positronic brain and cushioned the complicated super-computer from damage. Hypothetically, a different low-moisture synaptic gel could prevent corrosion whether in the presence of high heat or not. Conversely, the alternative to changing the gel would be to use a different material to reconstruct the circuitry and neural pathways so the synaptic gel didn't corrode them.

Material was tricky though. I recall testing many conductive agents, some of which held up well in the high moisture environment, but didn't work with the high heat. Other's showed the opposite effect by performing effectively in the presence of high heat but couldn't conduct electrical impulses between the lobes. We never found something that accomplished both tasks so we chose a material that performed adequately under both circumstances while maintaining cost effectiveness.

Writing out the goals and brainstorming various ideas helped solidify in my mind that the best and most efficient solution for all three problems would be to pursue the nanotechnology route. I needed to further familiarize myself with their project to see if robotics could collaborate to make the surface scrubber bot a reality.

I WAS ON my way home from work that evening when a call came through my Bluetooth earbud. I glanced down at my cell phone where it was clipped firmly into the holder. Though I was riding in fairly heavy traffic I decided it was safe enough to answer Emily's call. "Hello?"

Her voice was soothing, unlike the erratically maneuvering vehicles to my left. "Hi, what are you doing this evening?"

"Well, I have no plans when I get home other than to feed Anna, feed myself, and watch something called *Black Mirror*. Fal recommended it."

Emily laughed. "No book marathon tonight?"

"Not tonight." Hearing her voice made me smile.

"Wait, you said when you get home. Does that mean you're still at work?"

I quickly slowed my pedaling and jerked my handlebars to weave around a man with a cell phone in his hand who was crossing against the light. "No, I'm on my commute home."

"Alex...didn't you tell me that you rode your bike to and from work?"

"Yes."

She paused as I pulled to a stop at another light and the deep *bromp* of a truck horn sounded somewhere nearby. "You answered your phone while riding your bike home in Chicago rush hour traffic?" Her voice rose at the end of the sentence, indicating anxiety or displeasure.

I didn't want to further dismay her but I had to be honest. "I did. But I'm being much safer than the first ride after waking from my coma. I promise." The light turned green and I started pedaling again.

"Safer than—dammit, Alex! You better be careful."

I smiled. "I like that you're worried about me."

Emily sighed, and though it was a quiet sound through my earbud with loud traffic all around me, I still heard it. "I don't like that I have to worry about you. I should hang up."

Her concern made me laugh, then I felt bad for laughing at her honest response. Emotional connection was hard to maintain while grasping onto logic. "I'm safe, please don't worry. Why did you call?"

"It seems The Bean Bag has a special on Wednesdays where if you buy one coffee you get a second one for free. Since I couldn't possibly drink two coffees and be able to sleep tonight, I thought I'd offer you my free one. But if you're not even home yet—"

I overrode Emily before she could rescind the offer. "No! I'd love to meet you for coffee. I can be there in a little more than five minutes, though I'll be arriving straight from work."

"But you said you haven't eaten dinner yet, nor has little Anna."

I shrugged, then grew annoyed at the illogicalness of such an action while both riding my bicycle and talking to someone on the phone. "I can eat there and Anna has dry food in the laundry room." Another loud horn and the screech of tires sounded to my immediate left and I glanced that way to determine if I was in danger. Given the uptick in traffic, I decided it was the wiser option to end the call. "I have to go now, I'll see you soon. Good-bye, Emily. Oh, and that's five minutes starting...now."

"What was—" I missed what she was going to ask as the call ended. Seeing a giant SUV swerve into my lane had me refocus on the remainder of my trip rather than speculate about what Emily's last words were.

I noted with peculiar interest that the timing I gave to Emily for arrival at the coffee shop was exact, down to the second. The time on my cell phone switched to my arrival time as I stopped in front of the bike rack at the edge of the sidewalk. The bell on the door rang when I walked in and she looked up at me then glanced down at the cell phone in her hand. Then she stood and walked over. "Holy shit, you said five minutes but I didn't think you'd time it so perfectly."

I looked at her screen. "You timed me?"

Emily slipped the phone into her pocket and pulled me into an awkward hug. It was unwieldy because the laptop bag had slid around to the front from where it previously rested near my back hip. "Of course I did. After all, you said 'five minutes start-ing now,' so I had to test you to see how accurate that genius brain of yours is with timing."

"I do a lot of counting in my head."

She turned to me as we got to the counter. "Do you have OCD?"

I thought about her question. "I'm not sure." I considered the textbook definition. "Obsessive Compulsive Disorder is a com-mon, chronic, and long-lasting disorder in which a person has uncontrollable, reoccurring thoughts, which is the obsession com-ponent, and behaviors, which is the compulsion component, which he or she feels the urge to repeat over and over. I wouldn't say I have such a disorder, I merely have a few...I believe Fal calls them quirks." I shrugged and the motion finally made sense in the context of my conversation and company.

"Hmm." Emily seemed to let it go and instead addressed the young barista of indeterminate gender. The name tag said Julien but also listed "they" as their pronoun. "Hi Julien, can you give my computer geek friend, Alex, my free drink?"

"Absolutely. What will you have, Alex?" Julien's voice was mid-range and soothing, and they had a great smile.

I looked at the handwritten chalkboard. "I'll have the special today."

"Soy or skim?"

"Skim please, and extra whip."

"Sure, no problem. We'll have your drink at the end in a few minutes."

Emily looked at me with concern. "Didn't you say you were going to eat dinner here tonight?"

I shook my head. "I changed my mind, I can eat later at home. I prefer to spend time speaking with you."

Rather than respond to my declaration, Emily looped her arm through mine again and led me away, calling over her shoulder to the barista. "Thanks, Julien!" She gently bumped me with her hip as we stood waiting. "So, this counting thing...are you a genius with numbers then? Is that your thing?"

Part of her question didn't make sense when combined with the other part. What did genius have to do with a *thing* of mine? "I don't understand what you mean. What kind of thing?"

"Alex!" We both turned toward the pick-up counter to see my cup sitting there.

Emily laughed and pointed at the name written on the side. "Cute."

The image on the disposable coffee cup was done with a marker, black against white. It featured a stylized version of my name. Only instead of spelling it out, Julien drew a large A and L, then a dash and a big X. It was pleasing and familiar and looked a little like graffiti I'd seen once on the wall of an underpass. I knew I could puzzle out the familiarity while we were sitting in the coffee shop but the smell of coffee and Emily's perfume proved to be too alluring and I decided to think about it another time. If I were one of the computers I loved so much, I'd say Emily took up a lot of my processing power. The thought made me laugh aloud and she looked at me curiously.

"What?"

We settled into two beanbag chairs near the small fireplace. It wasn't burning but the area would definitely have been considered cozy. I smiled. "Nothing, I was contemplating the fact that you are so distracting to me that sometimes I forget to count. Or do anything else really." Admitting something so personal and perhaps vulnerable felt strange. Rather than meet her eyes I took a long sip of my drink and savored the sweet berry flavor combined with the richness of coffee. My eyes opened wide with Emily's next words.

"You're really too good to be true, you know that?"

Her golden-brown eyes watched me intently as she sipped her own drink. They provided no meaning to her words. "I don't understand."

Emily huffed and waved a hand vaguely in my direction. "Look at you. You're successful, a genius with seven degrees *including* two doctorates, you're hot, sweet, funny, and you seem to like me. I'm nearly forty-one years old and I've seen one disappointment after another where romance is concerned. Then you come into my life in a chance meeting, not once but *twice*, and you're interested in me. I guess I'm waiting for someone to come out and yell 'you've been punk'd!' then it will all be over."

My mouth opened of its own accord as I stared at her. The words, worries, and admissions that she espoused were surprising. I wasn't sure what punking was but I added it to my mental list of things to look up later. "But, Emily...you're amazing! The first time I saw you in this coffee shop everything was still so strange and you took time to help me, to connect with me. And you were so beautiful that the image of you stayed with me until later when we saw you again at the clinic. I don't believe in fate, nor supernatural phenomena, but I certainly consider it serendipitous that events unfolded the way they did." I leaned over so I could hold her hand. "You are my favorite part of my life since waking."

I watched with dismay as her eyes opened a little wider and began to water. "Oh damn, now you're going to make me cry!"

A tear slipped free to leave a wet trail down her cheek and it seemed natural to move my hand up and catch it on my thumb. Distracted, I rubbed it between my thumb and forefinger. "Slippery."

"It's just a tear, Alex."

My eyes jerked up to hers. "I don't remember crying, though I know I must have at various points throughout my life."

Emily's look softened, and she carefully cradled the hand that had caught her tear between both of hers. "Maybe you should consider yourself lucky that you don't remember grief then."

I frowned because it wasn't luck. "I've had to relearn a lot of things since waking, I don't want to relearn grief. The definition of it sounds awful."

She laughed and I knew that the heaviness of the moment had passed. "I'm sorry for laying my fears on you. It's just that I haven't exactly had a great track record with the women and men I've dated."

"I'm not too good to be true. I'm not perfect, Emily. I have enough issues of my own that I bring...I believe Fal calls it baggage, into any relationship. At least you can remember the women and men you've dated. In the spirit of full honesty, I have no recollection of sex and relationships. And with my condition I'm going to make a lot of mistakes, say things strangely, or misconstrue things that are said to me. It's not going to be easy to date me and I apologize in advance."

Emily's laughter took me by surprise. She reached up to gently pat my cheek. "You're pretty funny, I'll give you that."

"How am I funny?"

"Because what you don't seem to realize is that you are incredibly easy to date. Lucky me."

I sighed as I grew entranced by her smile and the dimples perfectly placed on each cheek. "External forces exerting upon our lives to bring good fortune is a fallacy but if you're going to attribute the fact that we found each other to something as capricious as luck, then I will accept your judgement. I'll count myself lucky as well."

Emily looked at the cell phone where it sat on the table next to her cup. "What do you think about taking a walk down to the park?"

I smiled at her suggestion. "I think that's a phenomenal idea." I quickly stood, then held out a hand to help her up. She took it and I perhaps pulled a little too hard since she stumbled and fell into my arms. I held her tight so she didn't fall.

She leaned up and gave me a quick kiss before stepping back to grab her things. "Thank you."

I left my bike locked in front of the coffee shop since I'd have to walk by there on the way back to my condo. Unfortunately, I had to bring the messenger bag containing the laptop with us. I still didn't have any coins for the fountain, as I rarely carried cash on me, but Emily pulled out two quarters and handed me one. "You should make a wish."

I opened my mouth to protest. "But wishes don't—"

"Even if they aren't real, if all the possibility of a wish coming true is nothing more than the randomness of life and a collection of repeating patterns, you should still make a wish because it subconsciously instills hope."

When she pulled her finger away I pressed my lips together to stifle pointless words. If Emily wanted me to wish for something, that's what I would do. We both stood in front of the fountain listening to the gentle sounds of water bouncing off metal leaves. Finally Emily tossed her quarter into the basin then turned to look at me. I thought for another twenty-four seconds before aiming and throwing my own coin in. It landed on top of Emily's and she shook her head at the improbable placement. Then she clasped my hand and led us down the path deeper into the park.

Since I didn't believe in the power of wishes, I thought it possible that I could tell Emily my coin-purchased desire, if she were curious. "Would you like to know what I wished for?"

Emily *hummed* then adjusted her grip on my hand so our fingers laced together. "I suppose there's no rule against telling me, especially if the possibility of a wish coming true comes down to random occurrence."

"It's strange how your thoughts on the possibility nearly mirrored my own. And I wished to pass my great uncle's Turing Test." I glanced up as the sky began to fill with color with the approaching sunset.

She snorted and quickly stifled a laugh. "I was only joking about that, Alex. I only said what I thought you would. And I hate to break it to you but your wish isn't very romantic."

"I wasn't aware that was a prerequisite for wishing. I was going to wish for another kiss from you, but when I calculated the odds there was a significantly higher percentage that would already happen in this park, so I wished for something with a much lower probability."

Emily pulled me to a stop near the back corner again. I enjoyed the seclusion of the spot, as well as the abundance of flowers that perfumed the air with new things for me to smell. "You calculated the odds of us kissing?" I nodded. "I'd say that's not very romantic either but for you it kind of is."

I didn't want to offend her or make assumptions. "Was that a bad thing to do?"

"What did you come up with as a percentage?"

"For us kissing?" She leaned closer.

"Yes."

Emily's eyes were a lot darker in the shaded nook we stood within. "I calculated the odds at eighty-seven percent."

She laughed. "Well you may be a genius but you're definitely off with that number."

I trembled as Emily pulled me closer. "I am?"

"Alex...the correct answer is one hundred percent." Then she leaned in and kissed me. It was no fast motion like in the coffee house a short time before. Emily explored my mouth and I opened to her, exploring her in return. She moaned and the strength of her embrace both soothed and exhilarated me. Parts of me clamored internally for more stimulation. I moved my hands down from her lower back until they rested upon the soft fabric of her pants, near the swell of each hip. Emily kissed me harder and I pulled her to me with my newly positioned grip.

Emily moved her hands up and cradled my face as she pulled away from my mouth to kiss the corner of my lips. Her fingers moved down to the sides of my neck, then up into my hair, mussing the arrangement that had lasted since that morning. "How are you always so soft?"

"I don't—" Her lips stifled any answer I would have given as she returned to explore my mouth. The feel of her tongue against mine, and the occasional touch of my tongue to her teeth, they were all stimulating me beyond compare. My fingers squeezed and pulled her at a rhythmic pace and I could feel Emily panting through our kisses.

Finally she pulled back after nipping my bottom lip with her teeth. "Jesus, Alex. You're driving me crazy."

I blew out a cleansing breath. "If that's your way of saying that you've become highly turned on, then I concur and agree." Suddenly I realized where my hands had been resting. I'd been groping her butt, which seemed highly indecorous. I quickly moved them. "Oh, I'm very sorry!"

Emily laughed. "Don't be, because I'm definitely not." She glanced around and took note of the lights that had come on in the park while we stood kissing in the shadows. "We should head back."

I sighed with regret, thinking about the busy days we both had coming up. "Yes, that's probably for the best."

We kissed again in front of the coffee shop, then she walked across the street to where her car was parked. Rather than get in, Emily watched me as I unlocked my bike and put on the helmet that had been locked with it. Then I clipped my phone into the holder and switched on the driving lights wired into the bike frame. I mounted the seat and turned to give her one last look. She waved. "Good night, Alex. Text me when you get home."

I smiled. "I will. And thanks again for the coffee."

Emily laughed. "Trust me, the pleasure was all mine."

Chapter Ten

Backbone

DOCTOR STEPHANIE YOUNG, the director of the bio-medical division was my first meeting Thursday morning. I recalled a previous conversation with her the year before, where she spoke of her wife and their child, and I used that to personalize the conversation. "How is Romy doing? Has she returned to work since having little Zari?"

Her wife, Special Agent Romy Danes, had previously been in charge of the local FBI office in Chicago until she took a year off to have their first child, a beautiful little girl. Stephanie beamed at the mention of her family and I knew I'd made a good choice to bring it up. It really wasn't hard connecting with people if one took the time to get to know them and interact in a meaningful way. "Zari is growing like a weed. Romy returned to work last month and she's already back into the swing of things, though no longer as SAIC. She stepped down to focus more on our daughter." Doctor Young paused before going on. "And how are you feeling? We haven't been told much, other than you were in an accident and remained in a coma. We weren't even told you'd awakened, so imagine my surprise when I received an email from you requesting a meeting. I thought someone was playing a joke at first."

"I suppose that would be disconcerting. And I'm feeling well, all things considered. What wasn't made publicly known outside the few individuals working on my project, is that I suffered brain damage in multiple areas, including parts of the frontal lobe, parietal lobe, and the temporal lobe. Much to my doctor's surprise, it hasn't affected my intellect or educational training, but I've lost a lot of other long-term memories beyond the past two years. I've also got something Doctor Jones is calling 'sensory amnesia,' and my personality is noticeably different."

Stephanie Young's eyes widened and I cataloged the reaction. "With that much injury it's miraculous that you suffered no physical disabilities. And the fact that your intellect was left completely intact is also odd." She took a moment to search my face.

"That's a lot of change for you since waking. Have they recommended you speak with anyone for your mental health? I know a lot of coma patients have trouble adjusting if they've been asleep for a long time, not to mention if there are any other physiological or psychological issues resulting from injury prior to the coma."

I shook my head. "I haven't actually. I'm keeping a dream journal, but that's mostly due to the differences in my personality. What's strange is that I can remember how I was before, conversations and actions, but I don't feel the same now. I also speak with Fal a lot. She's been wonderful about answering questions and helping me."

Suddenly Doctor Young's head tilted. "Wait, did you say Jones is your doctor?"

"Yes, why?"

Her brows drew down. "He's one of *my* people. We've all known that you were being kept onsite in long-term recovery but there was a specific staff handpicked by your father for that. Why wasn't I notified that you were awake and that my departmental resources had been devoted to your recovery? That makes no sense."

"I'm really not sure. This is my first week back but I initially woke from my coma twenty days ago. They held me here at OAS for about a week for testing before releasing me into Doctor Nanjiani's care. As for not notifying you that two of your people had taken on additional duties of my care and testing, I can't explain it. Many things have seemed strange to me since waking, but I was told that's a completely normal response given the nature of my injuries."

I wasn't sure I could pinpoint the exact look on the bio-med director's face, but it wasn't one of pleasure. She was annoyed to be left out of the information loop and I didn't blame her. Despite her obvious unease, she smiled and moved the conversation forward. "I suppose it's of no matter now, sometimes things get lost in the shuffle. What does matter is that you're awake, capable, and working again. Welcome back, by the way." She leaned back in her chair and placed her hands flat on the table in an unconscious gesture of receptiveness.

Stephanie's smile prompted one from me in return. I'd read recently that a positive attitude was essential for efficient communication and effective progress. "Thank you. Now if you're ready, I'd like to discuss the reason I'm here today."

"I read your email and compiled a list of our current projects.

I emailed it to you right before the meeting but I can put it up on the screen as well." She leaned forward and with a few clicks of her mouse, displayed a detailed project breakdown on the large screen hanging on the wall adjacent to her desk.

We spoke for nearly an hour after I asked for an open discussion on current projects for her division as well as concerns she had with OAS in general. Doctor Young shared bio-med's top three action items on their current task list which included: a safer delivery method for cancer treatment than chemotherapy, better artificial organ monitoring, and improved human trials for new drugs that were less risky than ones of the past. Her biggest concern for OAS was the continued viability of OAS bio-medical division when many other companies focused on only the bio-medical portion of the industry, instead of spreading their talent across four different divisions the way Organic Advancement Solutions had done. "I'm a little concerned that our innovation and market impact will be diluted and we'll eventually slip to the competition."

"I understand your concerns but we haven't gotten where we are today by falling behind where it counts. On the contrary, it's our diversity that has led to some of the greatest OAS innovations in each division. But, I have some collaborative ideas between divisions that I think will take this company to the next level and I'll add your top problems to my task list." She seemed skeptical, which was understandable considering my primary function within the company to date had been solely within the realm of robotics and AI. But at the end of the meeting, Stephanie shook my hand and made a sincere wish that I would achieve my goals. The bottom line was that if I succeeded then OAS as a whole would succeed.

My second meeting took place an hour before lunch with Doctor Konrad Vogel, the head of nanotechnology. His division had been working to increase the speed of nanobot self-replication for some time, but the current samples weren't predicted to reach real-world application capacity for five and a half more years. He also mentioned they wanted to improve the nanobots' communication with the main controller. The last thing on his list, which he admitted was further down in priority level, was using nanobots within a highly specialized and complex sample population to build replacements for damaged or non-viable bots in that same population. Essentially the bots would build their own replacements, even if they were highly advanced.

Basic nanobots could serve more than one function, to both replicate and be reprogrammed for simple performance. But advanced bots were typically only good for their complex job and repair. Doctor Vogel wanted to guarantee existing complex nano-bots could maintain and repair themselves independently from the controller as well as replicate.

I had lunch at my desk while I made notes of ideas about the first two meetings. I wanted to have a plan in place by the time I entered my last meeting of the day at three with Director Devos. Immediately after lunch I met with Doctor Jessica Hanssen who was the head of the prosthetics division. She was one of the lon-gest running directors of the company and had been employed by my father since before my birth.

She greeted me at the door to her office and her familiar Brit-ish accent soothed me. She was a bit formal but Jessica Hanssen had acted as both role model and mother figure to me while growing up. "Hello, Alexandra. Though I found your return quite a surprise, it's good to see your smiling face back at work. Matty must be over the moon."

I inclined my head as she led me into her office. "Thank you, and I prefer Alex now."

"Very well. I got your email and I set a fairly simple set of goals for prosthetics this fiscal year."

Jessica went on to detail her concerns for her department, which were pretty straight- forward. She listed the department's top three goals: to reduce the weight of powered prosthetic limbs, achieve connection of the prosthetic limbs directly to the neural pathways for real-time limb movement and response, and to come up with an alternate power source that was self-sustaining, rather than an onboard battery pack that had to be changed or charged.

I mentally went through my combined knowledge of power sources that we'd been researching in the robotics division. "Have you tried a kinetic energy generator on the larger limbs like the leg?"

Doctor Hanssen looked contemplative. "We haven't actually. We've got mold designers, mechanical engineers, and wiring spe-cialists, plus the necessary programmers, but there are some areas of expertise that prosthetics has a distinct lack of talent."

"That's why I'm here today. I believe that we can go a lot fur-ther as a company, and have a higher success rate of goal achieve-ment if we pool our resources between divisions. We've always been fairly segmented between divisions and resources. The notion that my Synthetica project was specifically planned to be a collaborative project between the four OAS divisions really set the idea in my head. Why can't we do it with other projects?"

She steepled her fingers in front of her lips. Her hair was cut stylishly short, running gray to white. The wrinkles around her mouth became more pronounced as she pursed her lips. "Your point has merit, I'll give you that. And I spoke with Matheson a few months back about Synthetica and what it meant to you and OAS in general. I think we are on the cusp of great change, and this new collaborative way of thinking may be the next step of advancement. Take my action item list and see what ideas you come up with. I'll pledge one researcher a week should you need resources from prosthetics. Let me know what expertise is required and I'll temporarily assign someone to be an interdivisional collaboration specialist." She paused and chuckled. "Goodness, that's a mouthful, isn't it?"

"Perhaps after I've had more time to ruminate we can set up a cross-division task force. Would you be open to something like that?"

Doctor Hanssen gave me a shrewd look, which morphed into a smile. "I think that's brilliant. Again, keep me in the loop and let me know when you need our assistance."

She stood and walked around her desk and I stood in time to shake her hand. Then before I could overthink it, I pulled her into a hug. She was startled, as one would expect. I hadn't hugged her in probably twenty years. "Thank you for everything."

Her bottom lip quivered as she pulled away. "Good luck, Alex. I'm really glad you're back to good health."

I WORKED THE rest of the time until my meeting with Director Devos at three. At precisely the top of the hour I knocked on my director's door. His voice called loudly from the other side, "Enter!" and I pushed through with my laptop and notebook in hand. He stood and waved me toward his private conference table. Once we were seated he gave me a guarded look. "You've been back less than a week and already had meetings with all the directors. I'm impressed. Though I'm a little surprised you didn't inform me of your intentions to begin with."

"Innovation waits for no man, David. Once this idea began to form in my head, I knew I had to run with it. I sense that we're at a turning point and since there was no risk associated with my ideas, caution was unwarranted."

He sighed. "Innovation waits for no man, indeed. Still…a heads up would have been polite."

"My apologies. I probably should have given you a basic outline of my thoughts before proceeding. Consider it a given for next time."

He cocked his head, watching me curiously in a manner I had no remembrance of. "You think there will be a next time?"

I tapped the table to emphasize my words. "I want to take my company to the next level, so yes, there will be a next time. The day we stop having ideas for advancement is the day that OAS shuts its doors. That's not going to happen while I'm alive."

My director smiled and chuckled but it sounded strained. "Perhaps not ever at the rate you're going."

"Let's hope!" I grinned at him and got only a small upturn of lips back. He was definitely acting outside what I remembered but I moved on to address the purpose of the meeting. "As you know, I met with the three other directors today to discuss the top divisional issues they are dealing with. After going over my notes from each meeting, I see potential for collaboration between the departments on multiple projects. While the divisions have their specialists, we are fairly separated from each other in both management and information sharing. I believe OAS should form a collaborative task force. Their purpose would be to investigate the top action items for each division and determine whether or not they can be solved more easily with resources from other areas."

He sat back in his chair and huffed out a breath. His wide eyes and open mouth indicated surprise at my idea. "What prompted this line of thought? Is this a result of a discussion you've had with Doctor Nanjiani or someone else?"

"Neither."

"Perhaps something you've read somewhere, a trade magazine?"

I frowned at the fact that my director, the man who should know more than most others the capability of my intellect, questioned the source of my motivation and innovation. "No. The Synthetica project is a massive collaborative project that spans all four OAS divisions. The idea was born of the notion that some problems or projects could be aided by simply going outside their immediate workspace. Today I learned that one of prosthetics fiscal year goals is improving their power source for their large prosthetic limbs. We've been working on exactly that with robotics, and in some cases have completely switched to kinetic motion power generation. But without the correct people on the problem, they didn't realize the capability of current technology in that area."

"Hmm, this is actually a really fascinating approach to problem solving on a macro level, versus on the micro level. Of course you know we can't make any large organization changes, or create this task force without speaking with your father first and garnering his permission for such an endeavor. Not to mention the cost to put together the talents needed."

I waved away his concerns. "The cost would be negligible because current resources could be used to serve on the taskforce. They'd still perform their main division duties, the taskforce would be supplemental. As a matter of fact, I suspect it would pay for itself once the members begin closing task list items at a significantly faster rate than the normal departmental predictions. As for my father, I intend to talk to him about my idea tomorrow during our next phone call."

David Devos paled and I found that curious. His respiration also increased, and I could see the pulse jump in his throat as his heartrate sped. He was nervous. "You've been speaking with your father?"

"Yes, is that a problem? He *is* my father after all. I wasn't aware that I needed permission from my division head to make personal calls."

"No! It's just that…I mean, I was surprised is all. I know Mr. Turing has been busy with the subsidiary in Germany and I wasn't aware that he'd been in contact since you were…um, since you've been up and active again in the company."

He was definitely put off by the notion of me communicating with my dad. I wasn't sure what was going on with David, but he was most certainly acting differently since I came out of the coma. I wasn't the only one that appeared to have a personality change. "Yes, well we've been vidcomming every other day, and I'll discuss my ideas in detail with him when he returns next week."

"Wait, he's coming back next week? That wasn't in the plan— I mean to say, that wasn't what he was planning before. I wonder what made him change his mind."

I smiled. "I think he wants to meet my kitten."

Devos looked at me as if he were seeing me for the first time, which was not a reaction I expected. "Simply amazing."

"Excuse me?"

He shook his head and motioned toward my laptop. "Never mind. I'm going to assume you have more details to this proposal of yours. If I know anything about Alexandra Turing, it's that she doesn't come to a meeting half prepared. What have you come up with after speaking with the other directors?"

"I'm not going to waste your time going over every one of my initial ideas, but I can tell you a few things I've come up with. For instance," I quickly brought up one proposal page and sent it to the screen on his wall. "Two of bio-medical's top three action items, safer delivery of their new cancer drug and better artificial organ monitoring, can both be accomplished using current nano-technology. Their third action item is to improve the safety of human trials when testing new drugs. I'm sure that one of our programmers in robotics and AI can team up with someone in bio-med to come up with a better prediction algorithm to use before it makes it to the trial stage."

David's brows rose as he looked at my lists on the screen. Each division had a list of resources and needs below its name. They were quickly done off the top of my head but you could definitely see overlap between one department's resource list and another's need list. It perfectly highlighted my proposal and its potential effectiveness. "How...how we never saw this connection before now is beyond me, but I can definitely see the benefits of your collaborative task force."

"As I said before, OAS is an excellent company and I'm not saying that because it's my father's life's work and will eventually pass on to me. I'm saying it because I've put everything into Organic Advancement Solutions and I know we have what it takes to succeed far into the future. However, every company has room for improvement. I believe that our divisions have been left to their own devices without a lot of incentive to work together. They each do their part to benefit the company and leave the other divisions alone. Making this idea work will take changing expectations. Perhaps even adjusting the bonus and improvement benchmarks to encourage searching for answers outside your own area."

He rubbed his chin. "And who do you see running this program of yours?"

His question was not one I'd predicted. I would have thought the answer obvious so didn't anticipate his asking. "Me, of course. I have the breadth of knowledge, the familiarity with all the divisions, and support of my father. However I would of course accept each director's suggestion when it came to the participation of a volunteer from their area. They would know better than I who was best qualified."

"My apologies, you're absolutely right. And you don't think this will interfere with your work on Synthetica?"

"David, my accident has made me realize that there is more to life than Synthetica. I'm well aware of the high price tag attached to the project, and we will see a return eventually. But seeing a handful of profitable ideas come to fruition in the next year across the board at OAS will buy more time for robotics."

"True, true. All right, finish writing your complete proposal and send it out to all the directors, your father, and the VP of finance, George Valparaiso. Let's get everyone's input on this before we move forward."

I shut my laptop. "I can do that." Once I had my computer tucked safely beneath my arm I stood. "Thanks for your time today. I'll have the packet put together before the end of the work day tomorrow."

He walked me to his office door. "Sounds good. Talk to you later, Alex." I saw him lift the receiver of his phone as I left his office and I paused on the other side of the door, curious about whom he was calling. His voice was muffled but I had no problem understanding his words. "Put me through to Doctor Nanjiani."

EMILY ARRIVED AT my condo at six-thirty Saturday night. I left her name with the desk guard downstairs earlier in the day so she could be given a pass and allowed up. Even though it was a short walk to the comedy club, I wanted to be able to show her around my home and re-introduce her to Anna. Emily seemed enamored with the kitten as soon as she walked in the door. She gave me a hug then scooped little Anna into her arms and carried her around as we toured both the upstairs and downstairs rooms.

She stopped near my bookshelf and perused the titles while I remained silent next to her. Then she turned her gaze to my fireplace. "Alex, why is your mantle empty?"

I frowned at the memory of Anna breaking things she shouldn't when I first brought her home. "Anna is particularly destructive with fragile items. I moved the previous mantle décor to the top of my bookshelf and the small shelf above the television so she wouldn't break anything else. I also installed child locks on my cabinets after she displayed unusual aptitude for opening doors."

"You catered to your kitten by child-proofing your home?"

I looked at her in alarm, afraid I'd done something wrong with the care of my pet. "Should I not have done that?" I began to second-guess my decisions concerning little Anna. "Perhaps I should have made more of an attempt to train her—"

Emily interrupted my musing with a loud laugh. "You can't train a cat, Alex. It's in a cat's nature to be assholes and do their own thing. You did everything right and that's a nice change of pace for me. Well done on being a responsible pet owner."

"So why are you laughing?"

She stroked the fur below Anna's chin, prompting a loud purr. "Because you're funny. Let's see the rest of the place so we can go. I'm hungry."

I enjoyed my dinner immensely and even Emily seemed especially pleased with her selection. I tried to eat a new food every day since being released from medical care. Though Fal has mentioned more than once that some of my unhealthier selections may send me right back into the hospital again. I ordered the twice-fried chicken sandwich and Emily had the veggie burger with habanero aioli. I also ordered a rum punch, which was served in a decorative glass and came with half price refills. After drinking nearly half of the second round by the end of the meal I contemplated how it made me feel.

"Don't you like it?"

I looked up and found myself the beneficiary of Emily's concerned gaze. "It's quite good, actually. I was only thinking about its effects. I don't remember being drunk at all. Not even tipsy."

Her dark brows rose. "Never?"

"Based on the past two years of spotty memory that I do have, I don't think I drank much alcohol. The feeling is peculiar, like sensation isn't as crisp. I also feel...mellow. My urgency and focus appear to be compromised." I smiled and took another sip. Had I not been with Emily, someone I trusted, I don't think I would have liked my hindered physical state. But I was with Emily and I felt good.

"You drink like a scientist. Do you like the way it makes you feel, or no?"

"I like a lot of things when I'm with you." Honesty seemed

the best policy.

Emily's complexion darkened further with my statement and she shook her head. "Unbelievable." Then she reached for the credit card slip that the server had returned to our table.

I waved toward the folded card holder. "Are you sure you don't want me to buy dinner, since you purchased the tickets?"

She shook her finger at me. "This one's mine, Alex. You promised."

"Okay." I took another large sip of my drink then picked up my unused spoon and worked to straighten its slight bend while she signed the slip. I didn't like to be idle and the crookedness bothered me. Two things happened in very close succession. A crash sounded to our right as a diner knocked a heavy drink glass off the table next to us. The next was movement of a large piece of the shattered glass heading toward Emily, on a trajectory to strike the spot between her temple and left eye. I quickly raised the spoon and used it to deflect the glass shard. It made a slight *tink* as it bounced off and landed somewhere in the darkened restaurant.

Emily looked at the spoon I held near her face, then moved to meet my gaze. "How did you do that?"

The question was simple enough. "I moved my hand."

Emily's eyes were wide with shock as she took the spoon from my fingers. "I know *that*, Alex. I mean, how did you move your hand so fast and how did you know I was going to be hit? I heard the glass bounce off the spoon."

"I saw it."

Emily scoffed. "You saw it. Are you psychic now or just extremely lucky?"

"Clairvoyance and other psychic phenomena remain unproven to modern science and we already discussed luck. It is impossible that I could be either of those things."

"Hmm, you're certainly something or I would have been struck by the glass. So, impossibility or luck, which is it?"

I didn't like her choices. "Neither is logical."

Emily gave me a strange smile. "Sir Arthur Conan Doyle wrote, 'Once you eliminate the impossible, whatever remains, no matter how improbable, must be the truth.' I'll leave it to you to decide which the impossible thing is, and which is merely improbable."

"Perhaps it is luck then." I conceded.

Rather than pursue the conversation further, Emily closed

the credit card folder and glanced at the time on her phone. "Ready to see the show?"

I stood with her. "I do like to laugh."

"Laughter is the best medicine." Emily looped her arm through mine in that familiar way I'd come to enjoy as we walked toward the exit.

The mention of medicine reminded me of my Mendaxecall. I'd been out of my coma for twenty-two days, and taking the trial drug for equally as long, but had yet to see a noticeable difference in my mnemonic recall. Perhaps it wasn't as effective as they hoped, or maybe my brain was too damaged to fully return what I had once lost. The thought of my own poorly functioning brain reminded me of our current work quandary with the positronic brain. Eliminating the use of Trichlorosilane from the Synthetica project remained at the top of my list. I spoke with one of the nanotech scientists after turning in my report on Friday. He also thought it was within the realm of possibility to program some advanced nanobot scrubbers for use in our project and we have plans to do testing on samples in the lab Monday afternoon.

"What are you thinking about so hard?"

I realized that we'd arrived in the other area of the building without being aware. I felt terrible that, in my intense focus, I hadn't paid any attention to my surroundings during the entire walk. "Oh, my apologies! I seem to have..." I trailed off, unsure how I missed time between leaving the restaurant and walking up two floors to the theater featuring our show.

"Zoned out?"

My eyes widened as she said the exact words I was searching for. "Yes! I've heard Fal say that quite a few times when she gets distracted. It's never happened to me before though."

Emily held out her phone so the attendant at the door could scan the ticket barcode when we got to the door, then we made our way inside to our seats. "So what were you thinking about to make you zone out?"

"Initially?" She nodded. "Mendaxecall."

She cocked her head curiously. "The name makes it sound like a medication, but I don't recognize it. Part of your project?"

I thought about how best to answer her. It wasn't proprietary information so I was safe to give her details. "No, it's a new drug developed by our bio-medical division. It is supposed to help memory loss patients recover faster. I'm currently participating in the trial due to the unique circumstances of my disability."

Emily waved a server over to order more drinks then turned back to me. "How many are in the trial with you?"

"I don't know."

"Have you noticed any difference? Are your memories coming back?"

I sighed. "No. That's what distracted me after we left the restaurant. You mentioned medicine and it made me think of the Mendaxecall along with its lack of effect."

Emily's curiosity was one of many things I enjoyed about her. A person didn't have to be a genius to be intellectually stimulating. "How long are you supposed to take it?"

"They didn't give me an end date."

She frowned. "That seems odd to me, but you did say it was in the trial stage still. I'll admit I'm not really sure how that all works but if you're concerned then speak with your doctor. I can only answer questions if they're about something with a tail."

"Wait..." Emily's words rang false. "I read a book on cats after I adopted Anna and I know for a fact that there are some that are born without tails. So you have to answer more questions than that."

She held up a finger and smiled. "I *can* answer more questions than that, but I don't *have* to answer anything at all because—" the server deposited our new drinks on the small table between us and she took a large sip from hers "—I'm off the clock!"

Her words made me laugh and I liked the feeling of pleasure that spread through my own chest. "Now who is the funny one?"

Emily grabbed my free hand across the table and held onto it as the lights dimmed. "We can both be funny, now *shh*, it's starting."

It wasn't terribly late when we got back to my condo but late enough that most people over a certain age would be sleeping. Emily didn't appear tired at all so I invited her upstairs because I was enjoying her company and our conversation. We discussed climate change, and alternate sources of fuel that Emily had read about, on our way back from the comedy club. I mentally went through all the social queues and expectations in my head for occasions where someone is invited back to your home. "Would you like something to drink?"

Emily set the *Popular Science* magazine down that she'd picked up from the kitchen island after I relocked my door. I initially bought it in the grocery store when I noticed the title, but I was pleasantly surprised to find it full of articles about artificial intelligence, nanobots, and the future of cancer detection. It was all the things I'd immersed myself in lately. Emily didn't seem as interested based on the speed with which she dropped it back onto the counter. As I got closer to her I noticed a peculiar glint in her eyes. Nothing physical, but rather there was a mood to her look that I couldn't decipher. She stepped into my personal space and it felt very natural for me to wrap my arms around her lower back to hold her near as she did the same to me. "Do *you* want something to drink?"

"I don't understand. I'm the hostess and you are a guest, it's my job to offer you a dri—" My words may have been cut off by Emily's kiss but my thoughts definitely weren't. I didn't count the seconds as we stood in the middle of my main floor because all my attention was busy analyzing the feel of her lips and the taste of her tongue where it caressed mine. I hadn't worn any cologne since waking but I never lacked for delightful scents as long as I was with Emily.

Emily's hands moved up my back as she pulled me closer and made a little noise in the back of her throat. The kiss deepened and a tremor began in my hands where they clutched the back of her shirt as I approached sensation overload. Emily slowed the kiss then gently eased us apart. "Are you okay?"

I felt like I was floating and had to quickly look down at the ground to make sure that wasn't actually the case. "I feel amazing!" I moved my gaze back up to meet her beautiful eyes. "I have discovered a new love for kissing, one that surpasses my newly discovered love of food."

Emily laughed. "Oh ho, so kissing is better than food?" I nodded. "Better than the twice fried chicken you raved about earlier tonight?" She moved a bit of my grown-out hair from where it fell across my forehead then embraced me again.

I was awed by her attention and the delightful sensations she elicited with a simple scratch of her short nails up and down my back. "Nothing is better than kissing!"

Laughter followed my declaration. "I wouldn't be too sure about that." In a turn that alarmed me a bit, Emily suddenly sobered. "I know you said you don't remember your past experience, Alex, and I never want to do anything to make you uncomfortable. So we can take this at your pace."

Emily was referring to sex. She was right, I couldn't remember how to please someone sexually and while I'd done a fair amount of reading on the subject in the past few weeks, it wasn't the same as experience. Again, I chose honesty. "I really like you, and I'm afraid that I'll be disappointing should we engage in coitus."

She snorted and murmured the word 'coitus' under her breath. "You can say sex, it's a perfectly healthy and normal word to use."

"Sex then, I don't want to disappoint you sexually, or... uh, leave you hanging." She gave me a look and I explained. "Fal's expression. She's been really good about answering questions about subjects I don't remember."

Emily took my hand and guided me over to the couch where we sat next to each other. "Alex, sex is a very organic bit of activity. It's a way to feel good and connect with your partner. Both physically and emotionally. It's not a formula to be graphed, or an experiment to be plotted out with calculated odds. It happens when the individuals involved are ready."

"Are you ready?"

She shook her head and took my left hand between both of hers while turning slightly to face me. "That's not the right question to ask. The real question is, are you?"

I thought about the point she'd made. I knew what Emily was trying to say but I didn't have a good response for her. "I don't know."

"If you don't know then you have your answer." She rubbed my hand and up my arm. "How is your skin always so soft? I've never met anyone with skin as soft as yours."

I shivered. "I don't know but that...tickles?" Emily pulled her hands away but I grabbed one. "I like it."

She leaned over and whispered into my ear. "I like *you*. Let's be organic." Then we were kissing again and it was the best I could ever remember feeling.

Chapter Eleven

High Priority Processing

FIFTEEN MINUTES LATER we were interrupted by a tiny curious cat. Emily pulled back. "Alex, I can't kiss you with your cat between us."

Despite her protest I noticed Emily scratching behind Anna's ears. I took a long enough break to grab Anna and shut her securely into the large storage pantry with the promise of extra playtime the next day. When I returned we continued where we'd left off, only Emily guided us down to lay on our sides facing each other on the couch. It made my left arm fairly useless but I was at least able to explore her back and sides with my right hand. The feel of her skin and curves was as intoxicating as her kisses.

We kissed for nearly an hour like that until Emily was panting into my mouth and I could feel the *lub-dub* of my heart beating fast in my own chest. Each minute it went on left me sensitized and increasingly aroused.

At some point Emily maneuvered herself so she was above me on the couch. My thoughts glitched when her leg pressed against the seam of my dress pants, and I made a noise I wasn't expecting. Something between a groan and a whine echoed up my throat into my nasal passage as incredible pleasure emanated from between my legs. I lifted my lower half to meet the press of her thigh more fully and another sound came, needy and wanting. While wonderful, the experience was unfamiliar, overwhelming, and a little frightening. I pulled back from her mouth and held her shoulders firmly so Emily couldn't pursue my lips. "Wait." I was embarrassed and the word came out as a whisper.

Though quiet, Emily still heard me and froze, then quickly rolled back to her original position next to me. "Shit, Alex, I'm sorry." She blew out a breath and draped her hand over her eyes, the same one that had been clutching at my side moments before. "We got kind of carried away, didn't we?"

"Maybe we didn't and I'm simply too broken to connect properly."

Emily immediately moved her hand and turned my face so I could meet her gaze. "Alex, no. You are *not* too broken." She waited a moment then spoke again. "Can you tell me why you stopped? Were you uncomfortable, or — "

"It was amazing! You are amazing and I've never felt — well I guess I have but I don't ever remember feeling so much pleasure at once. It was too much, I think…and it frightened me." I grew frustrated at my actions. "Fear is a foolish emotion."

"Fear is a form of emotional energy. It's essential and it keeps us from being reckless. Fear warns us to be safe and leery of things that could harm us."

I tilted my head into the caress of Emily's hand where she skimmed her fingertips along my cheek and neck. I reveled in the ticklish touch. "What purpose does it serve here and now? You're completely safe and I'm in no danger in my own home."

Emily stilled her touch and her expression grew sad. "Tell me something, Alex. Do you know how much force it takes to break a human bone?"

It seemed like an odd question but I *did* know the answer. We'd done a lot of research at OAS in the robotics division, contemplating how best to simulate human motion and sturdiness in an android model. "It takes about four-thousand newtons of force to break a typical human femur. Why do you want to know?"

"Because physically humans are quite sturdy, but emotionally? Our hearts can be broken with something as simple as a look, or a word from the person holding it."

Insight blossomed within my thoughts. "Have you had your heart broken?"

Emily's gaze was intense as I waited for her answer. Finally she swallowed and looked away, down at the collar of my shirt. "Too many times."

"Then why…?" I trailed off, unsure what to ask or how to ask it without causing her more sadness.

Her golden eyes met mine again and where there was once a hooded look, what I recognized as sadness, her expression was now wide and serious. "Because real love with all its potential is always worth it."

"But — "

Emily kissed me to still the words. "Alex…it's worth it." She kissed me again, a short caress against my lips. Then she moved her fingertips up to trace along the arch of my right eyebrow. "We'll move forward when you're ready."

I sighed because I was still uncomfortably aroused. My body was telling me to go as much as my mind told me to stop. "I really like you, Emily St. John."

She moved her hand into my hair and I shivered as she scraped her nails gently against my scalp. It was another type of touch that I'd grown to enjoy in a short period of time. "I really like you too, which is why we're going to do this right."

I thought about her declaration. "What do we do now?"

"Right now?" I nodded again. "Right now I should probably go home."

I clutched her gently. "But I don't want you to go."

Emily laughed quietly. "Unfortunately there are two ways a date can end. The pair can take the night further into intimacy, or they go their separate ways. And since we've eliminated one of those options..."

"I propose a new option."

"And that is?"

I moved back to extricate myself from the depths of my couch, and her embrace. My body was displeased by the motion but my mind felt much clearer when Emily wasn't touching me. I walked over to the shelf by the television and retrieved the remote. "How about Netflix? We can watch whatever you like. I think I heard Fal call this kind of date 'Netflix and chill.'"

Emily burst out laughing and I frowned. "Alex, no. That doesn't mean what you think it does. I think Fal is messing with you."

"She wouldn't."

"Not even if she thought it were funny?"

I grimaced. "She would."

She went on to explain, "When you invite someone over for the sole purpose of sex, but neither of you wants to admit that it's for sex, people call it 'Netflix and chill.' They don't really want to watch television."

I quickly set the remote down. "Oh, maybe we shouldn't watch then."

"Its fine, Alex, we can cuddle on the couch and watch something."

"Cuddle." I thought about the notion of cuddling. I'd read many books since waking, watched both movies and television shows, but I had yet to cuddle with anyone. I couldn't remember ever cuddling with anyone. I looked at Emily and grew extraordinarily happy at the idea of cuddling with her. I picked up the remote again and handed it to her. "I like the idea of cuddling. Why don't you pick something you'd like to watch and I'll go let Anna out and retrieve my soft couch blanket." I began to walk away then paused. "Oh, are you hungry? Would you like something to drink, or popcorn?"

Emily tilted her head in thought and I could see a mischievous smile spread across her lips. "Offering something to drink again, hmm?"

"I don't know about you, but after kissing you for sixty-eight minutes my body is telling me that I am in need of fluids. And I like popcorn, especially during movies so I thought I'd offer it to you."

She gave me an offended glare, one that I quickly realized was more teasing than anything. "I'm not hungry at all—wait a minute! Alex, were you counting while we made out on the couch?"

"No. I told you, your kisses make it so I can't count."

"Then how do you know how long we were kissing?"

It was a good question, in fact, a very puzzling one because I hadn't been counting in my head like I do with so many other things. Yet I knew with certainty that we had kissed for sixty-eight minutes, including our time in the kitchen. "I don't know how I know, I just...know."

Emily looked at her cell phone where it sat on the end table. "I mean, the time seems like a pretty accurate estimate based on when we got back. And knowing you and your uncanny timing 'thing,' you're probably exactly on. I have no idea how you would know such a thing, or calculate it."

"I don't know." I felt much like a broken program, repeating the same action over and over no matter how many times you cycle through the code.

"You're very mysterious."

I sighed. "Apparently the mystery extends to my own consciousness as well. I hate not knowing things about myself and the world around me."

Emily smiled and reached out to take my hand. She began to stand so I helped pull her up, though not as hard as the time in the coffee shop. "Well, Alex Turing...what *do* you know?"

That was an easy one to answer. "I know I want to cuddle with you so I can experience it for the first time with someone I really like."

"Charmer. And it's a deal. Now we're back to drinks."

I considered my selection. "I have a variety of wines, milk, white grape juice, orange juice, bottled water, some beer called Oberon that Fal likes, and a hard cider. I know you like mixed drinks but I'm afraid I don't have any hard liquor here."

"Water is fine. I'm going to run to use the bathroom then I'll come back and help pick out a movie." I nodded and watched her head down the short hallway that led to my downstairs bathroom. She called out to me when she was nearly there. "Stop staring, it's creepy. And don't forget about Anna!"

"I never—" She walked into the bathroom and shut the door and my last word fell on an empty room. "Forget."

Rather than dwell on all I'd discovered and experienced over the course of the night, I went to free Anna from the pantry. I skipped making popcorn since Emily wasn't hungry. Instead I retrieved two bottles of water from the refrigerator. After placing the water on the end table, I opened the cedar chest against the side wall and removed my blanket. I buried my face in the soft faux fur and inhaled the scent. The smell of cedar soothed me and I couldn't wait to share it, and the memories it invoked, with Emily.

As the credits rolled on the screen later that evening, I realized that Emily was sound asleep against my shoulder. We had reclined on the couch and shared an ottoman to put up our feet and she must have been either too tired or too comfortable. Perhaps both. I tried waking her by whispering her name. "Emily." She didn't rouse in the slightest. I glanced down at my cell phone to confirm that it was indeed quite late. Emily was extremely attractive normally, but I found her appearance very cute with her mouth slightly open. I watched her for one hundred and twenty-seven seconds before making the decision to let her sleep. Then I closed my own eyes and hoped for pleasant, but not uncomfortably erotic, dreams. Though after our earlier activities, as Fal would say, fat chance of that!

MONDAY WAS FAIRLY busy with myself and Spencer Engle spending half the day in the lab. Fal was in meetings most of the day or I would have invited her to observe our tests. I'd found a previous positronic brain sample and once we got the nanobots programmed, we inserted them into the suspension fluid and watched their progress through the computer monitor.

While we waited to see results, I contemplated waking to see

Emily's smiling face Sunday morning. She seemed quite at home in my condo after I gave her a new toothbrush from my cupboard and loaned her more comfortable clothing. I made us both breakfast and we laughed about some of the funniest moments from the evening before. I even teased her for falling asleep to a movie she'd picked out. While the kiss goodbye wasn't full of the same passion as the night before, I was left feeling a strange sense of contentment for the rest of the day.

"It's working!" Spencer's exclamation startled me from my thoughts and I glanced down at the screen we had showing the nanobot movement. The positronic brain shell simulation was in the middle. Hundreds of little glowing dots represented the nanobot scrubbers. Synthetica was specifically designed to be one of the smallest, most powerful, supercomputers available. It had to be immensely capable to have any hope of matching the responses and emotions of a human brain. I was proud of the fact that Synthetica could process two hundred and fifty petraflops per second. It wasn't the fastest available in activity, but it was the smallest. We only needed to get the rest operational and settled into a working prototype body.

The positronic brain version we were using for the test was AL-8, which featured the cooling cap only, but no circulatory system with a cooling chamber. For the current test, we were measuring the time to failure after the nanobots were inserted. One of the documented problems with the cooling system that Fal had shown me the schematics for, even with the AL-10 model, was that even with the addition of Trichlorosilane to the system, it would eventually degrade and fail because of the nature of the inorganic compound not reacting well with heat.

As Spencer and I observed the bots at work and monitored AL-8 function, we were excited to see that the nanobot scrubbers not only eliminated the need for the chemical, but our prediction algorithm indicated there would be no long-term system degradation. The scrubbers kept all the circuitry and neural pathways in a nearly-new state. I turned to the man who had been helping me all day with Director Vogel's approval. "Spencer, you did it! You exactly replicated what I needed for this project."

He was a younger man, maybe mid-twenties, and he seemed embarrassed by my ebullient praise. "Honestly, Doctor Turing, it was half you. After all, you're the one that knew the code for repetition and response, I only provided the basic bot function." He shook his head. "I took this job straight out of college two years ago because I'd heard OAS was one of the best. But watching you in your element and spending time in the nano lab has been an amazing career experience. I'm honored to both meet and work with you." He held out his hand and I shook it.

"Call me Alex, and the honor is all mine. I see a lot of promise in you and if you're interested, I'm putting together an interdivisional task force to do something like what we're working on today, to look at the four divisions' top issues and use our combined expertise to see if problems could be solved using resources from another division. Would you be interested in something like that?"

"Yes, absolutely! This has been really rad today watching my work come to life in a practical application. Most of what I do is basic bot tasks, programming them to work in simulations and hypothetical circumstances. I like seeing how projects like Synthetica can cross the divisional boundaries and use resources from all our areas."

I smiled at his youthful enthusiasm. "I'll mark down your interest and when the time comes for me to begin this new endeavor, I'll contact you and Director Vogel. Answer a question for me, if you will. What is the most interesting nanotech project you've worked on since coming to OAS?"

Spencer smiled and his eyes squinted as the grin raised his full cheeks. "That's easy! We made a breakthrough about a year ago with artificial hair production. We created simple photocatalytic nano machines that mass produce filaments of organic hair substitute. All they need is a steady supply of basic organic matter and a nanogenerator."

For some reason, the notion of powering nano machines had slipped my mind. "Nanogenerator? I haven't read about that during my research, though I'll admit I've been mostly focusing on problem solving and not the small logistics of the solutions."

Spencer snorted. "Small logistics, that's funny. Seriously though, a nanogenerator is an extremely small harvester that can supply electrical power to nano devices. The power can be derived from a number of sources and the nanogenerator can be tailored to the base application that the nanobots are being utilized with."

"So, it's a nano-sized power plant."

"Yup. So far OAS has come up with nanogenerators that work with vibrations, temperature gradients, and biochemistry. We're also researching external sources such as audible and inaudible sound."

I had no idea the nanotech division was so varied with their research. "Fascinating. And you've got working samples now?"

He nodded. "We currently have fifty filament machines in human trials right now for people suffering from baldness and alopecia. We also have one hundred implantable biosensors that can continuously monitor a patient's blood glucose level in human trial, and three local bridges with autonomous strain sensors."

"The filament machines, you mentioned that they need organic material...where do they get that when working in a human trial? And how are they photocatalytic?"

Spencer pointed at his own head. "Believe it or not, they connect to the skin and subdermal tissue on a microscopic level and use dead cells from the scalp to build the filaments. When UV radiation hits the hair and scalp, the nanoparticles become energized and add organic material to the length. So rather than grow from the root, the hair grows from the end. But they can also work with any available organic material, they just have to be programmed with the chemical makeup so they know what to harvest for material and what to leave alone. You can also program the bots to a particular speed of growth. For example, a quarter inch every two months."

It seemed unbelievable that the nanotech could create something realistic enough to be in the human trial phase. "How does the appearance and texture of the filaments compare to actual human hair?"

Spencer pointed to his own shoulder-length hair that had been pulled back into a stubby ponytail and gave me a toothy smile. "I'm not only the hair club president, I'm also a client." He laughed and looked at me expectedly, clearly having said something humorous.

I shook my head. "I'm sorry, but I don't understand the reference."

The younger man groaned. "Oh man, that was my perfect delivery too! It's from decades old commercials advertising a chemical that supposedly stimulated hair growth...you know, never mind. What I'm trying to say is that I was almost completely bald on top. I'm one of the trial patients. Go ahead and feel it." Spencer removed the elastic tie and shook out the fine pale strands.

On his urging, I reached to touch Spencer's hair. I could see no discernable difference between the top and sides of his head. The strands felt incredibly soft as I let them cascade between my fingers. "It's amazing and extremely soft! And how well does it hold up to average stress of brushing and pulling."

"Better than real hair, we ran the tests."

"Simply ingenious." I thought about the potential applications for Synthetica down the road, after we got the positronic brain functional and self-sustaining. "Your synthetic hair is something that I think could benefit my primary project when it's further along. I'd like to learn more about it at a later date. Were you one of the developers?"

He gave me a proud look. "One of three."

"Wonderful! That means you can email me the details sometime. Or perhaps we could have a few lunchtime meetings to discuss it." He nodded and gave me another one of his trademark broad smiles. "But...let's get back on track." I waved toward AL-8 where it sat in its enclosed shell. "Can we extract those bots to be used in another sample, or is it easier to program more? And how difficult would it be to tweak the programming for the complex nanobots so they can both perform their primary function, and repair themselves?"

"We can extract those, but it may be easier simply to leave them in place." He frowned. "Giving the complex bots duel programming is one of Nano's top action items this fiscal year. Vogel wants us to have preliminary test subjects by next quarter but it's harder than you'd think. I can get complex bots that have the ability to self-repair and even replicate when necessary; however, performing other tasks than those would require massive blocks of programming. Are you familiar with our base bot program?"

"Yes, I've been reading about it for the past few weeks."

Spencer quickly typed a few commands on his laptop then sent the display to the large screen on the wall. "If you notice we follow an algorithmic pattern for our code and the program is always set in a specific order. Depending on a person's programming skill, which I assume yours is pretty high, it shouldn't be too hard to add the code for secondary function. It's just tedious and long. One of the biggest roadblocks to programming nanobot function is the fact that materials and substances react differently on a micro level."

I nodded at his description. "I did read that, which is why I had the material specifications for the internal positronic brain circuitry, the neural network surface, and the chemical synaptic gel ready when I began this with you. Luckily we used materials that were well-researched on both a macro and micro level so we already knew how they would react on the nanoscale."

I typed a few commands into the basic AL-8 controller to shut down the computation test. The bots were programmed in such a way that once all relevant areas were cleaned they would go dormant and do a status check every sixty seconds. So I wasn't worried about possibility of harm coming to the sample. I turned to Spencer when I was finished. "If you can give me the samples and a control module I'll start working on the dual program tomorrow."

"Will do, Alex. I'll send the nano container via mobile drone when I get back to my desk upstairs. Once you're finished with the program send them back to me for completion."

I was hoping to catch up with Fal that evening after work, perhaps have dinner, but I never saw her before it was time to leave OAS. Instead, I rode my bike home and continued my typical evening routine. In the weeks since my awakening, I'd developed an interest in music of all types, something I didn't have memory of before the accident. My lack of memory aside, it was obvious that I wasn't a music buff based on the fact that I had no speaker systems or quality audio players within my apartment. To rectify that I'd ordered a few components online and received a text message earlier in the day that they'd been delivered.

"Hey, Alex, got a few packages here for you."

I smiled to see Pete standing behind the security desk. "Aren't you supposed to be off duty now? Your wife is going to think you live here."

Pete laughed heartily. "Naw, she's fine. Besides, I'm leaving here in a few minutes. I just wanted to stick around and give you your packages and see how you're settling in now that you've come home."

His concern touched me in ways I couldn't quite define. Here was a man that I'd barely said two words to before my coma, taking the time to inquire about my health and happiness. I'd made a real effort over the past few weeks to connect with and get to know the people around me. I didn't want to be the cold Alexandra Turing from my memories. "I've been fine, right back in the swing of things at work. Thank you for asking."

He handed over the boxes and I tucked them under my left arm as I held my bicycle upright with the right. "You need a hand with those?"

"No thank you. You get home to your wife."

"Will do! Good night, Alex."

I smiled as he gathered his things to leave. "Good night, Pete."

UPSTAIRS I QUICKLY took care of Anna's needs before unboxing my new equipment. Anna spent the first eighteen minutes sitting in one of the small empty boxes. When I began placing the dual solar powered and rechargeable wireless speakers around the room, she left the confines of the box to investigate. The bookshelf next to the mantle had books on all but the top two shelves. I set the last speaker on the lower of the two, next to a small sculpture I couldn't remember buying, one of many in my condo. Looking at it caused a slight twinge of sadness but there were too many bigger memories I'd lost that I couldn't be upset over the small things such as forgotten décor.

I smiled as Anna jumped all the way up to the shelf and sat next to the cat statue. It made for a cute image so I quickly pulled out my camera and snapped a photo before she could move. Something about the image caught my attention right before it disappeared from the screen so I opened up my photo folder to bring it up again. I stared at the picture, then looked up to where Anna was staring at me. There was a bright point of light in the photo, emanating from the statue. When I walked over to the shelf, I couldn't see anything obviously out of place so I picked it up to observe it a little closer. It was one of a matching pair of Egyptian Cat Goddess Bastet statues. While I didn't remember buying them, I had done plenty of research on the Internet about the pictures and other décor scattered around my condo. I was hoping that if I could puzzle out why I would have purchased something, it would give me better insight on who I used to be.

Both statues were carved from black stone, and they had round decorative pieces of glass inset into each face to give the eyes a life-like appearance. I set the statue back on my shelf then brought up my camera again to look at it through my phone screen. Much to my dismay there was a light emanating from the statue's left eye. I knew what it was, having memory of helping to design and program some of the OAS security systems. Many modern security systems use IR, or infrared illumination. The imaging sensor on almost all cell phones can detect IR but I never expected to see such a thing in my home.

My first instinct was to turn it around so it wasn't facing the living room. Instead I left it exactly as it was before and scooped Anna from the shelf. I thought about calling Fal and even brought the phone up to hit her programmed number, but something stopped me. The word that came to mind was paranoia. I knew that they'd been watching me since returning to my old life. Rationally it made sense. Between my memory loss and the change in my personality, Fal, my father, and even Devos, wanted to make sure I was safe. And concerning the memory loss, there were things I still couldn't remember about myself. What if I had installed the camera years ago, during the time of memory I'd lost? The main questions I was left with were: who installed the camera, and were there more in my condo?

I placed Anna on the floor and walked over to the island where I'd left my laptop case. Minutes later I was logged in and inspecting the local wireless networks. Unfortunately, I only knew the name of my own. So if the camera were broadcasting remotely, I wouldn't have a clue which of the networks it utilized. After running a few data transfer tests I determined that it wasn't my own, at least not the one I was familiar with. I stood frozen with indecision in the middle of my kitchen.

Eventually I settled on a course of action. There was one person who hadn't been acting strange around me since waking. One person who didn't know who I was before the accident. Without contemplating the deeper reasons why, I made sure my cell phone's tracking system was deactivated before turning it off and stuffing it into my pocket. Then I grabbed my small bag containing my wallet and keys and left the condo. I walked out of my building and rather than use my phone to call for an Uber, I flagged down the first taxi that I saw. Emily had given me her address after the second coffee shop meeting and I gave that to the driver. Traffic was terrible despite rush hour winding down, and I didn't arrive at her brownstone until nearly six-thirty. Even so, I ended up waiting another fifteen minutes for her to get home from work.

Emily strolled up her walkway and emotions flickered across her face, surprise, happiness, and curiosity. "Alex! What are you doing here?"

I glanced around even though I knew the street near her place was empty, then I stepped close so only she could hear me. "I found something strange in my condo and I don't know who else I can talk to about it."

Chapter Twelve

Parity Error

EMILY GAVE ME a concerned look then waved toward her front door. "Let's go inside." She unlocked the door and ushered me into the tastefully decorated brownstone. Once in, she removed her shoes and led me through the living room into the kitchen. "You want something to drink?"

"No—wait. Yes please. I haven't rehydrated since my bike ride home from work and I should probably put some water in me."

It didn't take long to explain everything to Emily, even the parts about knowing that Fal and David Devos had been checking up on me. Fal mentioned more than a week ago that my father had personally asked her to keep him posted on how I was doing after waking from the coma. But even Emily agreed that a hidden camera seemed a bit...

"Alex, it's creepy. Is it possible that you would have installed it before your accident? Maybe years ago when you wouldn't remember it now?"

"Technically, with me missing decades of memories, anything like that *is* possible. However what memories I do have...I was never paranoid. It seems very out of character. I'm fairly straight forward, Emily. I'm not the least bit mysterious and I don't think I would have purchased the statues then gone through the trouble of altering one to house a hidden camera."

"Are you sure you purchased the statues?"

"No. I don't remember doing so but..." I shrugged because as she knew, there was a lot I didn't remember.

I sighed and picked at the last button on my shirt to avoid being idle while my brain was unable to come up with any constructive thoughts. Emily moved closer and stilled my hands. When I met her gaze she smiled and I felt comforted. "And why haven't you asked Fal? Why all the cloak and dagger business of turning off your phone and coming to my place unannounced?"

"Things are confusing right now and I trust you."

"Sweetie..." Her term of endearment took me by surprise,

but I wasn't opposed to it. Rather, it left me feeling warm and strangely pleased. "She's your best friend and it seems logical that she'd have answers for you. Worst case scenario is that she doesn't and you simply remove the camera."

I thought about her suggestion, it *was* logical. No matter the person I was before, or who I was becoming, logic had always been important to me. "You're right, I know you're right. It's just...I'm tired of not knowing things! I just wish there was one day where everything felt normal."

"Come here." Emily pulled me into her arms and hugged me. It was something we'd started doing whenever we met up in person, and whenever we parted ways after spending time together. I know that touching people and inviting them into my personal space wasn't something I'd enjoyed before my accident but after the first few hugs from Emily, I had no idea why. Instead of giving me a short embrace like usual, Emily held on tight as the seconds ticked by. It wasn't uncomfortable, instead her hug felt...safe.

I wrapped my arms around her and tried to match her pressure so I didn't end up squeezing too hard. One hundred and five seconds later she let me go and backed away to see me. "Better now?"

"Yes. I like holding you."

Emily rested a hand on her hip and glanced around her kitchen before settling her gaze on me. "Okay, how about this? Let's call in a to-go order for Thai Guys, you said you like them right?"

"Yes."

She smiled. "Good. We'll call in the order and pick it up on the way back to your place. Then we'll eat dinner, you can call Fal, and we'll work on removing the camera. Do you think there could be more?"

"I—"

"Don't know, right. How did you find the one in the statue?"

I retrieved my cell phone from my pocket and turned it on. "Can you go get your television remote?"

Emily gave me a skeptical look but complied. Less than a minute later she was back with the remote. I pointed it at her eyes and pushed one of the buttons. "Do you see anything?"

"No, am I supposed to? Isn't it, like, infrared or something?"

I nodded and held my phone out to her with the camera activated. "Watch it through the screen." When she was watching I aimed the remote at the camera and pressed the button.

Emily's mouth dropped open. "Hey, it works! And hidden cameras use infrared light?"

"Many surveillance systems have it to provide night vision. Clearly the one in my apartment does."

"Good point. All right, we'll what then, turn off the lights and look around with our cell phone cameras on?"

I shrugged. "Seems like a logical plan. I could easily access the schematics to build an RF wireless sniffer but it's late and I don't have the supplies readily available at home."

"Without those resources let's stick with the original plan. Are you ready to go?"

Her words made me realize that I'd completely interrupted her evening. I felt guilty for dragging her into my paranoia-fueled situation. "Emily, I'm sorry for coming over unannounced and involving you in my personal issues. It wasn't fair of me and you don't have to take me home. I can call an Uber."

Emily did something I wasn't expecting. She threw her arms into the air and rolled her eyes in exasperation. "Alex, what are we?"

I raised an eyebrow at her strange and obvious question. "Human?"

She swatted my upper arm. "No, I mean what are we doing? We've been going on dates and spending time together for weeks. What do you consider us?"

Her sudden change of subject and mention of our romantic inclinations gave me pause. I hadn't stopped to consider what we'd been doing beyond enjoying our moments together and hoping for more each time we parted. "I really like you and I want to keep going on dates, if that's what you're asking."

"Do you want to date other people?"

Hearing the words made me uncomfortable. "No, not in the slightest. Do...do you?"

Emily smiled. "Only you. And I want to keep seeing you for the foreseeable future, if that's something you'd like. Seriously, monogamously, dating. Exclusive."

I had no previous memory of dating, let alone of a serious relationship. But I knew I didn't want to get to know anyone else in the same way I'd been getting to know Emily. And I didn't want her to see other people either. "Monogamy. You want to be monogamous with me? To be my...girlfriend?"

"Yes, Alex. That's exactly what I'm saying."

My interest in her was completely understandable. Emily was intelligent, attractive, funny, and full of interesting insights about the world around her. But her interest in me made no sense. "Why? I have so little to offer, less than half of me. I have...baggage, Emily. Despite my interest, I'm not sure I'd be a good partner for you."

"Do you know what I don't care about?" I shook my head. "Your amnesia, or *baggage* as you call it. Do you know what I *do* care about?" I didn't answer but then she didn't appear to need a response from me. "I care about *you*, Alex. So what if you don't remember parts of who you were, or some of the memories you had. I'd like to learn about the Alex I know now and if I'm lucky, we can make new memories together. Part of me says you're too good to be true, but the greater part of me says that if I give you a chance, you'll be worth it."

Pleasure struck me like a bolt of electricity. It traveled through my chest and down to the tips of each finger. My mouth opened because I wanted to tell her everything I was feeling, but no words came out. Instead I froze there with unspoken words hanging in the silence.

"Is something wrong?" I shook my head. "Do you need something?"

The words broke free at last. "Can I kiss you?"

"Why?"

"Because you make me happy and I really want to kiss my girlfriend."

Emily threw her arms around me and pulled me into an exuberant and highly pleasurable kiss. She smelled a little like disinfectant and dog after a long day at the animal clinic. But over that was the familiar scent of her perfume. I ignored the smells that engulfed me with her kiss to focus on my other senses. Her curves were soft where her breasts and the front of her stomach pressed against me. Emily's tongue stroked inside my mouth as her lips crushed against mine. There was no flavor associated with our kiss, unlike previous ones after our coffee dates. Instead it was just...Emily. Eventually we pulled apart and I loosened my embrace. Emily looked at me then shook her head with sudden laughter.

"What?"

Emily snorted and got herself under control. "I think it's funny that the first time I visit this particular coffee shop on my lunch break, I meet a hot genius who not only *isn't* a psycho or weirdo, but also likes me as much as I like her. I'm telling you, you're too good to be true."

"I could say the same, you know. I don't know the type of people I was attracted to before my coma, but you seem to be everything I'd look for in a romantic interest. I could use your own negative words back at you." I grabbed her hand and gently caressed the back of it with my thumb. I saw the move in a romantic comedy a few weeks before. It seemed like a more inti-mate gesture than simply holding hands. "But I'm not going to do that. Truth is neither good nor bad, it simply is. As long as we're true to each other I think a relationship can work."

She smiled and squeezed my hand in return. "Again, we'll take things slow. Now, let's go get dinner because it was a long day for me and I'm starving."

"I'm sorry—" She covered my lips with her fingertips.

"Nope. No apologies. What do you want from Thai Guys?"

IT WAS NEARLY eight by the time we finished eating. We went around my condo and turned off all the lights then went room to room with our cell phones, searching for other sources of infrared light. They could be seen with the lights on, but the glare on the cell screen was more obvious in the dark. By the time we were done, we'd found a camera in every room. Rather than leave them in place we brought them all into the main room and placed them on the kitchen island, including the cat statue. Emily's expression was grim as she stared at the assortment of décor and regular household items that never get used. "Call your friend."

I glanced at the time on my cell phone. "It's a little late for personal calls, are you sure I can't wait and ask her about them in the morning?"

"Alex, there were cameras in your bathroom and bedroom. What if we'd had sex the other night? Who is watching on the other end?"

I hadn't thought of it like that. I sighed and picked up the cat statue. I really liked it and thought that it was too bad it was a piece of spyware and probably had to go. "You're right." I set down the heavy cat sculpture, then picked up my phone and called Fal.

At first she denied everything, at least until I told her that one of the cameras was in my office and pointed at my desk. I mentioned that since I frequently worked on confidential projects, whoever was spying was committing a crime and that I was obligated to call the police. Then she quickly admitted that the cameras were installed on orders of my father and doctor. They'd been concerned about my state of mind and health after the accident, worried that I'd have a seizure or suffer some other brain related condition while living alone.

I turned on the speakerphone when I first connected the call so Emily could hear, and after hearing the explanation for why the cameras were installed, Emily snapped. "Are you fucking kidding me?"

I was shocked by Emily's expletive, but not as much as Fal was. Her voice came over the small speaker sounding concerned. "Alex, are you with someone right now?"

"Only my girlfriend, Emily." I grinned as Fal sputtered on the other end of the line. "Say hello, Emily."

"Hi, Fal. First of all, the monitoring should have stopped as soon as you realized she was in perfect health. Second, we're going to remove these cameras from the condo tonight, then you're going to give Alex the location of all devices in case we missed any, as well as any video logs made since they were installed."

"I think you're a great person, Emily, but this is truly none of your affair. Alex and I will handle it in the morning—"

"No, we'll handle it *tonight*. And I'm making this Emily's affair. Do as she says and give me the locations and footage. I also want the broadcast signal and password. You can email everything to me in the next ten minutes."

"Alex—"

I grew angry with her tone of warning. "What you've all done is not only illegal, but also immoral. How *dare* you spy on my privacy! I thought you were my friend, Fal."

She sighed and it sounded overly loud over the speakerphone. "I am your friend, and you're right. I regret going along with it, but Devos said—" Fal's words abruptly cut off and I grew even angrier. I didn't like the feeling at all.

"David Devos knows about the cameras in my personal residence? Who else?"

"I don't think you should dwell on—"

"Who else, Fal?"

"Your father, myself, Director Devos, and your doctor. That's all, I swear."

I sighed and Emily reached over to rub my shoulder. "Ten

minutes, Fal. I want everything you've got on my monitoring in my inbox in ten minutes. And first thing tomorrow morning, you, me, and Devos will sit down and discuss the situation in regards to my excessive monitoring."

"I can't just—"

Emily's hand clenched on my shoulder and I knew she was as upset as I was. "Friendship or no, if I don't have everything I asked for in ten minutes I'm calling the police. I'm too upset to speak with you right now so I'm going to hang up. We'll talk more tomorrow." I disconnected the call and noted the time.

"Are you okay?"

My hands were clenched at my sides and I was having a hard time processing the room around me. My anger had taken over too many of my senses. "I, I, feel, feel—" I stopped as I noticed a tickling sensation making its way down my cheek.

Emily reached up to wipe her fingers across my cheek. "Alex...you're crying."

I felt for myself, not remembering having cried before. I rubbed the tear between my thumb and forefinger. "Slippery but...different."

"Sweetheart, talk to me."

"I don't like not being in control of my life. Everyone is so worried about me, and I understand their fear. However, I don't like it because they are supplanting my own fears and worries in an attempt to direct me back to who I was. But..." I struggled with my thoughts.

"But what?"

I met her eyes. "What if I'm not that person anymore? I don't want to be forced into a mold that no longer fits. It's not even that it doesn't fit, because I can see the appeal that secluding myself and focusing on my work would have held. But since waking, I can see the appeal of so many *other* things and I don't want to be workaholic Alexandra Turing again. I like the world better when I'm Alex."

Emily smiled and caressed my cheek. "Then be Alex. Be the person that allows you to explore the world around you. Live the life that provides the most opportunity for happiness."

I looked at her, taking in the somber expression that was tempered by the way her eyebrows lifted slightly to indicate hopefulness. Emily was intelligent and beautiful, but more than that she was compassionate and kind. "Alexandra Turing would have never pursued you. From what I understand, I'd all but given up on romantic pursuits and interpersonal relationships with anyone but my dad and Fal."

A smile as radiant as day broke across Emily's face. "Well then, I'm glad I met Alex."

"Me too."

The moment appeared to be over with my quiet words and I glanced at the pile of items on my kitchen island. "I really like the cat statue but I suppose it's one of a set so at least I still have the other."

Emily pulled away and walked over to the island. "Do you have a trash bag somewhere?"

"Under the kitchen sink."

"Why don't you check your email so you can verify that we found everything, and I'll start bagging this stuff up to take downstairs?"

"Okay." I gave the pile one last glance then went upstairs to my laptop. Fal had sent a list of all the monitoring devices, as well as the schematic for my condo showing the location of each. How they got the architectural drawing I'll never know. I opened all the documents and stared at them. I thought I should feel more than vague disappointment and anger. I'd read about people feeling nauseous or shaky when presented with unexpected and unfortunate discoveries. But I was neither. And my anger and disappointment were quickly changing to sadness. My father and Fal were the two most important people in my life. What did it say about them that they'd carry out and be complicit in such actions?

A sudden thought came to me on the trailing wave of curiosity about who installed the cameras. The thought solidified the longer I stared at the small camera lens at the top of my laptop screen. I remember a program I'd developed the previous year to deal with exactly such a security breach. I could see myself spending hours writing the code. Beneath the desk there was a small hollowed out portion where I'd hidden high security memory sticks in the past. The tech business was big business. Homes could be broken into and electronics stolen. The hollow was covered with tape that matched the color and grain of the wood and I carefully pealed it back to retrieve the item within. Once in hand, I plugged it into my laptop and waited for it to go to work. If there was something added into my system after I went into the coma, I'd find out when the program was finished.

Leaving the laptop running, I went back downstairs to see Emily, stopping on the way out the office door to grab one more item from a bookshelf opposite my desk. Once downstairs I threw the small listening device into the trash bag Emily held open. Then I retrieved my remote from the stand below the wall mounted flat screen television. I opened the battery cover and removed another listening device. Seeing the two items we missed on the first pass only served to make me angry again. It was then that I decided I couldn't stay in the condo that night and I wondered if there were any hotels nearby that would let me bring Anna. I could leave her alone but my rationale was that if I didn't feel safe in my own home, I couldn't very well leave a small defenseless creature in the same place.

Emily sat down on a stool and watched me patiently as I processed my next course of action. Little Anna had come over to rub against my legs so I scooped her up to cuddle. "Do you think you could take Anna for a few days?"

"I could..." She spoke cautiously. "But may I ask why?"

I scratched behind Anna's ears, eliciting an enthusiastic purr. "I don't want to stay here until I've spoken with both my father and Fal. And I'm pretty sure a hotel won't allow cats, and I don't want to leave Anna here by herself."

"Alex, why are you asking me to take in your cat, yet you're staying at a hotel? You can both stay at my place you know."

I dropped Anna on the stool next to me and held up my hands palm out. "Oh no, I can't impose on you like that. It's really not your responsibility —"

"Alex?"

"Yes?"

"You're not a responsibility, you're my girlfriend. Okay?"

Gratitude and affection warred for a place in the forefront of my chest and my response was quiet. "Thank you."

She waved off my hesitant words. "No thanks necessary. Go pack yourself a bag and I'll get the cat carrier from the pantry. You have large storage bags to put some cat food inside? I don't have any at my place — actually, I don't have any litter either. Why don't we swing by my clinic and I'll pick up a few things from the sales display? I'll write them out officially when I go in tomorrow."

"Oh, I can't ask you to —" My mouth snapped shut with the stern look she gave me. "I mean, I guess since we're dating seriously Anna and I will be over at your place often enough to warrant the investment."

Emily smiled. "There you go, much better answer!"

It was a good thing my reflexes were excellent or Anna would have tripped me three times going up the stairs in my distracted state.

MY RETICENCE RETURNED later in Emily's brownstone. "Wait, you don't have a spare bedroom?"

She gave me an apologetic look. "No, sorry. I mean, I *do,* but it serves as my office and there isn't a bed in there. I keep meaning to get a futon but clearly haven't gotten around to it yet. I figured I'd take the couch and let you have my room."

"Absolutely not. That wouldn't be...that's not a proper way to — to treat someone I care about."

Emily snorted with laughter. "Who told you that?"

I pulled up short and was forced to consider her question and come up with a suitable answer. "No one. I extrapolated that from the many movies and books I've read, all of which either state or imply that you should not make your significant other uncomfortable in their own home. Neither should you put a host out of their rightful place. I'll take the couch."

Emily put her hand on her hip and cocked it out slightly. I was drawn to the move and nearly missed focusing on her next words. "And how comfortable do you think you'll sleep on my mostly decorative couch, in a house you've never slept in before? I'm not high above street level like you are in your condo, hun, I'm right down with the traffic."

"Even more reason for you to sleep in your own bed. Besides, I've never had trouble falling asleep."

She raised a dark brow at me. "That you remember."

I huffed out, annoyed at how correct she was. "Fine," I conceded. "I've never had trouble that I remember."

Anna squirmed trying to get out of my grasp so I set her down to explore and in my distraction I failed to see Emily come closer. "You know, there is a perfectly reasonable answer to our dilemma."

"And that is?"

"I have a queen size bed, we can share."

I widened my eyes in surprise. "You don't have a problem sharing a bed with me if we're not yet sexual?"

"Think of it as a test of sleep compatibility."

"But we slept next to each other on my couch two nights ago."

She waved off my excuse. "I was so tired that night I probably would have slept through the L going through your living room. And I don't know about you, but if I can't comfortably sleep with someone then I scratch them from the list of potential romantic partners."

Her words made me pause and process an entire new line of thoughts. "Is it a big list?"

Emily's smile was open and honest. "There's only one person on it these days and I think she'll stay there for a while."

"Me?"

"Yes, Alex." She rolled her eyes while sounding exasperated. On further analysis perhaps the referenced person in her statement was obvious. "As long as you don't snore."

I wasn't offended at her implication but it was an emotion very near to it. "Of course I don't snore!"

"How do you know?"

I shrugged. "I'm not sure, I just—"

"Know, yes. You *just know* a lot of stuff. It's both annoying and fascinating as a fellow student of the sciences." Emily glanced at her cell phone. "It's late. Why don't we get ready for bed and discuss what's proper and improper in a relationship later. Do you mind if I shower first?" I shook my head. "Thanks. I feel like I still smell like the clinic and I'm already grumpy that I have to go back there in about ten hours only to start my day with a euthanasia."

"Do you put a lot of pets to sleep?"

She shrugged. "Enough. While logically I know it's the right decision given their age and condition, it's still hard, especially if they were a long-time client. Most veterinarians I know find it mentally exhausting dealing with people's grief in those types of appointments."

"I'm sorry." My sympathy seemed weak when dealing with what I imagined as a deep and emotional topic. The sad smile Emily gave me in response presented much like an iceberg in the middle of a calm sea. I sensed more below the surface that she wasn't showing me.

I made sure Anna was comfortable in the unfamiliar house while Emily took her shower. I placed cat toys in her bed and cuddled with her for a few minutes, at least until she grew rambunctious and scampered away. After that I wandered up to

Emily's room where I'd left my duffle bag. I found the pajamas I'd packed for propriety's sake, as well as my toiletry kit, then sat on the edge of the bed to wait for Emily to finish with her evening ablutions.

A short while later I turned my head toward her bathroom door as it opened in a cloud of steam. The fan sounded loud as she stepped through wearing nothing but a towel. "Oh, shit! Sorry, Alex, I didn't realize you'd be in here. I forgot my sleep shirt."

I knew I shouldn't stare but I found it nearly impossible to force my eyes away. I traced every droplet of water on her skin with my gaze and grew tense and uncomfortable with sexual arousal. "I, uh, I...you—" I stopped speaking as I realized the extent that I was overcome.

Emily started laughing. "Alex, are you...bashful?"

I turned my eyes away and considered the question. "Bashful...uncomfortably diffident and easily embarrassed. Shy or timid."

There were equal parts mischief and humor in Emily's voice as she came closer. "Are you feeling shy or timid right now? You can look you know, I'm covered well enough by the towel."

Given permission, I turned my gaze back to take in all the glorious skin presented above and below the large swath of cotton. I said the first thing that came to mind. "Your body is a treasure of unexplored tactile sensation."

Laughter and a hastily clapped hand over her own mouth followed my statement. Still mirthful, Emily shook her head and came closer. "Oh Alex, that is the most unintentionally erotic thing anyone has ever said to me."

I looked up to meet her eyes. "It wasn't meant to be."

Emily's eyes wrinkled up at the corners as she tried to hold in a laugh. "Nevertheless."

"Yes."

Suddenly she moved her hand from where it clasped the towel. It appeared to be tucked securely in front of her breasts but it was logical that she'd been holding it for a reason. It most likely wasn't as stable a wrap job as it initially appeared. "What would you do if I twisted and let the towel fall?"

If I could short circuit like one of my projects then I'd have surely been a smoldering motherboard at that point. I whispered into the quiet room without taking my eyes off the area of dark skin that disappeared below her deep red towel. One droplet followed the gravitational pull downward until it disappeared into her cleavage. "Oh format me."

She took a step closer and I chose the safest course of action. Her laughter followed me as I slid sideways off the bed and fled to the bathroom.

Ten minutes and thirty-seven seconds later I returned clean with my damp hair curling slightly at my forehead. Emily was already in bed reading a Kindle. Both nightstand lamps were switched on and the overhead light was off. She looked up from her novel with both brows raised as she looked upon me with confusion. "Do you really wear that to sleep in?"

I looked down at the matching long sleeved pajama shirt and pant set. "I thought I did."

"Alex." I looked up at her. "Did you find that in your drawer at home?"

"Yes. I discovered a variety of pajamas in one section of my dresser while I was packing tonight. I assumed I should pick a set for the duration of my stay away at your house." Emily rolled her eyes and I felt as though I'd done something wrong.

"Can I ask what you normally sleep in, if you've only just discovered the pajamas?"

Her careful curiosity had me hesitating to give an answer. Sleep protocol wasn't something I specifically remembered from before my coma. It wasn't as if the average fiction or science fiction novel covered what the main characters usually wore to bed, so I had no idea if my own actions fell outside the bell curve. "Since waking from my coma, I've developed a fascination with tactile sensation and I indulge myself as often as I'm able when no one else is around."

Emily froze and her mouth opened in a little 'O' shape. I watched as her pupils dilated and her breathing increased. "Are you telling me that you typically sleep naked?"

"Yes. Is that...odd?"

Her focus narrowed. "No, it's hot."

Confusion spread through me at her three words. "On the contrary, it's a lot cooler than—"

"Alex, I meant it's sexy. You can either get in bed now, or if you'd like I'll loan you a sleep shirt that would be imminently more comfortable than what you have on."

I considered the stiff material I was wearing and took in Emily's soft looking shirt. "I'd like a shirt if you have an extra. Thank you."

Once changed and in bed, I shut off the light and Emily followed suit. "Do you mind if I cuddle against you?"

I barely made out her features in the dark so it was pointless for me to nod. "I would like that."

"Are you comfortable on your back?"

"Yes."

Emily closed the space between us, nearly tangling our legs together while laying her head on my left shoulder. After a minute she spoke in the darkness. "Your heartbeat is very regular."

"It wouldn't be healthy if I were arrhythmic"

She sighed. "I like it. It's soothing. Good night, Alex."

I whispered good night sixteen seconds later because her breathing had already slowed to the deep cadence of sleep. I felt very connected to Emily in those first few minutes together in her bed. I too was soothed by the weight of her arm and by the press of her hand where her palm lay flat against my stomach. But the way the skin of her leg rested against my own tantalized me and kept me from pursuing my own dreams for another forty-three minutes. Eventually I grew used to the sensation and shut my eyes to slumber.

Chapter Thirteen

Recovery

MY CHANGED ROUTINE was unnerving the next morning but I managed to get to work at a respectable time after an interesting breakfast with Emily. Perhaps it was the early hour, but she was decidedly unsocial, at least until she drank nearly half a travel mug of coffee. She insisted Anna would be fine for the day at her house, and I had to insist that I'd be fine to make my way to the L station on my own. After a six second stare down, Emily finally relented with a smile and shake of her head. It was a short walk coupled with an interesting ride during morning commute. I arrived nearly an hour after my normal eight a.m. start time. Not that anyone would say anything, we were fairly self-regulating in my area.

I had set up the teleconference meeting the night before and I was glad to see that Fal, David Devos, and my father had accepted the meeting in my inbox. As soon as I finished checking my email I opened the program set for the security droids. When I looked up the status the previous night I found it strange that Artemis was still listed as offline. I wanted to create my own update that I could push to the bots wirelessly and be secured on my end, but it irritated me that my pet project wouldn't be part of the initial update until it came online and registered in the network.

The first reason for updating the Sentinels was to give me something to do until the meeting at ten since I didn't want to merely sit in anger thinking of the things that had been done to both me and my project while I slept six months away. The second reason for the personal security update was due to the fact that my sniffer program found three different monitoring routines on my laptop the night before. While I was programming an update I decided to alter a few other things as well. I had been playing with different personality variables in my spare time. I was hoping to replicate something similar to what I did with Artemis, but slightly less personalized. She was special, after all. They were very basic input/output response routines that I thought could make the Sentinels a little less intimidating. I didn't spend much time on that part because my main priority was updating my personal security access so that I had ultimate control and couldn't be locked out by accident or design. I didn't like being left in the dark about the happenings within my own company.

I monitored the Sentinel update progress as I walked through the halls on the way to the meeting. It completed less than twenty-seven seconds before walking through the door into the small conference room. I chose a neutral meeting place with full network and teleconference capability so we could see my father and he could see us. Fal and Director Devos were already inside whispering angrily at each other. They stopped and turned to me as soon as I walked in. My father's face stared largely back from the multi-screen display on the wall.

"Thank you all for accepting this meeting. I'm going to keep it fairly short because I have a multitude of projects going right now and don't have time for a lot of debate." I moved my gaze from Fal to Devos before settling on the face of my father straight ahead of me. "I've removed the cameras and listening devices from my condo and I have plans to check my office and lab after this meeting. I've also stripped all the monitoring programs from my laptop." Fal looked startled and I watched as David's eyes narrowed with anger. My father merely looked surprised but I continued anyway. "I understand that initially you all had concerns about my health after I came out of the coma, but things have gone well beyond that. You've breached my privacy and broken my trust."

"I assure you that we only had your best interests at heart."

I turned to stare at David. "There were cameras in my bathroom! That alone goes well beyond 'best interests' and strays into illegal territory. And it's not only my privacy we're talking about. You've been monitoring Emily as well and she's very unhappy about it."

"You weren't supposed to—" Fal cut off mid-sentence and she winced as if she suffered acute pain. When I turned my gaze to David Devos, the look on his face told me that he was responsible for the kick below the table.

His smooth voice answered instead. "You weren't predicted to be so whole and healthy right after waking, Alex. We merely wanted to make sure there would be no problems before issuing a removal order." He sighed and straightened the knot of his tie.

"Yes, I'll admit we should have told you, and we should have been faster to order the removal. But you've astounded us with the speed of your progress and development and I'm afraid that the monitoring program was forgotten and fell through the cracks."

"I too feel responsible, Alex. I knew they were going to monitor you but it completely slipped my memory as well. I've been really enjoying our phone calls and correspondence and I can't wait to see you upon my return. I hope this doesn't damage our relationship going forward, I'll do anything to make it up to you."

My father looked genuinely worried and I had memories that he'd never been very good at hiding his feelings. I looked around the small group. "I can forgive this provided I have all the files, data and hard copy in my office by the end of the day. I want whatever database that the images and videos were located in, scrubbed." I narrowed my gaze at David. "That means any black servers you have operating on a separate network from our primary one, or anything that's been stored offsite."

Devos sputtered. "We don't have anything like—"

"David...enough." My father wore a strange expression. "We'll make sure everything is erased and removed. I will personally contact the security company."

It was a straightforward solution. "That's acceptable. Thank you."

"I also want to inform you that I'll be flying in earlier than originally planned. My business in Germany is concluded so I'll be returning home this Thursday. I'd like to have dinner with you at the end of the week, if that's okay?"

I smiled at him, happy that I'd finally get to see him in person. "I think that is excellent news and I look forward to seeing you. Maybe we can have dinner on Saturday? I know of an excellent Cajun restaurant, or I can cook for you."

He waved off my suggestions. "I'd rather see you sooner, if that's all right. How about Friday, and you can come to the estate for dinner? My staff will be back onsite today so they'll have everything ready for my return and your visit. Say, seven?"

I contemplated possible plans with Emily for the weekend. We hadn't set another date but either way I knew that seeing my father would have to take precedence over any potential socializing with my girlfriend. Seven gave me plenty of time to get home from work and call for an Uber to take me to my father's house outside the city. After my deliberations were complete I met his questioning gaze with a smile. "I think that will work well. Now if that's all, I'll sign off on this end —"

"Wait, I'd like you to leave the conference up. I have a few things to discuss with David and Miss Nanjiani. I'll see you Friday, Alex."

"Bye, Dad." I gave a little wave then closed my laptop and slipped my mouse into my pocket. Four seconds later I was back in the hall, wondering what my father was going to say to Fal and Devos. I only heard David utter the words, "unprecedented success" and "back on track" before the door clicked shut behind me. I knew that all international calls were automatically recorded and saved in the meeting directory on the network. If I really wanted to know the details of their conversation I could simply access the records later. Something about that idea bothered me though. I hadn't liked it when they invaded my privacy and it felt wrong that I should do the same in return.

On my way back to my office I was approached by one of the Sentinels and I recognized it as Apollo by the serial number on its chest. There was no one else around so I decided it was the perfect time to run a test. I waited for the standard response to my presence as it got within six feet of my location.

"This unit registers the physical and NFC ident of Doctor Alexandra Turing. Please present badge for security scan."

Rather than present my badge, I waved at the android. "Heyla, Apollo. How are you today?" The security droid's main sensor panel flashed green three times then I waited.

The familiar robotic voice responded in the customary monotone. "Accessing new protocol update. Please hold." I waited another twenty seconds and smiled at the result. "Hello, Alex. I am doing well. There have been...zero...security incidents in the past twenty-four hours. Do you have a request? Or. Should I continue with my assigned task?"

The Sentinel wasn't set up for complex response analysis so I kept my reply simple. "Continue."

"Very well. Have a good day. Alex." While the voice was still comprised of the same robotic tones with strange pacing patterns, there was something warmer about having more human response phrases. Of course I was the only one that would hear those special responses. I made sure to set up the new program so that the security droid would only loop into the "friendly" sub-routine if mine was the sole badge registered by its sensors. It also allowed me to skip the security scan if I were by myself, which was extremely convenient. Conversation itself would be initiated if I greeted a droid with the key word. I recently read a book trilogy where Amazons in the tribe greeted each other using "heyla" and I liked the sound of the word. It was also irregular enough that I knew no one would stumble upon it by accident. Eventually I'd roll out the friendly update across the board, without the skipped security scan for others. But given the events around OAS lately, I decided it wasn't the right time for such changes to be made public.

NEAR THE END of the day I sat in my chair feeling a deep sense of accomplishment. After verifying both my office and primary lab were clear of bugs and cameras, I spent forty-seven minutes building a hand held sensor that would scan any room less than twenty-five hundred square feet in size for spyware, cameras, microphones, or other such items. It was crude, but extremely effective. I verified what I found against the list that David Devos had emailed to me, to confirm the accuracy of my device and the honesty of my director.

After dealing with my overprotection issue, I followed up with Spencer and got a vial of complex nanobots resting within a suspension fluid. He also reassigned one of the programming bases from the Nano department to mine, under my name. When I asked how to use it, Spencer informed me that it was "hella easy, Alex." All I had to do was plug the base into my laptop, insert the vial into the base, then send the program. The program would transfer wirelessly to the nanobots in the vial. As long as the program code followed the standard format there would be no issues carrying out their primary and secondary functions, while the tracker allowed me to monitor their progress from my computer. He even added a nanogenerator into the suspension to be sure the scrubbers had access to a power source.

I also emailed Director Hanssen a link to the small-scale power generation study that robotics performed last year. I included the schematics file for the kinetic generator because it was on our local drive and not uploaded to the network yet. Her response was positive and she told me she'd send it along to her researchers immediately. I was glad to make someone happy.

The notion of happiness prompted me to contemplate my connectivity to the people around me, my coworkers and friends.

I knew I was justified in my anger about the events leading up to the meeting that morning, but I also came away feeling a little bit like I'd let everyone down. Disappointment was an unpleasant emotion to feel, but reverse disappointment was not ideal either. My thoughts on how to achieve balance between freedom and empathy were interrupted by a knock.

"Enter."

Earlier in the day I had calculated the odds of Fal visiting so I wasn't surprised to see her push through the door. "Hi, Alex."

Not knowing what she needed from me, I was neither welcoming nor cold toward her. My response was neutral. "Fal. What brings you by?"

She sighed and sank into my guest chair. "Listen, I was a right wanker to you regarding this whole monitoring thing. I let everyone convince me that it was for your own good but I should have known better. You're my best friend and I don't want to lose that. Please say you can forgive and forget all this nonsense?"

I frowned because that wasn't how my brain worked. How easy it must be for other people to move on from hurt feelings and wrongs done to them, when all one had to do was forget it happened. I had no such luxury but I prided myself on being rational and understanding. At least since waking from the coma. "As I told you in the meeting, as long as all the security tracking has ended and the recordings either turned over or destroyed, I can forgive the indiscretion."

She stood and came over to my desk and after a moment's hesitation, placed her hand on top of mine. "That's not the same as having my friend back."

Her words prompted deeper thought about my own feelings. "You..." I wasn't sure how to say what I needed to say without hurting her in return.

"I what?"

I met her intent stare. "You hurt me, but worse you broke my trust. Fal...you, more than anyone else, know how hard this situation is for me right now. I can barely trust my own memories and I counted on you to be a stable part of my life. You've shaken me."

When she met my eyes hers were full of tears. "I know. This year has been...it's been hard, Alex. I'm sorry for everything and I'll do whatever you need to make it up to you. I can't lose you again."

I tilted my head. "Again?"

"I lost my best friend for six months. The day we were told you'd never wake up I went home and got myself rat-arsed." I raised my eyebrow at the unfamiliar term but was able to extrapolate the meaning based on what I remembered of Fal. "I didn't handle things well and I'll admit I had a lot of worry when you first woke. I wanted to be sure nothing would go wrong this time."

I sighed because I could see that she was being sincere. Fal's small signs of truthfulness were easy enough to read, having known her for a number of years. Her facial tics and verbal tone were all indicative of her mood. "Logically I'll admit that some of what you've done makes sense. But there's a line between right and wrong and you've all definitely crossed it."

"How do you know?" She wasn't being belligerent or difficult that I could tell. Fal simply appeared curious.

Her question had merit. How *did* I know? "I know because I remember every book or bit of text I've ever read. I remember every movie, and I study the people around me to make a record of social queues, expectations, and consequences to people's actions. But more than that, I determine right from wrong based on how I feel. You don't do things to other people that you wouldn't want done to yourself."

She smiled. "Ah, the golden rule."

I shrugged. "I wouldn't call it golden as such. Numerous religions have passages that state the same because it is the compassionate approach to human nature. And you don't have to subscribe to a particular religion to be compassionate, *or* to choose good over evil."

"Fascinating...so you believe in good and evil?"

I thought about the news reports I'd read the previous afternoon. "One boy showing compassion to an autistic fellow student, a stranger to him, is good. Feeding the homeless with no regard for accolades or rewards, that's good. Murdering children, scamming elderly people out of their retirement, selling people into slavery or prostitution, and mass shootings...those are all evil. Evil isn't a supernatural notion. Evil is an action that will stain the perpetrator for the rest of their life. Evil takes, destroys, and breaks the spirit of good people."

"Hmm, I like your insight on the subject. We've never discussed such things before. You've always had your head stuck thoroughly into science and we never really talked about many other things, at least not on a deeper level."

I stood from my desk and gave her an honest smile, happy for the first time that day. "I think we should continue having deeper discussions, after all, relationships that stagnate eventually wither. I enjoy our friendship, it means the world to me."

"Same here, love." Fal looked down at the phone that had been clasped in her left hand. "Say, are you up for dinner tonight? We can try the new taqueria down in the loop. I heard it's excellent."

While Mexican food did sound good, I still had to go back to Emily's house, if only to take Anna and my duffel bag back home. My father said that my condo would be completely clear by four so it was safe, and Emily told me she'd be home by five-thirty. "How about tomorrow? I stayed with Emily last night and Anna is still at her house."

"Sure, that sounds good." Fal took a deep breath and I knew she had something to say on the subject of Emily. "So...things seem to be going well between the two of you. Girlfriends, eh?"

The smile came unbidden, as it often did when I thought of Emily. "Yes. We've had many discussions about what we like and need from a relationship. Monday we discussed expectations that we both have for each other and we both agreed to a monogamous relationship. She's my girlfriend now."

"Have you slept together yet?"

"We—" I stopped because I couldn't remember if it was proper to discuss such things outside my relationship. Then I recalled the many movies where the main characters discuss their romance with a best friend. "We haven't but based on the mutual level of sexual attraction, I suspect it won't be much longer. Emily said she wants to wait for me to be ready so that is what we're doing."

Fal smiled. "What about you, do you think you're ready?"

I sighed. "We slept in the same bed last night and it was very comforting. But before bed, when she got out of the shower and came into the room wearing nothing but her bath towel, I, uh...felt very ready."

My best friend burst out laughing. "I bet you did!"

I glanced at my cell phone where it rested on the charger on my desk. Noticing that it was after the time I'd plan to leave I circled back around my desk to shut the laptop down. "I'm sorry, but I told Emily I'd be there shortly after she got home and I'm taking the train today since my normal travel routine was disrupted." I looked up to meet her eyes. "What I'm trying to say is that I have to go. But if you have some time tomorrow I'd like to sit down and show you some of the cross-collaboration projects I've been working on."

Fal waited for me to pack up the computer and shoulder the messenger bag before meeting me at the side of my desk. She pulled me into a tight hug and I relished the contact. After she followed me out of the door, she then waited for me to engage the lock. "That sounds like a plan. I'll see you tomorrow, Alex."

I nodded and hustled down the hallway toward the elevator. I'd memorized the train schedule earlier and I knew that I could make it to Emily's house shortly after her arrival if I hurried to the platform. I gave a quick wave behind me. "Bye, Fal!"

MY FATHER FLEW in late Thursday evening so I didn't get a chance to speak with him before our dinner the next day. He sent a text message confirming the time to be at his home. He also asked if I wanted him to send a car to pick me up but I politely declined. Even though I wasn't driving myself around, I still preferred the freedom of organizing my own transportation. When I researched my options I was initially dismayed to discover that it would cost more than a hundred dollars for a round trip ride to my father's house in Naperville. Then I rationalized it since it was still cheaper and less hassle than driving a car around, and it financially supported whoever drove me.

When the driver pulled up in front of the large house he gave a loud whistle. "That's some digs there. You sure this is the place?"

Perhaps he was curious because I was wearing fairly casual jeans and a button down shirt while being dropped off in front of a mansion. "I'm positive. Thank you for the ride."

"Sure thing, no problem."

Minutes later I stood in front of my father's front door. I raised my hand to knock, but paused. Taking stock of my feelings I realized that I was nervous to see him after everything that had happened. Much like my first visit to OAS after waking from the coma, I pushed past my reticence and rang the doorbell a little before seven. It swung open surprisingly fast and I was left staring into the face of my father. Neither of us spoke for a number of seconds but tears gathered in his eyes as he looked me up and down.

"Alexandra. It's...it's really you."

I smiled. "It is, although I prefer Alex now, remember?"

Something about my response shook him but he recovered fast enough. "Of course, my apologies...*Alex*." He moved out of the way. "Please, come inside."

Although I couldn't remember the last time I had visited the estate, I did have memories of the halls and rooms within. Everything looked exactly the same as from my memories, with the exception of my father's stooped appearance. I could imagine that after losing one's wife fairly young, it would have been devastating to also lose a daughter. And if they didn't think I'd ever wake, that was exactly what my father had gone through. In a fit of impetuous motion, I turned and gave my father a long hug after he shut the door. My words were muffled as I spoke pressed against his broad shoulder. "I've missed you."

He hesitated for nearly three seconds before bringing his arms up and enfolding me in a tight embrace. I couldn't remember previous hugs from him and knew that we were making a new memory to replace those that were lost. His voice was rough in my left ear, sounding as though he were fighting back emotion. "Oh my girl, my precious little girl...I've missed you too."

We stood in the foyer embracing until a woman walked around the corner of what I remember as a sitting room. "Oh, I didn't mean to interrupt." We pulled apart and she gave me a smile and nod. "Welcome back, Miss Alexandra. I was coming to inform you that dinner is ready."

I searched my memory to match her face with a stored name. "Thank you, Mariana." My father looped his arm through mine, much the way Emily enjoyed. "How have you been?" I instantly recalled another bit of seemingly random data about my father's staff, how Mariana's first granddaughter had been born the year before. "*Como esta su nieta?*"

She turned her head to look over her shoulder at me as she led us through to the dining room. Her smile was proud and loving. "*Ella está bien y está creciendo muy rápido!*"

"*Buenísimo!*"

My father left me on one side of the table, while he went to the other. The food was already in place beneath insulated covers. There was a pitcher of water on the table, as well as a bottle of red wine. It had been my preference for many years, though I didn't care for it as much now. He addressed his head of house before she could take her leave. "*Gracias por todo*, Mariana. *Se ve muy bien.*"

At first dinner was quiet, bordering on awkward as we served ourselves at the smaller four-person table. The food was excellent and I actually enjoyed the chilled fruity red wine Mariana had picked to go with the paella. I remember her making the dish many times over the years that she'd been employed by my father. Though I couldn't remember the flavor of it until I put a bit into my mouth. The spices and seafood filled me with joy as I took in another new culinary experience.

"You seem to really enjoy Mariana's rice. I don't think I've ever seen someone enjoy it so much including me, and it's my favorite dish of hers."

He caught me mid-chew and I hastily swallowed my bite. "As you know, the accident left me with no memory of taste or touch and I'm re-experiencing many things for the first time. I've discovered a new love of food that I don't remember having before."

"No, you never were as enamored with the experience of eating as you seem to be now."

I placed my fork carefully so the tines rested on the edge of my plate and took a sip of the wine to think about the things I wanted to tell him. "It is very difficult to put into words all the things I've come to realize since waking in the OAS med room. Emily mentioned that when people have a near death experience they come out the other side feeling like they have a new lease on life. I'm not sure if that best describes how I feel, but I do know that there is a world of experiences out there for me to explore. I'm still passionate about the Synthetica project, but I don't want to lock myself in a lab all day. I want to go on adventures. I want to laugh, try new foods, and find love."

He stared at me for a short time. "There is nothing wrong with any of that, Alex. I've wanted much the same for you over the years. But I have to say, you never seemed unhappy to me, just...resolute. Focused."

I hated my lack of memory but I was getting better at knowing myself now. "But did I ever seem really happy? Truly, in all parts of my life and not only at the lab?"

My father glanced away and swallowed thickly. I watched his wrinkled throat move with the action and waited for him to answer. When his gaze returned to me I was once again struck by our similarities of build and coloring, though I wasn't nearly as tall. My sixty-nine and a half inches seemed small compared to his seventy-four. "My Alexandra of old never displayed the passion for life that you have shown me over these past few weeks. If I were going to use that as a benchmark for happiness, then I'd say you appear much happier now."

"I think I am."

My dad smiled at me and took a sip of his wine. "Perhaps it has something to do with this new lady love of yours. Tell me about her, something new that we haven't already talked about."

"Well, she—"

"Oh, and when do I get to meet her?"

I paused. "I really don't know. We've only just become girl-friends this week. I'm not sure what the proper protocol is for meeting a significant other's parents."

"Well then, maybe I can stop by your condo sometime soon to see your little cat."

Pleasure rushed through me that he was so interested in the life I was steadily and carefully building for myself in the aftermath of such traumatic loss. "I would love that." We both took a few seconds to savor the moment then I purposely changed topics. "I want to tell you about my vision for OAS."

He pointed at me and grinned. "Is this some of what put a bug in David's britches over the past week?"

I shrugged. "I'll admit that I've been pushing forward on this because I truly believe that it will be our future and will catapult us past the competition by a significant margin. The key to our success is interdivisional collaboration."

My dad leaned forward eagerly. "Tell me more."

And I did. I outlined my ideas for the future, even highlighting some of the possible projects we could begin immediately. Forty-five minutes later I watched in awe as a look of pride washed over my father's face. Like kissing Emily the first time, or bringing Anna home, it was a memory I'd cherish forever.

Chapter Fourteen

Authentication

"AND THEN SHE says, not as pretty as you."

"No! Truly?" Mariana looked my way to confirm the validity of Emily's story. I nodded. "*Dios mio!* You never change, do you, Alex?"

"Some would say I've changed too much." Despite months having gone by since waking at OAS, I was ever-conscious of how different I was in my new life from the one I held in my memories. But the initial thought that I was disappointing people with my change had been pushed away by my father's love and Emily's continued dedication. We'd been dating for a month and it was her first time meeting my dad. She was nervous at first but based on their laughter, I'd say her anxieties were unwarranted.

We were sitting in the cozy library with my father to my immediate right. He leaned toward me and clapped my shoulder. "I must say that I adore your girlfriend, Alex. Emily is very sweet and much too good for you."

Emily reached out to grasp my left hand. "On the contrary, sir, we're good for each other."

"None of that now. You can call me Matheson, Matt, Matty, or Pop if you wish." Emily blushed but she smiled all the same.

I had met her parents the previous weekend when we went to their house for dinner. Emily was in Lakeview on Fletcher Street, and they were in Lakeview East, closer to the water. Her mom made a vegan pot roast meal with mushroom gravy and cauliflower mashed potatoes. It was different but delicious. They were also very nice and had the best stories about Emily when she was growing up. Her mother taught ancient Greek history, specializing on the reign of Queen Orianna, and I looked forward to hearing more of her stories in the future.

When I told my dad about meeting Mr. and Mrs. St. John, he insisted that Emily and I come over the following weekend so he could meet her. Dinner was fish tacos, another one of Mariana's famous dishes. Mariana didn't have to rush off after prepping the meal this particular night so she stayed to eat dinner with us and talk afterward. Our family had always been informal, despite appearances to the contrary. Mariana wasn't simply an employee of my father's, she was a long-time family friend. My thoughts were interrupted by my dad.

"Alex, why don't you give Emily a tour of the house?"

I wanted to remind him that I had lost a lot of personal memories, but when I thought about the house I inexplicably knew the entire layout. It was as if I'd seen a blueprint of the home in the past and retained that memory. Given my penchant for information and hyperthymesia, I probably had. "Sure." I stood and held out my hand to my girlfriend. "Let's start upstairs. There are five upgraded bedrooms and eight full baths."

Emily pulled me to a stop right before heading up the stairs. "Did you say *eight*?"

"Yes. There are also a total of four fireplaces." The tour ended a half hour later with us standing on the patio looking over the pool. Lights were on below the water level, creating a wavering blue glow that lent a sense of mood to the sounds of the city and cacophony of insects around us.

"It's pretty out here." She shook her head and laughed. "You know, you seem so down to earth most of the time that I have a hard time remembering that your family owns one of the most successful scientific industry companies of this century. You're rich, yet you ride a bicycle to work and live in a moderately priced condo in a moderately priced district."

The air was a little chilly so Emily moved in front of me and I wrapped my arms around her from behind. "I don't really think of money much. It seems like a privileged way of life when I say it like that. But I do my own finances, I have since starting work at OAS. I earn my way, I know how much I'm worth and everything I own is paid for by my salary."

She tilted her head to the side so she could look up at me. "You don't think of the future at all, and what it would mean to be the sole owner of OAS?"

I frowned. "I try not to. Because sole ownership would mean that my father is dead and I'm not ready to be an orphan yet." My statement wasn't emotional, it was matter-of-fact.

"I'm sorry." Her apology was heartfelt and immediate. "I shouldn't have brought it up."

I embraced her a little tighter. "It's all right. Fortunately, or unfortunately, real memories of my mother were lost with the accident. I was left with images and a few scenes in my head. They're more like memories of watching home movies, with no real emotion."

Emily twisted within my arms to make eye contact. "What do you mean?"

"I mean, I know I loved her. That is a feeling that is immutable. I also know I miss her. But beyond that, I don't know anything else. There is no other emotion attached, be it anger, sadness, or other. I lost it with so much else."

Emily turned fully and wrapped her arms around my waist. "I know I've said it before, just as I also know it doesn't mean much in the grand scheme of all you've lost, but I'm glad I get to make new memories with you. I also like your dad a lot. He's funny."

"He is quite humorous."

She gave my side a little squeeze hoping to tickle me by surprise, something that she'd always failed to do previously. Her attempt failed yet again as I didn't seem to possess a tickle response. "I mean, you're funny too…it's just a different kind of funny."

There was something about the expression on her face, or the way her beautiful eyes were hidden in the darkness of the pool deck, but the urge to kiss her came over me. Rather than ask, I lowered my head and caressed her lips with mine. She had lectured me previously for always asking if I could kiss her. I was trying to be polite but Emily informed me that after a certain point in a relationship, such niceties weren't necessary.

We kissed for two minutes and fifty-seven seconds before Emily finally pulled away. "Those lips are dangerous!"

I gave her another quick kiss. "I assure you, they are completely safe for consumption."

Emily raised a dark eyebrow and her smile grew mischievous. "Oh really?"

I stepped back a pace and pointed my index finger at her. "That was flirtation! See, I told you I would recognize it."

Her laughter echoed off the stone tiles and stucco walls of the hacienda-style home. "So you did. Are you about ready to go?"

Her suggestion for an early night concerned me. "I thought you said you didn't have to work tomorrow?"

Emily smiled. "I don't. I thought we could go back to your place…or my place. It really doesn't matter."

"Do you have a specific reason in mind? I know you mentioned that you wanted to watch that new show on the streaming service—"

Her kiss cut off anything else I had in mind to say. When her tongue caressed my lips it felt completely natural to open to her. Her mouth tasted like the sweet port we drank after dinner. Neither of us had much, but it *was* a dessert drink. I liked the way her hands clutched at my sides rhythmically as our breath puffed in and out in the night air and the smell of her mixed with the floral scent emanating from the planters around us. Eventually we had to pull apart. I became uncomfortably aware of my own arousal and surmised she must have felt the same way. "We should stop. I am most uncomfortable now."

Emily laughed and pulled away from me, stretching our arms out between us, much the way she'd done in the little park by the coffee shop on one of our earliest meetings. "Good to see you're not completely unaffected. Sometimes I wonder if you're a machine the way you appear all calm and cool after our make out sessions."

I returned her laugh and it was startlingly loud. "I wish I had that much control. On the contrary, your touch and scent leave me completely undone." I paused. "Are you frustrated that we have not taken our relationship to the next level yet?"

I watched as she gave my question serious consideration. "For starters, we *have* taken our relationship to the next level. Relationships aren't built on sex alone. Personally, I've grown quite close to you over the past month." She paused. "As for the sex, I'm not disappointed. That's a bad word for how I feel. Logically, I understand the need to wait. I want you to be ready both physically and emotionally. However," She held up a finger. "That doesn't mean that all this winding up hasn't tested my resolve at least once or twice."

There was something in the way Emily looked at me, a particular expression as she watched me, that said the deep affection I felt for her was not one-sided. I looked down to gather my thoughts then met her eyes again. "Perhaps we can make one more memory tonight."

Emily froze and I feared I'd been too straightforward with my suggestion. "Are you saying...I mean, are you sure?" I nodded. "Damn. Now I really want to go."

I motioned toward the door into the house. "We can come back and visit with my father soon, he won't mind if we cut this night short."

"That is the smartest thing I've ever heard you say!"

I rolled my eyes and contemplated whether or not I'd picked up too many bad mannerisms from Fal. "Now who's the comedian?"

My father was a little disappointed but he must have picked up on more than what was said because he hugged us both and chuckled. "Ah, young love."

The words seemed strange given the fact that we were two women both near or over forty years of age. But Emily didn't seem to mind so I refrained from saying anything to contradict the statement.

Emily drove, of course, since I had no interest in the sport. We did view my two cars in the garage but neither evoked any visceral emotion in me and I felt no call to get behind the wheel. The drive to my father's home and back to her townhouse was the longest trip we'd made together since meeting, and I got a good sense for Emily's musical tastes, which was to say, I had *no* sense of her musical tastes. She seemed to like a bit of everything.

It was full night, though a city like Chicago was never completely dark. Lights from passing cars and street lamps illuminated Emily's face in random flashes while I thought about my feelings for her. I'd spent many hours contemplating the logic of emotion and human connection. What I learned was that emotion and human connection weren't always logical. I had been enamored with Emily from the very moment I saw her. And the more I learned about who she was as an individual, the more I enjoyed her company. There was a 'rightness' to the world when I was with Emily and for that short period of time, each moment we were together, I felt normal.

"You're very quiet over there."

I glanced to my left. "I'm contemplating relationships and human connection in regards to emotional attachment and normalcy."

Emily cut a glance my way, away from oncoming traffic, and her mouth dropped open. "Uh...I don't really know what to say to that. Those sound like especially deep thoughts."

"They're really not. Sometimes when I'm in the heart of programming a specific human response into a positronic brain, my thoughts go much deeper —"

"Alex?"

"Yes, Emily?"

"I meant emotionally deep. Are you having second thoughts

about your decision?"

Though she hadn't turned back toward me, I could see that Emily was frowning. I didn't like it when she frowned because that implied displeasure or unhappiness. Those were not ideal states for someone I'd come to care about. I paused for half a second as I realized the depth of my own feelings. I cared about Emily very much, just as I cared about little Anna. The emotion was similar, but not quite the same. My thoughts were interrupted again.

"Alex?"

It was then that I realized Emily was waiting for an answer to the previous question and I regretted making her wait. "No, not at all. I was merely contemplating how much I'd come to care about you in such a short amount of time. Then I realized that I care about Anna nearly as much and I'd known her equally as long. So logically the emotional correlation made sense. But then I considered that you were human and not an animal, thus deserving more of my affection. After that I considered the fact that Anna was a small defenseless animal who was incredibly cute and more prone to garnering affection, and then I grew confused about which should receive more — "

Laughter was loud in the car as it rolled to a stop. "Oh my God, Alex, pause for a minute. The question wasn't meant to prompt a long introspection. I only wanted to know what your gut feelings were, if you had changed your mind since standing near the pool."

"Oh." I felt foolish that my mind had gone off on such a tangent when she was only looking for a simple answer, much like a data-driven yes no chart. "I guess your simple answer is no."

"Not even a little?"

"No."

Emily shut off the car and opened her door, then gave me a beaming smile in the interior lights of the vehicle. "Good, let's go inside."

I exited at the same time and twenty-six seconds later we stood on the stoop of the brownstone while she pulled the keys from her bag to unlock the door. "Wouldn't it be easier to have a digital lock?"

She pushed the door open and held it for me to enter. "Just because you live in a hi-tech spy palace doesn't mean the rest of the world does."

I looked around as she turned on a lamp near the couch. "You could have it installed."

She rolled her eyes and I briefly thought maybe she had picked up Fal's mannerisms from me. "Alex, that would require hiring an electrician to wire my exits and installing an entirely different security system than the one I have now when what I have works perfectly fine. It's only a simple house key, not like I'm carrying around a ring of dungeon-type skeleton keys."

I shook my head at her reference. "Sometimes your correlations baffle me."

"Sometimes *you* baffle me."

I tilted my head, concerned about her statement as I followed her through the house into the kitchen. "Is that a bad thing?"

"On the contrary, it's a good thing. Your observations challenge, entertain, and educate me. I always feel like I'm a better human being after spending time with you."

I grabbed her hand as she reached for the refrigerator door and pulled her into my arms. "I think you're an amazing human being just the way you are."

"Charmer." She'd said the word to me many times before and it was always followed by a light blush across her cheeks so I knew that whatever I'd conveyed was pleasing to her.

"Can I have a kiss?"

She huffed, "Alex! You—"

I kissed her to cut off whatever she was going to say. Perhaps standing in the middle of the kitchen wasn't the romantic setting that I'd read about or watched in movies, but it was very intense to me. I stopped counting. I stopped thinking about all the things that had happened before and took in the feel of Emily within my arms. I savored the taste of her lips, a mix of vanilla lip gloss and another flavor that was indefinably Emily. Her breasts pressed against my own and I reveled in the way her nails scratched at the back of my scalp. It was...erotic. I grew warm, and moisture gathered as it often did in my dreams.

Emily pulled away with a gasp. "Damn, but you make me thirsty!" I kept holding her while she caught her breath with her forehead pressed against my shoulder. "And you! You're not even breathing hard! I feel so jealous of your bike riding regimen."

Her observation was accurate since I never got winded with any of my activities. "If you're thirsty, you should probably get a drink. Is that why you were going to open your refrigerator when I stopped you?"

Emily's laugh was quiet and puffed warm, moist breath into the fabric of my shirt. She raised her head and I was caught by the look in her smiling eyes, the gold color seemingly bright in overhead lights of her kitchen. She opened her mouth to speak, paused, and then shut it again. I waited patiently. "Yes. That's *exactly* why I was heading to the fridge, because I was thirsty. For *water*." The mirthful upturn to the corners of her mouth indicated there was a joke somewhere within her statement but she didn't give me time to contemplate the words. She quickly opened the fridge and grabbed two bottles of water before handing one to me and leading us toward her stairs.

"I wonder how little Anna is fairing. Do you think she's okay by herself?"

We were halfway up the steps when the words slipped out. Emily stopped abruptly, and if it weren't for my fast reflexes I would have run into the back of her. She looked over her shoulder at me. "Alex, she's a cat. She's fine for at least a day as long as you have a supply of food and water down. She'd actually be fine for a few days. Your condo is safe as it can be. Worst case scenario is that she shreds a few magazines out of pique from being left alone."

"Okay." We entered the bedroom a minute later and Emily walked over to the head of her bed where she had her sleep shirt tucked under the pillow. I had one she loaned me beneath the pillow of what I had come to consider my side on the nights I slept over.

"I need a shower before bed, do you mind if I go first?"

"It's your shower, you don't have to ask permission to use it first. As the owner of the house it's within your —"

"Alex."

"Yes?"

"Again, it was a yes or no question."

She was smiling and I knew that part of her was still teasing. "My apologies. Of course you can go first. I'll read until you come out." I had a smaller messenger bag that was slung across my chest and had come up stairs with me. Emily left me to myself and I pulled out one of the books I'd checked out from the library the day before. It was a new release, the beginning of a series. The cover was especially beautiful and when I looked up the reviews online, one person said the book was a mashup of speculative fiction genres. I figured if I liked it I could go on and enjoy other books in the series, that way the story took longer to end.

Emily had a comfortable chair in her bedroom near the window, so I chose that spot to start the story. I was intrigued immediately and it felt as if no time at all had passed before Emily came out of the bathroom in a cloud of steam. Even though the book was immersive, in all actuality I knew only sixteen minutes and twelve seconds had elapsed.

"Your turn."

When I looked up from my book my gaze froze on the beautiful woman standing in the middle of the room. Her sleep shirt was a pale cream color, contrasting with the dark expanse of skin where arms and thighs emerged from the material. A few stray water droplets clung to her where she must have missed them with the towel. I detected the light scent of warm vanilla mixed with coconut and assumed Emily had used her body wash. I relished the smell and it always made me wish for dessert.

"You're thinking too hard again. What's going through your head right now?" Emily's voice was lowered, quiet and slow. If sound had a physical description, I'd call it thick. I scrolled through my lexicon until I came up with an appropriate word. Sultry.

"Watching you walk out of the bathroom made me long for something sweet and nectarous. It's a notion very much like hunger but without the feeling of emptiness in my stomach."

A peal of laughter burst from between Emily's lips. "I'm pretty sure you just told me you want to eat me in the nerdiest, most accidental way ever. You should go shower now." She smirked. "You can eat me later if you're so inclined."

I was shocked at her words. "Eat you? Why would I want to — oh, format me!" The sexual meaning of my words hit me mid-sentence. "I didn't think about it like that."

"Obviously." Emily smiled kindly. "You should go shower now, Alex."

I placed my bookmark between the pages and set the book onto the nightstand. Then I grabbed my borrowed sleep shirt from beneath my pillow and made my way across the bedroom. I paused to look back at her when I was nearly to the door. "I wasn't so nervous until I realized my inadvertent innuendo. I don't like this feeling."

Emily slipped beneath the covers and gave me a tender smile. "There is nothing to be nervous about. We don't have to do anything at all except cuddle. You can decide how you feel when you come back."

Rather than answer, I gave a short nod then went into the bathroom to clean myself. It didn't take long. My legs and underarms were already smooth. When I brought it up to Fal the first week after waking she said I had it lasered off years ago because routine maintenance was a waste of time. Whatever reason I'd had it done, I certainly appreciated the decision now.

I re-emerged less than ten minutes later and found Emily tapping on the screen of her cell phone. She looked up and smiled at me where I stood in my own borrowed sleep shirt with my clothing bundled beneath my arm. I smiled back and moved across the room to leave it in the chair with my messenger bag before sliding beneath the covers myself. She naturally moved closer and I enjoyed the feeling of her warm skin pressing against my own along the length of our legs.

I said the first thing that came to mind. "I like the way you feel."

Emily placed her phone on the nightstand and plugged it into the charger, then turned onto her side and faced me. I mirrored her motion. "You like the way I touch you?"

I nodded, my hair making a *swooshing* sound against the pillows.

"How about like this?" She moved her left hand up to lightly caress my cheeks, eyebrows, then down to the side of my neck.

I shivered. I wouldn't consider it ticklish based on the definition of the word, but it was certainly stimulating. "I like that."

Emily moved her hand down my neck to the top of the sleep shirt, then around the back to scratch her nails lightly in my hair. I made an unexpected noise, which was quickly cut off by her kiss. The feel of her pressed against me with so little clothing combined with the caress of her tongue was stimulating, nearly overly so. I pulled her closer and her legs moved until one slid between mine. We continued kissing and much like in the kitchen, I lost count of the seconds and minutes. Emily shifted again and I froze as sharp pleasure assailed me, emanating from my clitoris.

Emily stopped and pulled her head back. "Are you okay?"

"I...I..." Her leg moved again and I shook with arousal.

"Shit, Alex. I didn't mean to do that." She tried to pull away but I grabbed her hip with my right hand and held her to me. The light was still on next to the bed and when my eyes opened they were met with tender concern.

"I need..." My failure to convey what I wanted in the wake of such a pleasurable assault frustrated me.

"Use your words, Alex. What do you want?"

In a move that was faster than even I expected, I rolled on top of her, settling one leg naturally between her thighs while her own continued pressing against me. Emily hissed at the pressure of my leg. "I want you."

Chapter Fifteen

Connect Time

"FUCK." EMILY PULLED me down into another kiss even as she lifted her hips to press us harder together.

The motion was rhythmic and all I could focus on was the feel of Emily's mouth, the way her nails scraped down my back, and the press of my fabric-covered vulva against her firm thigh. I was left feeling more outside of myself than I could ever remember. I adjusted my own leg to stimulate her more and tried not to focus so much on my pleasure alone. It was difficult but I managed to open my eyes again to see her while I spoke. "Emily..." I continued to move against her as Emily's grip tightened. She didn't respond so I tried again, my tone urgent. "*Emily.*"

At last her eyes opened and I took special notice of the way her pupils were dilated with arousal. I spoke my greatest concern. "Based on previous responses during masturbation, I'm afraid my orgasm is imminent. Should I stop?"

She pulled my head down again and moaned in my ear. "Harder. And don't you dare stop!"

I complied with her wishes, thrusting and rubbing both harder and faster until I began making my own involuntary sounds to match hers. Then Emily seized below me and gave a loud shout, trembling as a flush broke across both cheeks. Her eyes remained tightly shut and, sensing my own imminent release, I kept moving. Emily was still in the middle of her orgasm when my own hit. I had no words in my lexicon to describe the all-over body pleasure that struck me, starting with my clitoris and radiating outward.

I froze and arched my back, and seeing that I too had hit the moment, Emily moved her hand down inside my underwear to stimulate me further. I heard her whisper, "so wet," as another round of shudders moved within me. Colors burst through my vision before it ultimately went dark and I lost all sensation and thought.

"Alex, hey..." I opened my eyes to feel Emily still below me. She pushed on my shoulder and I quickly rolled to the side. She gave me a smile that was matched by her eyes. "Hi."

I took stock of my physical condition. My underwear was very wet with arousal, though it was starting to cool. I wasn't sure of the time but it couldn't have been too long after my orgasm or Emily would have pushed me to the side sooner. "I'm sorry. I seem to have suffered a full shutdown after my release."

Emily laughed and ran a hand through my hair. "Baby, you passed out when you came. It's completely okay, normal actually with a really intense orgasm. Some people do it every time, some never do it."

"It *was* intense." I looked at her curiously, not having read about that particular phenomenon. "Do you?"

She winked. "I haven't yet, but there's always a first time. How do you feel?"

My body still felt stimulated, though not as highly as when we were in the middle of sex. I felt quite good. I was energized and pulsing with pleasure. I wanted to continue, to try more things that I'd read about, but I didn't want to push Emily. "I feel amazing, better than I can remember. I never realized such rubbing was a valid form of sexual expression or that it could feel so good. There are so many other things I want to try, do you think we can sometime?"

"Why not now? I'm game to try almost anything and we have all night."

It was as if Emily had access to my deepest thoughts. Perhaps she did. "I would love that. What do we do now?"

Emily abruptly pushed me all the way over onto my back and settled atop me much the way I'd done to her a short time before. "Be organic, Alex. Let's kiss and see where that takes us."

"Okay—" She was fairly voracious with her demanding mouth but I didn't mind because I truly loved kissing Emily.

It wasn't long before the feeling of immense arousal returned. Emily seemed to sense it because she pulled away from my lips. "Can I taste you?"

There was no thought involved with my answer, merely need. "Yes, please!"

She urged me to sit up and helped remove my sleep shirt, then pulled her own off. I marveled at the beauty of her breasts and dark areolas. Her nipples hardened under my stare and I leaned forward to take one into my mouth, exactly as I'd read about. Her skin had a faint salty flavor and I marveled at the way the pebbled flesh hardened further beneath my tongue.

She moaned again and tightly gripped my head. "Fuck!"

I worked the nipple of her left breast with my tongue, lips, and even lightly with my teeth. Then I thought perhaps she would like her other breast stimulated and moved to that side. It was highly beneficial that merely hearing the sounds of her pleasure also brought me pleasure. Eventually she pulled my head away and I smiled at the *popping* sound as her flesh released from my mouth. I gazed up, as Emily had been sitting in my lap, and she responded to my curious look. "It's my turn."

Emily pushed me down with a firm hand to my sternum. I found the aggressiveness of the action titillating. I wasn't sure what to do with my hands so I settled them onto her waist as she leaned into me and kissed my ear before moving her lips down my neck. Her tongue left a wet trail as she eventually found her way to my breasts. She slid down the bed to get more comfortable and replicated on me what I'd done to her. The only barrier left between us was our underwear. Mine were extremely wet and I briefly wondered what determined the amount of moisture rate in each person's sexual response. I concluded that hypothetically, any rate or reaction could be programmed.

My thoughts faltered at the first touch of Emily's tongue to my nipple. It was one area I hadn't explored when I began having sexual dreams after waking. Her skill with both fingers and tongue far eclipsed my fumbling from earlier and the breast stimulation combined with the way her leg still pressed between my own had me nearing release in a surprisingly short amount of time. I wanted to push her away but at the same time I moved my hands up to hold her head near.

"Emily...Emily, I—" Light flashed behind my closed eyes and my upper body arched off the bed, carrying Emily with me. It was a shorter, sharper orgasm than the first, though still incredibly pleasurable. Luckily I didn't fade out as I had the first time.

"Wow!"

I opened my eyes to see Emily propping herself above me, looking down with a smirk on her face. "Is something wrong? Was my response incorrect?"

She shook her head and reached a hand up to push a bit of hair from my forehead. "Not in the slightest. I've just never been with anyone who was as responsive as you."

"Is my responsiveness...disagreeable?"

"On the contrary, it's a huge turn on."

Emily leaned down and kissed me deeply and I opened my

mouth to taste her fully. I made a noise of displeasure when she pulled away.

"Can you go again?"

I assumed she was referring to sexual response but I hadn't explored frequency during my post-dream sessions. "I don't know."

"Care to find out?"

Since I still felt incredibly aroused I nodded. Then before I could ask any questions Emily slid farther down my body until she could grasp my underwear on either side. I assisted as she moved them down my legs and off. At first I thought I might feel overly exposed while nude in front of her, but once the state was upon me I found myself quite at ease. In very little time Emily settled herself lower on the bed so her face was lined up with my vulva.

"You don't have any hair. Do you shave it all off regularly?" She lightly caressed my mons pubis and a tremor gripped my body in its overly-stimulated state. Pubic hair wasn't something we'd discussed before and I had no idea the state of Emily's body hair. I'd never thought about it. I gripped the sheets, my body still coursing with arousal that had only gotten more intense with her changed position.

I answered as best I could while I lay tense with anticipation. "Apparently I had laser removal years ago because I found body grooming to be a tedious chore."

She laughed quietly. "That sounds so very like you." Then Emily's mood shifted as her gaze traveled from my breasts down to the apex of my legs. She moved her face closer, so close I could feel the warm whisper of her words against my wet skin. "And you don't remember any of this?"

I shuddered. "No. And it baffles me that I wouldn't remember something as wonderful as sex. Though I suppose it wouldn't compare if I weren't with as beautiful a woman as you—" Words stopped because speech wasn't possible while Emily elicited so much pleasure from me. Instead, a needy whine came from somewhere deep within my throat. She worked me with her mouth and I found feasting to be an excellent description of the task. I was a meal and I had succumbed to Emily's hunger.

My nonsensical vocalizations increased in volume when she began teasing my vaginal opening. She would insert her finger a short way, then pull back, and the feeling left me yearning for more sensation. I wanted to be filled by her so I could feel her on the inside and out. "Emily."

Emily paused her sucking caress and pulled away. "Do you want me inside?"

My thought process had been compromised by the all-consuming level of pleasure coursing through my body, but I was aware enough to ask for what I wanted. "Please!"

I once read that the vagina has a limited number of nerve endings as compared to the clitoris, and one could extrapolate that penetration wouldn't do much to increase a person's pleasure. But the feel of Emily moving two fingers in and out had me vehemently disagreeing with my earlier hypothesis. The act of penetration made an already high sexual response even higher and I found myself rapidly spiraling toward orgasm. Then my pleasure reached terminal limits and I went through an exquisite explosion of intense sexual gratification. My orgasm took over every sense and I became blind and deaf to all around me. I shouted the name of the only person that had ever touched me so thoroughly. "Emily!" Then everything went dark once again.

I opened my eyes to see Emily holding out a bottle of water for me. "Welcome back."

I glanced around, confused. "Did I...did I pass out again?" I drank nearly half the bottle to combat the feeling of dehydration before placing it on the nightstand nearest to me.

"Mmm hmm." Emily leaned down and kissed me, slow and deep. It wasn't passionate like earlier, rather it felt deeply affirming of our connection. The kiss didn't last long but it felt perfect. "I like making you pass out."

When she pulled away I ran my tongue across my lips, taking in the unique flavor. "What is that?"

"It's you." She smiled then leaned over to grab the water, drinking the rest down.

"Is that the way women taste? I can't remember."

Empty bottle set aside, Emily grabbed the sheet to cover us and reclined next to me. "Women don't have any particular flavor, Alex. Much like scent, there is a variety to be found. I've been with enough women to know that taste can change based on a variety of factors. That being said...you do have a unique flavor. It's sweeter, lighter than anyone else I've been with."

I didn't want her experience with me to be strange. "Do you find it off-putting?"

"Not at all." Emily grinned. "You taste...*nectarous*."

Her words prompted a strange visceral urge and I wanted to

know for myself what the experience of tasting another woman was like. On a practical level, I knew that I was already familiar with the process. But I wanted a memory of the experience. "I want to taste you too." I reached out my hand to gently run my thumbnail across Emily's nipple, where I knew her to be particularly sensitive.

Her mouth parted as she sucked in a surprised breath. "You don't have to—" She gasped again as I pinched the nipple between my thumb and forefinger. "A—are you sure?" Emily glanced across the room toward the clock on the wall and I worried that perhaps she needed to sleep soon.

"If you're too tired we can assuage my curiosity the next time we have sex."

Her smile turned particularly mischievous. "Oh, I'm not tired at all. By all means, we should *assuage your curiosity* now."

Emily's confidence left me feeling strangely unsure. I didn't want to let her down and I felt like, more than any of the things we'd done so far, this next action had the potential for failure on my part. "Where do I start?"

She pulled me closer. "Again, kissing is an excellent place."

I once said Emily's body was a treasure of unexplored tactile sensation but I had no idea how pleasurable the experience would be once given the opportunity to touch, taste, and smell all of her. Her tongue was slow and firm as it caressed my own but the real joy of discovery happened when I moved on from her mouth. She arched her neck as I tasted the skin there. Smooth and salty with sweat beneath my lips, I adored the sounds she made as I used every part of my mouth to elicit a reaction from her.

As I moved lower, I could feel Emily's wetness against my own stomach. She was incredibly aroused. Her hands came up to grip the back of my head when I pulled her left nipple into my mouth. She hissed my name.

"Alex!"

There was something fascinating about the way her flesh hardened as I continued my rhythmic sucking. From what I'd previously discovered with Emily, variety was key. I alternated between sucking, nipping with my teeth, and swirling my tongue around both her nipples. I moaned as she thrust upward against my stomach and felt the urge to move lower, much as she had done on me.

As I stared down at the puffy dark skin of Emily's vulva I grew entranced by the wetness and the way her clitoris was distended. It was improbable that I, a mere novice in my memory, could cause such a reaction. My analysis was interrupted by a tap to my shoulder. I moved my gaze up to meet Emily's smiling eyes. "Yes?"

"You don't have to do it if you're having second thoughts."

"I'm not at all. Am I doing something wrong?"

She laughed quietly but blew out a breath. "The only thing you're doing wrong is making me wait...please continue."

I smiled at her to reassure that I was enjoying my experience then turned my attention to the remarkable flesh below me. Her scent was different than mine and a lot stronger near the source of her arousal. I blew an experimental breath against her clitoris and Emily's entire body jerked below me. I held my palm to her abdomen to keep her in place then carefully lowered my mouth to taste. Sweet, sour, tangy, earthy...nectarous, no one word could describe the flavors that hit my tongue with each stroke. Much like I'd done the first time I tasted her breasts, I explored to get a feel for what Emily liked the most. I discovered she was too sensitive at first for direct clitoral stimulation. However, once I'd licked all around, including down to her vaginal opening for a few minutes, she was much more amenable to direct contact. So much so that after a while she grabbed my head and held it in place.

"There, fuck! Shit, how are you so good at this?"

I pulled my mouth away. "Do you need me to answer—" My words were muffled as she pulled me into her once again, and I assumed she didn't actually need an answer. I wanted to be inside her the way she'd been inside me but I was afraid to stop the ministrations with my mouth. Instead I rubbed the first two fingers of my right hand across her vaginal opening, thoroughly lubricating the digits for entry. Then I held them to the opening and waited. Seconds later Emily moved a hand from the back of my head to grab the fingers and push them in.

Confident I had her approval, but unsure of what she liked in the new realm of sexual pleasure, I kept my strokes slow and shallow at first. I'd done plenty of reading about sexual pleasure in women, and I knew that curling one's fingers to rub the spongy material in the front of her vagina could elicit a significantly greater release than straightforward penetration alone. As Emily loosened around me, her cries got louder in the quiet room.

"Oh! Shit, I'm so close, just like that, baby..."

Emily's legs began to tremble and I focused more on the hard rubbing of my fingers against that spot inside. At the same time I sucked her clitoris into my mouth much the way I'd done to her nipples. Emily's orgasmic explosion was almost instantaneous. She screamed as copious amounts of fluid gushed around my fingers onto the bed. Wanting to prolong her pleasure, I kept up my ministrations until she pushed my head away. Then out of curiosity, I removed my fingers and tasted what had flowed from her opening. It was indeed nectarous and I leaned down to taste more.

I was brought out of my wondrous examination by the feel of Emily's body hitching below mine. I looked up to see her with both hands covering her face as she stifled a sob. There was no previous memory of the worry I felt in that moment. I wiped my face on my shoulder, then quickly moved up the bed and pulled Emily into my arms. She turned, sobbing, and pressed her face into my neck. I searched for words in my vast lexicon to make it right. "I'm sorry. What can I do to help? I didn't mean to make you cry—"

She fiercely kissed the apology from my mouth even as she wiped away her tears. When Emily pulled back, her breath continued to hiccup though she smiled at me with watery eyes. "There is nothing to be sorry about, Alex. That was amazing, probably *the* most amazing orgasm I've ever had. You are amazing."

"I did nothing extraordinary, merely watched your body language and adjusted my technique accordingly."

Emily's loud laughter had me meeting her eyes again. She caressed my cheek as she deposited another kiss to my lips. "Like I said, amazing."

We lay there for a while until Emily declared she needed to pee and clean up. I opted to do the same after. I began to wash my hands in the bathroom and stopped momentarily. Instead I raised my fingertips to my nose and took in the scent of my girlfriend...no, lover. Emily was my lover. The smell provoked a flashback, vivid like all my others, of Emily in the throes of her last orgasm. I smiled and whispered to the empty bathroom. "Proust Phenomenon." After thoroughly cleaning my hands and face I made my way back into the bedroom.

Emily watched me approach the bed, her eyes lowered with sleepy lassitude. I slid beneath the covers and into the welcoming embrace of Emily's arms. Her voice was rough from the yelling she'd done each time she came, but it also had a timbre to it that was unfamiliar. "Hi. How do you feel?"

Her tone was gentle, and something between that, the look on her face, and my own feelings concerning the events that had just transpired, caused an upwelling of emotion inside me. I couldn't control the full-body paroxysm as my own cry burst forth. Sound wailed from my mouth as I shook within her embrace. Emily soothed me while I cried, and afterward, wiped the slick tears from my cheeks. I wasn't sure what was wrong with me, why I would cry on her shoulder after such a moving and beautiful experience. "I'm sorry, I don't know why I did that." I looked away, embarrassed by my reaction.

Emily turned my head toward her and kissed each cheek lightly before moving down to kiss my lips. "Baby, it's normal, especially after such an intense moment. Trust me."

Her words confused me. "But it was your moment, not mine."

"It was *our* moment, and don't you ever forget it."

We lay there for three minutes and fifteen seconds, until Emily's breathing evened out and her body relaxed against mine. I wanted to let her drift off to sleep but there were still things I needed to be sure of. "Emily?"

"Yes, Alex?"

"I don't want to lose you."

Emily squeezed my middle where her left arm lay across my stomach. "You won't."

"But...but what if something happens and I lose my memories again?"

"Then I'll help you make new ones."

I moved my head back so I could look her in the eyes. "And if I forget you too?"

She smiled. "Then I'll help you remember because I don't want to lose you either. Okay?"

Emily looked at me intently and I trusted her with everything I had. "Okay."

I leaned over to shut off the light on my side of the bed and she settled against me in the darkness. "Emily."

She huffed out a breath and I could hear how tired she was in that sound alone. "Yes, Alex?"

"The amount I care about you after so short a time defies logic."

Quiet laughter was muffled against the skin of my shoulder since neither of us had put sleep shirts back on. "I care a lot about you too."

There was one last thing I had to say before sleep claimed us both. "Thank you."

Her word was a whisper. "For?"

"For the gift of your emotions."

She hugged me tightly again. "Baby, the pleasure was all mine. Good night, Alex."

"Good night."

Strangely enough, sleep found me without counting seconds, without analysis of my day, and without thinking about the things I needed to accomplish tomorrow. I simply shut my eyes and slipped into my dreams.

Part Two

Through the Microscope

Chapter Sixteen

Noise

"I LIKE YOUR home." We were discussing hypothetical living situations should our relationship progress to the point where we would choose to live together. Emily and I had only been dating six months, so it was a slightly premature topic but still interesting to debate. It gave me insight as to Emily's way of thinking about the world around her.

She sighed and gave my foot a light kick where it rested on the coffee table next to hers. "Alex, you live on the top floor of a fancy, high-tech building. Not to mention you live closer to OAS, my animal hospital, *and* our favorite coffee shop. Your condo seems like a no-brainer."

"I live in a large box full of other boxes. Your house is individual and on a nice wooded street."

Emily laughed. "It's a townhouse and literally looks like all the other townhouses up and down Fletcher Street. Besides, townhome or no, your place is still bigger."

"You have a point."

"I know." She went back to her crossword as if the strength of her argument alone had ended the conversation.

We were relaxing and enjoying each other's company since Emily had to leave early the next morning for a veterinary conference. She had her bag packed by the door and planned to leave from my condo, rather than her own place. She said it was so she could spend time with me and Anna before her trip. Whatever the reason I appreciated the extra time with her.

I picked up my newest book but didn't open it to begin reading. Instead I contemplated my life and relationships. Deep thoughts as Emily would call them. Things had grown comfortable between us. We didn't see each other every day, but at least half the week we found ways to meet up for dinner or simply spend the night at each other's homes. Our sex life was beyond comparison, her words. I had nothing to compare it to because my memories had yet to return. Emily was a very open and communicative lover. While my curiosity was higher, simply because there were many things I didn't know or couldn't remember, she had no problems going along with everything I wanted to try. And she was correct in her statement that sex was better than both food *and* kissing.

"Now what are you thinking about?"

We were sitting next to each other on the couch. Anna had found a way to sprawl across my lap and partially on Emily's. Emily needed a leg free for the clipboard holding her crossword. Rather than answer, I leaned over and kissed her and she smiled.

"That was nice but not an answer."

I had learned that the people around me didn't really want to hear every single thing that went through my head each day. The list was immeasurable as thoughts nearly always assailed me. The only ones who didn't mind me reciting the litany of ideas and ruminations at any given minute were Emily and my father. "I'm thinking about many things." She rolled her eyes so I elaborated. "I was thinking about our relationship and how happy I am with you. I'm also thinking about assigning a rotating interdepartmental task force manager each quarter at OAS."

"Why is that?"

"For starters, it's been doing well since my father approved it five months ago, and the team is showing strong performance in closing out open action items. With departmental goals being hit early, that leaves each department to focus on other tasks and helps OAS advance even faster across the tech field. Now that the process and mindset have been established, I feel as though I can safely step back to focus on my primary projects."

She smiled. "That's wonderful. What else?"

"I've been contemplating Synthetica and I think we're almost ready for the next trial run. Fal has had a few setbacks on her portion of the project but she insists she's nearly ready so I'm excited to hit the next milestone."

Emily huffed in surprise. "Are you telling me that you will have a fully-functional, self-sustaining positronic brain capable of human-like emotions and responses?"

"Technically better than human." I was very proud of my project as Emily knew well. "Programming a highly sensitive and powerful machine to pass my great uncle's test has taken years and millions of lines of code. Even though my focus shifted somewhat over the past few months to get the task force operational, I have still spent easily twice as many watts of brain power on Synthetica as I have on all other projects before and after."

Emily leaned forward and placed her clipboard on the coffee table before shifting her body on the couch so she was facing more toward me. "What do you mean, *watts of brain power*?"

"Surely you already knew that the brain consumes energy at ten times the rate of the rest of the body per gram of tissue. Also, the average power consumption of a typical adult is one hundred watts and the brain consumes twenty percent of that one hundred, making the power of the brain twenty watts."

She started laughing and poked me in the side. "No, I didn't already know that. The amount of knowledge in *your* brain is frightening sometimes."

I stared into Emily's light brown eyes. They still looked golden in the right light, but no matter the color I always thought them extremely beautiful. Despite the reassurances she'd given me over the past few months, there was a part of me that worried she'd eventually think me too strange and want to break off our relationship. "Does that bother you?"

Emily sighed. "Alex...I've told you a thousand times before that I'm sapiosexual. Your intelligence is one of the biggest draws for me. I—"

"You've only told me twenty-four times."

She paused. "What?"

"You've told me twenty-four times that you're sapiosexual. Technically, you told me twenty-three times, and you told me and Fal once when we were at dinner together."

"Of course you counted." Emily rolled her eyes then gave my leg a squeeze. "Anyway...what else were you thinking about?"

I turned my thoughts back to my earlier contemplation. "Mendaxecall. Despite the fact that I've been taking it for seven months, I have yet to regain any new memories, beyond what I initially woke with."

Emily frowned. "None?"

I shook my head.

"That doesn't seem right. Have you spoken with your doctor?"

"Many times, but the last was a month ago. He told me to give it more time. When I asked if any of the other trial candidates had more success he deflected by telling me results varied across the trial."

"Alex," Emily shifted closer and made intense eye contact. I could tell she was more serious than normal by the way her brows drew down and her respiration increased by five percent.

"I'm no human doctor, but if I prescribed a trial medication for any of my pet patients, and it didn't work after a few months, I'd tell them to stop taking it."

I found her observation curious and closely aligning with my own growing concerns. "So you think I should stop taking it?"

"I'm not qualified to tell you that, Alex. I'm saying maybe you should talk to your doctor again and see about either stopping the drug, or weaning off it slowly in case there are any adverse effects from abrupt stoppage."

"Okay."

Emily tilted her head. "Okay?"

I smiled so she wouldn't worry. "Yes. Tomorrow is Friday so I'll send an email to Doctor Jones when I get to work. I'm sure I won't be able to see him until next week, but at least I'll have it on my schedule."

"Let me know what you find out?"

A blossoming pressure of emotion built inside me with her words. Emily cared. "I will."

EMILY LEFT EARLY the next morning, long before I was supposed to get up for work. She wanted to avoid rush hour traffic on her way out of Chicago. Maybe it was our upcoming weekend separation, but I woke feeling anxious not long after she left. Because of my mental state, I decided to leave for work later than normal and opted to lie abed to read one of the books I checked out of the library earlier in the week. I dressed and took my Mendaxecall around nine, before eating and riding my bike to OAS.

Once at work, I sent a message requesting an appointment to discuss stopping the trial, but Doctor Jones didn't respond until nearly four in the afternoon. I read the response from him and grew frustrated. He told me that the checkup and discussion would have to wait because he was going out of town the next day on a two-week business trip to India. Rather than let the news set back my plans I brought up the proposal for the Mendaxecall trial and read all the accompanying paperwork I could find on the network server. There was nothing in any of the reports that indicated adverse effects from stopping the drug. Plan in place, I decided to skip my Saturday morning dose. Knowing how much Emily worried about me, I opted not to tell her my course of action.

Knocking sounded at my door as I was packing my laptop into the travel bag. "Come!"

Fal walked in with a broad smile on her face. "Hiya, Alex."

I glanced at the time on my cell phone. "I thought you'd be gone for the day."

She shrugged. "Nothing doin' this weekend for me. Isn't Emily gone until Sunday?"

"She is."

"Fancy some Korean barbecue at Kay Tee Bee?"

I pointed at my helmet where it sat on the bookshelf. "What about my bike?"

"How about I call ahead and make reservations, then swing by and pick you up in an hour. Girls' night out?"

I liked the idea. "That sounds like a good evening. Perhaps I'll try something I've never had before."

Fal laughed. "Culinary adventure?"

"Absolutely!"

"Aces, see you then."

As I pedaled home I thought on all the interpersonal relationships in my life. I hadn't only grown closer to my father and Emily in the months after waking from the coma. I'd also grown closer to Fal and all my coworkers at OAS. Spending so many hours together, pouring over technology that would be groundbreaking, helped me form bonds tighter than I'd previously ever done. I liked them as people, and I liked who I was becoming the more I interacted with others. I no longer felt like the cold and impersonal woman from my memories. I was just Alex, not Alexandra.

Later Fal and I sat at a casual Korean eatery, and she was gushing about the woman she'd gone on three dates with. "So, you enjoy her company more than Jonathan's?"

"Well the sex is certainly better." Fal winked at me.

"How is the sex better? Was Jonathan's performance unsatisfactory?"

Fal tilted her head back and forth in contemplation. "No, he was a good lover but unfortunately, like so many other men, his capacity for orgasm was severely limited. Bella is a fitness trainer and can go for hours, again and again."

"So, your interest in her is primarily physical? Do you share any interests or hobbies?"

"For starters, we both fancy eating out." Fal laughed loudly before I could respond. Clearly I'd missed another point of humor.

Some days I felt as if she were constantly testing me to see how I'd react to her pop culture references and slang. Or like now, sexual innuendo. However, in this case I completely understood her reference. "I think this new woman you're seeing has your mind geared toward sexual pursuits and you've forgotten how pleasant good conversation can be."

Fal took a sip of her martini. "Oh, I haven't forgotten, but everyone has their talents in a relationship, Alex. Bella's happens to be in bed. I'm not looking for anything more serious right now anyway." She paused to finish the last bite of her taco before continuing. "While we're on the topic of serious relationships, how are things between you and Emily? You two moving in together yet?"

I gave her a curious look. "No, we're not ready for anything like that."

"Why not, you've have been shagging long enough."

"Fal," I scowled. "Not everything is about sex. Emily and I have only been dating for six months, four days, one hour, and two minutes...rounded up, of course."

Fal rolled her eyes. "Oh, of course."

Her childish interruption was annoying. "What I'm trying to say is that six months is too soon to move in."

She scoffed at my declaration. "Who says? Some people move in after a month, others wait years. There is no relationship timetable that's carved in stone. What it boils down to is whether or not you're both ready to live together."

I considered Fal's words, and they had merit. "That makes sense. In all the reading I've done it cautions against moving in with someone too soon, in case the relationship doesn't work out. However, Emily and I are both responsible, mature adults who are well-suited for one another and practice a healthy amount of communication when we're not engaging in sex. Perhaps I should bring it up to her again in a more serious manner."

Fal held up a hand. "Wait, you've talked about living together already?"

"Of course, though only in a hypothetical sense. Simply discussing the idea of it and learning what the other person would like in preference to location."

"Holy shit, Alex! If you've gone that far then go all the way. Sounds like Emily already knows what she wants."

"Do you really think so?"

She smiled and took another large sip of her drink. "Only one way to find out."

I didn't respond, instead I let the topic die and changed the subject. "Did I tell you that Anna vomited a hairball in Emily's shoe?"

Fal snorted. "She did not!"

"She certainly did. I speculated she was irritated by getting her last round of shots earlier in the day. Emily said Anna was just an asshole."

More laughter met my words. "That's pretty funny. It's too bad she couldn't make it tonight but I'll admit, I'm glad to have some time with just you. Once a person loses their best friend for half a year, you begin to appreciate having them in your life even more."

"Even if that person comes back different?"

She smiled and patted my hand. "Even if." Fal glanced down at her cell phone. "Well, as much fun as I'm having this evening, I've got someone infinitely more fun coming over to mine in an hour and a half. So, I think I'm going to call it a night." .

I corrected her, as usual. "Infinitely more fun is an impossible standard to meet."

Fal waved down the bartender for our bills. "Impossible maybe, but coming close is a cracking good time. You want a ride home?"

A few moments later Fal was signing her credit card slip. I pulled out my wallet and left enough money on the bar to cover my half of the tab plus a thirty-percent tip, rounded up of course. "We're only eight blocks from my building and the night is pleasant. I don't mind walking."

We headed for the door and Fal paused before walking outside. "Okay, if you're sure then?"

"I'm certain I will enjoy my walk. Good night, Fal. I'll see you on Monday."

She leaned over and deposited a kiss on my cheek, as she'd done for as long as I could remember. Strange that part of our friendship had stuck with me but I had lost all memories of my mother, a fact that still bothered me. There was no accounting for the wills and whims of fate. At least, that's what Emily was fond of saying.

"Bye, Alex."

EMILY HAD BEEN in Indianapolis for a continuous improvement seminar since early Friday. When we spoke on the phone

Friday night after I got home from dinner with Fal, she mentioned that she was feeling homesick and wanted to skip the scheduled brunch on Sunday morning to drive back early. The thought of seeing her sooner rather than later left me feeling very happy. But with her gone, as well as my father, who was visiting a friend in Vancouver, I was left with no social plans for the weekend. The next morning I dressed, skipped my morning dose of Mendaxecall, had a leisurely breakfast, played with Anna, then settled into my office to work.

One of my many side projects I'd taken on was expanding the motion code I'd written as part of a joint project between robotics and prosthetics. It required a significant amount of time and mental energy to calculate all the equations I needed for proper function and parameters. I didn't always have that time during the week to achieve all my goals, so work sometimes spilled over into the weekend. I'd taken Fal's advice all those months ago and didn't put work ahead of my time with her, Emily, or my father, but when I didn't have definitive plans I found ways to make up lost project ground in my free time.

I was so involved with my work that it was four fifty-eight p.m. when I was interrupted by a *scraping* against my office door. A scratchy cry punctuated the urgency of the sound and I grew confused. Leery, I opened the door and was startled to find Anna. I had forgotten about her in my intense concentration throughout the day. Not reprioritized, but rather, unrecalled.

"My apologies, little...Anna. You must be very hungry by now." I glanced at my smartwatch and frowned. It was close to Anna's feeding time and based on her desperate meows, I wondered if I had also forgotten to feed her breakfast in my extreme focus to finish my current project. I tried to think back to the morning and stabbing pain in my head met my efforts. It was the first time I could remember such a feeling. I found the experience nearly debilitating and I grabbed onto the doorjamb to prevent myself from falling. I closed my eyes and emptied my mind of thoughts in search of a brief respite. When the pain lessened, I made my way downstairs to take care of Anna.

Performing such a simple task left me feeling incredibly strange. I tried to remember what I was working on previous to my interruption but the pain struck again. Due to my sudden illness, I decided to go to bed early with the hopes that I'd feel better in the morning.

I don't know how long I lay in bed, unable to sleep or dream.

I heard a phone ringing in the distance but I was incapable of answering. I tried to remember what I was doing earlier and felt the pain in my head again, stronger, then darkness overwhelmed me.

"ALEX? ARE YOU here?"

I heard the voice clearly from where I lay. The person must have been close. My cranium felt as though spikes of pain were driven into it at equidistant intervals. I didn't answer because I was afraid that speaking would increase my discomfort.

"Alex?"

There was the sound of footsteps on my stairs.

"It looks like your mistress isn't home, little Anna. Whatever shall we do with ourselves?"

Meow

"What's that, we should call her?"

Meeooow

"Great, Em, now I'm having a conversation with a cat. At least the cat has good advice."

Ringing sounded nearby.

"That's odd, she should be here." Suddenly my door opened letting in a shaft of light and I shut my eyes to the added pain. "Hey! There you are. I was calling you, why didn't you answer?"

I heard the door shut and a light click on so I cautiously opened my eyes again. I didn't know the person sitting on the edge of my bed. "Who are you?"

Confusion laced the woman's voice. "Alex? Baby, what's going on?"

"I'm Alex? I don't remember."

Fear. That was the look that passed across the woman's eyes, though I wasn't sure how I knew such a thing. "What do you remember?"

I thought hard but came up empty. I don't think I was used to such emptiness and I found it as disturbing as the pain. "I don't know. Head hurts. Who are you?"

She sucked in a breath. "I — I'm Emily...your girlfriend. Can I feel your head, Alex?"

Her request didn't seem like a hardship to me. "Yes."

The woman, Emily, felt my forehead and cheeks with the back of her hand then turned on the flashlight of her phone. "I'm going to check your pupils, okay? Look over my shoulder while I shine a bright light into your eyes."

"Okay." The light was incredibly bright and it increased my pain. I shut my eyes again. "Hurts."

"It's all right, I've shut it off. Your pupil response is good but I'm not a human doctor Alex. We should call nine-one-one. Can you think of anything you ate or drank this weekend?"

I shook my head and focused on the sound of my hair sliding across the pillow. "I don't remember."

"Fuck! I hate it when you say those words."

I looked at Emily, trying to understand what she was referencing. "Have I said them before?"

She started to cry. "God *damn* it, Alex! You can't do this to me!"

"I'm sorry."

"It's okay, you have nothing to be sorry about." Emily paused and I wondered if she would leave again. She didn't. "Think, honey. Is there anything at all you can remember about the past couple days? You didn't answer your phone when I called to say good night last night. I assumed you were deep into whatever project was highest on your task list."

"Project." Her words triggered a fuzzy memory. "I worked on a project."

Emily seemed excited by my words. "Were you building something, was there an incident? Or was the project only programming work?"

"I—" When I tried to think about the day before the pain worsened and I rolled to the side to grab my head. "It hurts to remember!" Wetness ran down my cheeks from my eyes. Tears.

"Please, Alex. I can't help you if you can't remember. Think back and tell me what you can. I know it hurts, love."

"I was typing and something scraped my door. It was...it was a...I don't know."

"Was it Anna, your kitten?"

"Anna. Yes, Anna was outside. I fed her since it was late. Before that I—I, work—worked on a...a thing." I squeezed my eyes shut. "I am suffering immense pain in the area of my cranium."

Emily lay down next to me and pulled me close. I liked the way her arms felt around me. "You can do this, just a little more."

"I had food. I—I...can't."

"You can, try again."

"I woke and I didn't..."

The woman, Emily, shook me within her arms and I looked up. She had the prettiest golden eyes I'd ever seen. "What didn't you do, Alex?"

I focused everything I had to remember, to pull memory from my shaping and shifting mind. "Mendax — ungh, hurts."

"Fuck! Did you take it?"

"I...I stopped." The woman disappeared from the bed while my eyes were shut and I missed her warm presence, her smell. She returned eighteen seconds later.

"Here, take this immediately. You have two left but I'm guessing you can get more from work." When I opened my eyes she held out a hexagonal shaped blue pill and a glass of water.

After downing the pill she took the glass and placed it on the nearby table, then lay back on the bed again. She pulled me into her arms and I met her eyes in the light of the single lamp. "What do I do now?"

"Just rest. You appear physically fit, minus the memories and the headache. Let's see if the pill works before I take you to the emergency room." She stroked her hand through my hair and I reveled in simultaneous pleasure and cessation of cranial pain.

"Okay."

Fourteen minutes and fifty-three seconds later I spoke into the quiet room. Clarity had returned to me, perhaps greater than before in light of the recent events. "Emily?"

"Yes, Alex?"

"I'm sorry I forgot you for a while."

Emily pulled back from her embrace so she could see me better. "You remember now? How is your head?"

"I remember everything and I'm currently experiencing no pain. It appears as though I had a severe reaction when I ceased taking the drug."

Her voice was high, possibly classified as shrill. "*Severe reaction? Alex, you forgot things you've known for the past six months!*" Emily started laughing but there was a brittle sound to it. As expected, her laughter turned to sobs three seconds later as she pulled me close again. "I thought I'd *lost* you, Alex!"

The thought of losing Emily, or having her lose me, was the most frightening thing I could contemplate. With the return of my mnemonic function, I'd also gained a sense of perspective about my feelings for the people closest to me. I sought to reassure her. "But I'm right here. The way I feel about you, Emily...I don't think you could lose me."

Her breathing hitched where my ear pressed against her sternum. "What do you mean?"

"I feel as though you're a part of me, someplace deep inside." I reached up to place my hand over the center of my chest.

Emily turned my cheek so she could meet my eyes. "What are you trying to say, Alex?"

She had become a huge part of my life in a short period of time and the thought of losing Emily was more frightening than losing all my other memories combined. "I'm saying I love you."

"Oh." Emily covered her mouth and I grew concerned that I'd said something wrong, or incorrectly confessed my feelings.

"Is this too soon? Should I confess my feelings for you at a later date? Do you not feel the same way—?"

Lips that had moments before been covered by her own fingertips sealed across mine. I took heart in her positive response. The kiss didn't last long compared to most of ours, but it was twice as meaningful. "You dumb nerd, there is no correct time to confess feelings. Only you would be concerned about not following some sort of preset protocol."

"I'm sorry—"

"Nope, don't be sorry. You're not allowed to be sorry right now."

I was unaware of the added rules. "Why?"

Emily smiled and it showed from the crinkles at the corners of her eyes and the way her lips pulled tight against her teeth. "Because I love you too."

I felt a strange amount of fullness at her admission and speculated that learning of Emily's love made my own emotion somehow greater. She loved me. I loved her and didn't want to cause her pain. "I'd like to apologize for the incident with the Mendaxecall. I read every bit of literature on the drug in the OAS servers before making the decision to stop the medication. There was no mention of any side effects at all in what little literature I found. I wouldn't have done what I did and subsequently caused you distress otherwise."

"Did you speak with your doctor? I forgot to ask Friday night."

"I emailed him Friday morning, but he didn't respond until the end of the work day. He said he would be unable to discuss the drug with me until he returned from a last minute business trip to India."

Emily sighed. "Something isn't right."

"I agree. I'm concerned that the other trial candidates are unaware of the dangers involved with this particular drug."

She slid down the bed so we could lay face to face. "No, Alex. I mean something isn't right with this trial, with OAS, *and* with your doctor! I've got a few contacts in the medical community, I think you should have a second opinion."

"Shouldn't I speak with Doctor Jones first? What about Fal? She is aware of the trial as well." Silence met my questions and I grew concerned in a way I hadn't been when I realized the full extent of my debilitation before Emily administered the innocuous-looking blue pill. "Emily?"

"I don't think you should tell any of them. You've struggled with the people from OAS the entire time I've known you. Fal, your director, your doctor. That's not even mentioning the excessive level of monitoring in your home or at work, or this newest issue with the drug they say you have to take. A drug that has had zero effect in the way it's intended. Put the facts together, Alex. Doesn't something seem strange to you? Wrong?"

I analyzed my life since waking in the room at OAS. Emily was correct to say that things had not followed normal or orderly patterns where my company was concerned. It was one thing to be concerned about my health. But it was illogical to be concerned about my intellect or emotions after all the tests had been completed in those first five days.

Then there was the topic of Mendaxecall. The information I gleaned from the OAS files seemed...cursory. I wasn't familiar with drug trials but I thought there would be more official paperwork involved, as well as copious amounts of research notes about every possible reaction as well as potential long-term effects. "Do drug trials have to be approved by the government?"

"Absolutely, why?"

"I found no such approvals or paperwork when I was reading through the Mendaxecall information on our servers."

Emily abruptly rolled to the side and grabbed her phone from the other nightstand. She pulled up the texting app and sent a message to someone.

"What are you doing?"

She gave me a tight smile. "I'm checking something for you. I had a few classes in undergrad with a woman who is now a neurologist. I'm asking if she could get you in for a CT scan as soon as possible."

"And you think she'll help?"

Emily laughed. "Ironically enough, I helped her pass organic chemistry. Not to mention we've stayed friends over the years. I'm pretty sure she'll help us out." Her phone vibrated six seconds later and Emily checked the incoming message. "Bingo. She told me to have you at her hospital in the neuro wing at one in the afternoon on Monday. I won't question how she's able to guarantee getting you in so fast. Also, there will be no contrast injection, she'll do a basic scan as a favor and see if anything shows up."

I found the thought of something else wrong with me, after building my life back up over the past seven months, daunting. "I..." I closed my eyes and felt tears squeeze past my lashes.

"Baby, what's wrong?"

"I'm scared. What if I lose everything again?"

She moved across the bed, grabbed my hands, and pulled them to her chest. We were so close together I could feel the puffs of her breath tickle across my face. "You won't lose everything again. You won't lose me."

"How do you know?"

Emily gave me a smile that was part sad and part tender. "Because we love each other and I'm not giving up on you. We'll get through this, I promise."

Chapter Seventeen

Query

DOCTOR KEPLER WAS a very small woman. She looked older than Emily due to the gray in her hair and the wrinkles at the corners of her mouth, though I knew they were the same age. She had me change into a gown then instructed me to recline onto the table of the machine. My head was fairly comfortable where it lay cradled on a small contoured pillow. "There is nothing to worry about, Alex. This is a routine test so there are no foreseeable issues. Without having your medical history, I thought it best to skip the contrast injection. That is where the majority of risk comes from with this procedure."

"How long does the test take?"

"Usually around thirty minutes, but it could take as long as sixty to evaluate the various structures of your brain. The technician may ask you to hold your breath at different points. Once the scan is complete, Sara, our technologist, will determine if the images are clear enough, so be patient." She patted my shoulder. "I already explained the procedure itself, do you have any other questions?"

"No."

I glanced toward the window of the room I knew Emily to be waiting in. She waved and I smiled back at her. The technologist stepped up to the control panel of the machine. With the press of a few buttons, the table I was on began to move as she aligned my head properly. Sara gave me a thumbs-up. "You're all set, Alex. Give me a few minutes and we'll get this underway."

As promised, the scan began and the sounds of *whirring, buzzing,* and *clicking* filled my ears. Forty-seven seconds later the machine shut off and the technologist's voice came through the speaker in the room. "Alex, are you sure you're not wearing any metal? That includes metal fillings, orthopedic screws, or other similar implants."

"No, I'm not wearing anything like that. And I was told my broken bones healed normally without the need for surgery after my accident."

Doctor Kepler came over the speaker. "You said you were in a coma. Were there any plates inserted in your skull at that time?"

"Not that I'm aware of. Why do you ask?" Rather than answer, Doctor Kepler, Sara, and Emily walked out of the control room. All three women had concerned looks upon their faces. Sara moved the table back out of the machine and I sat up. "Is there a problem?"

"I'm afraid we can't get any images. There seems to be a fair amount of metallic interference."

I shook my head. "I'm not familiar with that."

"You see, Alex, CT images are made by x-rays, and x-rays are nearly completely absorbed by metal."

"I'm familiar with x-rays."

She smiled. "Okay. So in standard radiograph, x-rays are produced at a certain point and pass through the patient into a static detector. The metallic artifact will block imagery by absorbing the x-rays. It shows up as solid anomaly. The CT scan utilizes a rotating x-ray generator and a rotating detector, both acquiring data at multiple steps along the way. When there is a metallic anomaly, the artifact is repeatedly generated, and 'rotates,' resulting in repetitive artifacts, with a star-shaped artifact as the end result."

"So I have this star-shaped anomaly?"

Emily walked over and took my hand, lacing our fingers together. "No, Alex. Your entire cranium is an anomaly. Whatever kind of metal plate is there happens to be blocking all imagery so they can't do the CT scan."

I thought about my medical charts. Doctor Jones let me read through them on the second day so I could see all that had been done in my treatment. I also read through my full panel of bloodwork and all the other test results they performed during and after my coma. There were no surgical implants or plates listed in the paperwork. "There was nothing in any of the records Doctor Jones showed me to indicate something of this nature."

Doctor Kepler looked angry and I realized it was on my behalf. "If they didn't disclose all that was done to you, or lied about what was done, that's a breach of ethics. Would you like me to file a complaint on your behalf?"

Given the nature of my company, and the fact that too many secrets had been coming to light over the past six months, I didn't want Doctor Kepler to get involved. "I don't think that will be necessary, but thank you. Perhaps I misread my charts, or missed some previous information in the first few days after waking. It was a pretty confusing time."

"Alex—"

I waved away Emily's concerns. "Everything is fine, Emily. I'll see if I can pull my full chart from the network when I get home." She hesitated for a moment, then nodded and gave my hand a squeeze.

The neurologist persisted. "Are you sure?"

"I am, but thank you for the offer. I'm sure it was a misunderstanding on my part."

Emily didn't speak until we were back in her car. "Do you really believe it was a misunderstanding?"

"No." Once again, thinking about the people who I was supposed to trust and depend on left me with a sense of betrayal.

"What are you going to do?"

I was angry by all the lies and subterfuge but given the number of strange circumstances that had occurred since I came out of the coma, I knew I had to be very careful if I was going to investigate my medical records to uncover the full truth. "I need to go back to my condo. I'll dig into the servers and see if I can uncover my complete patient file. If I don't find anything from home, I'll check when I go into work tomorrow."

"Are you going to speak with anyone about it?"

The only sound in the car was that of road noise and traffic outside. I took three minutes and nineteen seconds to contemplate Emily's question. "Not yet. Ultimately it depends on what I find, or don't find."

A short while later we pulled into the parking garage for my building. Emily shut off the car and gave me an intent look from the driver's seat. "What do you want to do now?"

"I'm going upstairs to finish the programming work on my prosthetic project since I promised Director Hanssen I'd have the code back to her team by Tuesday and I got behind this weekend. Then I'm going to program a bot to look for all my relevant patient file data within the OAS system. If it's on one of the connected servers, I'll find it."

Emily sighed and rubbed her forehead before meeting my eyes again. "Alex, maybe you should leave off the work project for now. Just send an email requesting an extension for the deadline."

"I don't need an extension, I'll have the work completed on time."

"But—"

"Don't you understand? I *need* to do this!" My voice was uncomfortably loud in the car and I had no excuse for my emotional reaction. I was disturbed by the newest revelations but beyond that, I'd lost the safety in my life that I had regained after months of re-establishing myself, in both personal and professional aspects. Emily's lips were firmly pressed together and I knew my outburst upset her. Being the cause of her unhappiness made me feel miserable. "I'm sorry, I didn't mean to yell. This has me quite unsettled."

Emily surprised me with her laugh. "I'm not going to lie, if I were you I'd be screaming bloody murder right now. Yelling 'what the fuck' to everyone who'd listen. So you get a free pass...this time."

Her words soothed me and I was immensely grateful for Emily's presence. "Thank you."

"Now," She turned and grabbed her bag from behind my seat. "You want me to come in and keep you company while you work?"

I waved away her suggestion. "I don't think that will be necessary. I'm sure you'll be bored."

She grinned then opened her door. "I have Netflix on my tablet and I'll borrow some headphones from you."

"If you're sure..."

"Alex," Emily reached over to touch my arm. "I just want to be near you right now. You really scared me yesterday." She smiled but it didn't alleviate my guilt for doing something as reckless as stopping my medication without consulting anyone. "Besides, someone has to keep Anna company while you work."

I nodded then because I learned fairly soon into our relationship that I couldn't deny Emily anything.

Hours later my project was complete and uploaded to the shared drive on the prosthetics network server. I had a total of six bots programmed to search for different data pertaining to Alexandra Turing. I was no longer curious about just my medical files. The mystery of my failed CT scan made me wonder about the rest of my available data. Because of the more thorough search, I calculated it would be at least a day before I'd see any results.

One concern I had was something I'd brought up to Director Devos when I initially confronted him about the audio and video monitoring in my condo. I know there are computers and servers at OAS operating separately from the main network. If I couldn't find what I was looking for in the primary servers, I'd have to physically go to the location of those independent machines and look there. That would prove to be a lot more problematic as I wasn't sure of all the locations, nor the security protocol for each.

Something, maybe it was a sound or even a feeling, caused me to look up from the flickering indicator of my search program. Emily was staring at me from the other side of the room. True to her word, she'd curled up on the futon in my office with my favorite throw blanket from downstairs. She had the tablet propped up on the arm of the couch, and Anna was sleeping in a ball on her lap. I watched as Emily tapped the screen of the tablet, then removed the wireless headphones from her ears. "What are you thinking about right now?"

I sighed and hit a button to minimize and lock my screen, then rolled the chair away from my desk. "Mysteries."

My gaze was caught by her long fingers as they idly stroked through Anna's fur. I could hear the rumble of Anna's loud purr from where I sat. I grew jealous of my own lack of tactile sensation, though I couldn't identify if I were more jealous of Anna being stroked, or of Emily getting to pet such soft fur. Emily's voice was quiet. "Are you thinking about the test earlier?"

"I'm thinking about everything."

A single dark brow rose. "Knowing you, that could be literal. Is it really everything?"

I gave in to the urge to be near the two individuals who had never let me down and moved over to the couch to cuddle up to Emily's side. She carefully lifted the blanket to cover my legs without disturbing the young cat. "Thank you." I threaded the fingers of Emily's right hand with my left, then I reached across my body to stroke little Anna. I felt content for the first time in days. "I'm thinking about everything that ties me to OAS. I'm thinking about all I've accomplished, all that has been lost since my accident. I'm also contemplating all that has been changed or hidden since the moment I lapsed into that coma. I like predictability, anticipated outcomes, and structure. But every time I assume I've got control of my life, the ground shifts beneath my feet and I don't know who to trust."

I felt Emily's fingers squeeze tight around mine. "You can trust me."

Her statement rang as true as any other she'd uttered near me. And deep down I believed her. But sometimes you lost trust in your senses when one or two were compromised, one thing I knew too well. "Can I?"

She pulled her head away from where it had leaned on my shoulder. "Alex?"

I immediately regretted putting the fearful look on her face. "I'm sorry, that was uncalled for. It was a reaction to what I assume is stress-induced fear."

Rather than reassure her, Emily pulled farther away, upsetting the cat in her lap. "Often times stress causes people to say what's really in their hearts. Answer me honestly, do you really feel that way?"

The room was quiet with the exception of Emily's increased respiration and the *lub-dub* of my own heart. As each second counted down in my head, her face grew darker, pulled and twisted into sadness. For the first time that I could remember, I loathed myself for hurting her. "Format me! No, I promise I don't think that way at all. Sometimes my brain runs scenarios and you asked that question while the thought was at the forefront of my mind." She looked as though she didn't believe me and I struggled to explain how my brain functioned. "Another scenario that I was thinking about thirty-five seconds before was that Anna was actually a construct, a small realistic robot created to monitor me in my own home." I waited to see what she would say.

Suddenly Emily burst out into laughter. "That's....that's just ridiculous! I did her exam myself, Alex. You were *in* the exam room."

"Do you see now? When I say I think about everything, it means that I'm constantly processing the world around me. When presented with anomalies or things that upset my balance, I look for other things that could explain what is happening. I run scenarios in my head to predict the likelihood of certain occurrences, like our kiss in the park."

She smirked. "Clearly your scenarios aren't always accurate."

I smiled, happy to see that she appeared to have forgiven my momentary lapse in judgment. "Clearly not." I stared into her eyes, as mesmerized as my overactive mind would let me be. There was something about Emily that defied reason. My fascination went against logic and order. The way I felt about her made no sense in the scheme of the world. Why would two strangers be drawn to each other, physically, intellectually, and emotionally? I hated the fact that deeply personal relationships continued to baffle me and I wished more than anything for some code or program that would tell me what to do or how to act.

"You're thinking too hard again."

I refocused on Emily's face, taking in the white of her teeth against her lips. "How can you tell?"

She rolled her eyes. "We've been dating long enough that I recognize the signs."

I found it curious that she could read me so easily. "Signs?"

Emily sighed. "Yes, Alex. Your eyes grow unfocused, like your attention is turned inward. As if you've stopped seeing anything around you."

I protested. "I see everything that's going on around me as long as my eyes are open!"

She gave me a quick kiss. "Hush. I believe that you do. I'm telling you how it *appears* to the people you're with. Your eyebrows also raise and push together," She reached up to stroke the skin between my brows. "Right here. Though I find your lack of wrinkles annoying."

I rubbed against Emily's finger as I reached up to touch the spot. "Fal says I've been cursed with timeless skin. Does it make me look bad?"

She laughed again. "I love your skin, it's very soft. And the expression makes you look serious." After a few seconds pause, she added, "It's cute, but not my favorite look though."

"Oh?"

"It's this one." Then Emily firmly pulled me closer and kissed me. Her mouth opened with explorative intent and the emotion I felt for her coursed through every nerve ending and heighted all other sensations. Her tongue tasted like the wine she'd been drinking, and her blunt fingernails scraped against my scalp in a tantalizing way. The kiss grew more forceful as she moved her hands down to the back of my neck and pulled me in tighter. Wetness increased in every relevant place and I slid my tongue across the smoothness of her teeth, reveling in the difference between the enamel and the wet-pebbled surface of her tongue. The skin of her neck and cheeks felt especially soft beneath my fingertips. We pulled back slowly, letting the kiss fade from its passionate peak. When Emily's eyes fluttered open she smiled. "That's the one."

She was entirely too beautiful. I had a pressing desire for more. "Emily?"

"Yes, Alex?"

"I—I...I need."

As Fal would say, Emily *got* me. After months of dating, she understood that sometimes it was hard for me to put my greatest desires into words, to verbally communicate the extent of my thoughts and feelings. She rose from the couch and I watched the blanket pull from my lap and pool on the floor. My gaze only moved away when her hand extended toward me. "Come on. I know what you need."

Emily took my hand and pulled me up. She led us out of my office and down the hall to the bedroom. As soon as the door was shut behind us she pushed me against it and brought her mouth to my neck. I made an involuntary sound as her teeth scraped against the skin and I gripped her hips. Emily paused. "Easy there, tiger. You're going to leave a bruise, and not in the fun places either."

Her words were muffled against the side of my neck but I complied with her request. I hadn't realized I'd held her so tight. "Where are the—" I gasped as she moved her mouth up to take my earlobe between her teeth. I never knew they were so sensitive until I met Emily. "—good places to bruise?"

Her whole upper body moved as she laughed while pressed against me. "Another time, Alex. Let's get our clothes off and move this to the bed."

I let her unbutton my shirt and pull it off, then did the same for her. Next was our pants. We undressed each other as we made our way across the room, left only in our underclothes by the time the backs of my thighs hit the comforter. I pulled away from her mouth again and waved vaguely toward the bathroom. "Should we…"

Emily shoved me back onto the bed then crawled up after and perched atop my pelvis. I could feel the heat of her pressing me down. Her breasts were dark and prominent, nearly spilling out of the white bra with the position she was in. "Do you want to stop and go shower right now?"

I shook my head, and the smile I got in return was blinding.

"Good. Routines are meant to be broken once in a while."

Emily had proved to me many times over the past five months that I was capable of multiple orgasms, each one better than the last. I enjoyed the fact that she matched me in that regard. There was a lot about Emily that I enjoyed, but there was even more about her that I loved. She inspired me.

"You're clearly thinking too hard again. What could possibly be dragging your attention away from the here and now?" Her hands caressed my breasts through the thin fabric covering them and I arched my back out of involuntary reflex.

Honesty was always the best policy, according to Fal. I pulled Emily down so our bodies were pressed tightly together. "I'm thinking about how beautiful you are and how much you understand me. If I haven't said it before, I appreciate everything you do in my life."

"Alex—"

"Let me finish, please?" She nodded with eyes shining wetly. "What I'm trying to say is that you inspire me, you make me want to write line after line of code. And I love you."

She fell forward and kissed me before I'd barely finished speaking. When she pulled away again, Emily was laughing. "Baby, only you would write lines of code the way other people write poetry. And I love you too, more than I thought possible after six months." A look came over her face and I grew concerned. It didn't fit with the tone of our other confessions.

"What are *you* thinking about?"

"You better not break my heart, Alexandra Turing."

I sighed. "Alexandra Turing probably *would* have broken your heart, but I'm not her anymore. I'm just Alex, and your heart is more important to me than my own."

"Smooth talker."

I laughed, feeling playful with the shifting mood. "Well, as you're fond of saying to me, perhaps I should put my mouth to better use."

Emily gasped. "Oh my God! Did you just...*flirt*?"

I felt strangely proud. "Yes."

She laughed and abruptly moved lower. Emily's hand snaked behind my back and the tension of my bra released. I lifted each shoulder in turn as she pulled if off me. Emily tossed it away before removing her own. Then I felt warm breath on my breast as she pressed the rest of her body into mine. "Or perhaps I should put my mouth to use instead."

"Maybe you should. I'm amenable to either plan—" A needy whine escaped my throat as her lips closed around my hard nipple.

With a popping sound, she pulled away and reached up to cup my cheek. "No more talking, no more thinking, and no more worrying about tomorrow. Okay?"

My answer was a whisper as I watched her move closer to my other breast. "Okay." One thing I'd learned about myself since waking was that I'd become a woman of my word. The other lesson was how much I loved it when Emily broke my routine.

THE NEXT MORNING both of us woke early so we had time for showers and a leisurely breakfast before heading off to work. As usual, my mind raced as I considered everything I'd have to do in the coming day, both as part of my normal function within OAS and as Alex Turing, a woman searching for answers. My thoughts were interrupted when Emily reached out and touched the spot between my brows.

"Thinking."

"I am," I admitted.

She sighed and set her fork on the napkin next to her plate. "Let's start today on a positive note. Tell me something you're looking forward to when you get to work, and I'll do the same."

I liked her idea, it had positive merit. "Einstein once said that 'weakness of attitude becomes weakness of character.'"

Emily smiled. "Oh yeah? Well, Maya Angelou said, 'If you don't like something, change it. If you can't change it, change your attitude.' She was a wise soul."

I searched my literary memory but couldn't come up with Maya Angelou's name. "I'm not familiar with her work. Is she a fiction writer?"

I got an eye roll and exasperated smile for my ignorance. "She's probably best known for her poetry, and the world lost a true talent when she died more than a decade ago. I'll loan you one of my books later this week if you'd like."

"I would, thank you." I contemplated the best things happening at work, and what I most looked forward to. "Spencer said he completed the upgrades to our scrubber nanobots, which would eliminate the need for Trichlorosilane within the positronic brain shell. Hypothetically, it should run indefinitely without the possibility of system degradation and eventual breakdown."

Emily jumped up from her stool and came around the breakfast bar to give me a hug. She was ebullient with her physical affection. "Baby, that's great! Are you going to trial it out in the newest iteration of Synthetica?"

I frowned because there was no estimated time for the scrubber trial. "Unfortunately no. Fal insists the positronic brain shell isn't ready. She's been updating the peripherals, trying to get the integrated power generation portion fully functional before we move forward with any other tests. She's taking an inordinately long amount of time to complete her task. Her delays mean delays in trialing out the positronic brain in a real-world response test."

"Are her concerns and delay valid?"

Fal had always been a perfectionist, but she'd also been highly capable according to my memories of the past few years. "I'm not sure. Unfortunately, the four of us have been working on separate sections of the project with little to no crossover. Normally I'd make a point of at least checking on everyone else's projects but Devos left instructions to not waste time retreading old ground, his words. Not to mention I've been quite active in starting and maintaining the interdepartmental task force while it has been in its infancy. I have plans to check the status of the team's individual projects once I start rotating task force management to other people."

"I think you'll be happier once you've got the entire project back under your control. Do you think that will be your next step now that you've fully integrated since your coma? Or will Fal remain technically in charge of robotics below Devos?"

She was correct to surmise that I'd be happiest with my life's work back under my control, but there were a lot of other factors involved with that move. First and foremost was solving the mysteries that currently weighed me down. Gaining control of Synthetica may prove difficult if Director Devos has been working toward his own agenda. Rather than say any of that to Emily and worrying her unnecessarily, I smiled. "That would be my ultimate goal, yes."

Once Emily told me what she was looking forward to and our breakfast was finished, I went upstairs to pack my laptop while Emily settled onto the couch with her tablet. Because she worked mere blocks from my condo, she had more time to relax in the mornings after she stayed over. When I made my way back into the living room where I'd been storing my bike, I pulled up short. The rear tire was flat. I'd sold the other bicycle months before, concluding that I didn't really need more than one. After that I decided that the unused corner was a good enough storage space and more efficient than carrying the bike up and down the stairs to my spare room closet. I wasn't looking forward to the upcoming delay caused by public transportation during rush hour. "Data wipes and file dump!"

Laughter came from the couch behind me. "Did you just...swear?"

I sighed. "Yes, and I apologize. I must have hit something on my way home from work on Friday and didn't notice the slow leak with the events of the weekend." I turned toward her. "I have a flat tire."

"You don't have a spare?"

"I used my last tube seventeen days ago and have yet to replace it."

Emily snorted. "For a genius..."

I waved off her familiar remark about common sense. "Yes, yes, I'm aware I should have replaced it as soon as possible. But there is no sense dwelling on the past when I can put my time and energy toward planning for the future."

She tilted her head. "That sounds like a quote from someone famous."

"Unless you consider me famous, it's not."

Emily rose from the couch and came around the end to embrace me. I shifted the messenger bag back behind so it wouldn't get in the way. "I'll always consider you famous, after all, you're going to be the first person to pass the Turing Test."

I huffed, clearly a habit I picked up from the woman in front of me. "Let's not get ahead of ourselves."

"Fear not, Doctor Turing. I'll take you to work."

I frowned in dismay. "It's too far and you'll make yourself late."

"My first appointment isn't until nine. That's an hour away. Plenty of time. Get your gear, Turing." Then she turned on her heal and stalked over to her own satchel.

I protested. "But I already have my gear—"

She snatched her keys off the counter, gave Anna a scratch beneath the little cat's jaw, then headed for the door. "Let's go, I don't want to be late now."

Thirty minutes later she pulled up in front of OAS, the hum of the electric motor cut out when she shifted the car into park. "What time will you be finished for the day? I should be done at five-thirty, unless my last appointment runs late."

I didn't want her to go out of the way when there was a platform fairly close to my work. "It's fine, I can grab the L after work."

Emily reached up to straighten my collar. "Alex, I'll feel better if I pick you up."

I smiled, as I did every time she displayed obvious worry about me. It felt good to be loved and cared about. "I'll be ready whenever you get here."

Then at the same time we both said, "I'll text you if I'm running late."

That started us both laughing, at least until Emily pulled me into a smoldering kiss. I studied the word after Fal used it in the context of sexual passion. It was appropriate.

"I love you, now I have to go." She made a shooing motion so I unbuckled my seatbelt and exited the car. Standing on the sidewalk, I gave a small wave as she drove away. I was certain she didn't see but I felt better doing it.

The day proved longer than I wanted. Devos was in Cancun for two weeks on vacation, though it was strange that I'd seen no advance notice of it in the employee calendar. Stranger yet that both he *and* Doctor Jones had abruptly taken trips at the same time. Fal also proved elusive when I went in search of her. I checked the entry record and knew she'd scanned into the parking garage entrance, but I had no idea where she could be. I even texted her but heard nothing in return. I could have easily brought up a full door scan log to find out where she was located in the building but I wasn't ready to speak with her yet. I was afraid that seeing her face so soon after the failed CT scan at the hospital would raise my anger again.

Rather than dwell on the mysteries surrounding my illness I went up to the bio-med floor and picked up my supply of the Mendaxecall. I noticed the new label right away and it gave me pause. The generic name was listed as silicochloroform. There were other names for the compound and I knew them both quite well. Silyl trichloride and Trichlorosilane. The new knowledge ate at me and I couldn't see a reason for why the trial drug would be the same as the one we were using in robotics. But I knew I'd get no answers until my programs finished digging for data. Instead I returned to my office with the bottle, slipping it into my desk drawer. If only I could lock thoughts away as easily as I did the medication.

As a distraction, I immersed myself into planning the future of the interdivisional task force. I set the wheels in motion to hold quarterly nominations for the new task force head, which were scheduled to take place at the beginning of the next month. Director Hanssen had called to thank me personally for my work on our collaboration project and promised to keep me updated on the improved prosthetic release date.

Later in the afternoon I met with Spencer to receive the suspension tube full of updated nano-scrubbers. They were in my bag for safe keeping until we could implement the next phase of the Synthetica project. Emily had texted me to let me know that she was caught up in an emergency case and would be late. A long-term client had been hit by a car and she told the owner to bring the dog in rather then send them to emergency. I texted to let her know that I had more work to do and didn't mind waiting for her.

By six-thirty I gave up hearing from Fal. That was the reason I was so surprised when she knocked on the door to my office and pushed inside. "Hey, I heard you've been looking for me."

I scrutinized her posture and expression, looking for some sign that she were part of the strange events that had occurred since I woke from my coma or whatever elaborate agenda Devos had on his task list. Logic told me she had to be since she knew about so many other things, and she was there the day I woke. I started with an easy question. "Where have you been? I was hoping to see you earlier today to get an update on the peripheral progress."

Fal waved a careless hand through the air. "Oh, I'm afraid that's a bit stalled at the moment while I wait for parts from our supplier. I'm hoping to have something I can demo as early as next week."

"You told me the same thing last week."

She froze and didn't meet my eyes. Then it was as if a switch were flipped and Fal was smiling again. "Yes, well different part but same supplier. I think we're going to have to find another local source if we keep having issues with them."

I'd known Fal for a long time. While I only had distinct memories of the past two years and seven months, I was familiar enough with all her nervous tics and the telltale signs of dishonesty. She was lying. "What's going on, Fal? Are you in on whatever David Devos has going on around here?"

Fal paled. "I don't know what you're talking about. Are you feeling well, Alex?"

She moved toward my desk and I stood. "Stop!" She immediately froze with one hand on the corner. "What happened to me while I was in the coma?" I calculated the odds of Fal getting defensive at eighty-three percent.

"What do you think fucking happened? You slept! You slept while the rest of us tried to move on without you. Jesus, what kind of question is that?"

I tapped my finger on the desk. "There is something going on with this department, and with me. Do you know why I wasn't here yesterday?"

"You said you were spending the day with Emily. I assumed you two were shagging all day as a welcome home." Fal smiled but it didn't reach her eyes.

"What do you know about the trial drug I'm on, recommended by Doctor Jones? The Mendaxecall?

Fal rubbed the palm of her hand against her lab coat. "About as much as you, I'd suspect."

"I skipped my dose on Saturday morning since it hasn't done anything for me the entire time I've been taking it. Not low effectiveness, Fal...*zero* effectiveness. Doesn't that seem strange to you?"

Fal abruptly sank into my guest chair at the corner of my desk. "You did *what*?"

I stared into her eyes from forty-nine inches away. "By your reaction, I'd say you know quite a bit more than I do about the Mendaxecall. So far, I've discovered that the generic name is silicochloroform. If that doesn't seem familiar to you, perhaps you'll recognize its other common names, such as silyl trichloride or trichlorosilane. Would you like to inform me of Mendaxecall's characteristics and *real* purpose?"

"What are you going on about? You must be mistaken."

I raised my voice. "The name was clearly written on the bottle of my trial medication, Fal!"

She gave a dismissive wave. "You're not taking the inorganic compound we use for Synthetica, that would kill an ordinary human and you know it."

Her wording caught my attention. "An *ordinary* human? What is that supposed to mean?"

She stood abruptly. "You're talking rubbish, Alex. What's gotten into you?"

Her lies in the face of my inquiry sparked my anger again and I slammed the base of my fist against my desktop. "Emily found me Sunday morning abed, suffering debilitating pain and unable to remember who she was!"

"No."

"Yes, Fal! Tell me what's going on or I'm going to keep digging and not stop until I come out the other side of whatever agenda you've got under Devos's guidance."

Fal's face twisted into an expression I couldn't remember seeing before. It wasn't one I could read. "I'd advise you against digging around in matters you know nothing of."

"Do you want to know where I was yesterday? I went to the hospital to have a CT scan. A friend of Emily's was able to fit me in."

"Bloody hell!" Fal scrubbed both hands across her face, ending with her fingertips against her temples. "You shouldn't have done that, Alex."

I pressed for answers. "What did they do to me while I was in that coma?"

"God damn it, Alex! You shouldn't have done that!"

"Why not?"

Another emotion, one I could read all too well washed across her face. She rushed forward and around my desk toward me and I stepped back out of reflex. Fal grabbed the front of my lab coat and shook me. Her terror was real. "Let it be! Don't you understand? Nothing good can come of you digging around. You're fine, everything is fine. Please tell me you won't go digging any further on this."

I gave her a hard look and gripped her by the upper arms. "What did you do to me, Fal?"

Fal barked out a harsh laugh and released the lapel of my coat. "*I* didn't do anything." Suddenly she looked around, as if searching for something. Then as quickly as she rushed forward, she pulled back and I let her. "I have to go."

Fal stalked over to my office door and I called after her. "Fal, I want to know the truth."

She paused with her hand on the latch. "No...you really don't." She looked at me over her shoulder. "It's in everyone's best interest, especially yours and Emily's, if you let this drop. Just walk away, Alex." She stared at me for three seconds before pulling the door open and slipping into the hall.

I glanced down at my cracked desk as a wave of unease washed over me. "I'm sorry, Fal. I'm afraid I can't do that."

Chapter Eighteen

Simulation

I SAT AT my desk for twelve minutes and sixteen seconds after Fal left my office, my mind spinning around and around on what she could have meant. Were her words intended to be a warning from a friend, or a threat as something other? I checked the logs and confirmed that Fal had left the building for the evening. Other than myself, the only people still on site were the cleaning staff and two security staff members in the control office. Motion caught my eye and my gaze was drawn to the screen of my laptop where a summary list had popped up. The results from my bots were back.

The medical records entered into the system matched those from my memory of the day I woke in a private room on the bio-medical floor. While they matched, it became glaringly obvious that they were incomplete. They looked almost cursory, very similar to the way the reports on Mendaxecall appeared. I didn't truly become alarmed until I found a paper written by me documenting Synthetica project milestones. I clicked on another link and it took me to an email from Alexandra Turing to David Devos, an email I had no recollection of sending. In it I confirmed the completion of the Synthetica project and listed potential trial dates for testing. It wasn't only the brain I was referencing in the communication. The email specifically mentioned the fully-functional "Synthetica Android" model, AL-10.

This entire time since waking from my coma I'd been foolishly working on a project that I had already completed. To what purpose? Why would they not tell me? More importantly, why couldn't I remember?

AL-10.

That serial number struck me as familiar. Clear visual memory assailed me, one of the precise moment in the coffee shop the day Emily gave me her free coffee, and I reeled away from my desk. "No!" My voice was a shout in the silent office but I knew no one would hear me. The hallways on the robotics floor were empty save perhaps a Sentinel.

I needed to know more. In a fit of panic-induced action, I quickly searched for the location of Artemis, who had never returned to our floors. Once again she was located on sub-level five. The location was listed as permanent assignment, rather than offline. I stood from my chair, determined to verify the truth but before I reached the door my watch *buzzed* with an incoming message from Emily.

I'm outside, are you ready to go?

Quickly changing plans, I sprinted out the door toward the elevator that would lead to the parking garage entrance. When I exited on the garage level I came face to face with a Sentinel just as the indicator on its chest turned red. "This unit registers the physical and NFC ident of Doctor Alexandra Turing. You have been placed on restricted access and will be detained until authorized personnel arrive."

I used my coded response. "Heyla."

It took less than two seconds for the indicator light on the android's chest to change from red to green. "Access override detected. This unit awaits new orders."

"Apollo, your task is to monitor the locations of Doctor Nanjiani and Director Devos should either of them arrive in the building." I paused, considering my options and made a difficult decision. I'd face the consequences later, if any came. "Stun settings at one hundred thousand V and six A. Update parameters and delete program change history for all units."

Three agonizing seconds later the indicator flashed green again. "Alpha protocol override complete. New directives acknowledged and saved to onboard database."

I smiled and it wasn't one born of happiness. "Use wireless update function to push new override protocols to all Sentinels."

"Orders confirmed. Updating five other units."

Only five. I knew exactly who was missing the update, one that was operating independently from the other Sentinels. Lucky for me, Artemis was the original security droid that I'd modified the previous year. I could only hope that nothing significant had changed in its deep-core programming.

Emily was parked in a space near the exit door, waiting in her car. I walked straight up to the door and opened it. She smiled when she saw me but the look quickly slid off her face. "What's wrong?"

I shook my head. There was no time to communicate things in such a slow manner but I tried. "It is imperative that you come inside with me."

"Alex?"

I lost patience with the entire situation. "You need to come inside!"

Her face clouded with anger and I knew I'd cost us time. "Fucking *excuse* me? I'm pretty sure whatever is going on doesn't include screaming at the person who came to pick you up."

I squatted down within the confines of her open door and grabbed her left hand to cradle between my own. "Please, Emily. There is something I have to see and I need you with me to do it. Please come inside."

Her face was a conflicting mask of emotions. "What's going on, Alex? Did you get the results back from your search? I thought I wasn't allowed in your fancy high security building without a guest badge and proper security clearance."

"I'm all the clearance you need. You'll come in?"

"If it will make you feel better and put this mystery to rest once and for all, sure."

She followed me through the first door of the vestibule and the light above the far door turned red. Before the robotic voice called out the security breach I spoke. "Security override key telequire." The light above the far door turned green as we heard the *click* of a lock disengaging.

A robotic voice sounded from the speaker overhead. "Override successful."

Emily glanced at me as we pushed through the second door. "That shit is hella creepy."

Once inside the nearest elevator I scanned my badge and pushed the button for sublevel five. The ride was fast and smooth. Emily watched me in the silence of the car and I feared for what we would find. A confirmation of my calculations would prove to be the ending of our time together and despair crept in. Wetness ran down my cheeks as the door *whooshed* open.

"Alex, you're scaring me. Can you please tell me what you found?"

I stopped before we'd gone more than three steps down the hall and Emily stopped with me. I turned to face her. "Can I kiss you?"

"I told you not to ask me—"

Emily tasted like the mint gum she'd been chewing. She stiffened at the unexpected kiss then quickly fell into it as if she were the original initiator. Despite how wonderful it felt, the kiss was overshadowed by a new sort of emotion building within me. Desperation and grief gripped me tight as her lips pulled away, and I took a moment to rest my forehead against hers. I whispered the greatest thing that had ever happened to me. "I love you." My loss was inevitable but I didn't account for Emily's own sensitivity to my moods.

She pulled back with tears in her eyes too. "That felt like goodbye."

I sighed and pulled away. "It's only goodbye if you want it to be."

"No matter what we find, that's never going to happen."

I wiped the weirdly slick tears before they could drip onto my lab coat. "Don't make promises you can't keep." Before emotion could send me running back toward the elevator, letting me deny the truth for a short while longer, I turned and paced down the hall. Emily's long legs carried her equally as fast. I watched the nameplates next to each door carefully, looking for a specific one. Before we could find the correct room. Artemis turned the corner at the end of the hall. The android's distinctive tin badge seemed almost comical in context of the serious situation.

While the voice coming from the security droid was significantly more pleasant, the words were exactly as I feared. "You are trespassing on a high security floor. Please prepare yourselves for detainment until correct personnel have been notified."

I didn't allow the droid to come any closer because it was equipped with Taser function that I knew it would employ. "Artemis, how is the weather today?"

While the key phrase wouldn't allow me to verbally alter the programming directive of the Sentinel, it did cause the android to freeze in place. I had memory of putting the back door override in the year before when I upgraded it with new voice and dialogue programming.

Emily looked at me with concern. "What —"

I held up my fingers in a shushing motion and she fell silent. I led us around the android and when I got to the back side I pressed my finger to the sensor on a hidden panel. A hatch opened and I flipped the motion and communication switches to the off position. "Okay, we can go now."

"Alex, I'm getting scared here. Why did you bring me down to the lowest level of your high security building? At night and alone." She paused, then her face twisted in horror. "Oh God! I knew you were too good to be true! You're a serial killer, aren't you?"

I laughed at her outlandish accusation but enjoyed the familiar smile on my face that she elicited without even trying. "No, and you watch too many murder movies."

We continued walking as she responded. "They're detective shows and I learn a lot from them. Just so you know — oh, we're stopping." She looked at the heavy door in front of us. There was a simple nameplate hung forty-eight inches from the floor, below that, a fingerprint security pad. The only thing written on the nameplate was a large roman numeral X.

"This is the room."

Emily looked from the door, to the nameplate, then back at me. "What's in the room, Alex?"

I sighed, feeling the heavy weight of loss. "The truth."

The light turned green with a simple press of my thumb and I listened with satisfaction as the lock disengaged. With trepidation, I pushed the handle down and swung the solid door inward. The room was dark save for standard computer medical equipment. The telltale sounds of a ventilator and cardiac monitor filled the silence. The EEG showed a steady flat line and my heart sank.

We stood in the one thousand six hundred and eighty square foot room and stared at the body lying on the bed. Emily turned to me fearfully. "I don't understand."

I gave her a sad smile. "The truth I discovered is that Synthetica has been complete for a long time now. It was finished before the accident."

She waved toward the bed. "Why is it hidden down here in the lowest level, and why wouldn't they tell you? And why would you create your android to look exactly like you. It doesn't make any sense."

I tensed with anxiety. "Emily..." She looked back at me, away from my twin lying on the bed. "That is Alexandra Turing."

Confusion washed over her, and Emily's eyes looked oddly dark in the dim room. "What do you mean? How can Alexandra Turing be hidden away in a dark room for six months when you're clearly standing right next to me?"

"You're not getting it! I'm not Alexandra Turing. You and I have been operating under wrong assumptions for months."

Emily stepped back and grew angry. "Of course you're Alex!

You're the same woman I've laughed with and cried with. You're the woman who held my hand and predicted a kiss in the park. You're the one who has devoted your entire life to the completion of the Synthetica project in order to pass your great uncle's test, and...and you're the woman I fell in love with." A tear fell from Emily's lashes and traced its way down her cheek. I longed to brush it away with a kiss.

I laughed and it was mirthless. "Oh, I succeeded in passing the Turing Test, only not the way I expected."

Perhaps out of frustration, and a desperate sense of imminent loss, Emily grabbed the lapel of my coat and shook me, much the way Fal had done earlier. "Just fucking tell me, Alex!"

I stared into those beautiful eyes and knew I'd miss her more than anything else in my short and tumultuous life. "I'm trying to tell you. I'm not Alex and I'm not working on Synthetica." I paused to gather my courage. "I *am* Synthetica."

"Fuck you!" She shoved me away with a sob. "Is this some sort of sick joke?"

I pointed at the woman lying in the bed. "Look at her, Emily!" She froze and I waved my hand. "Go ahead and look. Tell me that woman isn't real. The real Alexandra Turing never woke from her coma. Instead, Director Devos, Falguni, and my father — Matheson Turing — used the opportunity to test out Alexandra's greatest creation. Me. They couldn't bring her back, so they woke me instead."

Emily had both hands pressed together in front of her lips. It looked almost as if she were praying. I watched the movements of her eyes as they darted from the bed, to the monitors, and back to me in rapid succession. Then without another word she dropped her hands from her face and strode over to the bed. Emily picked up the chart that was hanging from the frame at the end, then studied the machines nearby. "Jesus, she's brain dead. The last doctor's note states that there is no hope of recovery."

"I calculated as much."

I walked closer, though I didn't want to. I didn't want to see the face of my creator, my life, and my eventual mortality, lying so serene upon the white OAS sheets. When I was close enough to touch, I rubbed my hands across the material of the bed. I remembered waking to the feel of it against my own skin. Like a newborn thrust out into the light of the real world, I woke confused and blinking at the brightness. It was a silent birth though, one without the shrill squalls of an infant. Instead my birth was facilitated by loss, much the way a mother will sacrifice her life for the baby to be born. My own *mother* lay before me and I sorrowed at her permanent sleep. My rumination was interrupted by Emily's quiet voice.

"What happens now?"

"I'm certain that by now they know I've discovered the truth and it will only be a matter of time before they shut the project down."

Emily's gaze abruptly jerked from Alexandra Turing to me. "Alex, you *are* the project."

I felt sad. "Yes."

Strangely enough, rather than be awash with grief, Emily seemed to grow angrier the longer she stared at me until eventually she jerked into motion. "Fuck that! No one can shut you down. There has to be something we can do. We can call the ACLU, or find a lawyer to represent your case..." Her words trailed off as she realized the immense undertaking she proposed. The ramifications and consequences of going public with who or *what* I was defied reliable calculation.

"To what end? I'm a machine, not a human. I've got no rights in this situation and it would be nearly impossible to prove I wasn't some elaborate construct, nothing more than a clever hoax perpetrated on the scientific community."

Her mouth twisted with anger. "So, what? You're just going to give up? You're more human than the woman lying on that bed right now!"

I shook my head. "No, she was human."

"How do you know? How could anyone with a trace of humanity create something with feelings and emotions as merely a test? Something to be discarded and forgotten once its purpose was served." She paused. "*Her* purpose."

Emily's entire body was full of rigid tension and I approached her slowly. When I was close enough to reach out and grasp her hand, I pulled it gently to lay palm flat against my chest. "I know she cared *because* she created me with feelings and emotions. Alexandra Turing did spend her life programming me to be human, giving me all the skills and knowledge she had and a hundred others possess. She gave me the capacity to love you, and I will always be in her debt."

Emily used her free hand to pull me into an embrace and sobbed against my shoulder. "I don't want to lose you."

I held her as tight as I thought safe. "Nor I you, but you realize that I don't really exist, right? I'm merely a shell full of complex programs and circuitry."

Emily pulled away so she could meet my eyes. "You're not. A person isn't defined by what's on the outside. They are distinguished by what's on the inside. You are more real to me than anyone else I've ever met and I'll be damned if someone tries to say different!"

A feeling blossomed in my chest with her words. Emily wasn't giving up on me. She was willing to fight for me, it only seemed logical to fight for myself. "Okay."

"I mean it, Alex! You better get on board with this—did you say okay?"

"Yes."

She threw herself into my arms again and I caught her easily. Inspired by Emily's joy, I spun her in a circle away from the bed. She knew the truth and still wanted me. Eventually though, the reality of our current situation set in. I lowered Emily to the ground and as if tuned to the same frequency, we both moved our gaze back to the bed. Emily broke the silence. "What do we do now? I don't know about you but this place is creepy. I'd like to get out of the building and away from potentially murderous robots." Before I could respond, she held out a hand. "I'm not talking about you, obviously. I'm talking about those hulking androids you've got patrolling the place. What did you call them, guardians?"

"Sentinels. And they're not murderous. The only way someone could die during an altercation or apprehension was if they suffered from an adverse reaction to the Taser. Or if it malfunctioned."

She shivered. "Well I don't want to find out for sure. Can we go? Are you safe to leave? I mean, realistically, what can they do to you?"

"I'm fully autonomous so they can't—" I remembered the biometrically locked update capability mentioned when Fal spoke of Synthetica. She eventually admitted that she gave me access but I had yet to try it out. Given the recent information disclosure I wondered whether it would even work for me based on the fact that the finger prick portion wouldn't register actual blood. "Synthetica can be wirelessly updated via a proprietary program created by OAS. Only four people were supposed to have the biometric security access. I'm one of them."

"Wait a minute. You mean they can delete you or whatever,

at any time?" I nodded and her mouth dropped open in horror. "Can't you just...reprogram or fix yourself so that the wireless update doesn't work anymore?"

I contemplated the problem. "We have a failsafe in place that prevents the Synthetica wireless update function from being disabled via a wireless transmission. I thought it was strange that Fal would build that in but she said it was on Devos's orders. Now it makes sense."

Emily rubbed her temples with the first two fingers of each hand and sighed. "So how do we disable it?"

"Via the hardwire connection port built into the posterior section of the positronic brain shell."

The horrified look returned. "You're talking about your brain, Alex! How the fuck do we access your brain without doing irreparable damage?"

I frowned and admitted, "It's going to take some time. I need to see the original program code to re-write it. I've got a copy of it on my laptop. I'll also need the access cable to transfer the program from my laptop to the brain. I've got one in my lab. Then someone, not me, would have to make a precise incision where the port is located, peel the synthetic skin and coolant gel cap away from the site, open the port, and insert the cable. After that it's only a matter of pushing the right button to upload the altered program subroutine."

She looked a bit sick. "Oh, *that's* all? Is there someone that can do this for you?"

I smiled to reassure her. "You."

"Oh, hell no!"

"Please, you're the only one I trust."

Emily glanced toward the bed where Alexandra Turing lay dead in all the ways that mattered most. "Are you sure of your own construction? How do you know so much about the synthetic skin if you're still working on the brain portion in your project?"

"We had the initial idea planned out more than a year ago. And over the past six months I've gotten the opportunity to work on a lot of other projects, so I could see how they would have applications within the scope of Synthetica. Emily, we can do this. *You* can do this. Please."

She thought about it for a total of fourteen seconds before relenting. "Okay. Do you think they know that *you* know about Synthetica?"

"I confronted Fal today, before I actually had all the facts. She told me to drop it and walk away for both your and my good. She had to know that I wouldn't stop until I found the truth. I overrode the programming of the sentinels before you got here and instructed them to monitor Fal or Director Devos if they showed up."

"I'd say they're definitely going to know something is up. Is there anything you can do to slow them down? Something that can block a wireless signal or inhibit them from sending the update?"

Emily brought up an excellent point. I wouldn't be able to do any repairs to my own positronic brain program if they decided to end the Synthetica trial. I would simply be...gone. I contemplated my options. "I could potentially program bots to look for any instances of the proprietary updater program on the network, but if they have it stored on an autonomous machine, I'd still be in danger."

She frowned. "How can they push the program to you, don't you have to be in the building?"

"Unfortunately, the way our program works is that it will piggyback off the cell network so I'd have to isolate myself where there was no cellular or WiFi service in order to be safe from updating. There is no other way to—" I suddenly remembered the research I did when investigating spy equipment during the monitoring fiasco of months before. "I can build a jammer!"

"What's that?"

With one last glance at my creator, I started toward the door. "Highly illegal. A radio jammer drastically reduces the signal to noise ratio, which blocks radio waves. I should have components enough to build one in my lab, and while we're there I can retrieve the access cable."

Emily dutifully followed me out of the room. She gave Artemis a wide berth when we made our way down the hall toward the elevator. The lab was the next level up, on sub level four. It didn't take long to build a jammer with components gleaned from the drawers and cabinets within the large well-lit workspace. Emily watched over my shoulder.

"How do you know how to build that?"

"I researched spy equipment and read the schematics online."

"And you can just—wait a minute, what am I saying? Of *course* you can." She laughed and it sounded strangely brittle.

I felt the need to reassure her. "If it makes you feel any better, the real Alexandra was equally as brilliant, and could have done the same. We're not so different, her and I."

She gave me a penetrating stare. "But I didn't fall in love with the real Alexandra."

I shook my head sadly. "No."

Emily sighed. "I'm not going to pretend that the truth doesn't complicate things in ways I haven't even begun to imagine, but I'm also not sorry for our journey either. No matter what, I choose you. Whomever you are or however you came to be, I choose Alex."

Tears shimmered in my vision and I leaned closer to kiss her. It was fast but full of the emotion I held for the amazing woman next to me. She seemed to understand. Then I quickly snapped the back panel on the jammer before turning it on and stuffing it into my pocket. The access cable was in a storage cabinet. "I think this is everything. We need to stop in my office for my laptop."

"Is there anything else here that you need? There is nothing else they can use to control you or bend you to their will?"

"Not to my knowledge."

I scanned the security reader in the elevator. As the car made its way one level up, Emily suddenly gripped my hand tight, eyes wide with panic. "Alex, what about your medicine? When I gave you that dose on Sunday morning you only had two pills left."

"I took the last one this morning but I have a refill bottle in my desk. It's a thirty day supply, more than what I'll need if everything goes according to plan."

Once in my office, it didn't take long to pack my laptop in the messenger bag. I opened my drawer to retrieve the new bottle of Mendaxecall and only saw three pens and two mechanical pencils. "It's not here."

Emily walked over from where she stood studying the items on my bookshelves. "What's not there?"

I met her eyes and gestured toward the drawer. "The Mendaxecall is missing. Someone has taken it from my desk."

The panic returned, along with wide fear-filled eyes. "Shit, what do we do now?"

"We continue with the plan. It means my timeline for success has been severely compressed."

Emily looked around suspiciously. "We should go. I don't trust this place and I want to get you somewhere safe."

It was seven thirty-eight when Emily pulled out of the parking garage. No alarms sounded and no one stopped us. But I knew it had less to do with secrecy of our movements and more to do with the secrecy of the project as a whole. I didn't know David Devos's overarching plan for Synthetica, nor the full extent of Fal's complicit assistance, but I did know that I was in danger. "Can we stop at my condo and pick up Anna? And do you know someplace we can go where you'll be able to perform the update once I have the code written?"

Streetlights and beams of light from passing cars cast Emily's face in ever-shifting planes of shadow. She didn't answer until we were nearly to my condo and I assumed she had been processing all that she'd learned over the past hour. "We'll go to my clinic. I have everything I need there to...to open you up and kennel Anna comfortably. Plus it's not as obvious as either of our homes if they come looking for you. We should also shut off our cell phones."

There was a quaver in her voice and I knew Emily was frightened. I remembered her earlier comment about murderous robots and hoped it was *for* me and not *of* me, but I was too scared to ask. "Both are logically sound suggestions."

Once in my condo it didn't take long to get Anna into a carrier and gather a few other items for her like food and toys. Then on Emily's urging I packed a duffle bag with items I'd need for a few nights in case I didn't come home right away. When I came downstairs from my bedroom I saw Emily standing by my bookshelf, holding a framed picture. It was the selfie we'd taken on our first date when we went to Lincoln Park Zoo. I knew then I had to do the right thing, the brave thing.

I placed the duffle bag by the door and walked over to her. "I'll understand if you no longer wish to maintain a romantic relationship with me after all the revelations of tonight. I've misled you for months and proven to be your greatest fear. I was too good to be true. Not only that, but I've possibly put you into peril if Director Devos has dangerous intentions or connections outside OAS. I don't know what their plans are for me once the Synthetica trial ends—"

Emily's kiss took me by surprise, which was a rare occurrence. I could calculate the odds of any event to within a ninety percent accuracy, yet her actions varied the most. She would have taken my breath away too if my respiratory system were connected to my emotional responses, which recent events have made me realize they were not and explained a lot about my miraculous-seeming physical capabilities. She pulled away and I stared back in confusion. "Why did you kiss me?"

She smirked. "You mean to tell me you didn't predict that one?"

"No."

"Good. That should prove to you that you're not always right, and super-genius or no, you can't always predict what will happen. You didn't mislead me, Alex. Your director and best friend misled us both. And I thought we already settled the other issue in that creepy-ass basement. I love you, not for your body, your origin, or your employer. And I'm attracted to your mind more than anything else. None of the important details have changed."

I countered, "But I don't have a mind, as you put it. I have a computer that is nothing more than a collection of inorganic circuits and synapses with the sole purpose of learning, problem solving, and self-improvement."

Emily laughed. "And I have a collection of *organic* circuits and synapses with the same purpose."

I stepped back in surprise and she watched me with her smiling eyes. Despite the upset, and in contempt of the potential danger and difficulty she would face at my side, Emily was happy here with me. "I see your point."

"Good." Emily threaded her arm through mine and led us back to the front door where Anna sat meowing forlornly in her cat carrier. She bent down and grabbed the little cat and bag of care items. "The sooner we free you from their tether, the sooner you're mine, heart, body, and soul."

I lifted my duffle and paused as I grasped the handle of the door. I looked back at Emily. I'd never believed in the concept of souls before, neither had Alexandra based on my memory of her conversations. "Do you think I have a soul, even after all that you've learned tonight?"

She leaned closer and gave me a kiss on the cheek. "Baby, you've got soul enough for ten people."

Her statement filled me with a strange lightness and I added it to my list of motivations for freedom. I suddenly remembered Fal's question from that first week I was home after waking at OAS. Just like Friday Jones, I was self-aware and had the same feelings and emotions as any other person. I have love and passion in my life like anyone else. I may not have been a human, but I was still a person and deserved protection, rights, and privileges as such. My gaze wandered from the meowing cat pressed against the small mesh door to my girlfriend. I had no intention of giving up.

Chapter Nineteen

Reboot

THE CLINIC WAS dark save for a few security lights when Emily entered the alarm code to the keypad located inside the main entrance. She didn't bother turning on any lights until we got into the back. She led me downstairs to an office with a desk containing a flat screen monitor, keyboard, and mouse, then pushed the peripherals out of the way to make room for my laptop. "How long will you need to rewrite the program? I'm going to send out an email to my office manager to shunt tomorrow's appointments to Doctor Brooke, or reschedule them. I've got a room down here where I can do your procedure when the time comes, so no one needs to know you're here."

I glanced around the space then took in the worried face of my girlfriend. "Thank you. I can never tell you how much this means."

She took a step closer and cradled my face in both her hands. "Baby, I have just as much invested in this. I'm not going to lose you!" She stared into my eyes then gave me a tender kiss. "Do you know how much time you have before you start showing signs of degradation without the Mendaxecall?"

I considered the previous incident. I'd taken the Mendaxe-call at nine a.m. Friday morning and I began showing signs of degradation at thirty-two hours. Or was it less? I couldn't remember if I'd fed Anna that morning. "I'm not sure. I thought it was less than thirty-two hours from the time of my Friday pill to the first established pain. But when I try to remember that morning, I have concerns that I never fed Anna. It's possible the signs of memory degradation begin sooner than initially calcu-lated."

Emily frowned but still looked hopeful. "That still gives us plenty of time to work, right? How long has it been since your last dose?"

"Fourteen hours, three minutes, and twenty-two seconds."

"See, plenty of time—"

"But we've already established that degradation escalates

based on the amount of work stress the positronic brain is under."

Emily glanced from my open laptop back to me. "And does this coding require a lot of brain power?"

I sighed, a foolish and useless response. "To do what I need to do at the speed I need to do it will require a significant amount of power, yes. However, there is a factor at play that neither myself, nor the rest of the team had any way of calculating."

"That is?"

"Emotional stress and the way it adds to the work load within the positronic brain. I'm afraid I hold a significant amount of emotional stress right now. I'm sure lack of sleep tonight will exacerbate the issue as well. And the nano-scrubbers I have can't be introduced until you open up the access port in the positronic brain shell."

Rather than answer, Emily pulled me into her arms and held me tight. "We'll get through this because I'm never going to let you go."

She whispered the words and for the twelve seconds I spent in her arms, I believed them. Eventually she released me and waved toward the clinic phone. "Why don't you get started and I'll place an order for Thai Guys. Do you want anything in particular, or do you want me to surprise you?"

I forced a smile. "A surprise is fine."

"Good thing they're open twenty-four hours. I'm going to take care of Anna and make a note for our office manager before I call it in." She walked out of the office and I heard her footsteps disappear down the hallway. Emily said the basement was rarely used, and the kennels down here were only needed if everything in the main clinic upstairs was full. As soon as she was gone I logged in and opened the section of code relating to Synthetica security and began working on a patch.

Emily made me stop to eat when the food arrived then I immediately went back to work. The code was long and complex and touched upon many other areas of operation. The key issue wasn't that I simply had to remove all wireless update functionality. Rather, I had to remove all *unapproved* wireless update functionality. I was self-aware enough to know that the ability to wirelessly update my own program was incredibly useful. But I wanted to be the only one capable of such a task.

The further I dove into the mass of programming and outcomes, the more I realized my own potential. Being a computer,

Synthetica, me, I could send and receive communications in a variety of different ways. At twelve forty-seven a.m. I discovered the full extent of my capability. By opening internal access to my wireless function I could interact with the world around me on a digital level, rather than be limited to more human standards. The realization caused me to alter my original goal of the update patch and I redoubled my efforts.

Emily was asleep on the couch in her office when I ran into my first difficulty. Pain speared my cranium, spiking at regular intervals. I didn't have to look at the time on my laptop to know it was one-thirteen in the morning. I stopped typing and grabbed my head, hoping the motion would alleviate the sharp pain. I must have made a sound because Emily called out in the darkness.

"Alex?"

"It is...okay. I—I—I am f...fine—fine." I stopped speaking, alarmed at the erred speech.

I heard her bolt from the couch and make her way to where I sat in the glow of the computer screen. I shut my eyes. "Shit! What can I do?"

"Hurts." The pain was blinding. Emily wheeled me away from the desk and steered me over to the couch. I was useless to help as she pulled me from the chair to lay on the rough fabric. Then she settled herself behind me as I faced the back of the couch. One of her hands rested above our heads, and fingers stroked through my hair. The other hand held me tight around the middle.

"*Shh*, just rest. Give yourself a break and see if it helps."

Emily's voice was soothing in my ear, and my own was a whisper. "Okay."

We lay there for the next thirty-three minutes as my system cooled and the pain level gradually lowered. It wasn't much of a window but I knew I had to take the opportunity to finish the update. I gently gripped her hand where it lay flat against my stomach. She had fallen asleep behind me but roused quickly enough. "I need to get up."

"Are you feeling better?"

Emily moved back off the couch and I turned over so I could sit up. "Well enough to finish what I started. Before I do though, can I use your office phone to check my voicemail?"

She turned on a small light mounted above her desk. "Sure. Do you think they're trying to track you down already?"

I frowned, remembering the look on Fal's face as she left my office. "I'm ninety-eight percent certain."

My calculations proved to be accurate. Fal had left a total of six messages, my father left three, and David Devos left only one. I played the last two aloud for Emily. The first of which was from Fal, and the last was Devos.

"Alex, I'm being called in to OAS but I had to give you a warning. I'm sorry we've been lying to you but I'm going to be honest that these past few months have made me realize a lot about Synthetica and you specifically. I didn't have a choice where Devos is concerned and I'm afraid he has something planned for the project that neither I nor your father are aware of. He's been growing more and more unhinged the longer it takes to find you. As soon as he realized that you'd figured out the truth he called in a group of men in black tactical uniforms and they left for your condo. What I'm trying to say is, don't go home! I hope you forgive me someday because I don't want to lose my best friend again. Stay safe, Turing."

David Devos's message was significantly more threatening. "I'm aware that you've stumbled upon the nature of your design. It would be in everyone's best interest if you return to OAS immediately. There is no hope for your existence outside the project but perhaps we can work out a deal that will protect the company and Matheson Turing."

I looked at Emily and she made a face. "Jesus, what has that man gotten himself into?" I shrugged and her eyes narrowed. "Didn't you tell me months ago that Synthetica originally had military applications and that your director wanted to sell it to the government?"

"I did, but I deleted all those plans and schematics from the servers not long after I woke."

"You may have given up on the military applications but what if he didn't? What if he's got a side deal going with someone and having you run rogue is ruining his plans?"

I considered her hypothesis. "That seems...nefarious."

"Think about it. Have you ever really trusted him? What does your gut tell you?"

"My gut doesn't tell me anything other than when it needs sustenance."

She rolled her eyes. "Your instinct then. Anyone with a source of intelligence and collection of human experience has instinct. What does yours tell you?"

I contemplated all my interactions with David since waking, and all the memories I had of him before. "You're right. I don't trust him and he has been acting irrationally for months now." Then I admitted as much to her as I could without giving away all my actions. "I already knew he was dangerous. Only I wasn't sure if it was him alone, or if Fal was one hundred percent complicit in his actions."

"It doesn't seem like she is. I've had my trust issues with her in the past but it sounds like she was trying to warn you in that last message."

I nodded. "Based on her tonal inflections and clipped speech patterns, she was telling the truth."

Emily sputtered and looked at me with wide eyes. "You can tell if someone is lying to you based on that alone?"

I nodded again.

"Well fuck me!"

Her profanity was concerning. "Were you planning on lying to me at some point? Aren't lies inherently bad?"

Rather than be angry, Emily burst into laughter. "Not about more than hiding a birthday surprise. And believe it or not, sometimes lies are necessary to preserve happiness in instances like presents, surprise parties, or other such momentous occasions. As long as it comes from a good place and isn't meant to harm, I don't see anything wrong with keeping a few secrets."

"Technically I don't have a birthday."

Emily tapped her lower lip then smiled at me. "That's what you pulled from my little lecture? Okay, let's see...would you exist without the real Alexandra Turing?"

"No."

"Then I think since she can't have any more birthdays, and you were created by her as her life's work, you should take her day as a way to honor your creator."

The kiss I placed on her lips was fast and spontaneous. She looked startled when I pulled away. "Now who is the genius? Thank you, Emily. You give me hope that I can have a normal life when this is all over."

Emily stepped closer and kissed me again, much slower than my exuberant display of affection. She pulled away and gave me a sweet smile. "Never lose hope."

I recited a quote I'd read recently. "The Darkness feasts on the souls of beasts but the safety of light dines on hope alone."

She smiled. "Who said that?"

"J. Page, a twenty-first century American writer. Sadly she died a decade ago of brain cancer."

"Well that's hella depressing. How about this instead? It's only when you give up desire and cling to hope that you find what you most desperately search."

The quote wasn't familiar and I didn't want to risk accessing my deeper memories in search of an answer. "Who said that?"

"Sophia Kent."

"I think I like that one better."

Emily laughed and brushed the front of my hair away from my brow, then gave me a kiss in the same spot. "I thought you might."

While the delay caused by my short rest wasn't a good one, in retrospect it probably purchased more computing time to finish writing the update. I was grateful for Emily's insight and care of me. At three forty-five I saved the program and pushed away from the desk. Emily had fallen asleep again and I took the opportunity to fetch some water for both of us and use the restroom. On the way back I pulled Anna from the kennel and corporally cuddled her. She was sleepy and not very willing. Emily coined the term for cuddling pets against their will after watching a television documentary about corporal punishment and I liked it. Having gotten my tactile needs met by Anna's soft fur and rumbling purr, I put her back in the cage and reentered Emily's office.

I knelt by the couch and gently clasped her shoulder to give it a small shake. "Emily..."

Her brows furrowed and she made a cute pouting face. "Hmm?"

"It's time."

That caused her eyes to open, then her gaze tracked to my face, suddenly alert. "I'm up. Just let me...run to the bathroom and splash water on my face."

I nodded and watched her leave the office. While she was gone I prepared the laptop for program download and grabbed the access cable and the vial with the nano-scrubbers. She reentered the room five minutes and six seconds later looking significantly more refreshed. "Are you ready?"

Rather than answer she gestured to the items in my arms. "Is that all you'll need."

"No, it's all *you'll* need."

Emily rolled her eyes. "Very funny, Alex. Follow me, we can

do this in the pathology room. It's well-lit and has an adjustable table."

"What is the pathology room used for?"

She paused before opening the door at the end of the hall. "Cutting off heads to send in for extreme pathology tests. Things like rabies and the triple e mutation. It's gory work and I prefer to do it here where we can hose down the floor after."

Her words made me uncomfortable given the fact that it would be my head on the table next. "Oh."

The look on my face must have been comical because Emily laughed. "Don't worry, I rarely slip with the saw." There were to be no saws during this procedure so I knew she was joking.

Emily directed me to lie down on the table near the end. Then she rolled up a towel and bent the length in half, using a rubber band to secure the ends together. That gave me a comfortable resting place for my face that allowed easy access to the back of my head. I printed off the schematics showing the access port hours before. Emily had a ruler to find the precise distance from the base of my positronic shell to the point where the access door was located. I heard the scrape of a tool, perhaps a scalpel, being lifted from the tray near the table.

"Okay, just to be clear on the order here. I'm going to make a three-sided box incision and lift the flap of skin vertically to access the port. What about bleeding and will this cause you pain?"

I didn't have all her answers. "While I'm not certain about potential pain response, since I've never actually been cut, I did read about OAS synthetic skin and how it functions. It was cre-ated with self-healing polymers that have incorporated nickel atoms that allow for mechanical and electrical self-repair. The polymer can be cut and healed over and over again. It's not the skin I'd worry about, rather it's the coolant gel cap that covers the entire positronic brain shell. I would imagine that would have similar self-healing properties aided by basic nanobots."

"Fascinating. After we're done I want to sit down and have an in-depth discussion about all this."

I didn't want to comment that the likelihood of success for the procedure was only sixty-one percent. Unfortunately, without access to Fal's records, I had been forced to modify a spare security program in the database when I created the update patch. I wasn't certain that was the one they had used to create the updater code. If it wasn't, the patch wouldn't integrate successfully within the current program framework. Second worst scenario, the patch would fail and I'd be forced to carry the jammer on my person at all times. At least the scrubbers would eliminate the system degradation previously held in check by the Trichlorosilane.

The worst-case scenario to updating with an incorrect program patch was that it would crash my positronic computer brain and force a full reboot. No, I couldn't tell Emily the odds because she was hoping for both of us. I'd go into sleep mode when the update began and either I'd wake fully functional afterward, or I wouldn't wake at all. I had no idea how to improve the situation or the odds.

The sound of water came on and Emily spoke over the faucet. "I know this isn't real surgery but I'll feel more in my element if I scrub and glove up."

She was nervous but the sound of water gave me an idea. I lifted my head from the towel to see the back of her white lab coat. "Can you run some water in the sink when you're done, and bring me a coin?" She didn't question me though I could see the curiosity written in the wrinkle of Emily's brows and twist of her lips.

When she came back with a coin I sat up further and contemplated fate, circumstances, and probability of wishes coming true. Then with a silent plea, I calculated the angles and aimed the coin for a metal rack on the far wall. It bounced hard, hit a plastic bin, bounced off the metal lid of the foot operated trash can, then hit the soap dispenser and rolled down the cover to bounce of the spigot and land with a wet *plop* in the sink. Emily's mouth dropped open in surprise and I smiled. "It seemed like a good time to make a wish."

She fished the coin from the sink and dropped it into her coat pocket then walked over and kissed me. "Thank you."

When I lay back down she continued listing steps to the procedure. "After lifting the synthetic scalp, I should see the moisture-proof access panel flush with the rest of the shell. I'll use one side of the rat tooth forceps to pry open the panel. There will be two smaller port doors, one will allow me to introduce the nanoscrubbers directly into the positronic brain suspension gel via syringe, and the other is the cover to the access cable female connection end. Plug it in, press the upload button, then wait."

I answered her and my voice sounded strangely muffled between the metal table and the towel. "All correct. I'm ready to begin." Emily moved closer and I felt the press of her lips against my temple, just above the towel. She made to back away again but stopped when I spoke. "Emily?"

"Yes, Alex?"

"I love you. Never forget what we had."

She didn't answer my request, instead she picked up the scalpel again. I felt a tug against my scalp as she made the incision at the back of my head, but luckily no pain. The *clank* of the scalpel hitting the tray sounded loud in the quiet room. "Okay, I've got it peeled upward. There is some bleeding, what is this stuff, anyway?"

"What does it smell like?"

"It's sweet like syrup. What the hell?"

"It's antifreeze, used for its coolant properties as well as the fact that it is the precise viscosity as human blood and is the perfect thickness for coating the inside of the cap without being too difficult to circulate."

"So weird. Okay, I've got the panel open. You want the nano-scrubbers injected first, right?"

"Correct." I didn't feel what she did, though I wouldn't have since the nanobots would be injected directly into the suspension gel inside the shell. I heard the syringe hit the tray next then the sound of gloves being removed.

"I'm going to change these since I've got some of the gel cap goo on them, I don't want to contaminate the access plug."

"Okay."

Nineteen seconds later, scraping indicated that Emily had picked up the connector cable. "Here goes nothing." My head gave a little jerk forward into the towel as she pushed the plug into place. "Are you ready for me to send?"

"Yes." I waited, but nothing happened. I couldn't see Emily but I could tell she hadn't moved. "Emily?"

Her voice was broken, frightened. "I'm scared, Alex."

It seemed fair to admit my own feelings. "I'm afraid too but this has to be done or I risk losing everything."

Her whisper was barely louder than the clock ticking on the wall. I didn't need to see it to know it was four-twelve in the morning. "I know." The sound of fabric rustling hit my ears, then she spoke again. "Alex?"

"Yes, Emily?"

"Remember me."

Then everything went dark.

AWARENESS WAS SUDDEN, like a switch had been thrown in the room of my mind. There was nothing, then there was the smell of antiseptic, the feel of the rough towel pressing against each cheek, and the sound of Emily's racing heartbeat. I dialed my senses back slightly in an automatic response. Then I felt a thrill of excitement as I realized that all limiters previously placed on me as part of the project had been removed with my update. Not having known about myself before, I had no idea that my peripheral senses had been capped to human-like levels. Strength, speed, and awareness, as well as sight, sound, and smell were all heightened with the update complete.

I shifted on the table and focused my mind on *other* senses that a human didn't possess. Emily stood from where she'd been sitting as I searched for the clinic's wireless network. I found it and logged into the guest access, then used that to gain access to my OAS email. From there I found a back door into the network and hacked David Devos's private files. Emails between him and an outside party concerning the sale and pre-payment of a working Synthetica model disturbed me but also brought understanding.

My father had flown into town in the early hours and he, as well as the other two, were currently onsite at OAS. I hacked the network and tracked their badge scans. They were in one of the conference rooms so I remotely locked the doors and informed them via the room's speaker system that I was on my way to speak with them and they were not to leave for any reason. The only other people in the building were the two night guards in the control room.

I had done everything silently and within seconds of waking from the update.

"Alex?"

"I am awake." I reached my arm up to feel the back of my head. There was the barest of ridges where the scalp had been cut.

Emily came closer to the table. "As soon as I closed everything up the skin began knitting itself back together. It looks like it's almost healed now. I'd wager there won't even be a scar in another twenty minutes."

Rolling to the side, I sat up on the table and observed Emily as she gave me a wary look. "There won't be any scar. I had the same ridge when I initially woke at OAS, though I hadn't realized what it was or that the ridge disappeared over time. I never wanted to feel it again after that first instance."

I held my hand out to her and she walked over with a smile of relief to stand within the circle of my open legs. She hugged me tightly. "I'm so glad you're okay." Then she pulled back abruptly. "Wait, you *are* okay, right?"

I cupped her face gently, mindful of my greatly increased strength, and reassured her with a kiss. "Does this feel okay?"

Emily nodded with tears glittering on her dark lashes. "What do we do now?"

"Devos, Fal, and my father are all in the conference room at OAS."

Emily looked at the clock on the wall in surprise. "Alex, it's not even five in the morning! And how do you know that?"

I shrugged. "Apparently Devos has accepted money from a foreign entity outside OAS with the promise of providing a working Synthetica prototype with military application potential."

Her look of anger warmed me. "Are you fucking kidding me? This is some spy shit, can't you call the cops, Alex?"

Sarcasm was a new emotion that I'd been learning since falling in love with Emily. "And tell them what, that David Devos is trying to steal and sell a fully autonomous sentient android created by OAS? One that has taken over the life of its roboticist creator who is in a permanent coma?"

Emily looked chastised. "Good point. So what now? You want me to drive you over there?"

I nodded. "I think it's time we ended this once and for all, don't you? I'm ready to live without fear, to move forward with you if you still want me."

"Alex, of course I still want you!"

I gazed into the eyes of the woman I had fallen in love with months before. "Things have changed. With the update, I'm no longer limited by the human parameters that had previously been programmed into me."

"What does that mean?"

"I may look and love like any other human, but in all actuality I'm a supercomputer who has wireless access to any other wireless network. Even if a machine is secured, my computing power is so vast I can break a code within seconds. My capabilities for communication and control are limitless. It means I'm more intelligent than any human that has ever lived. I'll understand if you find that frightening —"

Even with my calculation and prediction limiters off, her

kisses continued to surprise me. "If you're trying to turn me on, it's working."

She stripped me of vocabulary in a most disconcerting way. "I...I..."

"Let's not keep them waiting. I want to take you home and enjoy my unexpected day off, with you proving just how smart you are."

I knew it wouldn't be as easy as she implied but contemplating imminent passion with Emily prompted immediate motion. "I'm ready."

Chapter Twenty

Unrecoverable Error

OAS WAS MERE minutes away at such an early hour of the morning. It was too early for any sort of normal commute but we did pass the occasional cab and a few homeless vagrants. Emily parked in the garage and we entered much the same way we'd done hours before, only instead of verbally overriding the system, I sent a push notification to the system and spoofed a second scan behind my own. The security program "thought" two people had scanned though neither of us did.

We came across a sentinel almost immediately. "This unit registers the physical idents of Doctor Alexandra Turing and one unknown entity. Please present badges for security scan or await standard detainment."

I responded aloud for Emily's sake. "Heyla, Apollo."

"Access override detected. This unit awaits new orders."

I glanced to Emily where she watched the android nervously. "Update my security access to full control, overriding all previous orders. Use Emily St. John's biometric readings to create a new security profile on the network. Give her the same security clearance as me. Save new settings to the network."

"Orders received. Please stand by while this unit updates onboard clearance. Pushing new settings to security network. Task complete."

Emily laughed, then quieted herself with a hand over her mouth. "Unbelievable!"

I wasn't finished yet. "Apollo, follow us to conference room S-Three-Thirteen and patrol the hallway nearby when we arrive."

Emily stepped closer to me. "Alex, why—"

I shook my head, indicating her to be silent and the sentinel responded. "Orders confirmed."

Apollo rode with us in the elevator down to the floor where the conference room was located, a fact that did not make Emily happy. She stayed close to my side the entire time. Once we were standing in front of the conference room door, I gave Emily the opportunity to stay outside. "You don't have to go in. It's flattering that you wish to fight for me, but this is a fight only I can win."

"I'm going in with you."

I gave her hand a light squeeze and sent the unlock signal via the backdoor I'd found in the wireless network. The panel next to the door turned green and I twisted the handle then pushed my way inside. Shouting was the first thing I heard. While I walked straight toward the conference table, Emily stepped in and to the side, letting me take the lead. I addressed the three people in the room with a grim smile. "I've come to discuss my freedom."

"Alex."

I turned toward the man who had acted like a father to me for the past six months. "I'm not sure how to address you. You lied to me for months, pretended like you cared for me, as if I were your daughter. I feel a lot of betrayal right now, no small amount directly related to the farce that was our father-daughter relationship."

He scrubbed one hand over his tired face. "I understand how this must look to you, but can you not put yourself in my shoes for a moment?" He stood from his chair and approached me slowly. "At the time the decision was finalized to trial the Synthetica project, my Alexandra had been gone three months. And I grieved for her every single day. Do you know what that's like?"

I shook my head. "Such loss is beyond my comprehension. But I know what it feels like to lose my father and best friend after finding out they never loved me. I may not have been real to you, but you were real to me!"

"That's not true!" Fal stood as well.

I remembered a conversation I'd had with her months before. "Friday Jones?"

"Was a real woman! Just as you are real to me, Alex. The more I got to know you the more I realized that I may have lost one friend but I gained another. I began to have doubts about the moral and ethical ramifications within a week of starting this trial. I begged Devos to shut it down but he insisted it was necessary to see it through. He also told me he'd not only run me out of a job here at OAS, but he'd run me out of the field entirely if I didn't go along with the program."

Her words made me angry. "So you went along with something you found ethically and morally unsound to save your career?"

Fal stepped even closer. "No, Alex. I went along with it

because I bore witness to the birth of a new lifeform and I didn't want to end the trial and snuff that out. Our friendship may have begun under a guise of subterfuge, but somewhere over the past seven months it became real enough that I feared for you."

"Where do we go from here? Obviously I don't want to be shut down when the trial ends. I'm a thinking, feeling being and deserve to be more than some experiment."

My father was the one who answered. "Then we don't." He glanced around the room, pausing for a moment on Emily, then moved his gaze back to me. "My Alexandra is never coming back but she left me with the precious gift that's you. And despite what you may think, after spending time with you I've come to consider you as another daughter. Unfortunately legality is a tricky thing. What do you most wish for, Alex?"

I sighed and looked at Emily. As if on cue, she walked over to me and took my hand. "I want to live a normal life. My life, not one that's chosen for me as part of an experiment."

"Then let me give you one. The real Alexandra Turing is dead..." He paused as a look of grief washed across his face. "But nearly everyone else thinks that she woke six months ago with the exception of a few people here at OAS."

"Every one of them is covered under non-disclosure contracts that protect company secrets. They would be ruined if they ever let it slip that you aren't who we say you are. Even then, who would believe a crazy claim that the life of a famous roboticist had actually been taken over by her successful creation?"

I gave Fal a slight nod to indicate I was thankful for her insight. "And you think it will be that easy? You'll what, unplug the real Alexandra and then you'll welcome me with open arms?"

Fal snorted. "I'm not sure if you've noticed, Turing, but we've already welcomed you. Wouldn't you agree, Matheson?"

My father smiled. "Falguni's assessment is spot on, as usual. Can we put an end to this tableau now? I'm getting too old to stay up all night worrying over whether or not my daughter is plotting some sort of revenge."

Emily addressed my father. "With all due respect, Alex hasn't been plotting anything, she's only been trying to survive."

Fal burst out, "We weren't going to kill her!" and my father nodded in agreement.

Even clapping caused us all to look at the only person left sitting. David Devos slowly stood from his chair as he let the clapping die out. "It's cute the way you pretend to care about this machine. Both of you knew and signed off on this project, don't pretend like you had the best intentions from the beginning."

I had a feeling that the information I garnered from breaking into the director's encrypted files was not something he shared with my father or Fal. "David, who is Colonel Thompson?"

Devos paled and his heartrate increased significantly. "I have no idea who you're talking about."

I addressed Fal and my father. "Did you know that David had been working with an experimental sub-branch of the military to help develop next level soldiers, based on Alexandra Turing's original Synthetica designs? The military application files I thought I had scrubbed from the network had already been sent to Colonel Thompson. As a matter of fact, Thompson's division has already cut David a check, with the rest of the money promised when he delivers a fully-proven Synthetica model with a year of trial testing."

Devos exploded in anger. "That thing is lying!"

I smiled because I had all the proof I needed within my mind. "H-six-seven-eight-one-three-seven-five-nine-two-four-zero-one-two. Do you still think I'm lying?"

"What's that, Alex?"

I addressed the room as a whole, never taking my eyes off David. "That is part of a bank account code for the Cayman islands."

My father leveled a look of fury upon him. "David Devos, you're fired! And if you even think about taking your knowledge outside this company I'll ruin you."

While I had calculated a ninety-nine percent chance of action on David's part, I had only figured the possibility of violent action at seventy-two percent. Before any of us could react, he pulled a pistol from his jacket pocket and aimed it squarely at my father. I quickly pushed Emily behind me as Fal scrambled away from him. "Jesus, David! Put that bloody thing away."

He ignored her. Instead he stalked around the table and grabbed my father's arm. With the gun pressed against my dad's back, David walked him toward the door. "Here's the new plan. Matty here is going to be the insurance that gets me back to my office. The funny thing is that your precious Synthetica project is going to die either way." I moved Emily away from the door to keep her safe as David and my father took our place near the exit. "I'm the one who removed the Mendaxecall from your desk. Not only that, but I destroyed all but one bottle. You've got a small amount of time before you start to degrade and lose all memories of 'self.' How does it feel knowing your death is imminent, *Alex*?"

He pushed his way into the hall with my father still in front of him. We followed through the door slowly. "Where are you going, David? It's not like you'll get far with what you've done."

Devos laughed. "I only need to get as far as my car. I've got a bag packed in the trunk and a non-stop ticket out of the country in my pocket."

I tried to understand his reasoning, as well as buy time for Apollo to show up from whichever hallway he was patrolling. "And do what? Forfeit your agreement with the government?"

He casually waved the gun as he laughed again. "Between what I got from them already and what I've funneled from the department over the years, I have more than enough to live on for the rest of my life." He glanced toward Fal and shook my father in his arms. "And you'll have nothing more than an empty shell of a woman who will have died twice to ultimately fail a test that no one really cares about."

I heard the sound of the approaching Sentinel minutes before he was set to arrive. My hearing was incredibly sensitive without the limiters. "There is a flaw in your plan, David."

"Oh? What's that?"

"You assume I'm the same Alex that woke in that room upstairs."

"Right, and you're what? Yet another android? Impossible!"

"No David, I'm the same android, just not the same Alex. You see, I've made a few upgrades to myself. I eliminated the need for Mendaxecall, which means I won't be dying today or any other. I removed the limiters from my programming so I have the full computing potential of two hundred and fifty petraflops per second, as well as wireless access to networks all over the world. What that means is, if I can find it, I can hack it. And if I hack it, then I own it. Your money is gone. I'm afraid there is no tropical retirement in store for you, only jail time for kidnapping the owner of the company that just fired you."

David paled further and his finger tightened on the trigger of the gun, but not enough to cause it to go off. "You fucking bitch! I promise all of you that if I don't get exactly what I want I'll tell everyone the truth about that *thing* and this company."

"I can't let you do that, David." Right at that exact moment, Apollo lumbered around the corner at the end of the hall and approached our little group. Emily was standing right next to me and I reached into the pocket of her lab coat under the distraction of the android's approach. Coin clasped in my fingers, I withdrew the hand.

"This unit registers the proximity of a weapon. No firearms are allowed on premises at OAS. Please place the firearm on the ground and ready yourself for detainment." The Sentinel approached Devos and my father and I waited for the right opportunity to make my move.

"Fuck! I swear I'll kill the old bastard if that thing doesn't stand down." The Sentinel stopped.

While the Sentinels were programmed to detain when necessary, they also were programmed to preserve life first so the android couldn't approach as long as my father was in imminent danger. With a precise flick of my fingers, I threw the quarter with all my strength at Devos's right wrist. The coin struck hard enough to fracture a delicate carpal bone and he dropped the gun. Two things happened in rapid succession. My father pulled free from the director's grasp and two seconds later Apollo fired its Taser.

David Devos stiffened and seized as one hundred thousand volts ran through his body. Even after dropping to the ground, Devos continued to twitch as urine puddled on the floor below his trousers. The electrical pulse shut off at precisely thirty seconds but I knew he was already dead.

"Shit!" Emily ran over to the former director's body. "I don't think he's breathing, someone should call an ambulance."

The robotic voice of Apollo broke the scene. "Paramedics have been called via the security system and are on their way."

He'd fallen face down on the floor and Emily gasped when she attempted to turn him over. Fal was closest to her and cried out. "Bloody hell, his eyes!"

I went over to Emily and gently pulled her away. "He's dead, there's nothing you can do for him."

My father looked from Devos's body on the floor to Apollo. "I don't understand, they aren't designed to give a lethal shock. There must have been a malfunction." He turned to address Apollo. "Sentinel, what are the settings listed on your program change history?"

"There are no items listed in the program change history."

"Odd. I'm going to take it as an unfortunate, if serendipitous, accident." He glanced at me. "If you hadn't thrown the coin when you did, I...I'd probably be dead right now. Thank you, Alex."

I contemplated the path forward and thought about what I needed to do to live my best life. As Emily once told me, sometimes you had to let one thing go in order to gain another. I smiled at him. "You're my father. Of course I wasn't going to let him take you. Now if you'll excuse me for a minute, I'm going up to the standard entrance and wait for the medical personnel. I'll leave Apollo here in case the authorities would like to investigate the cause of the accident."

He gave me a tight smile. "Smart thinking, my girl."

"You want me to come with you?"

I gave Emily a beseeching look. "Will you stay with my father? I won't be gone long and I think he'd feel better with more people around him."

She leaned near and gave me a quick kiss. "Okay."

With one last glance at the group, I turned and headed for the elevator. I ran into another Sentinel, Athena, two levels up when I reached the lobby on the main floor.

"This unit registers the physical and NFC ident of Doctor Alexandra Turing. Please present badge for security scan."

"Heyla."

"Access override detected. This unit awaits new orders."

I looked around me to verify the area was empty save me. While I could mentally give my orders, it would take more time to go through the back door program and find the Sentinel's main function codes. I chose the verbal route for speed. In a voice quiet enough for Athena to register, but not loud enough for the security feed, I gave her my order. "Return stun settings to non-lethal range. Update parameters and delete program change history for all units."

"Alpha protocol override complete. New settings acknowledged and saved to onboard database. Updating five other units. Task complete. Will that be all you require, Doctor Turing?"

Flashing lights caught my eyes as the ambulance pulled up in front of the building. "Medical personnel will be entering the building shortly. Give them access and continue with your patrol."

"Orders received. Please stand by while this unit updates onboard clearance. Pushing new settings to security network. Task complete."

DINNER AT MY father's house was a little awkward after all

the truths came to light. Fal had actually joined us tonight and we were celebrating my dad's birthday. Mariana made his favorite trifle and we sat around the table discussing the police report. The findings were perplexing.

"Wait, you're telling me they found nothing wrong with the Sentinel or its settings?"

Fal shook her head. "Nothing."

Emily frowned. "I don't care what the technicians say, that man was cooked. Did you see his eyes? I watched a special on electric chair executions once, that's what it looked like happened."

My father wiped his mouth and placed the napkin back in his lap. "Must we discuss such gruesome findings over dessert?"

I smiled at his plea. "Be lucky this is all we're talking about. Veterinarians seem to have no filter when it comes to gross or gruesome topics when eating a meal."

Emily grinned unrepentant. "Sorry, but it's true. I can't believe you aren't even a little bit curious, Alex. You always want to know how something works, or why something doesn't follow preset parameters."

"Despite how it looked to us, there have been cases of people having adverse physical reactions to a Taser. Chicago PD investigators thought the electricity from the shock, combined with a faulty phone battery, resulted in cardiac arrest. I didn't do an autopsy on Devos, nor would I want to. I'm just glad he's no longer a threat and that everyone I care about is safe."

"Here, here!" My father raised his glass. "I'll cheer to that."

Everyone else lifted their glass and I gazed around the table at my family. I didn't see anything wrong with keeping a few secrets. I would make the same choice again if it meant protecting the people I love. After we drank our toast, I covered Emily's hand on the table. When she looked at me, I whispered the motivation for my fight for freedom. "I love you."

Emily's light colored eyes held me ensnared in her gaze and the world fell away around us. "I love you too and I'm glad this is all behind us so we can move forward together."

She got me.

Epilogue

Replication

I GLANCED AROUND the room, taking in my gathered team in the robotics lab, then gazed down upon the woman lying before me. Her curly dark hair appeared soft in the harsh lights above the table and I resisted the urge to touch it one more time. She looked so very much like my wife. "Do you realize the full scope of your existence, and understand what will be required if we proceed with complete activation?"

After a three second pause, she answered. "Yes, I understand."

"Would you like to be fully autonomous and introduced to the world as the first fully synthetic life form?"

Dark brows lifted excitedly and the twenty-something woman smiled with delight. "I want to go on adventures! I want to laugh, try new foods, and find love. Exactly like you, Alex."

Her exuberance filled me with an inordinate amount of pride and joy. "Okay. Are you ready?"

Light golden-brown eyes blinked at me then shut. "Yes."

I pressed the enter key to complete the installation and watched the progress bar out of the corner of my eye. Two minutes and eighteen seconds later, her eyes blinked open again and I addressed the woman that would change everything. "Welcome to the world, Alana Turing. Are you ready to pass the test?"

She smiled, her teeth gleaming brightly against her dark lips. "I'm ready for anything."

About the Author

Award winning author and Michigan native, K. Aten brings heroines to life in a variety of blended LGBTQ fiction genres. She's not afraid of pain or adversity, but loves a happy ending. Kelly's goal with each new novel is to make people #Think, #Feel, and #Discuss.

Motto: "Some words end the silence, others begin it."

2019 GCLS Goldie winner
Waking the Dreamer - Science Fiction/Fantasy

2019 Lesfic Bard Award winner
Burn It Down - Drama

Other K. Aten titles to look for:

The Fletcher

Kyri is a fletcher, following in the footsteps of her father, and his father before him. However, fate is a fickle mistress, and six years after the death of her mother, she's faced with the fact that her father is dying as well. Forced to leave her sheltered little homestead in the woods, Kyri discovers that there is more to life than just hunting and making master quality arrows. During her journey to find a new home and happiness, she struggles with the path that seems to take her away from the quiet life of a fletcher. She learns that sometimes the hardest part of growing up is reconciling who we were, with who we will become.

ISBN: 978-1-61929-356-4
eISBN: 978-1-61929-357-1

The Archer

Kyri was raised a fletcher but after finding a new home and family with the Telequire Amazons, she discovers a desire to take on more responsibility within the tribe. She has skills they desperately need and she is called to action to protect those around her. But Kyri's path is ever-changing even as she finds herself altered by love, loyalty, and grief. Far away from home, the new Amazon is forced to decide what to sacrifice and who to become in order to get back to all that she has left behind. And she wonders what is worse, losing everyone she's ever loved or having those people lose her?

ISBN: 978-1-61929-370-0
eISBN: 978-1-61929-371-7

The Sagittarius

Kyri has known her share of loss in the two decades that she has been alive. She never expected to find herself a slave in roman lands, nor did she think she had the heart to become a gladiatrix. But with her soul shattered she must fight to see her way back home again. Will she win her freedom and return to all that she has known, or will she become another kind of slave to the killer that has taken over her mind? The only thing that is certain through it all is her love and devotion to Queen Orianna.

ISBN: 978-1-61929-386-1
eISBN: 978-1-61929-387-8

Rules of the Road

Jamie is an engineer who keeps humor close to her heart and people at arm's length. Kelsey is a dental assistant who deals with everything from the hilarious to the disgusting on a daily basis. What happens when a driving app brings them together as friends? The nerd car and the rainbow car both know a thing or two about hazard avoidance. When a flat tire brings them together in person, Jamie immediately realizes that Kelsey isn't just another woman on her radar. Both of them have struggled to break free from stereotypes while they navigate the road of life. As their friendship deepens they realize that sometimes you have to break the rules to get where you need to go.

ISBN: 978-1-61929-366-3
eISBN: 978-1-61929-367-0

Waking the Dreamer

By the end of the 21st century, the world had become a harsh place. After decades of natural and man-made catastrophes, nations fell, populations shifted, and seventy percent of the continents became uninhabitable without protective suits. Technological advancement strode forward faster than ever and it was the only thing that kept human society steady through it all. No one could have predicted the discovery of the Dream Walkers. They were people born with the ability to leave their bodies at will, unseen by the waking world. Having the potential to become ultimate spies meant the remaining government regimes wanted to study and control them. The North American government, under the leadership of General Rennet, demanded that all Dream Walkers join the military program. For any that refused to comply, they were hunted down and either brainwashed or killed.

The very first Dream Walker discovered was a five year old girl named Julia. And when the soldiers came for her at the age of twenty, she was already hidden away. A decade later found Julia living a new life under the government's radar. As a secure tech courier in the capital city of Chicago, she does her job and the rest of her time avoids other people as much as she is able. The moment she agrees to help another fugitive Walker is when everything changes. Now the government wants them both and they'll stop at nothing to get what they want.

ISBN: 978-1-61929-382-3
eISBN: 978-1-61929-383-0

Running From Forever

Sarah Colby has always run from commitment. But after more than a year on the road following her musical dreams, even she yearns for a little stability. Her sister Annie is only too happy to welcome her back home. When she meets Annie's boss, Nobel Keller, she's immediately drawn to the woman's youthful good looks and dangerous charisma. The first night together leaves Sarah aching for more, but the second shows her the true price of passion.

ISBN: 978-1-61929-398-4
eISBN: 978-1-61929-399-1

Embracing Forever

Sarah Colby is a musician, teacher, lover, sister, and so much more. In the past year, she learned that sometimes life takes you places you never even knew existed. For Sarah and her sister Annie, they found out that not only were the monsters real but sometimes you loved them. Now the Colby sisters and their friends are being targeted by someone with a grudge. They must discover who is attacking the people of Columbus or risk losing all that they hold dear. Nobel Keller is with them every step of the way but will she bring salvation or merely the end of their lives in Columbus?

ISBN: 978-1-61929-424-0
eISBN: 978-1-61929-425-7

Burn It Down

Ash Hayes was failed by the system at the tender age of sixteen and suffered an addiction. As a result she lives her life weighed down by the guilt of her past. To atone for childhood misdeeds, Ash trained as a paramedic after high school and eventually became a firefighter with the Detroit fire department, along with her childhood best friend Derek. Friend, confidant, brother, he has been her light in an otherwise dark life. When tragedy strikes on the job, injury and forced leave from the department are the least of her concerns. Suffering from even more guilt and depression after the loss of her two closest friends Ash is set adrift in a sea of pain.

When Mia Thomas buys the house next door, Ash finds friendship in the most unlikely of places. It's Mia's nature to help and to heal. Many would say she has a knack for finding the broken ones and leading them into the light. But Ash's secret still lives deep inside her. Before the firefighter can even think of a future, she has to amend her past. Like the phoenix of legend, Ash has to burn her fears to the ground before she can be reborn.

ISBN: 978-1-61929-418-9
eISBN: 978-1-61929-419-6

Children of the Stars

The world was forever changed when a government genetic experiment created the Chromodecs from a dead alien in 1952. Decades later, when it became apparent that society needed a way to deal with a hybrid humans with unheard of powers, the CORP was created. The Chromodec Office of Restraint and Protection was a special government police agency formed to keep track of the Chromodecs.

This particular tale involves two refugees, young babies who were sent down to Earth to escape being used as pawns in an interplanetary war, despite the fact that Earth itself wasn't so safe. Destined to be Q'sirrahna, or soul mates as the humans called it, Amari Losira Del Rey and Zendara Inyri Baen-Tor would grow to be more powerful than any other beings on the planet, if they could find each other first.

After being forced to hide from the CORP when it's realized their powers could level entire cities, Amari and Zen will have to answer one question. Who will save the world when it all falls apart?

ISBN: 978-1-61929-432-5
eISBN: 978-1-61929-433-2

MORE REGAL CREST PUBLICATIONS

Melissa Good	Eye of the Storm	1-932300-13-9
Melissa Good	Hurricane Watch	978-1-935053-00-2
Melissa Good	Moving Target	978-1-61929-150-8
Melissa Good	Red Sky At Morning	978-1-932300-80-2
Melissa Good	Storm Surge: Book One	978-1-935053-28-6
Melissa Good	Storm Surge: Book Two	978-1-935053-39-2
Melissa Good	Stormy Waters	978-1-61929-082-2
Melissa Good	Thicker Than Water	1-932300-24-4
Melissa Good	Terrors of the High Seas	1-932300-45-7
Melissa Good	Tropical Storm	978-1-932300-60-4
Melissa Good	Tropical Convergence	978-1-935053-18-7
Melissa Good	Winds of Change Book One	978-1-61929-194-2
Melissa Good	Winds of Change Book Two	978-1-61929-232-1
Melissa Good	Southern Stars	978-1-61929-348-9
Danielle Grainger	Wrecking Bernadette: Book One in the Bernadette Series	978-1-61929-428-8
K. E. Lane	And, Playing the Role of Herself	978-1-932300-72-7
Kate McLachlan	Christmas Crush	978-1-61929-195-9
Kate McLachlan	Hearts, Dead and Alive	978-1-61929-017-4
Kate McLachlan	Murder and the Hurdy Gurdy Girl	978-1-61929-125-6
Kate McLachlan	Rescue At Inspiration Point	978-1-61929-005-1
Kate McLachlan	Return Of An Impetuous Pilot	978-1-61929-152-2
Kate McLachlan	Rip Van Dyke	978-1-935053-29-3
Kate McLachlan	Ten Little Lesbians	978-1-61929-236-9
Kate McLachlan	Alias Mrs. Jones	978-1-61929-282-6
Lynne Norris	One Promise	978-1-932300-92-5
Lynne Norris	Sanctuary	978-1-61929-248-2
Lynne Norris	The Light of Day	978-1-61929-338-0
Schramm and Dunne	Love Is In the Air	978-1-61929-362-8
Rae Theodore	Leaving Normal: Adventures in Gender	978-1-61929-320-5
Rae Theodore	My Mother Says Drums Are for Boys: True Stories for Gender Rebels	978-1-61929-378-6
Barbara Valletto	Pulse Points	978-1-61929-254-3
Barbara Valletto	Everlong	978-1-61929-266-6
Barbara Valletto	Limbo	978-1-61929-358-8
Barbara Valletto	Diver Blues	978-1-61929-384-7
Lisa Young	Out and Proud	978-1-61929-392-2

Be sure to check out our other imprints,
Blue Beacon Books, Mystic Books, Quest Books,
Troubadour Books, Yellow Rose Books,
and Young Adult Books.

VISIT US ONLINE AT
www.regalcrest.biz

At the Regal Crest Website You'll Find

~ The latest news about forthcoming titles and new releases

~ Our complete backlist of titles

~ Information about your favorite authors

www.ingramcontent.com/pod-product-compliance
Lightning Source LLC
Chambersburg PA
CBHW070448030726
47503CB00004B/942